About the Authors

USA TODAY bestselling author **Lucy Monroe** lives and writes in the gorgeous Pacific Northwest. While she loves her home, she delights in experiencing different cultures and places in her travels, which she happily shares with her readers through her books. A lifelong devotee of the romance genre, Lucy can't imagine a more fulfilling career than writing.

Jennifer Rae was raised on a farm in Australia by salt-of-the-earth farming parents. All she'd ever wanted to do was write, but she didn't have the confidence to share her stories with the world until, working as a journalist, she interviewed a couple of romance-writers. Finally the characters who had been milling around Jennifer's head since her long years on the farm made sense and she realised romance was the genre for her and sat down to release her characters.

Fiona Brand lives in the sunny Bay of Islands, New Zealand. Now that both of her sons are grown, she continues to love writing books and gardening. After a life-changing time in which she met Christ, she has undertaken study for a bachelor of theology and has become a member of The Order of St. Luke, Christ's healing ministry.

Boardroom
COLLECTION

February 2018

March 2018

April 2018

May 2018

June 2018

July 2018

Takeover in the Boardroom

LUCY MONROE

JENNIFER RAE

FIONA BRAND

MILLS & BOON

Published in Great Britain 2018
by Mills & Boon, an imprint of HarperCollins*Publishers*
1 London Bridge Street, London, SE1 9GF

Takeover in the Boardroom © 2018 Harlequin Books S.A.

An Heiress for His Empire © 2014 Lucy Monroe
Who's Calling the Shots © 2014 Jennifer Rae
A Tangled Affair © 2012 Fiona Gillibrand

ISBN: 978-0-263-26625-2

09-0418

MIX
Paper from
responsible sources

FSC
www.fsc.org

FSC™ C007454

This book is produced from independently certified FSC™ paper to ensure responsible forest management.

For more information visit: www.harpercollins.co.uk/green

Printed and bound in Spain
by CPI, Barcelona

AN HEIRESS
FOR HIS EMPIRE

LUCY MONROE

For Judy Flohr, a very special reader who I have long considered an honest friend. It's sort of amazing to me that you've been reading and sharing your love of my books since the very first one, *The Greek Tycoon's Ultimatum* back in 2003. When I'm doubting myself or the story, I know I can re-read your emails or online reader reviews and remember why I write and that maybe I'm not so bad at this after all. THANK YOU!!!
Hugs and blessings, Lucy

CHAPTER ONE

MADISON ARCHER SET her morning coffee down, hot liquid spilling over the rim, as she read her Google alerts with growing horror.

Madcap Madison Looking for New Master?
Archer Heiress into Heavy Kink
San Francisco Bad Boy Dumps Very Bad Girl

The articles made lurid claims about a lifestyle and relationship between Maddie and Perry Timwater. A completely nonexistent relationship.

The fact that Perry was the source caused the coffee to sour in Maddie's stomach.

His supposed exposé of their fictitious relationship claimed she was a submissive with a serious pain fetish and need for multiple partners. She gritted her teeth on the urge to swear as she read it was her inability to remain faithful that forced Perry to end things between them.

Maddie wouldn't mind ending Perry right that minute. Betrayal choked her.

How could he have done this?

He was her *friend*.

They'd met their freshman year at university. He'd made her laugh when she'd thought nothing could. Not after her epic fail trying to get Viktor Beck's attention. She'd started university with a broken heart and Perry had helped her paste over the cracks with friendship.

She'd helped him pass his accountancy courses. He'd played platonic escort for her and she'd provided him entrée to Jeremy Archer's world—an echelon above his own.

But never, not once, had their friendship ever taken a turn toward something heavier.

Pounding sounded on her front door. "Maddie! It's me, don't freak." Then barely a second later, the double snick of locks sliding back was followed by the door swinging wide.

Holding a bag from their favorite bakery aloft, her black bob swirling around her pixie face, Romi Grayson kicked the door shut behind her. "I come bearing the panacea for all ills."

"I'm not sure even chocolate and flaky pastry can make this situation better." Maddie slumped against the back of her chair.

Eyes the same vibrant blue as Maddie's glittered with anger. "So, Perry's lost his mind, right?"

"You saw the articles?"

"Only after reporters woke me from a dead sleep demanding my opinion of my best friend's darker sexual proclivities." Romi's mouth twisted wryly. "Proclivities I'm pretty sure you wouldn't have even if you *weren't* still a virgin."

"You've got that right. I've never been able to trust one man enough to have sex, much less multiple partners."

As ridiculous as that might seem at twenty-four, it wasn't going to change anytime soon, either.

"If you ask me, it's got less to do with trust and more to do with the fact you imprinted on Viktor Beck like a baby bird when you were a teenager and you've never gotten over him."

"Romi!" Maddie was in no mood to hash out her unrequited feelings for her father's dark-haired, dark-eyed, to-die-for-bodied golden boy.

"I'm just saying…"

"Nothing you haven't said before." Maddie's stomach grew queasier by the second.

Along with the rest of the world, Vik would see the articles, but she couldn't afford to think about that right now, or she really was going to lose it. "Father is going to kill me."

This new scandal was bound to crack even the San Francisco tycoon's icy demeanor. And not in the way Maddie had always craved.

He'd sent her away to boarding school months after her mother's death and Maddie had courted media attention in the hopes of gaining his. It had worked for her mother, Helene Archer, née Madison, the original Madcap Madison, but Maddie had come to realize the strategy had backfired pretty spectacularly for her.

In the nine years since Helene's death, Jeremy had developed a habit of thinking the worst of his daughter. When he wasn't ignoring her existence all together.

"If he doesn't die of a stress-related heart attack first." Romi put a chocolate-filled croissant in front of Maddie.

"Don't say that."

The other woman grimaced. "Sorry. Stuff just comes out. You know what I'm like. Your dad is wound pretty tight, though."

Maddie couldn't argue that.

"I think this time, Perry's diarrhea of the mouth has me beat anyway." Romi chewed her pastry militantly. "What was he thinking?"

Morose, Maddie stared at her friend. "That he wanted the money the tabloid paid him for the story?"

She'd had no idea that turning down his latest request for a loan would result in her utter humiliation. How could she? Friends didn't do that to each other.

"Jerk."

Maddie usually played peacemaker between her two closest friends, but she wasn't about to stand up for Perry this time. "What am I going to do?"

"You could threaten to sue and demand a retraction."

"Based on my word against his?"

Romi made a sound very close to a growl. "You two have never even kissed with tongue."

"But we have kissed, for the cameras." Perry had always made a joke of it.

He had been Maddie's go-to escort for years and more than one article speculating on their relationship had been run, often quoting anonymous sources and always accompanied by the joke kissing pictures.

"Do you think he's done this before?"

"Sold *confidential details* of your supposed relationship?" Romi asked.

"Yes."

"You know what I think."

Maddie sighed. "That he's a leech."

"Always has been."

"He was a good friend." Maddie couldn't make herself claim he *still* was.

Romi just gave Maddie a disbelieving look, no words necessary.

Ignoring it, Maddie said, "I probably can't prove we never had a relationship, but I can sue them for libel in the details."

"His word against yours."

"But he's lying."

"This is something new for the tabloids?"

Feeling hopeless, Maddie pushed her croissant away.

"You could always sic your dad's dogs on Perry. That media fixer of his could be cast in Shark Week on the Discovery Channel."

"I should." Even supposing her dad cared enough to assign his media fixer's precious time to helping Maddie.

Romi's expression turned knowing. "But you won't. Perry was your friend."

Maddie opened her mouth, but Romi put her hand up, forestalling words. "Don't you dare say he still is."

"No." Maddie swallowed back emotion. "No, it's pretty clear he's not my friend and maybe he never was."

"Oh, sweetie." Romi came around the table to hug her.

Maddie fought down stress-induced nausea. "I thought he was real."

"Instead, he turned out to be just another one of the plastic people." Romi's tone reflected her own experience with that. "All looks and no substance."

Maddie choked out a morbid laugh. "Yeah."

A bugler's reveille sounded from her smartphone.

With a snicker, Romi moved back to her seat. "Daddy's PA?"

"I thought it was appropriate." Maddie clicked into her text messages, unsurprised to see that there were dozens.

While she checked her phone periodically throughout the day, Maddie only had sound alerts set for certain people: Romi, Perry—who was going off the list today—Maddie's father, his personal assistant. Viktor Beck.

Not that her father's business heir apparent contacted Maddie these days. But still, if he did…she'd get an audible alert.

Ignoring the numerous messages from *friends*, acquaintances and the media jackals, Maddie clicked into the one from her father's PA.

Mtg w Mr. Archer @ 10:45—conf rm 2.

Mr. Archer. Not Mr. A, even though the PA had used text speak for the rest of the message. Not *your father*. That might have been too personal.

"He wants to meet this morning." Maddie bit her lip, considering what she'd have to change to make that happen.

Romi nodded. "Are you going to go?"

Maddie considered putting off her morning plans for the meeting with her father.

"No." It wasn't as if her showing up when he called was going to make Jeremy any less angry.

She shot a quick text back to the PA offering to come anytime after noon-thirty.

Fifteen minutes later, Romi was gone after a final pep talk when the strains of Michael Bublé's "Call Me Irresponsible" sounded from Maddie's smartphone.

Her father was *calling* her. Personally. Not texting.

Any other time, she would be thrilled. But right now? The crooner's smooth voice was as ominous as the sepulchre tones of a Halloween horror flick's sound track.

Maddie put the phone to her ear. "Hello, Father."

"Ten forty-five, Madison. You will not be late."

"You know I have a standing morning appointment." Not that he knew what it was.

Maddie had tried to tell him once, but Jeremy had mocked the very idea of his flighty daughter doing anything worthwhile. Worse, he'd made it clear how useless he thought it was to spend time volunteering at an underfunded public school predominantly populated by the children of poverty-level families.

Since then, Maddie had kept her two lives completely separate. Maddie Grace, nondescript twentysomething who loved children and volunteered a good chunk of her time, had nothing in common—not even hair and eye color— with Madison Archer, notorious socialite and heiress.

"Cancel." No give. No explanation. Just demand.

Typical.

"It's important."

"No. It is not." His tone was so cold it sent shivers along her extremities.

"It is to me." She wished she could be as unaffected by his displeasure as he was by hers. "Please."

"Ten-forty-five, Madison." Then he hung up.

She knew because the call dropped.

Wearing the armor of her socialite Madison Archer persona, Maddie got off the elevator at the twenty-ninth floor of her father's building in San Francisco's financial district.

None of the nerves wreaking havoc with her insides showed on her smooth face.

Makeup applied to highlight, not compete with, the blue of her eyes and gentle bow of her lips, she'd styled her chin-length red hair in perfectly placed curls around her oval face so like her mother's. No highlights had ever been necessary for the natural copper tones.

Her three-quarter-length-sleeved Valentino black-and-white suit wasn't this year's collection, but it was one of her favorites and fit the image she intended to convey. The wide black banded hem of the straight skirt brushed a proper two inches above her knees and the Jackie-O-style jacket with a statement bow was a galaxy away from slutty.

She'd opted for classic closed-toe black Jimmy Choo pumps that added a mere two inches to her five-foot-six-inch height. Maddie carried a simple leather Chanel bag, her accessories limited to her mother's favorite Cartier watch and diamond stud earrings.

Maddie didn't look anything like the woman described by Perry in his "breakup interview" with the press.

She walked into Conference Room Two without knocking, stopping for a strategic pause in the doorway to allow the other occupants a moment to look their fill.

She wasn't going to scurry in like a mouse trying to avoid the cat's attention.

The brief moment had the added benefit of allowing her to take her own *lay of the land*.

Seven people sat around the eight-person conference table. As to be expected, her father occupied one end. Maddie was equal parts relieved and worried to see his media fixer at the other end, but not happy at all to see the man seated to the right of her father.

Romi was right that Maddie had had a crush on the gorgeous Viktor Beck since he started working for Jeremy Archer ten years ago. The unrequited feelings had evolved from schoolgirl infatuation to something more, something that made it impossible for other men to measure up.

That first year, Maddie had still had her mother and Helene would tease Maddie for her blushes in the tycoon-in-the-making's presence.

Maddie had learned to control her blushes, but not the feelings the handsome third-generation Russian engendered in her.

Having him here to witness her humiliation tightened the knot of tension inside her until she wasn't sure it would ever come undone.

Less understandable, but not nearly as upsetting, was the presence of two of her father's other high-level managers in the remaining chairs on that side of the table. Her father's PA sat to his left, with an empty chair beside her.

The final man at the table had a powerful presence and a familiar face, but in her current state of highly guarded stress, Maddie couldn't place him.

Everyone had a stack of papers in front of them. It took only the briefest glance to see what they were: printed-out copies of the news stories Maddie had seen earlier on her smartphone. Underneath them was an individual copy for each person in the room of the actual tabloid the original story had run in.

Vik's pile was different. It had what looked like a contract on top. Looking around the table, Maddie realized everyone else had a copy of that as well, but on the bottom of their pile—the stapled corner was the only thing visible in the other piles.

She looked at her father and gave him the sardonic expression she'd been using for years to mask her vulnerability. "I don't suppose it occurred to you to discuss this with me privately before bringing in a think tank."

"Sit down, Madison." He didn't even bother to respond to her comment.

Which should neither surprise, nor hurt. So why did it do both?

She waited a count of three before obeying his brusque order, deliberately ignoring the stack of papers in front of her. "I assume we've already drafted a letter demanding a retraction?"

When her father didn't answer, she stared pointedly at his media fixer.

"Is it likely your ex-lover will recant his commentary?" the fixer asked in a flat tone.

"First, he was never my lover. Second, he doesn't have to recant his lies for us to sue the tabloid for libel." Though her chances of winning the suit weren't high without Perry's honesty.

"I am not in the habit of wasting time or resources on a hopeless endeavor," her father said.

"The story is out there and that can't be changed," she agreed. "But that doesn't mean we leave Perry's lies unchallenged."

Her father's eyes were chips of blue ice. "If you wish to challenge your ex-lover's *lies*, you may do so, but that is not my concern."

"You don't believe the stories?" she asked with a pained incredulity she couldn't quite hide.

"What I believe is not the issue at hand."

"It is for me." There were only two people in that room whose opinion Maddie cared about.

Her father's and Viktor Beck's, no matter how much she might wish that wasn't the case.

Her gaze shifted to Vik, but nothing from the stern set of his square jaw to the obscure depths of his espresso-brown eyes revealed his thoughts.

There had been a time when he might have tried to encourage her with a half smile or even a wink, but those days were gone. There'd been no softening in his demeanor toward her since her first trip home after going away to university.

And while that might be her own fault, she didn't have to like it.

Her father cleared his throat. "Those tawdry stories may have precipitated this meeting, but they are not the reason for it."

Maddie's attention snapped back to her only remaining family. "What do you mean?"

"The issue we are here to address is your unacceptable notoriety, Madison. I will not sit by while you attempt to rival other heiresses for worldwide infamy."

"I don't." Even when Maddie had tried to court her father's attention by gaining that of the media, she hadn't gone that far.

Okay, so she and Romi were known for their participation in political rallies of the liberal variety, which included a well-publicized sit-in protesting cuts in local school funding. That Maddie had gone further, bungee jumping from the Golden Gate Bridge with five others and unfurling a giant banner that read Go Green or Go Home, was beside the point.

There were videos online of her bungee jumping in less politically motivated and slightly more risky circumstances. The snowboarding had been a total failure, but she'd always loved downhill skiing and learning to jump had been fantastic. Of course, only her tumbles made it into the media.

But she hadn't done a thing to get herself in the papers in over six months. Not since hitting the headlines with a nighttime adventure in skydiving that had resulted in her hospitalization with a hairline fracture to her pelvis.

Her father had not only ignored her exploit, but he'd also ignored Maddie's injury. And not only had he refused to take her phone calls from the hospital, but he'd also made it clear, through his PA, that Maddie was not welcome at the family mansion for her recovery.

She'd been forced to hire a nurse to help during the weeks of her limited mobility. Romi had offered to stay with her, but Maddie refused to take advantage.

"Am I to understand you didn't read Madison in on the contents of this contract?" Vik asked, unexpected disapproval edging his deep tone. "Do you actually expect her to agree?"

"She'll agree." Her father gave her a stern glare. "Or I will cut her out of my life completely."

The words were painful enough to hear, but the absolute conviction in her father's voice stabbed straight through Maddie's carefully cultivated facade to the genuine and all-too-vulnerable emotions underneath.

"Over this?" she demanded, waving her hand toward the printed articles. "It's not true!"

"You will not continue to drag my name and that of my company through the mud, Madison."

"I don't *do* that." While she'd managed a certain level of media notoriety, it had never before been because of anything even remotely like the lies Perry had spewed to the tabloids.

Her father began reading the headlines out loud and weak tears burned the back of her eyes. Maddie refused to give in to them, wishing she could be as genuinely emotionless as the steel-gray-haired man flaying her with other people's words.

"I told you, *he lied*."

"Why would he?" the media fixer asked, sounding interested in an almost clinical way.

"For money. For revenge." Because she'd turned him down one too many times and compounded that by refusing his latest request for a loan. "I don't know, but lied."

How many times did she have to say it?

"It is time for definitive measures to be taken," Jeremy said, as if she hadn't spoken.

"On that at least, we can agree, beginning with the demand for a retraction. I can do my own interview." Even though she hated that kind of direct contact with the media.

She considered offering the ultimate sacrifice of integrating her Maddie Grace life with that of socialite Madison Archer in order to combat the negative image that clearly concerned her father.

Jeremy dismissed her offer with a slicing gesture. "I believe I've made it clear that the current scandal is not my primary concern."

"What is your concern?" she asked, confused.

"The capricious lifestyle that has resulted in your unacceptable and notorious reputation."

"You want me to come work for AIH?" she asked with zero enthusiasm and even less belief.

The last time the issue of Archer International Holdings had come up, her father had made it clear he no longer harbored dreams of her one day taking over.

His harsh bark of laughter was all the answer she needed. "Absolutely not."

"You want me to get a job somewhere else?" She could do that.

She preferred using her education as a volunteer teacher's aide, but if it would help her relationship with her father, she would get a paying job—which hopefully wouldn't conflict with her volunteering schedule.

More derisive laughter fell from her father's lips. "Do you really think any reputable charity or business would hire you right now?"

Heat climbed up her neck, ending in a very rare blush. She'd become adept at hiding her emotions, even suppressing her blushes of embarrassment a long time ago.

But suddenly, she realized that if it *did* become known that Madison Archer was Maddie Grace, the school might be forced to disallow Maddie's volunteering. All because a man she'd thought was a friend had turned out to be a lying, manipulative, opportunistic user.

"He wants you to get married," Vik informed her, no indication in his tone or demeanor that he was joking.

Her father did not jump in with a denial, either.

For the first time, she looked around the room to see how the other occupants were reacting. Her father's media fixer and PA were both busy on their tablets, ignoring the conversation now, or giving a pretty good pretense of doing so.

One of his managers was looking at her with the type of speculation that left Madison feeling dirty, but the fact he had the articles about her spread out in front of him could have something to do with that, too.

The other manager was reading through the paperwork and the man who Maddie did not know was looking at her father, his expression assessing.

Vik's expression was enigmatic as always.

She met her father's gaze again, finding nothing there but implacable resolve. "You want me to get married."

"Yes."

"Who?" she asked, unhappily certain she already had an inkling.

"One of these four men." Her father indicated Vik, the two other managers and the man she did not know. "You know Viktor, of course, and I am sure you remember Steven Whitley." Jeremy nodded toward a manager she was fairly certain had been divorced once already and was nearly twice her age.

Maddie found herself acknowledging both men with a tip of her own head in some bizarre ritual of polite behavior. Or maybe it was just the situation that was so bizarre.

He indicated the manager whose look had given her the willies. "Brian Jones."

His expression was benign now, almost pitying.

"I thought you were engaged," she said, her voice almost as tight as her throat. But that couldn't be helped.

Hadn't Maddie met his fiancée at the last Christmas party?

"Are you?" her father asked, annoyance clear in his tone. "Miss Priest?"

His PA looked up from her tablet with a frown. "Yes, sir?"

"Jones is engaged."

"Is he?" Miss Priest didn't sound concerned. "He is not married."

"But I will be." Brian stood. "I don't believe I'll be needed for the rest of this meeting, if you'll excuse me, sir?"

"Did you read the contract?" her father demanded.

"I did."

"And you are still leaving?"

"Yes, sir."

A measure of respect shone in her father's eyes even as he frowned. "Then go." He nodded toward the stranger on the other side of Maddie as if the introductions had not been interrupted by the defection of one of his candidates. "Maxwell Black, CEO of BIT."

Maxwell smiled at her, magnetism that might actually rival Vik's exuding from him. "Hello, Madison. It's good to see you again."

He wasn't overtly sexual, but there was a vibe to him that made Maddie wrap her arms protectively around herself. This man carried power around him the same way Vik did, but with a predatory edge she hadn't experienced from her father's heir apparent.

Then, she'd never been his business rival.

"I don't believe we've met?" She forced her arms to fall to her sides.

"I saw you at the Red Ball last February."

She remembered going to the charity event that raised money for research into heart disease, but she didn't remember seeing him.

"I would have remembered."

"I'm glad to hear you say so." His teeth flashed in a blinding white smile. "But I meant what I said. I saw you there. We were not introduced."

"Oh."

Her father cleared his throat in that disapproving way he had, but if he expected Maddie to say it was a pleasure to meet the man—under these circumstances—he didn't know her very well.

But then that had been her problem most of her life, hadn't it?

CHAPTER TWO

THE MORNING HAD gone according to Viktor's plans so far, but the spark of temper in Madison's brilliant blue eyes threatened to derail it.

If Jeremy had evinced even one iota of the concern Viktor knew the older man felt for his daughter's current predicament, she would be reacting very differently. But then if father and daughter got along perfectly, or even very well, Viktor's own plans would by necessity be very different.

"You know, I never even entertained the fantasy that you called me to help me, to take *my side* for once, to protect me because I mattered to you." The beautiful redhead offered the emotionally laden words in a flat tone Viktor almost envied.

She would be one hell of a poker player.

She was lying, though. Madison wouldn't have shown up if she didn't think her father would help her.

"You never were a child taken with fairy tales," Jeremy said.

Viktor could have reined in the older man's prideful idiocy, but that wouldn't further his own agenda. However, he felt an unexpected pang of guilt at Madison's barely there flinch and flash of pain in the azure depths of her eyes.

She recovered quickly, her expression smooth—almost

bored. "No, that was always Mom's department. She lived under the fallacy that you cared about us. I know better."

It was Jeremy's turn to flinch and he wasn't as fast at hiding his reaction as his daughter, but then he had to be in shock. Madison didn't go for the jugular like that. In fact, in all the arguments between the tycoon and his daughter Viktor had been privy to, he'd never heard Madison use her mother's memory against her father before.

No triumph at the emotional bloodletting showed on Madison's porcelain features.

Instead, she looked like she wanted nothing more than to get up and walk away. The fact she stayed in her seat was proof the heiress might be criminally flagrant in her personal life, but she wasn't stupid.

She knew her father well enough to be aware that Jeremy's arsenal of threats wasn't empty.

"You have five minutes." Madison's words verified she did indeed realize her father had more *encouragement* to lay on the table, but also that she had little patience in waiting to find out what it was.

Color washed over Jeremy's face. "Excuse me?"

"She wants the other two prongs to the pitchfork," Viktor informed his boss.

Jeremy's scowl said he knew that's what she'd meant, but he didn't like the time limit or implied ultimatum that Madison would get up and leave if it wasn't met.

"Pitchfork?" Black asked.

Viktor could have answered, but he didn't. Giving Maxwell Black any kind of information wasn't on his agenda for the day. Viktor had ignored the presence of the other *candidates* at the table as superfluous, and planned to continue to do so.

Madison wasn't so reticent. "Jeremy never enters a fight he isn't sure he can win. To that end, he stacks the deck.

He'll have three scenarios in the offing, none of which will I want to eventuate."

"You call your father by his first name?" Black asked.

Madison flicked a meaning-laden glance in the tycoon's direction. "As he pointed out, I'm the not the one in the family to wallow in sentimental fantasy."

What she didn't say was that until that morning, Madison had called Jeremy Archer *Father* and sometimes even *Dad*. That she would no longer do so could be taken from her words as a given.

No question that the company president had seriously messed up in his approach to his daughter.

Viktor might have suggested the current course to protect AIH's interests and future, but he would not have blindsided Madison with it during a meeting with strangers.

He'd been angry when he realized Jeremy hadn't even bothered to brief his daughter about the meeting's agenda before her arrival. She might be flighty and prone to inauspicious, risky behavior, but she deserved more respect than that.

Viktor had no doubts that Jeremy would ultimately get what he wanted, not least of which because Viktor would make it happen.

However he had a nascent suspicion that the personal cost for that success might be higher for Jeremy than the president of Archer International Holdings anticipated.

Madison flicked a glance at the Cartier watch on her wrist. "Your time starts now, Jeremy."

"Golden Chances Charter School."

"What about it?" Madison asked with caution, the barest crack in her calm facade finally showing.

"Over the last three years, you have donated tens of thousands of dollars from your Madison Trust income to school improvements and projects."

"I am aware."

But Viktor hadn't been. He began to wonder what else he didn't know about Madison.

Jeremy's eyes, the only feature truly like his daughter's, reflected subtle triumph. "The school's zoning is under scrutiny."

"It wasn't as of yesterday."

"Things change."

"I see." Madison glanced pointedly down at her watch.

"Are you pretending that does not matter to you?"

"No. You have two more minutes."

Viktor was impressed. Madison would have done a better job negotiating a recent deal with a Japanese conglomerate than the project manager they'd sent to Asia.

Jeremy frowned. "Ramona Grayson."

"What about her?"

Viktor would be crossing his legs protectively if that tone and look had been directed at him.

"Her father is a drunk," Jeremy pointed out with well-known derision toward a man Madison had made no bones about considering a second father.

"And mine is a conscienceless bastard. I guess we both lost in the masculine parent lottery, though given a choice I'd pick Harry Grayson. His emotions might be pickled with alcohol, but at least he has them."

Viktor had seen Madison angry. He'd seen her hurt, embarrassed and even seriously disappointed. He had never seen her this coldly furious.

The Madison that Viktor had known for ten years was in no way reflected in the harshly dismissive woman in front of them.

Despite the implication of her words, she loved her father. In the past, she hadn't been able to hide her need for his attention and approval. Her mistake had always been how she went about getting it.

She'd followed in her mother's footsteps, not realizing

Jeremy Archer had been too traumatized by the loss of his wife to want to see her audacious nature reflected in their only child.

"Do you think Ramona sees it that way?" Jeremy asked. "Or perhaps she would prefer a father not lost in a bottle."

Madison shrugged. "It's not something we discuss."

"Nevertheless, the destruction of her father's business, followed by him losing everything to bankruptcy, would hurt her a great deal. Don't you think?"

Madison pulled her phone from her purse with an almost negligent move belied by the blue fire in her gaze. "You have exactly fifteen seconds to take that tactic for coercion off the table."

"Or what?"

"Ten."

And for the first time in Viktor's memory, infallible businessman Jeremy Archer made a mistake in negotiating. He silently called his daughter's bluff.

He believed that because she had no interest in business, Madison was not capable of the same level of ruthlessness as he was.

Viktor knew from personal experience that just because a parent and child lived very different lives, it did not mean that they shared no common personality traits.

Madison pressed her phone to her ear.

"Don't," Viktor said.

Madison just shook her head. "I'm sorry, Viktor."

There would be only one reason for her to apologize to him. Whatever she had planned would have a detrimental effect on AIH and, by default, Viktor's job and livelihood.

The possible implications were still firming in his brain as she made contact with the lawyer in charge of the Madison Trust. "Hello, Mr. Bellingham. I need you to draw some papers up for me. I'm texting you the instructions now."

Seconds later the lawyer's agitated tones came through her phone.

Madison listened for a moment in silence and then replied. "Yes, he knows. He's sitting right here. In fact, he's the one who put this in motion."

The fact the unflappable Bellingham was still speaking loudly enough for Viktor to almost make out his words said something about the nature of Madison's instructions.

"I am absolutely certain, and Mr. Bellingham? If your firm wishes to keep the Madison Trust as a client in sixty-five days when it falls under my control, I suggest you have those papers ready for me to sign when I stop by your office later this afternoon."

Another spate of conversation, this time quieter.

"Thank you, Mr. Bellingham."

Madison tucked her phone back into her purse and faced her father, her expression daring him to ask what she'd done.

Jeremy remained stubbornly silent, or maybe he was in too much shock to react. He had to realize the likely content of those papers, or maybe he didn't.

Maybe Jeremy Archer was under the mistaken impression that Archer International Holdings was important enough to his daughter that she would not do what Viktor was almost positive she had done.

"What do the papers say?" Viktor asked, unwilling to make decisions based on assumptions.

"As you know, because of the financial deal Grandfather Madison made with Jeremy upon his marriage to my mother, the Madison Trust holds twenty-five percent of the privately held shares in Archer International Holdings."

"Those shares are your heritage," Jeremy said.

"Romi is my friend."

"So you gave her some of your shares?" Viktor asked with no real hope it could be that simple.

"If Mr. Grayson's company is under threat from AIH or any company remotely affiliated with it, at one minute past midnight on my twenty-fifth birthday, all of those shares will be signed over to Harry Grayson personally. Not his company."

"You cannot do that!"

"I can." Madison looked more like her father in that moment than at any other time Viktor had known her.

"And if his company is not under threat?" Viktor asked, suspecting that Jeremy's calling his daughter's threat had precipitated some kind of permanent action on her part.

"Half of my shares will be signed over to Romi."

Jeremy stood up, his face flushing with color, his eyes narrowed in fury. "You will not sign those papers."

"I will." Conversely, Madison relaxed back into her chair. "You had your chance to take my friend's happiness off the table as a negotiating point, but you refused to take it."

"That's insane," Steven Whitley said, speaking up for the first time since his introduction to Madison. "Even half of your shares are valued at tens of millions."

"Romi won't have to worry about her drunk of a father ruining *her* life, will she?" Madison asked her father, as if he'd been the one to bring up the point of the shares' value.

Jeremy slammed his hand on the table. "I am not ruining your life, Madison, you've done a fair job of that yourself."

"No, I haven't, but I don't expect you to believe me."

"You are not giving away twelve and a half percent of my company!"

Viktor didn't know if Jeremy realized he'd just effectively taken the third prong of his threats off the table. No way was he going to allow Harry Grayson Sr. to own twenty-five percent of AIH.

Jeremy and Madison were too much alike. Both would

go to extreme measures for what was most important to them. The problem was that while Madison was very important to Jeremy, she did not believe it and Jeremy was willfully blind to what Madison needed from him.

Beyond that Archer International Holdings came first with Jeremy, and the people she cared about came first with Madison. Right now, those two priorities were in direct conflict.

Things were going to go completely pear-shaped if Viktor didn't take control.

"Sit down, Jeremy," Viktor instructed the older man in a tone that was respectful, but firm.

With a glare for his daughter, Jeremy returned to his seat.

"This meeting has derailed and I believe it is time to regroup."

Jeremy nodded.

Viktor stood and straightened his suit jacket before walking around the table and offering his hand to Madison. "Come with me."

"What are you doing, Viktor?" Jeremy asked, his expression considering.

The man knew that AIH sat near the top of Viktor's priority list, too. The company was the conduit for his own plans and no chance was he starting over because of the father-daughter issues of its owner.

"Madison and I have some things to discuss."

Steven frowned at him. "You are not the only candidate, you know. This contract was offered to four of us."

"I am the only one who matters."

An infinitesimal quirk of his boss's mouth said he knew that was true, but he said, "I believe that is up to Madison."

The lady in question made a sound of disparagement. "Right. If the decision is mine to make, I assume it's to be from the men you included in this meeting. One of whom was already engaged, another is old enough to be my father with a history of failed marriages and the other a complete stranger. And then there is Viktor."

"Maxwell Black is a man worth knowing."

While it might be true, Viktor didn't appreciate Jeremy pointing it out. Two half-Russian boys, raised to appreciate a culture not fully American, Maxwell and Viktor had grown up together, their families close, their goals similar.

Friends of a sort, but too alike for comfort, both men were determined to make their mark on the world, to be at the top of the food chain.

Because of the different paths they took to dominant positions in the business world, Viktor's and Maxwell's interests had not conflicted before today.

Thankfully, Madison didn't look impressed by her father's words.

She shifted so she could make eye contact with the CEO of BIT. "Mr. Black, do not be fooled by Jeremy's mistaken ignorance. Those articles are lies made up by a man I believed was my friend. Perry and I never had any sort of sexual relationship, much less a BDSM one."

The pain underlying her measured tones prompted Viktor to make some plans in regard Perry Timwater.

"I believe you." Maxwell's assurance proved he was every bit as intelligent as Viktor had always known him to be.

Madison relaxed infinitesimally. "Good."

"Regardless of the reason for our meeting, I would like to get to know you, Miss Archer." Maxwell, damn his hide, smiled charmingly at Madison. "You seem like an interesting person."

She inclined her head. "Thank you, but—"

"Don't dismiss the possibility of our compatibility out of hand," Maxwell interrupted her with another of his lady-killer smiles. "I bet I could teach you to like some of the things you've been accused of needing."

Madison's gasp said she was shocked by Maxwell's words.

Whether the words themselves or where he chose to speak them, Viktor didn't know and it didn't matter. *He* wasn't surprised. Maxwell played to his strengths and exploited the weakness of others.

Turning the lurid headlines into something forbidden but potentially exciting was a solid tactic for handling the current situation and the humiliation Madison had to be experiencing. Though she'd done nothing to let it show.

Unfortunately for Maxwell, Viktor wasn't going to let the ploy succeed.

Nothing was standing between Viktor and control of AIH. Not even Madison herself, but particularly not Maxwell Black.

Clearly upset with Maxwell's words, Jeremy made a sound of protest.

Before the older man could say anything Viktor was in front of Black, blocking his line of sight with Madison. "That is not something you are going to discuss here, or with Madison at all."

"You think not?" Black challenged back.

"I know not."

"I don't need your protection, Viktor," Madison said quietly from behind him.

He turned to face her, but didn't move so Black would have to stand and sidestep to see her. "Nevertheless, you have it."

She shook her head, whether in denial, or frustration, he didn't know.

"I'm nowhere near taking him up on his offer. I'm pretty sure even the mildest form of that kind of relationship requires trust and I don't have any. Not for men, particularly men with the same priorities as Jeremy Archer. *Businessmen.*"

She made the word sound like a slur.

Viktor didn't believe her regardless. Madison trusted *him*. She always had; even if she no longer realized it.

And while Maxwell's words hadn't surprised him, Madison's willingness to meet them head-on did. But then maybe it shouldn't have. She'd already shown her willingness to stand against her father.

Maxwell got up, his pose too damned relaxed for Viktor's liking. Even less did he like the way the other man moved around him to face Madison. "I see."

"Good."

"Nothing in the contract states we must share a bedroom."

Madison's eyes flared with...was it interest?

Viktor cursed under his breath. "In order to receive the shares stipulated, Madison and her husband must provide an heir for Archer International Holdings."

Madison gasped, anger shimmering around her like electric currents.

Before she could say anything, Maxwell shrugged. "There is always artificial insemination."

"While we live two entirely separate lives?" Madison asked in a tone Viktor recognized, but from the reaction of both Maxwell and her father, they did not.

Jeremy puffed up with renewed anger while the other Russian-American nodded with smug complacency. "Exactly."

"We would be married in name only?" she asked, the disgust levels rising enough that the others should have recognized them.

They didn't.

"No." Viktor was done with the verbal games.

Madison gave him a look like she was questioning his right to make the pronouncement.

"That sort of relationship would be too uncertain for the health of Archer International Holdings," Viktor pointed out.

Disappointment dulled the blue of Madison's azure gaze, but she masked the emotion almost immediately. Viktor cursed silently.

Her father, however, nodded vigorously. "Precisely."

"I think your daughter has already proven she is more than capable of her own decisions." Maxwell's admiration was annoyingly apparent.

"I won't sign the contract," Jeremy said in implacable tones.

The BIT CEO didn't look worried.

Madison's features had gone smooth with a lack of emotion once again as she stared at her father. "You believe I would agree to that kind of marriage?"

For once Jeremy seemed incapable of speech, perhaps realizing finally how little interest Madison would ever have in such a cold-blooded bargain.

"But then you believed the lies Perry spewed, didn't you?"

"I never said that." Jeremy's voice had an alien quality.

Realization of his colossal error in judgment in the handling of his daughter must be settling in, but being who he was, Viktor's boss wasn't going to back down, either.

Madison pulled her copy of the contract from the stack of papers in front of her and stood. "I assume you aren't going to do anything to mitigate Perry's lies."

"I have done it. Do you think this agreement is only about AIH? This is as important for you as it is the reputation of my company." Jeremy clearly believed what he said, but then Viktor had made sure his company's president saw things exactly that way. "Once you are married to a powerful man with an impeccable reputation, you can begin to live down your youthful excesses."

"My life has nothing to do with your company."

Viktor wasn't about to let the conversation degenerate further and there was only one direction it was headed if the two kept talking. Down.

"Conrad will put out a press release categorically denying all of Timwater's allegations," Viktor inserted before another word could be said.

The media fixer looked up from his tablet. "I will?"

Severely unimpressed with the man's lack of dedication to the protection of the company president's daughter, Viktor let Conrad see his displeasure. "You will do a hell of a lot more than that. If you'd been doing your job properly to begin with, this situation would not have happened."

"Protecting Miss Archer from her own excessive behaviors has never been in my job's purview," Conrad claimed in snide tones.

"Did you notice the loss of confidence in AIH articles in the online press this morning?" Viktor asked. "The first of which went live within thirty minutes of that tabloid hitting newsstands. Or did you think that was just a coincidence?"

The media fixer swallowed audibly and shook his head.

Jeremy didn't look too happy, either. He'd been too focused on using the current situation to bring his daughter into line, and had ignored the bigger picture. Something that was anathema to him.

"Your job is to protect the image of this company and anyone affiliated closely enough with it to impact our reputation in the financial community," Viktor reminded Conrad in a hard voice.

"Yes, sir."

"Maybe it's too much for you. Perhaps you'd prefer to move to a PR position working for a nursing home?" Viktor allowed the implication that was the only type of job Conrad would be able to get to hang in the air between them.

The usually unflappable media fixer paled, showing the man still had some of the intelligence he had originally been hired for. "I'm on it."

"You should have been on it at four-fifteen this morning after the scandal sheet went on sale."

Conrad didn't argue. He'd screwed up.

"I don't know what you spent this meeting doing on your tablet, but whatever it was, it wasn't as important as getting ahead of Madison's situation."

"I was writing the engagement announcement."

"I see. Not nursing homes then. Maybe you should be writing puff pieces for online dating sites," Viktor opined.

Nervous laughter filled the room and Jeremy made a sarcastic sound of approval, but it was Madison's genuine amusement that Viktor enjoyed the most.

"I'll need your signature on a civil suit against Perry Timwater," Conrad told Madison.

"No."

Viktor wasn't surprised by Madison's answer and forestalled any arguments from the media fixer or Jeremy. "The man was her friend. She's not going to sue him."

"Some friend." Conrad snorted.

The tiny wounded sound that Madison made infuriated Viktor. "We have other avenues of influence to bring to bear. I want a retraction from Perry in time for this evening's news. Play it off as a joke perpetrated by one friend on another."

Viktor turned to Madison. "For real damage control, you are going to have to do an in-person interview for one of the big celebrity news shows and meet with a journalist with a wider readership than the original article."

"Whatever I can do," she said with more conviction and none of the disagreement he expected.

Viktor's brow wrinkled in thought. Something about this scandal concerned Madison enough that she'd come to her father to ask for help.

While Jeremy might not see Madison showing up for this meeting as that, Viktor was certain of the truth.

Unlike her other escapades, Madison wanted this one cleaned up and her father's refusal to take it seriously had bothered her. A lot.

Viktor needed to figure out why it meant so much to her.

He put his hand out to her again. "Come with me, we'll talk your father's plan through and make some decisions from there."

She looked ready to argue.

He smiled at her. "Is that really too much to ask? I've got Conrad working on fixing this for you."

"Are you going to tell him to stop if I refuse?"

"No." Madison needed an act of good will.

It was important she realized that she could trust Viktor to watch out for her. He had to be the only candidate for her fiancé that she seriously considered.

Because her husband was going to take over AIH eventually and Viktor had every intention of that man being him.

Madison tucked her purse under her arm. "Okay."

"Just a minute," Jeremy said.

Viktor turned to face him. "I know what you want."

"But—"

"Have I ever neglected your interests in a negotiation?"

"No." Jeremy got that implacable look he was known for on his face. "Just remember that Madison's cooperation isn't the only thing on the line right now."

Viktor wasn't surprised by the threat, or even bothered by it.

He'd spent ten years working for this man and his ultimate goal was finally in reach. Viktor wasn't about to let it pass him by.

CHAPTER THREE

MADDIE FOLLOWED VIK into Le Mason, not at all surprised when the maître d' found them a table in a quiet corner in the perpetually busy restaurant, popular with tourists and locals alike.

"Did you eat breakfast?" he asked.

She shook her head, not even pretending to herself that shredding Romi's offering of chocolate pastries counted as actually ingesting calories.

He ordered the restaurant's specialty pancakes for her and coffee for himself.

"Did you bring me here to remind me of friendlier days?" she asked, sure she knew the answer.

"I brought you here because you used to crave their banana pancakes and I hoped to tempt you to eat." His six-foot-four-inch frame should have looked awkward in the medium-sized dining chair, but he didn't.

With his dark hair brushed back in a businessman's cut, his square jaw shaved smooth of dark stubble and a body most athletes would be jealous of covered in a tailored Italian suit, nothing about Viktor Beck could be described as awkward.

Doing her best to ignore his sheer masculine perfection, Maddie adjusted her napkin over her lap. "How did you know I hadn't already?"

"I guessed."

"I used to stop eating when I was stressed." She was surprised he remembered.

"Are you saying that's changed?"

"No." Too much was the same, but she wasn't about to tell him that.

She had to remember that Vik's interests here were aligned squarely with her father's. Not Maddie's. He'd made that clear six years ago and nothing had changed since.

Yes, Vik had gotten Conrad focused on curtailing the media frenzy around Perry's supposed breakup interview, but he'd done it for the sake of the company. Again…not Maddie.

Whatever his agenda now, it had the welfare of AIH as the end goal, she was sure of it. And if she got swept along with the tide, so be it.

"Give me the bullet points of the contract." She was morbidly curious about what her father had done to entice a man like Viktor Beck, or Maxwell Black for that matter, to marry her.

Vik's dark brows rose. "You trust me to tell you everything important?"

Answering honestly wouldn't just make a lie of her earlier words, but it would make her a fool. "I'll read it later to make sure."

"Your father accepts that you will not be his successor."

"What was his first clue?" She'd refused to get a degree in business and had fended off every request, demand and even plea for her to take a job at the company.

"Do you really need me to enumerate them for you?"

"No."

"Suffice it to say, Jeremy has finally accepted you are never going to be CEO of Archer International Holdings." Vik's deep tones were tinged with more satisfaction than disappointment at that pronouncement.

"It would certainly set a roadblock in your own career path if I were."

His espresso eyes flared with quickly suppressed surprise.

She smiled, pleased that he hadn't realized she knew. "You don't seriously think your desire for that office is a secret?"

"It's a family-owned company."

"That you plan to run one day and if Jeremy doesn't realize it, he's being willfully blind."

"That is one of his failings."

"You think?"

"He does not see you for who you are or what you need from him."

"You tried to tell him, once." The year before her clumsy attempt at seduction.

She'd thought Vik standing up for her meant he cared. But looking back, she had to conclude the friendship he'd offered her had been in pursuit of his own goals. Gaining Jeremy Archer's unmitigated trust.

She could have told Vik befriending her wouldn't do anything for him. Her father would have had to care about her for that to be the case. And he didn't.

The only thing that mattered to Jeremy Archer was the company. He'd married her mother to gain the necessary infusion of capital to make AIH a dominant player in the world market. His only interest in Maddie had been as a potential successor.

"He's given up on me personally because he realizes I'm never going to be his *business* heir." As much as it hurt, it also made sense of how unconcerned he'd seemed to be by "Perrygate."

"The only thing Jeremy has given up is his plan to try to lure you into the business."

Maddie shook her head, not buying it for a second. "You

heard him. He had no intention of having Conrad help me until you stepped in."

"Your father can get tunnel vision."

"And all he could see was the endgame." He hadn't even noticed that her scandal had adversely impacted AIH's reputation.

"Yes."

Maddie waited for the waitress to place her pancakes on the table and walk away. "Which is?"

"You married to a man who can and will be groomed to take over as Jeremy's successor."

"If my father can't get what he wants out of me, he'll use me to get it, is that right?"

"That's a very simplified view and not entirely accurate."

She wasn't going to argue something she knew to be true, as did Vik, even if he was too loyal to admit it.

"Jeremy wants his successor to be family." Hence the marriage. "How old-fashioned."

"It ensures his grandchildren will inherit his legacy intact."

"And that's important."

"To him."

The smell of pancakes, fresh bananas and syrup had her mouth watering. "What about you?"

"You need to ask?"

"AIH is your life." As much as it had always been her father's.

"Say rather AIH is the vehicle for my own dreams."

"I didn't know men like you dreamed."

"Without visionaries at the helm, companies like AIH would atrophy and eventually die."

"So, you think my father is just a very dedicated dreamer." Sarcasm hanging thick from her words, she took a bite of her pancakes and hummed with pleasure.

Vik laughed. "That is one way to put it."

"And your personal dreams include being president of AIH one day."

"Yes."

His easy honesty surprised her and charmed her in a way. She'd always thought of men like him as having goals. Solid, steady, unemotional stepping stones that marked their success.

"Wow. I guess the heart of a Russian really does beat under that American-businessman veneer."

"My grandparents like to think so."

She offered him a bite of pancake with a slice of banana. "And your parents?"

Vik took the bite just like he used to and memories of a time when they'd been friends, and all *her* dreams had centered on this man, assailed Maddie.

"My mother has been out of the picture for all of my memory. My dad is like a computer virus. He keeps coming back."

She smiled. "I should say I'm sorry, but having a father who drives you nuts makes you more human."

Vik shrugged, but she couldn't help wondering if he'd told her about his dad on purpose. To build rapport. She thought Vik had outclassed her dad a long time ago in the manipulation department.

After all, Jeremy Archer still thought he ran AIH. However anyone with a brain—not blinkered by willful blindness—and access to the company would realize it was actually Vik's show and had been for a few years.

"Whose idea was it to offer Steven Whitley and Brian Jones up on the chopping block?"

"It's hardly a sacrifice to be offered this kind of opportunity." Vik drank his coffee, his expression sincere if she could believe it.

But then what was to say she couldn't?

"Marriage to the prodigal daughter for an eventual company presidency?" That might well be worth it to a man like Vik.

"You don't exactly fit the distinction of prodigal."

"Don't I?"

"You haven't blown through your inheritance. In fact, you are surprisingly fiscally responsible."

"Thank you, I think."

"You haven't abandoned your family to see the world."

"I moved out of the family home."

He winked at her. "But stayed in the city."

"What can I say? I love San Francisco."

"And your father."

"I'd rather not talk about that."

"Understood." He smiled and her nerve endings went *twang*. "Your media notoriety isn't even of the truly scandalous variety."

"Until Perrygate."

Vik waved his hand, dismissing the importance of Perry's lies. "That will be handled."

"Thank you for that." The thought of being forced to give up her volunteerism because of an unsavory reputation hurt deeply, compounding her pain at Perry's betrayal.

He knew how important working with the children was to her.

"But seriously?" she asked, refocusing. "Whitley and Jones?"

Vik shrugged, but his lips firmed in a telling line. "They're the most likely men within the company to do the job."

"Marrying me?"

"Becoming the next president."

"Besides you."

"Besides me," he agreed.

"You're the only *real* candidate."

"I would like to think so."

"And then there is Maxwell Black."

Vik's eyes narrowed, the brown depths darkening to almost black. "Your father is never going to approve the kind of marriage Black suggested."

"And if that is the only kind of marriage I'm willing to agree to?" she taunted.

"Jeremy will hire a surrogate and have his own child in hopes of succeeding with him where he failed with you."

Wholly unprepared for that answer, several seconds passed before Maddie felt like she could breathe again. "He's not a young man any longer."

"He is fifty-seven."

"He would not be so cruel." And she did not mean to her.

No child deserved to be born merely as a player on the chessboard. She should know.

She'd taken herself out of play, but she'd had the strength of the memory of her mother's love to bolster her own courage.

This child would only have Jeremy Archer.

Maddie shivered at the prospect. "I'm not having a child simply for him or her to be put in the same position."

"You want children." There was no doubt in Vik's voice.

"Someday."

"Whenever you have them, or whoever you have your children with, Jeremy will want the company to ultimately pass on to them."

"I know." Her father's role in her life and that of any children she might have was something she'd already spent several hours talking to her therapist, Dr. MacKenzie, about.

"That is not a bad thing."

She'd come to realize that. While Maddie's feelings about AIH were too antagonistic for her to ever want to be a part of it, as she'd always seen it as the entity that kept her father from her, it did not automatically follow that her children would feel the same way.

"You said something about me having a child being necessary for the man I marry to take over AIH."

"Upon the birth of our first child, my succession to the presidency will be announced. Your father will shift into a less active role as chairman of the board on his sixtieth birthday."

"And if I haven't had a child by then?"

"My becoming company president will not happen until we have had our first child."

"What if we can't have children?"

"We can."

"You sound very certain."

"I am."

She remembered the ultrasound her doctor had ordered as part of her last physical, at the company's request. She'd thought it was odd, but since her medical insurance was through AIH, Maddie hadn't demurred.

"Jeremy had them run fertility tests on me."

"Just preliminaries, but enough to know that aside from something well outside the norm, you should have no trouble conceiving."

"That's so intrusive!"

Vik didn't reply and, honestly, Maddie didn't know what she wanted him to say. She wasn't entirely sure the test had been all her dad's idea. If Vik had suggested them, she wasn't sure knowing would be of any benefit to her.

"What else?"

"The contract gives five percent of the company to me on our five-year anniversary. Another five percent on the birth of each child, not to exceed ten percent."

"How generous, he'll allow me to have two children." She'd always dreamed of having, or adopting, at least four and creating a home filled with love and joy.

"The contract does not limit the number of children you have, only the stock incentive to me for fathering them."

She ignored the way Vik continued to assume he was her only option. "What else?"

"On your father's death, if we have been married for ten years, or more, I will get another five percent of the company. The remaining fifty percent of the company will be placed in trust for our children with voting proxy passing only to our children actively involved in the executive level of running the company. I will hold all outstanding family-voting proxies."

"But the other children will receive the income from the shares."

"Yes."

"It sounds complicated." But then her father wasn't a simple man, not by any stretch.

Vik took a sip of his coffee. "Jeremy wants a legacy and you've made it clear you won't be part of it."

"So he wrote me out of the will."

"Only insofar as his ownership of Archer International Holdings is concerned."

"I see." Honestly, she didn't care.

The Madison Trust provided all the income she needed to live on. That income would decrease once half of her shares in the company transferred to Romi, but Maddie didn't mind.

The biggest expense she had was keeping up her appearance as Madison Archer, socialite. As far as she was concerned, that part of her life could go hang. If her father wanted her to keep up appearances, he could pay for the designer wardrobe and charity event tickets.

"Is there anything else pertinent to me in the contract?"

"Your father would like us to live in Parean Hall."

The Madison family mansion, named for the pristine white marble used for flooring in the oversized foyer and the risers on the grand staircase, had stood empty since the death of Maddie's grandfather from a massive coronary upon hearing of his daughter's accidental death nine years ago.

"I have plans for the house." It was part of the trust and would come to her when she turned twenty-five.

"What plans?"

"That is none of your business."

"Indulge me."

Maddie didn't answer, but concentrated on finishing her pancakes. Vik didn't press.

His patient silence finally convinced her to tell him.

She said, "I want to start a charter school, this one with boarders from the foster-care system."

"An orphanage."

"No, a school for gifted children in difficult family circumstances." A place the children could be safe and thrive.

Vik sipped at his coffee pensively for several moments.

"How will you fund it?"

"A large portion of my trust income will go to it annually, but I also plan to raise funds amidst the heavy coffers of this city. I've learned a lot about fund-raising since my first volunteer assignment on the mayoral campaign when I was a teenager."

"Your father has no idea how full your life is."

"No, he doesn't." And Vik had barely an inkling as well.

She'd stopped telling him about her plans and activities when he'd rejected her so summarily six years ago.

Vik relaxed back in his chair. "The Madison family estate is a large house, even by the elite of San Francisco standards, but hardly the ideal location for a school. Either in building architecture or location."

"Oh, you don't think poor children should live among the wealthy?" she challenged.

He didn't appear offended at her accusation. "I think it will cost more than it's worth to get zoning approval."

"That section was zoned for the inclusion of a local school, but none was ever built."

"And you think that zoning will remain once your neighbors learn of your plans?" he asked in a tone that said he didn't.

"I don't intend to advertise them."

One corner of his lips tilted just the tiniest bit. "A fait accompli?"

"Yes."

"You have to apply for permits, hire staff…it's not going to stay a secret long."

"And then the fight begins, you are saying?"

"Yes."

"But why should the residents care if there's a school in their neighborhood? The city planners clearly intended there to be one."

"And the fact there isn't should tell you something."

"But—"

"I can find you a better building."

She didn't want to sell her grandparents' home. Her memories there weren't the greatest. Her Grandfather Madison had often made Jeremy Archer look warm and cuddly by comparison, but Maddie's mother's stories of her own childhood had been filled with delight.

Maddie always wished she'd had a chance to know her grandmother, Grace Madison.

"I'll have to sell the mansion to finance another purchase." No matter how much she might not want to do it.

The school was too important to give up and Vik was right, as he so often was—the opposition to a boarding school in that neighborhood for the underprivileged was bound to be stiff.

Vik shook his head decisively. "I'll buy the other building."

"In exchange for what?"

"Consider it my wedding gift to you."

"Presumptuous."

"I'm the only man I will allow you to consider." Dark brown eyes fixed on her with unmistakable purpose.

She ignored the way his words sent shivers through her insides. "You're assuming I'll agree to marry."

"Your father doesn't realize it, but I know he didn't need anything beyond his first threat to convince you to fall in with his plans."

"You don't think so?"

"Are you in another relationship?" Vik asked, the words clipped, something like anger smoldering in the depth of his gaze.

"No." Maddie saw no reason to hedge.

"Dating anyone?" he pressed.

"No." She frowned. "Why are you asking about this now?"

"Because if you were in a relationship with someone who mattered to you, no pressure your father brought to bear would sway you into marrying someone else."

He was right, but it rankled. "You think you know me so well."

"I know that your dad means more to you than you want him to believe."

"It's not a matter of what I want." Her father didn't think he mattered to Maddie because she wasn't all that important to *him*. Not in a personal way.

"Jeremy isn't going to back off on this."

"Why now?"

"You need to ask?"

"Yes." Her father had been too unconcerned about

Perry's scandal for it to be what tipped him into must-get-my-wayward-daughter-married mode.

"Jeremy has been worried about what will happen when you come into your majority for the Madison Trust for a while."

"Now he knows."

"I don't believe he saw that one coming."

"No. It wouldn't have occurred to him that I would purposefully put Archer International Holdings at risk."

"No."

"But apparently the idea that I might marry someone who might do that had already occurred to Jeremy."

"Yes." Something about the quality of Vik's stillness said he might have had more to do with that than her own father's paranoia.

"So, he was already considering how to get me to marry the man of his choice?" Maddie surmised. "He's using Perrygate as a vehicle for his own agenda."

She wasn't surprised by her father's mercenary motives, but she didn't have to like them.

"You would have to ask him." Vik indicated to the waitress to bring their bill. "I think the reality is more that he is afraid you'll end up with Mr. Timwater. Your father will do anything to prevent that."

"To protect the reputation and future of the company." Considering Perry's poor luck with his own business ventures, she could understand her father not wanting him to get even shallow hooks into any part of AIH.

"Sometimes, I think you are as willfully blind as your father." Vik shook his head. "He wants to stop you from marrying a man who would go public with the kind of claims Perry made in his interview."

"And Jeremy believes you're a huge improvement."

"You don't?" Vik asked, his tone more than a little sardonic.

She wasn't about to answer that. "Perry has never been in the running."

"Several articles in the media over the past six years would suggest otherwise."

"And the media *never* gets it wrong."

"You've never denied it, not publicly and not to your father."

"That's where you are wrong." And she had no satisfaction in that truth. "I told my father that Perry was just a friend, but he never believed me. He's always been more interested in his own interpretations and those of the media than anything I might have to say."

"I don't think that's true, but he is stubborn."

"So are you, in the way you defend him."

"Would you respect me if I had no loyalty for *my* friends?"

"Is my father your friend?"

"Yes." The single word wouldn't let her doubt his sincerity.

She used to think Vik was her friend, too.

Then things changed.

Now, she was facing the reality that it wasn't just that her father wanted her to marry Vik, but so did the man himself. Both had their reasons, but while different those reasons all centered around AIH, not Maddie.

She wasn't sure where, if anywhere at all, she came into the picture, other than as a minor piece on the chessboard. She certainly didn't feel like the queen.

CHAPTER FOUR

"I'LL BE BACK at three to take you to the lawyer's office," Vik informed Maddie as she unlocked her door and stepped inside.

"Are you sure that's not a conflict of interest?"

"Would you rather go alone?" he asked, a mocking twist on the masculine lips she'd spent far too much time studying as a teenager.

"No." Especially not after witnessing the media circus outside her building.

The paparazzi had always found her interesting, but it had never been like this.

And it was only getting worse as the morning wore on.

She'd managed to sneak out of the back entrance earlier, but the story and her location had spread in just that amount of time. There were almost as many media leeches haunting the other entrances to the building as in front now.

Even the parking garage hadn't been free of their presence.

She'd expected Vik to have his driver drop her off, but she could only be grateful he had insisted on getting out of the car and escorting her all the way to her apartment door.

He'd kept his body positioned protectively between her and the reporters stalking her. Vik was also very good at remaining silent no matter what was thrown at them and Maddie found it easier not to react with him as a buffer.

"Security will have the parking garage cleared," Vik said after a short text conversation on the elevator.

"Thank you."

They stepped off the elevator into a thankfully empty hallway.

Vik looked both ways before leading her toward her door anyway. "You need a security detail."

She shrugged, not wanting to get in to this argument right now, and not at all sure she would win it.

"When was the last time you had this lock changed?" he asked as she opened the door.

She looked up at him, wishing it didn't feel like all the oxygen got sucked out of the air every time she did that. "Why would I have it changed?"

"At least tell me you had new locks installed when you moved in."

"Why would I?" she asked again. "I'm sure the building management took care of it when the previous tenants moved out."

His expression said he didn't share her confidence. "You don't own the apartment?"

"No." She'd always planned to move into the mansion once she'd turned it into a school after she got control of her Madison Trust inheritance.

"Who has a key to this door, besides any previous tenant?" he asked with sarcastic emphasis on his last words.

Maddie leaned against the doorjamb when he showed no signs of following her inside. "Romi." She grimaced. "Perry, but he's not going to show his face."

Vik just shook his head before pulling his phone out and making a call. "Get the building access cards affiliated with Madison Archer's apartment deactivated and new cards issued for her, Ramona Grayson and myself."

He listened in silence for a moment. "Yes, have Ms. Grayson's delivered to her and the others to my office. I will pass Miss Archer's on when I see her later this afternoon. I want a security system installed, along with high-grade safety locks while we are gone."

The day before, Vik's high-handedness would have made Maddie livid. Today? It just felt like someone was watching out for her.

"You know, for a corporate shark, you're pretty good at this white-knight stuff," she observed as he tucked his phone away.

"I make a good ally."

"But a terrifying enemy, I bet."

"You'll never have to find out."

"Even if I refuse my father's ultimatum?" She didn't bother to point out that if she did agree, she could still choose to marry a different man.

They both knew how unlikely that was.

Her youthful affections notwithstanding, she wasn't about to marry a stranger or a man who had multiple divorces under his belt.

Vik reached out and cupped her nape, stepping forward until mere centimeters separated their bodies, the heat from his surrounding her in a strangely protective cocoon. He didn't say anything, just caught her gaze, his dark eyes compelling her to some sort of belief.

Her breath escaped in a whoosh, unexpected and instant physical reaction crackling along her nerve endings while her heart started a *precipitando*. "Viktor?"

"You will never be my enemy, Madison."

"You're so confident I'll do what you want?"

"I'm confident *in* you, there's a difference."

There so was. He couldn't have said anything more guaranteed to get to her. People who believed *in* Maddie were a premium in her life. And less by one after this morning.

Dark espresso eyes continued to trap her even more effectively than his hand on her neck. "Trust me."

"Do I have a choice?" she asked with an attempt at sarcasm.

"No." His reply held no responding humor. Tilting his head, he stopped only when their lips almost touched. "You don't, and do you know why?"

"Tell me," she said in a voice that barely registered above a whisper.

"You already do." Then his mouth pressed against hers and the drumbeat in her chest went to the faster paced *stretto,* while electric pleasure sparked from his lips to hers.

A sensation she'd only known once before despite the fact she'd tried kissing other men. Six years ago when she'd thought the best way to celebrate becoming an adult would be to tell the man she'd been infatuated with for years that she loved him.

Even the memory of that old humiliation could not diminish the feelings of ecstasy washing over her from this elemental connection.

The kiss didn't last long, just a matter of seconds, but it could have been hours for the impact it had on her. When Vik pulled away and stepped back, Maddie had to stop herself from following him.

"Three o'clock. Turn your phone ringer off. I'll text."

She nodded, her mind blown by a simple kiss. Which did not bode well for her emotional equilibrium.

She fought acknowledging the possibility that tycoon Viktor Beck might well be more dangerous to the almost twenty-five-year-old Maddie as Archer business protégé Vik had been to her as a teenager.

"Go inside and lock the door, Madison."

She nodded again, but didn't move as she tried to reconcile the present with the past.

He shook his head, a curve flirting at the corner of the usually serious lines of his mouth. "You're going to be trouble."

"That's what my father says."

"I was thinking of a very different kind of trouble." Vik traced her bottom lip. "Believe me."

"Oh, really." Her lip tingling from his touch, warmth infused her that corresponded to the heat in his voice.

His smile became fully realized, and it was almost as good as the kiss.

She wasn't the one who was going to be *trouble*.

"Oh," she said again, this time without intending to, her body reacting to that warm expression in ways she just *didn't* with other men.

Vik waited in silence, no sense of impatience in evidence, but Maddie knew every minute he spent with her cost his tightly packed schedule.

She nodded to herself this time. "See you later."

Maddie stepped back into her apartment. Closing the door on him was a lot harder than it should have been.

She threw the dead bolt and a second later there was a double tap on the door. Vik's goodbye.

Using the pay-as-you-go cell phone she'd bought to provide Maddie Grace, volunteer, with a contact number, she called the school and let them know she wouldn't be in for at least a couple of days. She couldn't risk being caught in her Maddie Grace persona and having the best part of her life exposed to the media furor.

The next call she made was to Romi, who started cursing in French when Maddie told her friend that Jeremy Archer was using Perrygate to try to push Maddie into an *approved* marriage.

Maddie didn't tell Romi about the threat to her own

father's company or Maddie's response to it. Romi would demand her friend not sign the papers.

"Are you going to do it? Are you going to marry the man you've been crushing on for the last ten years?"

"That was a schoolgirl crush. I'm twenty-four years old now."

"And still a virgin. Still avoiding relationships."

"I'm not exactly alone in that."

Romi's silence was as good as a verbal acknowledgment.

"Besides, I *could* marry one of the others."

"Right."

"Maxwell Black offered a marriage of convenience with children by artificial insemination." She couldn't help a small smile at the memory of her father's reaction to that offer.

She knew Romi would get a kick out of it as well.

"Max was part of your father's deal?" Romi demanded in a tone a couple of registers above her normal one.

All of Maddie's humor fled. "You know Maxwell."

Silence. "A little."

"More than a little if you call him *Max*."

"We went out a few times."

"You never told me."

"It's no big deal." But, threaded with vulnerability, Romi's tone said otherwise.

Maddie warned, "I think he found Perry's claims about our supposed sex life *intriguing*."

"I know."

"You what?" Maddie practically screeched, her own problems forgotten for the moment. "How do you know that?"

"Do you really need me to spell it out for you?"

"You're still a virgin."

Romi had said so and the woman might be a hyperactive, borderline political anarchist and more than a little eclectic in her dress style, but she never lied.

"Technically, that is true."

"Technically?" Maddie drew the word out.

"Look, Maddie, I don't want to talk about it." Vulnerability now saturated Romi's voice, defenselessness that Maddie could not ignore.

"Okay, sweetie. But I'm here for you. You know that, right?"

"Always. SBC."

"SBC." Sisters by choice.

Maddie's mom had called them that the first time when she was explaining to the elementary school principal why the girls would do better with the same kindergarten teacher.

He'd refused to change their assignments and Helene Archer had called in the big guns.

It was the only time Maddie could remember her father stepping foot in her grade school. Mr. Grayson had come down, too, threatening to withdraw his company's support from the prestigious private school.

Romi and Maddie had never been assigned different classrooms again.

They had shared everything, including their grief at the loss of the only mother either girl had ever known when Helene Archer's speedboat had crashed into rocks invisible under the moonless sky.

Maddie hadn't gotten her propensity for risky behavior from nowhere.

She understood now that her mother's increasingly erratic behavior had been Helene's way of crying out for help. Help neither Maddie, nor her father, realized Helene needed.

It was a failure Maddie was still coming to terms with.

Vik's text came in at ten minutes to three.

He was on a conference call he could not reschedule,

but two bodyguards would be at her door in a few minutes. They had AIH indigo-level security IDs and she was not to open the door unless she saw the familiar badges through her peephole.

Specially trained for protecting people rather than corporate property and secrets, the indigo team was her father's personal security detail. It used to be hers, too. Wanting to live as normal a life as possible, Maddie had refused to be assigned bodyguards when she moved out of the family mansion.

Her father had argued, but ultimately given in.

She didn't think Vik would be as easily swayed. If he thought Maddie needed a bodyguard for her security, she'd have one.

The same way the company's on-site security system had been upgraded because Vik deemed it necessary. Her father had been all for it, though.

Nothing was too good for Archer International Holdings.

The limo was waiting in front of the elevator bank in the parking garage. Thankfully, no enterprising reporter had managed to keep vigil. Which probably had less to do with the parking garage guards than the two additional indigo-badge bodyguards standing at attention on either side of the elevator doors.

One of them stepped forward to open the door to the limo and she stepped inside, only then realizing that Vik had taken the conference call on his mobile.

Every dark hair perfectly in place, his designer suit immaculate, he nodded at her while carrying on a conversation in Japanese.

His words did not falter, his Japanese smooth and unhesitating, and yet she felt the weight of his full regard. Like his attention was fully on her.

Like she mattered.

Succumbing to the desire to sit beside him, Maddie settled onto the smooth leather seat across from AIH's media fixer. Relieved that none of the bodyguards had instructions to join them in the back of the limo, she was still grateful the other occupant gave her an excuse to give in to the irresistible urge.

The need to be near Vik was verging on ungovernable, just like it had been six years ago.

Maddie wanted to chalk it up to the exceptional circumstances. She just wasn't sure she could.

Which was not enough of a caution to move to the other seat. There was simply no comparison between Vik and Conrad, who until that morning she had found slightly annoying but now considered flat-out obnoxious.

The PR guru took a break from typing madly on his tablet to silently acknowledge her. If his smile looked more like a grimace, she wasn't interested enough in interacting with him to call him on it.

Besides, Perry's fake exposé had triggered an ugly media frenzy beyond anything Maddie had ever experienced for her far more innocent escapades.

There was even speculation now that some of her riskier endeavors had been the result of orders from her *master*. That wasn't even the worst of it. Maddie did not know how a virgin could be labeled a sex addict with obvious intimacy issues, but she'd stopped reading her Google alerts after that headline.

The limo had exited the parking garage and pulled away from her building when Vik ended his phone call.

"Are you okay?" he asked Maddie.

Honesty would reveal a level of vulnerability she wasn't comfortable sharing with Vik, much less Conrad. She had no idea how her life had spun out of control so fast.

And Perrygate was only part of it. Her father's ultimatum and the realization their relationship would never be what she wanted had been followed too closely by the equally alarming, if for different reasons, acknowledgment that she was actually considering marrying her girlhood crush.

"I'm fine."

"Good," Conrad said, as if he'd asked the question. "Containing this media bloodbath is going to take serious effort and you need to be on your top game."

He didn't have to tell her. Maddie had spent the time since Vik had dropped her off earlier worrying about what would happen if she couldn't reclaim her reputation.

The all too real prospect of losing her dreams of opening a small charter school tightened Maddie's throat, so she just nodded.

Once the media started looking more closely at Maddie's life, her alter ego was bound to come to light and the probability of losing her volunteer position was pretty much guaranteed.

While she enjoyed the anonymity of her Maddie Grace persona, she'd only taken rudimentary steps to keep her two lives separate. She wasn't James Bond, after all, just a socialite who craved time contributing as a *normal* person.

The only reason no one had cottoned on to Maddie Grace and Madison Archer being the same person before was that the news simply wasn't all that interesting. Or it hadn't been.

Her notoriety as Madcap Madison had been of the innocent variety, good for filler pieces in the social columns, but not salacious enough to really impact circulation numbers. Therefore *she* had not been interesting enough to be targeted by any serious digging.

She'd no doubt reporters were getting out their sharpest spades now. Perrygate was all that and a bag of chips for the gossipmongers.

The most painful part of Maddie's predicament was

that it wasn't just her dreams on the line here; Romi was equally invested in the charter school.

Vik sent a text and then pocketed his phone. "Our lack of an immediate response opened the door to other spurious claims from supposed former lovers."

Vik gave Conrad a look that left no doubt exactly who the VP of Operations for AIH blamed for that mistake.

Maddie felt no smugness at the media fixer being so obviously in the doghouse with Vik. Her life was too out of control to harbor even a hint of that, but she couldn't help the small thrill of pleasure at him taking her side.

From the moment he'd stepped in and ordered Conrad's cooperation that morning, Maddie had known she wasn't alone in facing the painful consequences of her onetime friend's betrayal.

Conrad tugged at the collar of his shirt. "We're working on retractions, but the best strategy for solidifying the prank angle is to give the media hounds another story."

"What do you mean? Like a two-headed baby from outer space, or something?" Maddie asked as her phone chimed to indicate a text from one of her select group.

Thinking it was Romi, she pulled out her phone and checked the message. It wasn't from her SBC; it was from Vik and said, You are not fine. We will talk. Later.

She texted back. If you say so.

Vik pulled his phone out and replied to her text while speaking. "Or something. A glossy celebrity gossip magazine has already offered a two-page spread announcing our formal engagement in exchange for exclusive photos of a lavish, well-attended wedding reception."

"We're engaged now?" Had she missed something between the text convo and their in-person discussion?

Vik didn't answer, but waited in silence for her to come to her own conclusion.

"It's the best way to stop any more dirty snow falling in this avalanche," Conrad said unctuously.

"Dirty snow? Really?" she asked sarcastically.

"Do you have a better word for it?"

"Perrygate."

"Appropriate, but don't use it on your social networks," Conrad instructed her. "It implies a negative rift between you and Mr. Timwater. We're dismissing all this as a joke gone wrong."

"Then you can play it off as the bad joke that ruined a friendship. I won't play nice with Perry." She couldn't.

Conrad frowned thoughtfully. "It would be better for you to be seen as the forgiving friend. Waiting a few months to cut the man from your life will increase your popularity."

"I don't care."

"Timwater isn't coming within a hundred feet of Madison, not even to apologize." Vik's voice brooked no argument.

And Conrad proved he was more intelligent than other evidence to the contrary because he didn't make one. "Fine. Fine." He started taking notes. "'The Prank That Ended a Friendship.' I can use that. We can spin the angle even. 'The Bad Joke That Almost Ended an Engagement.'"

Maddie looked at Vik. "Is he for real?"

Part of her knew this was the way things had to be, that Conrad was just doing his job, but having her life reduced to clichés and headlines was not fun.

"It's going to be okay, Madison." Vik pulled her cold hand into his own. "Trust me."

He had never hesitated to invade her personal space, or to touch her, though she'd never noticed him being so free with others. It was one of the reasons she'd convinced her eighteen-year-old self that Vik might return her feelings.

She'd realized later that the small touches were probably the result of the way his Russian grandparents had raised him. Maddie had figured she hadn't seen him behave that way with others because he had so few personal relationships.

None but his grandparents and her father that she'd ever actually come into contact with.

That was one thing she and Vik had in common.

A very small inner circle.

She didn't comment on this now, just gave thanks for the fact he was willing to offer her the kind of comfort she needed and had never been able to ask for.

Vik squeezed her fingers. "Conrad is one of the best in the business. Before this morning I would have said *the* best."

Conrad flinched, proving he'd been listening even as he typed.

"And our engagement is the only way to restore my reputation?" she asked almost rhetorically.

She didn't see another way out, either.

Her father had more leverage for his plan than he could possibly comprehend. The realization of Maddie and Romi's dreams relied on a reputation Maddie could not afford to lose.

Vik frowned. "I'm sorry, Madison, but nothing is going to make the story go away completely."

"Why not?" Media fixers worked miracles.

Isn't that what everyone said? If they couldn't fix this, her and Romi's dreams were going to crash and burn. There was no way Maddie was going to let that happen.

Conrad looked up from his tablet. "Some people will always believe that where there is or was smoke, there had to be some ember of fire."

"But there isn't one."

The twist of Conrad's lips said he was probably one of *those* people.

Vik's hand moved to Maddie's thigh, bringing her attention careening back to him and him alone. "I believe you."

"No matter what the press has claimed, I've never even had a serious boyfriend," she admitted painfully.

Something flared in Vik's eyes, but he just nodded. "You've been too busy getting into trouble."

"Not *this* kind of trouble."

"I know."

"And not even my usual in the last six months."

Conrad's head snapped up. "Is that true?"

"I haven't done anything zany or even remotely newsworthy since I broke my pelvis in that botched skydiving landing."

Conrad narrowed his gaze. "What about parties? Random hookups?"

"Did you not hear her, Conrad?" Vik asked, dropping the temperature in the limo with the ice in his tone. "Madison does not do random hookups."

"She said she hasn't had a serious relationship, that the men claiming to have engaged in BDSM encounters are lying. Miss Archer never claimed to be celibate." Okay, so Conrad *had* been listening.

Vik didn't thaw even a little. "You can take *no random hookups* as a given."

"Can I?" Conrad asked Maddie, surprising her with his tenacity.

"Yes," she replied firmly. "I haven't been out in the evening except to attend charity events since my accident."

"With Perry as your escort?" Conrad asked, sounding unhappy by the possibility.

Which she could understand, in light of recent events. She wouldn't call the emotion she was feeling right now unfettered joy, either.

"A couple of times."

Vik's jaw hardened.

"Most events, Romi and I go together. Perry isn't all that interested in helping others." Maddie felt disloyal admitting that truth, but Romi had always said it.

Perry had never been as interested in the causes Maddie supported as the A-listers and potential business contacts he could meet at certain events.

"You've been at most of them, yourself," she offered to Vik.

He frequently represented AIH at that sort of thing, being an expert at making connections Perry only aspired to. Maddie knew that Vik also supported the causes in very tangible ways, both on behalf of the corporation and personally.

The gorgeous, corporate white knight nodded.

"That could work in our favor, unless you were photographed with your date for the evening," Conrad mused. "Even then, we could make it work."

"Vik hasn't had a date with him at one of these events in over a year." Knowledge that revealed how much attention Maddie paid to Vik.

A fact she'd done her best to hide even from herself, darn it.

His raised brow and knowing look said he realized that, too.

"That's good. We can back-engineer a budding relationship you've taken pains to keep out of the media spotlight." Conrad took more notes on his tablet. "This works."

Maddie turned toward Vik. "We're really getting married?"

"You tell me."

"Only it doesn't seem possible." Everything since her nearly spilled cup of coffee that morning felt like a dream, at times odd, unpleasant and bordering unbelievable.

"Believe it," Vik said, unconsciously answering her silent thoughts.

She narrowed her eyes, trying to read him. "How can you take this so calmly?"

"What am I supposed to be upset about?"

"Yesterday you were a free agent. Today you are engaged." Didn't that bother him, even a little?

Or was it something Vik had planned all along? Somehow, she couldn't quite dismiss that possibility.

"We are not engaged yet."

Something went tight in her chest. "But—"

"We will finish this discussion after you meet with the lawyer."

What did that mean? Did he think they were engaged, or not? *Were* they engaged? Had she said *yes?* She was pretty sure she hadn't. And she might know her choices were very limited, but did Vik? Really?

He returned his attention to his phone and sent a text.

This time she had no doubts it was to her.

Sure enough a few seconds later, her phone chimed. Trust me.

Trust him. Right. He thought it was that easy? "You aren't going to try to talk me out of signing the paperwork?"

"I told Jeremy threatening Romi could boomerang on him."

"He didn't believe you."

"He has a hard time backing off once he's set a thing in motion."

"Are you saying he's already started the wheels of destruction for Mr. Grayson's company? They used to be good friends."

Vik shrugged noncommittally. "He's done the research on how to make it happen."

"And he didn't want to waste his efforts?" Her dad could be so cold, but then that wasn't breaking news.

"You and I have agreed Jeremy could have no idea how spectacularly it would come back to bite him on the ass."

"But you aren't trying to change my mind."

Conrad stopped typing and listened as if he, too, was curious about what was motivating Vik's behavior.

Vik ignored the other man, his focus entirely on Maddie. "Those shares ultimately belong to you."

"My father doesn't see it that way."

"It never occurred to Jeremy that any child of his would consider AIH as a means to an end rather than the end itself."

What did he know? Did Vik realize she had always intended to use her income from the shares to run the school?

It wouldn't be a long stretch from what she'd told him that morning.

What he couldn't know was that Romi would do the same. She wanted the school as much as Maddie.

Vik's dream was something quite different, but obviously just as important to him. "You want the company."

"Like your father, I want to leave a legacy for my children." Some might think the lack of emotion in Vik's deep tones belied his words.

Maddie knew better.

His dark brown eyes burned with certainty. "Archer International Holdings will be that legacy."

"But we're not engaged." She couldn't help the small bit of sarcasm.

Maddie was unsurprised by Vik's lack of response.

CHAPTER FIVE

MADDIE'S TIME IN the lawyer's office went quickly, though the elderly man did ask if she was sure she knew what she was doing.

Maddie had no doubts.

Vik stood when she came back into the anteroom, no sign he was in any way upset about what she'd been doing. "All finished?"

"Yes."

"Do you have any plans for the rest of today?"

"No."

Vik put his hand on the small of her back and walked with her out of the law office. "Good."

"Why?"

"We have a photo shoot with the magazine photographer this evening. He'll join us for dinner at your father's mansion. My grandparents will be there."

"Playing happy families? Is that really necessary?"

"Yes."

When they reached the parking garage, he led her to his car, the limo and SUV full of bodyguards nowhere in evidence.

"Conrad is in the limo with a redheaded decoy." Vik opened the passenger door of the black amethyst Jaguar XJL for Maddie.

She settled into the luxury car. "Better her than me. I would have made a lousy celebrity."

"You think?" he asked. "Your father thinks you've been doing your best to become the next reality TV star."

"Just Madcap Madison, version two-point-oh."

Vik's expression went from smile to grimace, reflecting Maddie's own conflicting feelings about her mom's escapades in the light of adulthood. "In many ways Helene Madison Archer was an amazing woman and she raised a strong and impressive daughter, but the way she chose to cope with the things she didn't like in her life wasn't healthy. You must see that."

"I do." It had taken some time, but Maddie had come to that conclusion a while ago. The *Madcap* was something Maddie was doing her best to drop from her name. "Believe it, or not, I've always been very careful what part of my life I allow the media into."

"Perry isn't so choosy."

Vik was in the driver's seat, their identity obscured behind the Jaguar's tinted windows, when she replied. "Perry is an idiot who relied on our friendship to protect him from the consequences of his lies."

"It is."

"You think so?" She indulged in an old favorite secret pastime as he drove out of the financial district and through Chinatown toward Van Ness.

Watching Viktor Beck.

Memories of their recent kiss played over in her mind, a mental movie she could not seem to turn off and that caused a visceral reaction in her body. A reaction she wasn't sure if she should try to suppress, or not.

If they were getting married, reacting to his kiss was a good thing, right?

Thankfully, she didn't have to answer the disturbing question of whether she would marry him for the sake of her dreams if she *wasn't* attracted to him. How much of her father's ruthlessness colored Maddie's spirit?

She was sure Jeremy Archer would say the papers she'd just signed answered that question, but that wasn't how she saw it.

Vik shifted down, his car purring as it climbed the hills of San Francisco's streets. "You refuse to sue Perry despite his defamation of your character."

"Our friendship is over." Ultimately that would cost Perry more than any settlement she might get in court.

"Is it?"

"Yes."

"You sound very certain." Vik didn't.

"I am."

Vik turned onto Highway 101. "Good."

"And even if for no other reason than that he'll never get another loan from me, that's a serious consequence for Perry." One she really didn't think the other man had foreseen. He would have counted on her loyalty, but had made the egregious error of not giving her any. "He'll also never again be able to use being my escort as a way into events his own connections won't provide entrée."

"It sounds like it was a pretty one-sided friendship."

"That's what Romi always said, but it wasn't true."

"Yes?" Vik sounded genuinely curious, if doubtful.

"Letting people in isn't easy for me."

The business tycoon who had spurred more fantasies than any teenage heartthrob in her adolescent breast made a disbelieving sound. "You have a huge social network."

"And a total of two people I called friends, now only one."

"I think two still." Vik flicked her a glance with meaning. "Just not the same two."

Unexpected and not wholly welcome warmth unfurled

inside Maddie at the claim. Nevertheless, she admitted, "I'm glad to hear that."

She just hoped it was true. Chances were good. Viktor Beck might be a bastard in the business world, but he was no liar.

"He made me laugh," she admitted, falling back on old habits of sharing her uncensored thoughts with Vik.

"You have an infectious laugh," Vik offered. "I missed it."

It was weird to think of Vik missing anything about her. "You decided our friendship was over."

"Not over, just truncated."

"If you say so." But six years on, she could maybe share his point of view.

"I thought it for the best."

It was entirely possible it had been, no matter how much his rejection and subsequent pulling away had hurt. She hadn't thought so at the time, the combined loss of her mom, then her grandfather, what little attention she'd had from her father and then Vik's friendship had left Maddie with real intimacy issues. But if she and Vik had maintained their close friendship, she never would have gotten over him.

Nor would she have made her own way in life, building dreams completely independent of AIH.

"Looking back on it, it's kind of surprising I let Perry get so close." But then she'd needed a replacement for Vik at least.

"You loaned him money."

Which had taken their friendship into a different realm, she now realized—a realm where Perry saw Maddie as a resource rather than a friend. "In the interest of accuracy, we'll have to call them gifts, not loans."

"And that makes it better?"

She shrugged, though Vik's attention was on the road as

they joined the heavy traffic over the Golden Gate Bridge. "Perry's business ventures never seemed to work out."

"Selling this story to the tabloids is pretty stupid as a long-term plan if you were already bankrolling him."

"I wasn't. I turned him down the last time he asked for money." It had been a hard decision, but she'd had her own dreams to bankroll. "I'd come to the conclusion there were better places I could sink my money than down the rabbit hole of another one of Perry's unlikely business ventures."

"So, he betrayed you."

"Yes." She sighed sadly. "I had no idea my friendship was only worth a few dollars."

"Fifty thousand."

"That's how much he got paid?" She wasn't surprised Vik knew.

The man made it a habit to know everything of even peripheral importance to him. Maddie figured it would be a matter of days, if not hours, before he learned of her anonymous volunteering and even her therapist.

Uncertainty about his reaction to her secrets was the only thing stopping her from telling him herself.

"For the initial tabloid article. He planned to leverage the scandal into more paid interviews and even a book deal." Vik's voice was laced with disgust.

"That's ridiculous. I'm not exactly a celebrity." She hated this.

"No, but you are the Madcap Heiress."

"Madcap Madison. It's what they called my mother." She could still remember the first time one of the tabloids had used the moniker for Maddie.

It had made Maddie feel like maybe Helene was still with her in some small way. Only later had her own maturity and help from her therapist helped Maddie to see how distorted that thinking was.

"You share her penchant for making it into the press,"

Vik agreed. "Perry's book wouldn't have made him a million dollars, but someone would have paid him a hefty advance for it."

"That's just stupid."

"That's our reality-television, celebrity-drama-obsessed society." Vik shifted into the higher gear as they finally made it over the bridge.

San Francisco's gridlock could get really ugly, though it was better than the freeways that became parking lots during high commute times in and around L.A.

"I suppose. You talk about the book deal like it's in the past."

"It is." Definite satisfaction colored Vik's two-word answer.

She shouldn't be surprised Vik had worked so quickly, but she couldn't deny being impressed and only a little apprehensive. "What were Perry's terms?"

"Timwater didn't set the terms, trust me."

She had no trouble believing that, not when Vik was involved. Perry had no hope with the power of AIH brought to bear against him at the instructions of its VP. "What did Conrad get him to agree to?"

"Do you think, after his screwup this morning, I would trust this negotiation with Conrad?"

"*You* met with Perry? Wasn't that overkill?" Putting Vik and Perry in the same room was like pitting an alley cat against the heavyweight champ.

The cat might be wily and street smart, but he was still going to get pulverized.

And she wasn't entirely convinced of Perry's street smarts.

"From now on, anything to do with you goes through me personally." Vik exited the freeway, downshifting the powerful Jaguar.

"That's not how my father operates."

They were headed toward the Marin Headlands. Maddie recognized the route, though she hadn't been there since her school days, on the obligatory field trip to the Golden Gate Bridge and to view the city vista.

"I am not your father."

"But you're a lot alike."

"In how we do business? Yes. But you share more personality traits with your father than I do."

"You're kidding."

"No."

"I know we're both stubborn, but…"

"It does not stop there, believe me."

"So you say." She was *nothing* like her father.

"I do."

Typical. Vik felt no need to explain himself, or convince her, which only made her want to hear his justifications all the more. She wasn't going to ask, though.

Not right now.

Right now, she was far more interested in what they were doing in the parking area near Battery Spencer. "Is the magazine photographer here to get some color shots, or something?"

"No."

Vik pulled neatly into a parking spot and turned off the car, but made no move to get out.

He unbuckled his seat belt and turned to face her. "It is a good thing the friendship is over from your side. Timwater signed a nondisclosure agreement that covers every aspect of his association with you. The penalties for breaking it are severe."

"But he's going to talk about our friendship." It had spanned the same six years as the dearth of Vik in her life.

"No, he is not."

She had no desire to see the man again, but she wasn't sure how she felt about their friendship disappearing as if it had never been, either. "It isn't going to help with what he's already done."

Vik's eyes bored into hers. "He's signed a retraction, admitting everything he told the tabloid was a lie."

"Won't that leave him open to a lawsuit from them?" And why was she worried about someone who had so very blatantly not been worried about her?

"They don't get a copy of the confession…unless he screws up again." The threat in Vik's words would have been spelled out to her ex-friend in no uncertain terms.

"And that will protect him?"

"Do you care?"

"I probably shouldn't."

"You would not be you if you didn't," Vik said with something like indulgence and no evidence of judgment.

"I'm not a pushover."

"No one witnessing you facing your father down in the conference room this morning would ever question that."

"Okay."

Vik smiled. "You are a strong woman whose strength is tempered by compassion. My grandmother Ana is such a woman."

"And you love her."

"Yes."

Did that mean he might love Maddie one day? She did her best to quash that line of fantasy thought. Like she'd told her father earlier, Maddie wasn't the fairy-tale believer her mom had been. She had no expectations of marrying for undying love and irresistible passion.

So, she couldn't understand where the tiny ember of hope burning deep in her heart despite Maddie's strictest self-talk came from.

Unaware of the war going on inside of Maddie from that simple admission, Vik added, "Timwater will make a public apology for his prank after our engagement is announced."

Even though they *weren't* engaged, according to Vik.

It suddenly occurred to her that they hadn't come to the overlook for privacy to discuss Perry.

Even so, she needed to know one thing. "How much?"

"Did we pay him?"

"Yes."

"The way his apology will play, he'll get to keep his fifty thousand from the tabloid." Vik didn't sound particularly happy about that fact.

"And?"

"The only thing I gave Timwater was my word not to destroy his name in the business world. The nondisclosure agreement guarantees we will not sue him in civil court, either—so long as he keeps his side of it."

"He never would have believed I would do that."

"I would. Regardless of if it was on behalf of the company rather than you, Timwater would be just as screwed."

"You're ruthless."

"It's not just an Archer family trait. We do what we need to get what is important to us."

"Like marrying the owner's daughter to take control of a Fortune 500 company."

"Yes."

"Thank you."

"For?"

"Not trying to pretend this is something else." No matter what her heart wanted.

"What exactly do you think this is?"

"Necessary."

He nodded. "Yes, but it will be a marriage in every sense of the word. You do realize that?"

"You mean…"

"Sex. We will not be living celibate lives."

"No affairs?" Not that she would be willing to take this step if she thought he was a womanizer, if she herself had plans to look outside the marriage for that kind of companionship.

"No affairs," he repeated, making no attempt to suppress how disgusting he considered the idea.

Vik wasn't that guy.

He *was* the grandson of a very traditional Russian man. Vik would never do anything that would disappoint the old man. He thought his father had done enough of that.

He'd shared that, and a lot more she hadn't expected him to, when they were friends during her teen years. He'd never been like a brother, but he had been one of the few people she'd believed she could rely on back then.

Could she rely on him now?

"Be very sure you understand what I am saying here, Madison." Vik reached across the console and cupped her nape in a move that was becoming familiar. "I am not Maxwell Black. My children will not be conceived in a test tube."

"Of course not." Whatever their feelings for each other, this situation was very personal for him.

He nodded like that had settled everything still left unsaid between them. She wasn't so sure she agreed, but she didn't hesitate to get out of the car with him.

They took the path to the overlook, Maddie grateful she'd worn the sensible pumps and that the ground was dry. Neither of them spoke while they walked, but he kept his hand on the small of her back, moving it to her elbow in the uneven patches of terrain.

When they stopped, they were at one of the favorite overlooks that gave a view of both the famous bridge and the San Francisco skyline. A few tourists dotted the area, but none near enough to hear any discussion she and Vik might have.

Vik maneuvered them so he stood only a few inches from her, his body acting as a barrier against the incessant winds off the harbor. The close and clearly protective positioning felt significant.

"My grandfather gave my grandmother her first view of San Francisco in this very spot," Vik said after a moment of silent contemplation of the vista before them. "He promised her a future with food to put on the table for their family. A future without oppression for their Orthodox beliefs."

"He kept his promise."

"Yes." Vik went silent for several seconds of contemplation. "Grandfather brought my dad up here as a child. Misha told Frank he could be anything he wanted to, a true American with no accent, his name just like all the other boys'."

"Your grandfather gave your father the freedom to be anything he wanted to."

"Even a failure."

She couldn't argue that assessment, not when she knew Frank Beck had spent his adulthood running from responsibility. Unless something had changed in the last six years, Frank only contacted Vik when he wanted something. Usually money.

Placing her hand on his forearm, Maddie said, "He didn't fail when he fathered you."

"Misha and Ana raised me to be who I am."

"An undisputable success."

Vik turned to face her. "You believe that?"

"I do."

"That is good."

She smiled, not sure why she felt the need to reassure Viktor Beck, but determined to do it anyway.

"*Deda* brought me up here, too, when I was boy. Frank could not be bothered, but I made promises to myself, commitments to the children I would one day father. Promises *I* will keep."

"I have no doubt."

Vik's gaze warmed, his expression filled with unmistakable determination. "My grandparents were not in love when they married, but theirs is one of the strongest marriages I have ever witnessed."

"They are devoted to each other."

"And to their family, even my dad."

"I believe it."

Vik nodded, his dark eyes reflecting approval of her words. "That kind of dedication runs in my veins right along with the ruthlessness."

"I know."

Vik laid his big hands on her shoulders, creating a private world of two for them. "I believe our children will share those traits."

"No doubt." There was nothing she could do about how breathless her voice had become.

He was touching her, and even through the fabric of her Valentino suit jacket and the shell she wore under it, she felt the connection intimately.

"Considering it will come from both their mother and their father, our children have little hope otherwise."

"I'm not ruthless," she said, shocked by the accusation.

"The paperwork you signed today would say otherwise."

"You know that isn't the way I usually do things." It just had been...necessary.

"Ruthlessness does not have to be the dominant trait in your nature for you to have it."

"And it doesn't bother you?"

"That you'll fight for those who deserve your loyalty, even those who do not? No."

"You expect to deserve my loyalty."

"Yes."

"And will I get yours?"

His expression said her question surprised him. "Do you doubt it?"

"Six years ago…"

"You kissed me and I pushed you away."

"That's a simplified way of looking at it and not entirely accurate."

"No?"

"No. I told you I loved you. You told me I was too young and you didn't just push me away, you pushed me out of your life completely. Our friendship ended with one kiss."

"It was necessary."

"We could have stayed friends."

"No."

"Why not?"

"You were an eighteen-year-old, barely a woman."

"But I was a woman."

"I know." There was a message in his voice she couldn't decipher.

"You were also the daughter of a man I admired and who trusted me with you."

"Not to mention he was your boss," she reminded him a little snidely.

"Yes, my boss. The president and owner of a company I intended to run one day."

"A relationship with me would hardly have gotten in the way of *that* goal."

"It would have. Six years ago."

"But not now." No, *now* it was the opposite.

Marriage to her would give Vik exactly what he wanted.

"No, not now."

"I loved you." She wouldn't call it a crush; it hadn't been by then. She'd gotten over it, but at one time she *had* loved him. "Your rejection hurt me."

"I am sorry."

But he wouldn't change his past actions, even if he could. She knew him.

"Look on the bright side," he said almost teasingly.

She didn't remember anything bright about that time. "What?"

He smiled like a shark. "It should be easy for you to learn to love me again."

"Emotion doesn't work like that." And she was pretty sure falling in love with this man, even if she married him, wouldn't be the smartest thing she could ever do.

"Doesn't it?" He pulled something out of the inside pocket of his coat. A small lacquer box that fit in his palm. "My grandmother brought this *Palekh* over from Russia when she and my grandfather defected during the Cold War."

"It's beautiful."

"It is a reminder."

"Of what?"

"The beauty they left behind and the life they hoped to build. *Deda* always said *Babulya* was his frog princess."

The top of the box was decorated with an image from the Russian fairy tale where Prince Ivan ended up married to an industrious and lovely princess who had once been a frog. The magical princess outdid her aristocratic counterparts set to marry Ivan's brothers in every way.

Maddie thought maybe she understood why Vik's grandmother Ana had told Maddie the story of the frog princess the first time they'd met.

"Does this make you my frog prince?" she asked tongue in cheek.

Vik traced the rich image painted in egg tempera on black. "Perhaps it does."

"You know I don't believe in fairy tales."

"Maybe you should."

Now, *that* was definitely *not* something her father ever would have said to her.

"Your grandfather's promises seem to fly in the face of Russian pessimism." But then Misha Beck had never struck her as a pessimist.

The man who had changed his last name to reflect his new country and life had a decidedly forward-thinking attitude.

Maddie had only met Vik's grandparents a few times, but she liked them.

A lot.

Despite the fact Misha and Ana had raised their grandson, Maddie had always considered them the epitome of a *normal* family. The kind of family she'd always wanted.

The kind she wasn't sure Vik was offering with whatever was in that small lacquer box.

"*Deda* never believed the old adage that to speak of success cursed it." Though his shoulders didn't move, there was a shrug in Vik's voice.

"His life and yours prove his skepticism."

"That is one way to look at it."

"The other?"

"*Deda* gave up being a Russian and embraced the way of his new homeland."

"The American ideology does tend toward the positive."

"Remember that."

"You think I have to be a dreamer because of where I was born and raised?" she demanded.

"No. You have your dreams. I have mine. It is not about where you were born, but who you were born to be. I want you to believe in both of our dreams."

"And that takes some of the idealism this country is known for."

"Yes."

He wanted her to believe in his dreams.

It might be love between them, but this was more than a business proposal—no matter what had prompted it.

CHAPTER SIX

"And this?" She pointed to the *Palekh* that had to be at least fifty years old. "Is it a reminder for *me* now?"

No matter how unmoved she tried to appear about that possibility, it touched her deeply.

"Yes."

Her breath hitched. "Of the successful legacy you promised your unborn children?"

"Among other things."

"That kind of success is more important to you than it is to me." Maddie wanted promises of other things.

She wasn't naive. She wasn't looking for undying love, despite the odd feelings deep in her heart she was doing her best not to acknowledge. Even Helene Archer had been too pragmatic to promise her princess a knight in shining armor that would *love* Maddie. But there was more to life than building a company that dominated the world market.

"You think so?" he asked, sounding amused.

Though she didn't understand why. Maddie could only nod.

"It will take the *significant* results of that type of success to make your school a reality."

She couldn't deny it.

"You think money means little to you, but then you have never lived in fear of want." If he had sounded even a little condescending, she would have been angry.

He didn't.

"And you have?" she asked, wondering if there was something about his past she didn't know.

"Not like my grandparents, but let's just say the year between my mother's death and *Deda* deciding I would come to live with him and *Babulya* was not one I would ever allow my own child to endure."

"I'm sorry."

"Frank's inability to make anyone's needs as important as his own, including the basic need to eat of his six-year-old son, taught me as much about who I did not wish to be as *Deda* taught me about the man I would become."

"Your grandfather is a good man."

"He and *Babulya* raised me with an appreciation for the difference between working to provide and working an angle."

"Like your dad."

Vik grimaced. "Frank is very good at angles."

"You want your life to matter."

"It already does."

She couldn't argue that. Didn't want to. "I want my life to matter, too—we just have a different way of going about it."

"Yes, we do." He didn't sound bothered by that fact.

Why was she?

She wanted to tell him about Maddie Grace, but wasn't sure how she would handle it if Vik had the same attitude about her efforts as Jeremy had had.

"I have already promised to help you see your dream of a charter school realized," Vik pointed out.

Yes, he had, which put Vik miles ahead of her father in that regard already. Maybe their differences would make both of their lives better, rather than tearing them apart.

"What kind of promises are you making with that box,

Vik?" she asked, almost ready to believe in the possibility of the complete family she'd never had.

His handsome lips tilted a little at the nickname she hadn't uttered in six years, keeping it strictly private to her thoughts. Something she had not been able to let go of, but would not share with others, either.

"If you accept my proposal, I promise fidelity."

She nodded.

"I will expect the same," he said, as if there was any chance she didn't already realize it.

Interesting that he'd led with that one, though. Was that because he thought she needed it after Perry's betrayal, or was it more personal for Vik?

Either way, she said, "That's a given."

"I am glad to hear that."

When he said nothing else, but looked down at her with an expression that seemed to see into her soul, Maddie prompted, "And?"

"I promise to continue to grow AIH, leaving our children a legacy worthy of both my family and yours."

It was a promise meant more for and to himself and their future children, but she didn't dismiss it is as unimportant. Not after he pointed out her own dreams required money just like his did, if not on the same scale. "All of our children?"

"Yes." His brow furrowed. "Why would I distinguish?"

He could be one of those men who considered their eldest their only important child, or only their sons. But she knew he wasn't.

Her concerns were a lot more unpredictable.

"I am willing to have two children with you, but I want more and they will be adopted." This wasn't a deal breaker for her.

Not if she could have her school, but it was something she desperately wanted to do. Be open to the possibility of bringing children into her life that they could offer a family, not just support, encouragement and help.

Vik's brows drew together in thought, not a frown. "You want to adopt?"

"Yes."

"Babies or children?" he asked.

"Does it matter?"

"No."

Happy with that answer and the speed of it, she offered, "Most likely children."

"All right."

"That's it? You agree?" Shock coursed through her.

"I assume we will make any decisions in regard to bringing more children into our lives—both those born to us and adopted by us—together."

"Of course, but you're open to it?"

"Nothing would delight Misha and Ana more than a house full of grandchildren to spoil."

"There are a lot of bedrooms in Parean Hall." Which was her acquiescence to living there as a married couple.

His satisfied smile said he recognized that as well. "I do not anticipate filling them all with children, but have no objections to our family inhabiting half of them."

It was a ten-bedroom mansion.

Could it really be this easy? "You'll put that in the prenup?"

"If you insist, but I assure you it is not necessary." He placed the antique Russian keepsake against her palm. "Any promises I make you here will not be broken."

"So long as it is within your power."

"Yes." His tone and expression implied Viktor Beck considered very little outside his power and influence.

"And you will be a father to our children, not just the man with that title." He wasn't the only one with memories of neglect after the death of a mother.

Hers might not have been to her physical needs, but Jeremy Archer had let Maddie starve emotionally.

"I cannot promise to make every Little League game or sit-in your daughters organize, but I will make our children a priority."

"*My* daughters?"

"Mine will be too busy trying to take over the corporate world for social activism."

Tickled, she laughed like she hadn't with him in too long, but grew serious again quickly enough. "I won't have my child forced into dedicating his or her life to AIH. That has to be a personal decision."

"Agreed." But clearly Vik had no problem believing his children would be as dedicated to AIH as he was.

Who knew? Maddie herself might have wanted a career in AIH, at least in some capacity, if she'd had a different relationship with her father.

"I think we will have to accept that our children will be influenced by both of us," she told him.

"I can think of much worse things."

"I'm glad you said so," she replied cheekily, secretly touched by his sincerity.

"Open the box," Vik instructed.

"Are you done making promises?"

"Any other commitment I make to you would fall under the three I've already made."

"Three?"

"Fidelity. Dedication. Family."

Inexplicable emotion clogged her throat, but he was right. He'd promised the things that mattered most to her. With a few words he'd committed to building a *family* with her and all that entailed.

She took the lid off the box, incapable of hiding the way her fingers trembled.

Inside, nestled in a bed of black silk, were two rings.

One she recognized as a traditionally inspired Russian three-strand wedding band. Each diamond-encrusted ring interwoven with the others was a different shade of gold: yellow, white and rose.

It was beautiful, but not ostentatious. Perfect for her. Beside it rested a diamond engagement ring set in the pink-tinted gold that would sit flush against the curved wedding band when he put it on her hand.

She didn't ask how he knew the rose tint that used to be known as Russian gold was her favorite. Vik was scary like that.

She didn't ask if she would be able to wear the ring beside the wedding ring after they were married. She could see the curve in the band that would make that possible.

He'd melded the traditions of his homeland with that of his grandparents and taken her own preferences into consideration. It was so Vik. She might not still be in love with him, but it was no wonder she'd never been able to accept a substitute.

"It's beautiful," she breathed, the moment feeling unexpectedly profound.

"As is the woman it was designed for."

"You didn't have this designed for me." He couldn't possibly have.

This kind of custom work wasn't done in a few hours.

He cupped her hands with his own. "You will have to accept that my plans for the future have included you for much longer than you considered me in the same regard."

"I sincerely doubt that." He'd been *it* for her since she'd had her first real thought about boys and girls and how their lives came together.

Even when she hadn't realized she was still comparing every man to Viktor Beck. Darn Romi being right all these years anyway.

He shook his head. "You had a schoolgirl crush, but have not thought of me in that way for six years."

So, he *wasn't* all-knowing. "That shows how much you know. Romi always says I hold other men up to your example and they pale in comparison."

"And what do you say?"

"I always denied it."

"See, I told you."

"I've begun to realize she might have been right." No other man had a chance with Maddie.

Not Perry, not anyone.

Vik's expression dismissed her words as an exaggeration.

"I never forgot you." He'd been too deeply embedded in her psyche, if not her heart.

Maddie had honestly believed her issues with trust had prevented intimacy with another man, but now realized memories of *that guy* had been enough to keep others at bay.

"You avoided me like the plague."

"You did your own avoidance."

"For about a year," he acknowledged. "I missed our friendship. I thought enough time had passed that we'd gotten past the awkward incident."

And he'd approached her. She'd rebuffed him, doing her best to never be put in a position where they could speak privately again. She'd stopped coming home unless her father demanded her attendance and that happened rarely enough.

For at least two years, Maddie had turned down every invite that might put her and Vik in the same sphere.

"I wasn't on the same page." What had been awkward for him had been humiliating for her.

"You made that unmistakable."

"I was angry with you." She'd felt betrayed.

Perry's treachery hurt; Vik's rejection had devastated her.

"And now?" Vik asked.

What did he want her to say? She'd stopped avoiding him at social functions before she graduated from university, but she'd still made sure there was no opportunity for them to renew the old friendship.

"The world looks like a different place from twenty-four than eighteen." It was the best she could do.

"You will forgive me for hurting you?" he asked, like it really mattered.

So, she told him the truth. "I forgave you a long time ago, Vik."

"It did not feel like it."

She looked up into his espresso-brown eyes. "Do you forgive me?"

"For kissing me?" he asked, sounding genuinely confused.

Not a usual circumstance for him. She would take a moment to savor it and even tease him if the discussion wasn't so important.

She explained, "For mistaking your kindness for something more and making our friendship impossible."

"I never held it against you." His tone implied something else altogether.

"You thought you should have known I was falling in love with you," she realized.

"That wasn't the way I termed it, but yes."

Right. He'd thought her love was a crush. But if it had been only a crush, it would have taken months, not years, to get over.

"You're not omniscient, Vik."

"If I'd been paying better attention, I could have headed you off gently."

She wasn't sure that was true. Vik was right that she

and her father shared a stubbornness that resulted in a tenacity of purpose almost impossible to derail.

"If we'd remained friends, Perry would never have gotten the hold on you he did."

"You think you would have stopped us becoming friends."

"I would have prevented him from using you as his personal bank and he would have known that you had people looking out for you."

"People scary enough to abandon his plans for the phony exposé before he ever put feelers out for the first reporter?" she asked with a smile.

"You think I'm scary."

"To men like Perry? Oh, yes, definitely."

"But not to you."

"No, Vik, you don't scare me."

"Good."

He frowned. "Perhaps you would not have taken the chances you have in the past years if you'd had the stability of my presence in your life."

"You're pretty arrogant."

"Do you deny it?"

"Actually yes," she said firmly. "My actions are not your fault, or your responsibility."

He shrugged, clearly disagreeing.

"You really have a God complex."

"No, but I know my responsibilities."

"And I'm one of them?" she demanded, frustrated more with herself for seeing that as romantic than Vik for his arrogance.

His smile sent heat through her, reminding her of that lack-of-celibacy thing he'd taken pains to make clear. "I hope more than that."

"Friends again?"

"Yes, definitely."

"But you want more." Maybe not passionately and personally, though she was beginning to see that Vik *did* desire her, but to make his dreams come true, Vik was going to marry her.

"Yes."

"Okay."

"To?"

"Everything."

His expression turned even more heated and predatory. "Be careful what you promise."

"This is a special place. Promises made here stick, right?"

"Yes." No doubts.

"Then I promise to do my best to make both our dreams come true."

"I make this promise as well."

That was way better than him promising to build AIH into some world superpower, in her opinion. "Thank you."

His kiss took her by surprise. It shouldn't have. Wasn't it natural to kiss to seal an engagement?

But the kiss did surprise her. And then it overwhelmed her, his lips coaxing a response that radiated throughout her body. They took possession of hers, no longer coaxing, but insisting on the two things she'd said only that morning she wasn't capable of.

Submission and trust.

But then, like with so many other things in her life, the rules did not apply to Viktor Beck.

She found herself melting into him, no thoughts for self-preservation or holding anything back.

And he accepted her surrender with a forceful masculine desire that belied any claim for a lack of passion between them.

He devoured her mouth, his arms coming around her,

his hands pressing her body against his, one thigh pressing between her legs as far as her skirt would allow.

Maddie's knees would have given out, but Vik's hold on her was too tight.

She'd thought the kiss this morning had been hot, but it was nothing like Viktor Beck staking claim to the woman who promised to marry him and give him his dreams.

Viktor knocked impatiently on Madison's door thirty minutes before they needed to be at Jeremy's ostentatious home in Presidio Heights.

Viktor had not given himself time for a drink or idle chitchat on purpose. After the kiss at the overlook, he did not want to risk his self-control before the dinner.

If his grandparents weren't going to be there, as well as the photographer from the magazine, he would never have left Madison that afternoon. But she deserved to show up to her engagement dinner on time and *not* looking like she'd spent the hours before in bed.

He'd told her the truth earlier. Six years ago he'd seen her as barely a woman when she'd kissed him.

He'd been shocked by his own body's response to her overtures, realizing for the first time that she was an adult and *not* a child. Not that he'd given that revelation much credence.

Not at first, but after a year of avoiding her and indulging in more liaisons than his workaholic regime usually allowed for, two things had become obvious.

He missed Madison and she was the only woman he wanted sharing his bed. She was still too young and Viktor's plans didn't include marriage for at least a few more years.

Anything else with the daughter of AIH's president and owner was out of the question. And not just because Viktor considered the older, driven businessman a friend.

Viktor wasn't sure when he realized his own business ambitions included marrying Madison, but it was well before he broached the subject in any oblique way with Jeremy. The older man's concern regarding what would happen when Madison inherited full control of the trust gave Viktor the traction he needed for Jeremy's approval of his own future plans.

He'd had the rings commissioned and intended to launch his courtship of Madison in the coming weeks when Timwater sent a spanner into the works with his "breakup interview."

If Viktor had started his pursuit of Madison earlier, the opportunistic man would not have had a chance to hurt her with his lies. It was unacceptable bad timing that had left Madison vulnerable.

It angered him. Viktor did not do bad timing. And he did not get caught by surprise. But he had not anticipated Timwater's betrayal of his long-standing friendship with the heiress.

While it had not precipitated long-term action on Viktor's part that he wasn't already planning, the intolerable situation had brought things to a head before he intended. *And* it had forced him to work around Jeremy's knee-jerk response to his daughter's misadventure.

While that might have ended up working in Viktor's favor, it had come with additional emotional cost to Madison.

He might be ruthless, but that was not okay with him. Her well-being was his responsibility now.

The door opened and Viktor's thoughts scattered.

Madison's copper curls flirted around her face, her blue eyes vibrant and flashing with a response to his presence that found a corresponding reaction in his body.

Lips entirely too kissable despite the dark color staining them in a perfect scarlet bow curved in a smile of welcome. "Hi, Vik. Are you coming in?"

She'd encased her tempting body in a 1950s-inspired couture cocktail dress in a shiny dark blue that rustled as she moved.

The skirt was full, nipping in at the waist, and the bodice fitted, the artistically cut neckline dipping to reveal the hint of cleavage he found more sexually alluring than any woman he'd seen in a dress that revealed most of her breasts.

"You…" He cleared his throat, finding it unaccountably dry. "You look beautiful."

Only after he spoke did it occur to him that he had not answered her question.

"Thank you." She blushed, something she rarely did anymore. "It works?" The nerves that slipped in to tinge her smile were something else she didn't show others. "Only I wanted your grandparents to see *me,* not the…"

She didn't have to finish. "It will be all right. *Deda* and *Babulya* are eager to see you and welcome you into our family."

"They know we are engaged? Have they seen the articles?"

Ignoring his own best intentions, he pushed into the apartment and right into Madison's personal space.

She gasped and looked up at him, eyes wide, breath hitching. "Vik? What?"

He curved his hands around her waist, enjoying the soft slide of the fabric and the heat of her skin under it even more. "They know we are engaged and they are delighted."

"Oh."

"They know about the stories and they are furious with Timwater."

"They don't believe them? You told them he lied, didn't you?"

"I did and they don't." Viktor reveled in the implicit trust in his ability to make things right that could be read into her questions.

"Thank you."

Mindful of the crimson color on her lips, he bent down and pressed a soft kiss to the side of her neck, staying to inhale the subtle fragrance of honeysuckle mixed with orange and a hint of vanilla and her own unique scent. "You smell good."

"It's my perfume."

"It's you. Rosewater would smell just as delicious against your skin."

She trembled against him, her hands pressing into his chest. "Vik."

That was all she said. Just his name. But it was a plea, whether to step back or to do something about the electricity arcing between them, he did not let himself contemplate.

He stepped back. "We need to go. Everyone is waiting."

"Including the photographer."

"He has his instructions to be as unobtrusive as possible."

Madison grimaced, her opinion of how unobtrusive that could actually be very clear.

He looked around and spied her coat over the back of an armchair. Viktor had always enjoyed Madison's efficiency and was glad to see that she had not developed the habit of keeping a man waiting that he always found more irritating than intriguing.

Grabbing the coat, he offered it to her. "We need to head out."

"You cut it a little close." But she didn't hesitate to let him help her into the fitted wool trench coat the same crimson red as her lips.

He saw no reason to hide the truth. "Protecting us both from how much I want you."

"What are you talking about?" she asked, sounding genuinely confused as she did up the oversized black buttons and tied the belt on her coat.

"You must realize the prospect of having you in my bed has my libido in overdrive." The truth of that was never more blatant to him than in how hard he found it to lead her out of the apartment without once mussing the color of her lipstick.

However, nothing said he had to curb his desire to touch her completely. They made their way to the elevators with his arm around her waist.

"But why would it?" Could she sound more innocent? He didn't think so.

"You are an incredibly beautiful woman." But more importantly, she was the one woman who sparked desire hot enough to do his ancestors proud.

"You didn't want me before."

"We discussed this. You were barely more than a child." And he *had* wanted her.

"You're right," she said distractedly. "But—"

"Nothing. Trust me. I want you. Six years ago, the timing was wrong, but I will gladly offer you all the proof you desire later tonight, *after* dinner with our respective families."

"You want to come back to my apartment tonight?" she squeaked, charming him.

The elevator doors closed, giving a false sense of privacy he had to once again fight taking advantage of.

"You have no reason to be nervous," he assured her. "I am not an animal in the bedroom."

Even if he wanted her with heretofore untapped primal mating instincts.

"Vik…" She blinked up at him, her lips parted slightly. "I told you, I'm a virgin."

"What?" The elevator doors opened but he didn't step out, his brain short-circuiting.

"I told you—"

"That you hadn't been in a serious relationship." But that didn't mean she hadn't had sex. Things happened. She was twenty-four. This was not possible.

"No random hookups."

"Ever?" he asked in disbelief.

"I told you I had no experience."

"In BDSM."

"In anything."

"That will change." Viktor was not above using whatever means necessary to ensure the future he planned. Including being Madison's first lover.

The fact he wanted her more than any woman he had ever known was beside the point.

She stepped off the elevator into the parking garage. "I don't think being engaged to you is going to be anything like I was imagining."

"If you thought it was going to be without sexual intimacy, I'd have to say you are right," he said as he helped her buckle into the passenger seat of his car.

He gave in to the urge that had been riding him since the moment she'd opened her door and kissed her. He reined in his desire. Barely. And stepped back.

He closed her door and took several deep breaths before moving around the car to slide into the driver's seat.

Her eyes glowing with blue fire, she asked, "No pretense of waiting for our wedding night?"

"We made our vows at the overlook this afternoon. Nothing said later between us will be any more profound." He started the engine, but didn't back out of the parking spot, waiting with an odd feeling in his chest for her reply.

"I thought it felt that way…like it was profound."

"It was." He put the car in gear.

"So what? You consider us married now?" She sounded like she didn't believe her own words and yet he knew she had felt the weight of the promises they'd made earlier.

"As good as, yes."

"You make your own rules, don't you?"

"You are just now figuring this out?"

CHAPTER SEVEN

THE ENGAGEMENT DINNER was a lot more enjoyable than Maddie had expected it to be.

Especially considering the fact the guest list had grown to include some Archer second cousins, a Madison great-aunt, one of Misha's nephews and his wife, who just happened to be visiting friends who owned a vineyard outside of Napa, and Romi.

Maddie's father was all smiles, though underlying his bonhomie was an unfamiliar reticence with her that gave Maddie a certain level of comfort. He had not escaped this morning's debacle in the conference room unscathed.

Small winces indicated he did not like her new habit of calling him by his first name, either, but if he wanted her to stop, he'd have to ask. Nicely. And behave like a father. Somehow.

She hadn't started calling him Jeremy to hurt him, but because it simply hurt *her* too much to refer to a man who treated her like a stranger more often than not as Father.

Vik acted as a buffer between them, not exactly a new role for him, but one he hadn't played with any consistency in six years.

Taking it a step further than he used to, Vik actually physically stood between her and others in unconscious protection whenever she felt herself growing uneasy. While no one had the bad taste to actually mention the articles spawned by Perry's lies, family could manage intrusiveness in subtle ways strangers never could.

Thankfully, Vik seemed to recognize her moods—sometimes even before she did—and took steps to make sure the questions didn't get a chance to edge into being blatantly intrusive.

Tellingly, no one seemed to find it hard to believe they'd been carrying on a relationship outside the media's radar for months now. Not even Misha's nephew evinced surprise at the engagement.

Everyone was happy to congratulate Maddie and Vik, making her feel like maybe this thing could really work.

Regardless of what had precipitated the engagement, their friends and family considered them a good match. A big part of her agreed.

She only hoped she wasn't making a huge mistake… that Vik was the man she was discovering. More the white knight in Armani than the heartless tycoon following in her father's footsteps that she'd seen him as for the past six years.

Vik's grandparents were wonderful, as always.

Misha was a gray-haired, slightly stooped version of Vik with an exuberant warmth very unlike his more reserved grandson. A retired scientist, Ana was both highly intelligent and gently affectionate by nature. She wasn't as overt as her husband, but she would make a wonderful great-grandmother for Maddie and Vik's children.

The magazine photographer turned out to be extremely good at fading into the background and Maddie found herself relaxing and enjoying the first real family dinner she remembered since her mother's death.

"Your grandparents are such nice people." Maddie allowed Vik to remove her coat and his own before taking both of them and hanging them in the hall closet.

Such a simple thing to do. She'd done it hundreds of times for other guests, but never with the same homey feeling—or sense of irrevocability that washed over her as she closed the closet door.

Vik was staying the night.

And Maddie's heart was pounding in her chest like a bass drum.

Not from fear, though. No, nothing like it, though that surprised her. Shouldn't there be at least a little anxiety?

She'd never done this before, after all.

But all she felt was excitement.

Maybe it was because she knew Vik would leave if she asked him to. Only she didn't want him to leave.

She wanted him to follow through on the promise of passion in their kisses earlier. Besides, if they weren't compatible in bed, that could be a real problem.

Right?

Only what were the chances when his kisses turned her inside out. Self-justification much?

She made a sound of self-deprecating humor.

"Liking my family is a source of amusement for you?" Vik's hands landed on her shoulders before he turned her to face him.

His expression wasn't mocking or judging, just inquisitive.

She smiled up at the beloved handsome face as she shook her head. "No, I was thinking about the things we tell ourselves to justify doing what we want to do."

His look promised things she'd never experienced but was pretty darn sure she wanted to. "What *things* do you want to do?"

"Like you don't know."

He shook his head. "I'm still a little stunned you've never done them before."

"Pretty pathetic, huh?"

"In what way were you pathetic?" Vik asked in a tone that didn't bode well for anyone who might have used that word to describe her.

Including herself.

She liked the feelings his instant protectiveness engendered in her despite the fact she thrived on her independence.

Feeling a little odd about that, she moved away from him and crossed the living room, which was decorated in her favorite shabby chic. While she loved the perfect blend of distressed wood furniture, floral damasks, lifelike silk bouquets set in epoxy to look like water, the pristine whites and abundance of feminine styling screamed "single woman living alone" to her.

And while there was *nothing* bad about that, she wasn't as pleased by the fact she'd never even had a short-term relationship. She'd be happier if something in her home indicated the need to take someone else's preferences, or even needs, into account.

"What would you call a twenty-four-year-old virgin?" she asked, turning back to face him.

"Picky." His smile melted her.

She grinned up at him. "That's one word for it."

"You were waiting for me." She could tell by his tone he thought he was joking.

A sudden revelation hit her. Romi had definitely been right all along. "I was."

She might have been able to get over her first love, but Maddie had never moved on from thinking that Viktor Beck would be the ideal lover. And so she had turned down every other man.

Yes, trust was an issue for her, but right along with her lack of trust in other men had been a primal certainty of whom she wanted to share her body with.

A certainty she'd been consciously denying but living under for the past six years.

Espresso eyes darkened with unmistakable lust, blowing her mind. He wanted her. He'd said he did. He'd kissed her like he did, but that look?

It was imbued with the same primitive passion she'd acknowledged in herself. So predatory. It sent shivers chasing along her nerve endings.

"You were made for me," he said, confirming it wasn't her imagination.

The driving force between them was very mutual.

"A pity you didn't realize that six years ago." She regretted the words as soon as she said them and shook her head. "Forget I said that."

Maddie got why Vik had turned her down before. Wishing they'd already taken this step so she wouldn't be dealing with her public humiliation right now was both futile and borderline ridiculous. Because even if they'd gotten together then, there was no guarantee they would still be together now.

His jaw firm, his lips set in a determined line, Vik moved toward her with intent. "I was not ready for marriage and you were not ready for me."

"I—"

His finger pressing against her lips stopped the argument. "We both had living to do."

"You were really thinking about *this* then?" she asked with surprise she couldn't hide.

"Yes."

"But you weren't happy about it." Wasn't happy about the memory if his current expression was anything to go by.

"You were eighteen. I was still used to thinking of you as a child. It felt wrong."

"I was an adult, a grown woman." But even as she made

the claim, she knew that compared to Vik she *had* been a child.

"You could vote, join the armed forces and take on your own debt. That didn't mean you were ready for a relationship with a man like me."

"A relationship, or sex?"

"Same thing when it comes to you and me."

"Is it?"

"It has always been marriage or nothing between us, Madison." Vik reached out and traced the line of her bodice, his fingertip never straying from the sapphire-blue taffeta of her dress to the skin of her bosom.

Her breath hitched, but she didn't move away. "Because of AIH."

"Because my grandfather raised me to be a man with a sense of honor." The "unlike Frank Beck" went unsaid, but she heard it anyway.

Vik would never be like the father that had caused both him and his grandparents so much grief and disappointment.

"You may be a shark, Vik, but you're an honest one."

He smiled wryly, his fingertip resting on the point of the V dipping between her breasts. "And I don't eat guppies for breakfast."

"Am I a guppy?" she asked breathlessly.

"No." Satisfaction burned in his dark gaze. "You are a twenty-four-year-old woman."

The emphasis he placed on the word *woman* was a conversation all in itself.

"You planned to marry me before Perrygate ever happened."

"I did." Vik looked with significance down at the custom ring on her finger and she caught on.

There was no denying the truth in front of her eyes. "You really did have the rings made for me."

"I do not lie."

"No, but…" The scope of what he was saying left her grasping for words that would not come.

"Timwater forced me to move my plans forward, but only by a couple of weeks."

"You were going to ask me to marry you?"

"I planned to date you first," he said with some wry humor, almost self-deprecatingly. "We needed to rebuild the rapport we once had."

His thinking made him a different man than her father in ways she didn't feel like enumerating, but wouldn't deny. "You recognized before Jeremy did that the only way my father would have an heir to leave in charge of the business is if I married him."

"Yes."

"So, you made plans to play on my father's desire to leave his legacy to *family*." It was brilliant. And manipulative.

But he'd already shown that as important as his own plans for AIH were to Vik, he would not ignore Maddie's happiness. He'd offered to buy her a building for her dream as a wedding gift.

Calculated? Maybe, but *for* her benefit, not to her detriment.

Vik's silence was answer enough. Not only had he strategized, but he'd also started working on her father already. Jeremy had come to the whole "his daughter must marry to save herself and the company's reputation" pretty darn quickly otherwise.

"I'm not sure how I feel about this," she admitted.

She understood. To an extent.

But it still felt like she'd been maneuvered.

Vik's touch finally strayed entirely from her dress to the upper swell of her breasts, tracing the same path as before, only along her skin this time. "While you are deciding, take into account that if you had been a different woman, my plans would have taken a different direction."

She shivered, her breath quavering in her chest until another thought came to her. "You would have taken AIH out from under my father?"

Horrified because as much as she didn't get her father, she loved him, and she was certain Vik would have done exactly that. Rather than allow a stranger to come in and take over what he considered to be his.

Vik shrugged, neither confirming, nor denying. "It was not necessary."

"You said Jeremy is your friend."

"He is."

"But you would still take his company."

"I would not have betrayed him."

No. That wasn't Vik's style. "You still would have figured out a way."

"Does that upset you?"

"I said before that you're ruthless."

"This is not news."

No, it really wasn't. "My mind doesn't work like yours."

"Make no mistake, you have your own brand of ruthlessness, but if you were too much like me, we would not fit so well together." Both his hands moved to settle on her waist.

She was distracted by the sensation of his thumbs brushing up and down against her lower ribs. "You think we fit?"

"I know we do."

"So, you're saying you don't just want the company. You want me, too." Not just sex with her, but Maddie as a complete person.

At least the Madison Archer he knew about. What would Vik think of Maddie Grace?

"You will support my dreams in a way a woman of less strength could not do."

"Your plans would have been really messed up if I'd picked one of the other candidates Jeremy put forward." She gave in to the irresistible urge to poke at the bear.

Vik's gorgeous mouth twisted in disdain. "You were never going to choose another man."

"You don't think so?"

"I know."

"Another word for excessive confidence is arrogance."

"I prefer honest."

She laughed softly and then had a revelation. "You manipulated the choice of candidates."

"I was not expecting Maxwell Black."

"Neither was I." And she still wanted to know what the man had done to Romi. "He's intense."

"He's a good businessman."

"Is he honorable?"

"Yes."

"As honorable as you?"

Vik considered his answer for a second. "I would do business with him on a handshake."

"Good to know."

"Why? Considering your options?" He didn't sound too worried by the prospect.

"According to you, there are no other options."

"True." Vik looked like he was considering what he was going to say next. "We grew up together."

"What? Like in the same neighborhood?"

"Same Russian-American-dominated street, same school, same afternoons spent in activities sponsored by the Russian cultural center."

"Were you friends?"

"We still are...of a sort."

"You're too alike to be really close."

"We jockeyed for the top place in class until we went to different universities."

"No one else had a chance."

"No."

Maddie bit her lip, but finally decided she would be honest about her concerns. "Romi dated him."

Vik's gaze flared. "I see."

"He's intense," Maddie repeated.

"Are they still dating?"

"No."

"Then…"

"I don't need to be worried?"

"He is a good man."

When it was Viktor Beck making the claim, Maddie believed him.

"Are you really spending the night?" she asked, focusing on what mattered most in the present moment.

"Yes."

"After a single day." One day in which they had decided to get married, made that decision public and negotiated a future they could both live with.

"In one respect, but between us?" He pulled her body close so they shared heat. "Tonight is the culmination of ten years."

"We've barely spoken in six."

"When was the last time Frank was in town?" Vik asked her, like she'd know.

And she did. "Three months ago. He was in San Francisco for Christmas." Vik's father had attended Jeremy's holiday party along with Misha and Ana.

Vik nodded, his expression dour. "*Babulya* was pleased."

"But you couldn't wait for him to leave."

"You are the only person who knew that."

She found that hard to believe, but then…maybe not. Vik didn't wear his emotions on his sleeve.

But that wasn't the point, was it? "Just because I saw

your father at my father's home and knew he was in town doesn't mean you and I communicated in any meaningful way."

"Didn't we?"

Okay, so in the past two years, they'd had increasing numbers and depths of conversations. And it struck her. She'd thought she was just being grown-up about the past, but he'd been working on rebuilding that rapport he had mentioned earlier.

The man made Machiavelli look like a preschooler in the art of the deep play.

"Still." Not a brilliant comeback, but what she had.

Vik smiled that shark's smile. "When was the last time I took a date to an event?"

So, she knew the answer. She'd revealed earlier in the car with Conrad how closely she watched Vik without meaning to watch him at all. "That doesn't mean anything."

"Doesn't it?"

"Vik…"

"I believe both the fact that I have not had another woman on my arm in over a year *and the fact you know that* is significant."

"Really?" she drawled sarcastically even as she couldn't help wondering if he was right.

"I know that you haven't dated, either. I wasn't entirely sure about Timwater, but the way you two are together doesn't imply sexual intimacy."

"I should hope not."

"Besides, he was sleeping with other women."

She'd suspected, though Perry had always tried to play it like he didn't sleep around. She wasn't sure why. It wouldn't have mattered to her either way.

Vik knowing however, meant he'd been paying attention. "You have a file on him, don't you?"

"Naturally."

"And Romi?"

"Romi has been your friend for longer than me."

"You're saying you don't have a file."

Vik leaned down and spoke softly, right into Maddie's ear. "I'm saying I don't need one."

It wasn't exactly sweet nothings, but she still shivered from the sensation of his breath gently blowing across her ear.

"You know her well, too," Maddie said, not even sure why she was trying to keep the conversation going.

"Yes."

Curiosity and concern prompted her to ask, "Did you know she'd dated Maxwell?"

"No."

"Good. I don't feel like I was so oblivious."

Vik straightened, but didn't move back. "I'm sure if you did not know, they both took pains to keep it private."

"You're right." While Maddie was still worried, she didn't feel like a bad friend anymore.

She let herself fall into his deep coffee gaze, even as she relaxed more completely into his body. "I want to kiss you."

Bad friend, or good one, Maddie didn't want to think about anyone except her and Vik right now.

"What is stopping you?" He leaned down so their lips were a fraction of an inch apart, taking away the only barrier that mattered.

She moved toward him, speaking in a breath against his lips. "Nothing."

The first brush of her lips against his electrified her. It was the barest of caresses, but near unbearable in its intimacy. She was staking a claim with the featherlight touch and he was accepting that claim as surely as she'd accepted his promises earlier.

They were distinctly different, one set of lips masculine, the other feminine, and yet they fit with the perfection of molds aligned and cast simultaneously.

Vik's response was full-on alpha man, accepting her mouth with his and then turning it around and moving his lips against hers, driving the kiss to greater sensation and closeness.

Nipping oh-so-gently with his teeth on her lower lip, he demanded entrance. With no thought but to give it, she let her lips fall open.

His tongue swept into her mouth and just that fast Maddie was drowning in a sexual response only this man had ever brought out in her, thoughts and emotions overwhelmed by the onslaught of devastating sensuality.

Vik's hold on her tightened as he pulled her body completely flush with his, his big hands roving over her back and up to knead her scalp.

Her own hands slid of their own volition up his pecs, over his shoulders and to the back of his neck, pulling her body around so her breasts were crushed against his chest. Sparks of delicious sensation pricked her nipples nearly to the point of pain in their intensity.

It felt so incredible still dressed, she could not fathom what it would be like once they were naked skin pressed to naked skin.

Vik made a rumbling sound of approval in his throat before his body shifted and then she was being lifted into his arms as he stood.

The man was strong. Following on that thought came another.

They were really going to do this.

For the first time, Maddie was glad she was a twenty-four-year-old virgin.

She wanted no past experiences shadowing this moment with him. No memories of hands on her flesh but his.

Vik carried her unerringly into to her bedroom, lowering her back to her feet and pulling his mouth from hers. She didn't want to stop and used her hold on his neck to lift herself back up so the kiss could continue.

It was only natural to swing her legs up and around his waist, locking her ankles behind his back.

Something about her actions flipped a switch in Vik and the kiss went nuclear. His mouth devoured hers as he cupped her bottom through the rustling silk of her dress's full skirt.

Overwhelmed by sensation, Maddie lost her connection to anything but the kiss. She did not know how long their mouths ate at each other. Nothing registered but the sparks of pleasure he ignited in her rapidly fanning into a conflagration that consumed.

She wasn't even aware he'd moved them to the bed until he broke away from her and she didn't fall to the floor.

She mewled with her need to reconnect to his lips, a sound that would have mortified her if she was not too lost to desire to care.

"Vik!" she demanded, no other word coming to the forefront of her mind.

His smile was feral and hot. But the wink that came with it was hotter. "Clothes."

CHAPTER EIGHT

ONE WORD BUT it was all Maddie needed.

She sat up and reached back to unzip her dress. It was tricky at the best of times, the top of the zipper hitting her in the center of her back.

With her hands trembling from need, it was impossible. So frustrated she could almost cry, she struggled to unzip it.

All the while, she couldn't pull her eyes from Vik. He'd ripped his Armani sweater off and tossed it on the floor, the black T-shirt he wore under it joining the pile of cashmere a second later.

His belt made a whoosh as he pulled it out of his trousers and the buckle clunked against the wall when he tossed it. His tailored slacks were next, dropping to reveal a straining bulge behind dark designer briefs.

"Your body is beautiful," she breathed in awe.

Every muscle of his six-foot-four-inch frame was honed. Dark hair covered his chest, narrowing to a trail that disappeared into the waistband of his briefs.

She didn't know if it was the dark, clingy fabric or reality, or even her oversensitized emotions, but Vik looked huge.

Maddie's thighs clenched even as her fingers itched to touch. And she hadn't seen the actual package yet.

Vik looked back, his own expression filled with desire. "You're still dressed," he accused.

"I know," she said with pure frustration.

He winked again, the expression just as mind-bogglingly sexy this time as the first. "Need some help there?"

"Yes."

He stalked toward the bed like a big sleek cat, climbing on with the same grace. He reached around her and let his fingers trail down the shallow V of her dress to the top of the zipper. "Is this your problem?"

"I can't reach it."

"How did you get dressed then?"

"I wasn't hampered then."

"By what?"

"What do you think?" she asked, wanting to sound annoyed and only succeeding in revealing the need inside her.

"Me?"

"Desire," she clarified.

"Desire for me."

"Yes," she admitted, no real reason to pretend otherwise, but annoyed all the same at having to say it out loud.

"Good." He lowered the zipper inch by inch. "I like this dress."

"I'm never wearing it again."

"Please do."

"Why?"

"I have always enjoyed unwrapping my gifts. Just ask my grandparents."

"I'm not a Christmas package."

"No, you are something far more valuable." He kissed the corner of her mouth and then brushed her lips with his lightly. "You are the woman who will share my life."

"You're awfully good at romance for a corporate shark."

He wasn't kidding about enjoying the process of unwrapping. Time moved by in increments measured by her rising passion as he took off first her dress, removing it to reveal her body one slow inch at a time. His desire-filled gaze burned her with sensual appreciation.

The silk foundations she wore under the dress came next, but he took even more time with those than the blue taffeta, kissing bits of her flesh as it was revealed, sensitizing her body in ways she'd no idea he could do.

When he was done, she was a naked, quivering mass of sexual need.

And he still had his briefs on.

She tugged at the waistband, her voice husky with passion when she managed to force the words past the tightness in her throat. "Take them off."

"Not yet."

"Why?" she demanded, patience in another universe.

"You are a virgin."

"So?" He was going to change that, wasn't he?

"So, you need preparation and I'm on a hair trigger where you are concerned."

"You have to take your underwear off to make love to me," she spelled out slowly, like she wasn't sure he got it.

He bared his teeth in a smile that had no humor. "And before that happens I will make sure you are ready to receive me."

"But—"

"You will have to trust me on this." His eyes demanded her acquiescence.

She didn't know if she could give it. "I want you!"

"And you will have me."

Vik's hand slipped between her legs right then, fingers delving in the moist heat no other man had ever touched, and she cried out. He touched her in ways she'd only ever dreamed of being touched, caressed her to her first shattering climax before she even realized what that desperate feeling inside her was leading to.

She'd touched herself, but it had never felt like this. She was still trembling with spent pleasure when a single long masculine finger slipped inside her. Something shifted in her heart at the intimate intrusion.

He was not inside her, not the way she'd always imagined, but they were connected on a level that corresponded to a place inside her soul.

He pressed upward and she winced with pain.

"Hurt?" he asked, his own tone strained.

"A little."

"It will sting."

"Why?"

"I am going to break your hymen with my finger. It will make the actual penetration of my sex easier on you." The words were clinical, but his tone and the concern in his expression was not.

He'd thought this through and that touched her in the same place in her soul his intimate intrusion had.

He pressed a little harder.

A sharp shard of pain stabbed her. "It more than stings!"

"I am sorry." He grimaced. "It will be worth it."

She wasn't so sure about that, but trusted him enough to give him the benefit of the doubt.

That trust was sorely tested a moment later when the pain increased to the point that she felt like he was invading her with a hot poker, not his finger. She gasped and tried to pull away, surprised when she succeeded in dislodging his hand.

He leaned back on his haunches, the telltale traces of blood on his finger a testament to his success.

Grateful that the pain was already morphing to a low-level throbbing rather than stabbing, she asked, "Now?"

"Not yet. There is more to do."

The more included him stripping naked finally. In the bathroom, where he ran a very hot bath.

He looked even bigger jutting out from his body than he had with his erection tucked behind black silk knit.

He smiled at her with gentle humor. "Your eyes are as wide as saucers."

"You're as big as a baseball bat."

That startled a laugh out of him. "Not even close."

"Right."

"Your eyes are playing tricks on you."

Unsure where it came from, annoyance drove her stomping across the tiled floor and gave her the boldness to grope him in her fist. "My fingers are not touching."

The sound he made was not a word.

Viscous drops formed on the tip of the flesh in her hand. She touched it with her fingertip and brought it to her mouth, licking it cautiously.

Surprisingly it was almost sweet, with only a hint of the salty bitterness she'd heard about. "I like it."

He groaned and then jerked his body backward so his hard flesh slipped from her hand. "Bath. Now."

"Why?"

"Can't you just trust me?"

"I trust you more than any other man on this planet." He might be the only man on the planet she *did* trust. He had to know that.

"It will make it better for you," he explained.

"How do you know?" she demanded. "Have you had sex with many virgins?"

She found that possibility seriously disturbing.

"None," he practically snarled as he lifted her up and set her in the bathtub with surprisingly gentle movements, considering his apparent irritation. "I read up on it."

"Because you're a planner."

"Yes." He still sounded like a man ready to take someone's head off.

"Why are you mad?" she asked plaintively.

"I'm not angry!"

"You're snarling at me."

"I'm turned on." The low growl rumbled through her.

"So am I. The bath was your idea!"

"For your benefit."

Oh, man. "I'm sorry. This isn't easy for you, is it?"

"Waiting?" He stepped into the bath behind her, pulling her into his lap, his hands settling on her possessively. "No, my sexy little redhead, it is not easy, but you are worth it."

Another white-knight moment. "If you aren't careful, you're going to have me believing in fairy tales."

His only answer was one languid touch to her thigh. That caress was followed by another and another and another, all over her body and each touch accompanied by the ever-present presence of his hardness pressed against the small of her back.

Her nipples were aching and sensitive, her clitoris vibrating with pleasure, and her entire body melted over his by the time his hands stilled their insidious movements.

There were no words left in her brain when he drained the tub and lifted her back to the tile floor. They dried off in silence, bodies aware and straining toward each other.

She and Vik stripped the bedding back without acknowledging that was what they were going to do, and then together they fell to the mattress covered by the single sheet.

The lovemaking was everything she had ever dreamed it would be, his sex filling her so deeply she felt like they'd really bonded into one entity in that moment.

There was still some pain, but nothing stabbing and dark, and the pleasure pushed any lingering discomfort to the bottom register of Maddie's awareness.

This time when she climaxed, she screamed until her throat protested the strain. Vik grew impossibly hard inside her, his body going rigid just before he shouted his own release in the form of a single word.

"Mine."

She didn't even think about birth control until the next morning.

Viktor came to awareness in the dark, two things at the forefront of his mind. The woman he'd craved for years was now in his arms and they hadn't used birth control the first time they made love.

The former gave him satisfaction and the latter a twinge of regret. In a perfect world, they would have a couple years of marriage to enjoy their time together as a couple, to solidify their relationship.

In the real world, Madison had been forced into marriage by the actions of that bastard who had called himself her friend, and Viktor's grandparents were getting on in years. If his children were to have the time to enjoy them as Viktor had, they would have to come along sooner than later.

Viktor had taken advantage of Timwater's idiocy. He could deal with the consequences of other realities, too.

For him, family was everything.

It was the reason he'd been driven to succeed. The one thing that drove him most intensely was the desire to not only make his grandparents proud, but to also provide for his own family as his own father had not done.

Viktor had determined early in his life never to walk a single step in his own father's shoes.

When he'd first met Jeremy Archer, Viktor had believed he'd found the mentor he sought. And he had, but he had also come to the realization that as wrapped up in AIH as Jeremy was, his vision was still too limited.

Both in a business sense and when it came to family.

Jeremy had never understood that all of AIH's success

meant nothing in the face of his spectacular failure with his daughter.

Madison was Viktor's match in every way. They were not just sexually compatible, they were combustible. Just as he'd known they would be.

But equally important, they were friends with compatible, if very different, goals for the future.

Viktor felt an unfamiliar sense of having dodged a bullet with Maxwell Black's presence in the conference room that morning. Jeremy bringing in Maxwell—of all men—had precipitated actions on Viktor's part he hadn't intended to take until later.

But he couldn't complain about the outcome.

He in no way regretted making love to Madison and had every intention of showing her that no other man would be her match as Viktor was.

He wasn't just the perfect successor for AIH, he was perfect for Madison.

With that thought, he brushed his hand down her flank, leaning over to kiss the side of her neck and bring her to wakefulness for another example of how very well they meshed in bed.

For the first time in her life, Maddie had woken in another person's arms.

She lay, warm and secure as half of Vik's body covered hers, his breath still even and slow in sleep.

And she thought of babies and the possibility of family. Had he done it on purpose? Or had he been as lost to the final satiation of years' worth of unfulfilled desire that the idea of birth control hadn't even entered the picture?

Before she'd been made love to by a man who never seemed to get enough, she would have written the latter off as a complete improbability.

But Vik had woken her several times in the night and

pushed the boundaries of pleasure and her body on each occasion, his hunger for her something she would never again be able to doubt. There'd been no question when they *were* sleeping that they would do so skin-to-skin.

The one time she'd tried donning her sleep pants and tank top, he'd gotten this look in his eyes. Really intense, feral and determined. Her pajamas had been in a puddle on the floor moments later and her body humming the music of the Viktor Beck pleasure symphony.

Even now, his oversized sex…

No, she didn't believe him that he was no bigger than most men. She'd heard on one of those talk shows hosted by a group of interesting and mostly famous women that the average length was just about five inches erect. Well, she knew from five inches and his was nearly twice that. Average? She did not think so.

Right now, that not-at-all-average hardness was pressing against her hip, telling her that when he woke he'd be ready for more physical intimacy. Despite the twinges of soreness making her aware of muscles she hadn't known she had, nipples that ached from all the stimulation they'd enjoyed and a tender feeling in the flesh between her legs, she knew she wouldn't hesitate to respond.

Except…they hadn't used any form of birth control in the long night of passion. Not once.

"I can hear you thinking." Vik's early morning voice rumbled above her head.

"You said we would make any decision about children together."

Tension seeped into his big body, but he did not move away. "Yes?"

"We did not use birth control last night."

Oddly, he relaxed. "No, we did not."

"Vik," she said in warning.

He sat up, somehow getting pillows propped against

the headboard behind him and her sideways in his lap with a minimum of movement. It was a position he apparently enjoyed.

He tilted her chin up, bringing their gazes into alignment. "We made that decision together."

"I didn't make a decision at all. I didn't even think of it."

His eyebrows rose. "Neither did I."

She narrowed her eyes, trying to gauge the truth of his statement. She might be blind, but Maddie couldn't see the smallest flicker of deceit in the espresso orbs.

"It never once occurred to you that a condom might be a good idea?" she asked.

It was his turn for his eyes to narrow, but they glittered with anger not concentration. "You believe I would lie to you?"

"No, but you're ruthless enough to take advantage of an expedient situation."

He agreed, no sign of embarrassment at the truth. "Yes, but to what end would I ignore birth control?"

"You get five percent of the company when I give birth to our first child." Did she really have to remind him of that fact?

"Did you plan to wait to start a family?"

"No." She couldn't even claim not to have thought of it. Dreams were something even a woman who didn't believe in fairy tales could indulge in. And Maddie's dreams included building the kind of family she'd always wanted to have.

"I did not think you did." Therefore, he had no need to take advantage of circumstance.

"Okay."

"Okay, what?"

"I believe you."

He kissed the tip of her nose. "As you should."

She wrinkled her nose. "It might be old-fashioned, but

I would still like to wait until we are married to conceive our first child." Though if she *was* pregnant, she would accept that as the gift she believed it to be.

"Agreed."

"So, from now on, birth control," she insisted.

"Agreed."

"You're being awfully compliant."

"The truth? I would prefer to wait a couple of years before having children."

"Oh." She hadn't considered he wasn't keen on starting a family right away.

"But my grandparents are in their seventies," Vik continued. "If my children are to have the benefit of *Deda* and *Babulya's* presence in their lives, we cannot indulge me."

"I see." Wow.

Once again, she was reminded that while she and Vik might be motivated by different hopes for the future, they both had them. And lucky for her, they dovetailed, as surprising as that might be.

"I hesitate to point this out," Vik said. "Because I *do* want to gift my grandparents with the next generation of our family."

"What?" Maddie couldn't believe how comfortable she was having this discussion naked and sitting in his lap on the bed.

"Won't it be difficult to start your school if we have a baby right away?" he asked.

She gave him a self-deprecating grimace. "I say all the time that money doesn't matter to me, but the truth is, I'm counting on it to be able to 'have it all,' as they say."

"You plan to have a nanny?" He sounded almost shocked.

And she loved him all the more for it. "Probably, but not to *raise* our children. However, if we are ever going to be able to leave the house, we have to have someone besides your grandparents we can trust to care for our children."

"Yes."

"So, we'll have a nanny, someone who fits into our family, preferably matronly in both appearance and age." So, sue her if Maddie didn't want a beautiful young woman living under Vik's nose in their house.

"What do you mean about the money then?"

"I have every intention of hiring qualified staff who share mine and Romi's vision to run the school."

Vik's dark brow furrowed. "But you will both still give a great deal of time to the school. You will have to."

"Yes, but we'll make it work. Romi and I already discussed what would happen in the event one or both of us had a family."

"I'm not surprised."

"My father would be." He'd always assumed she had no business sense if she didn't want to be part of *his* business.

"Jeremy only sees part of the picture when he looks at you," Vik agreed pragmatically.

"That's all he's interested in." Jeremy Archer had never wanted to give the time necessary to get to know who Maddie was, not before Helene's death and definitely not after.

"He *can* break out of his tunnel vision."

"So you say. I've witnessed no evidence."

Vik shook his head, clearly done with the topic. "You'll need an efficient and knowledgeable personal assistant."

"Exactly." A nanny for convenience, not necessity, but a PA? That Maddie would *need* to make sure things got done.

Vik's phone rang before they could continue their discussion. It was Conrad, excited about the opportunity for a live interview with the newly engaged couple on an evening celebrity-news show.

And so it began.

* * *

The next weeks passed in a whirl of activity. Interviews as a couple, interviews by herself. The media furor around Maddie and Vik's engagement was even bigger than the initial craziness Perrygate had spawned.

Vik slept at her apartment every night while decorators and contractors worked overtime getting Parean Hall habitable for them. Maddie interviewed domestic staff while overseeing the changes to the main rooms and the master suite. She did her best to make sure both her and Vik's design aesthetic was incorporated in their new home.

And could hear his voice saying "I told you so" when she realized she knew enough about his preferences to do that.

Maddie went back to her secret volunteering in her brown wig and contacts, dressed in clothes from the local superstore. Every minute spent with the children cemented her determination to do more.

She also scheduled a visit with the therapist she'd seen in the immediate months after her skydiving accident, when Maddie had realized the time had come to break away from her past. Dr. MacKenzie was vocal in her praise for how far Maddie had come in dealing with both her mom's death and her father's emotional neglect.

However the therapist evinced some concern about the marriage that Vik said he intended to be *real* and yet was connected to a very lucrative contract for him. Dr. MacKenzie asked Maddie to consider carefully her reasons for agreeing to the engagement.

So Maddie did and, even more importantly, she talked to Vik about it.

"Yes, the contract your father offered is beneficial to me, but getting married right now is important for you, too."

"You think I said yes to the whole marriage thing because of the school, don't you?" Had she?

She'd told herself on that crazy, surrealistic day that was exactly why she needed to consider the idea seriously.

But Vik just shrugged. "Even if the scandal had blown up like it could have, you would not have given up on the school. Romi would have been the public face to run it and you would have been the silent partner as I now will be."

She loved his confidence in her. The pleasure of it masked the full import of his words for a moment, but then it settled in.

"*You* will?" When had Vik offered to partner with her and Romi in founding the school?

"We made promises to see one another's dreams fulfilled. Marriage to you will give me AIH. I've told you that I will ensure it provides for your dreams as well."

Maybe she should have expected something like this, but she hadn't. "You really are my white knight."

"I thought you did not believe in fairy tales." His voice and expression were teasing, but something told her he liked her claim.

"Maybe I just believe in you." He had always been the exception, the one man she trusted—even when she hadn't thought she had a reason to.

Refusing to admit it didn't make it any less true.

"You do," he said with a mix of implacability and smugness that should have annoyed her.

It didn't. She liked it. "So certain."

"Of you? Yes."

Ultimately, it all came down to that simple truth. *She* trusted Vik to keep the promises he'd made at the Marin Headlands overlook.

The fact that she was falling in love with Viktor Beck all over again? Well, that was something she didn't bring up even to Romi.

How could she help it? The man spent more time masquerading as a white knight than a business tycoon.

The wedding was going forward. And soon.

For the ceremony itself, they planned a very small gathering, but the reception would be huge and attended by the cream of society, the scions of the business world and even a few celebrities.

When Maddie's follow-up therapy appointment conflicted with a meeting with the caterers for their wedding reception, she told Vik she didn't want to reschedule her time with Dr. MacKenzie.

"You are seeing a therapist?" Vik asked. "Why didn't I know this?" The latter clearly the only thing that bothered him about her revelation.

"Because I didn't tell you?"

He made a scoffing sound.

"No one knows except Romi."

"When did you start seeing him?"

"Her. And right after the skydiving incident." Maddie had realized she was taking the same self-destructive path as her mother and she wasn't going to do that. "I saw her weekly for a couple of months and then a few more times after that."

"I'm impressed."

"You are?" She had worried a little he would think she was weak for needing to see someone.

"You realized you couldn't help children if you didn't deal with your own childhood issues."

That had been exactly it. "How do you know me so well?" she asked, falling a little more in love with him right then.

"You know the answer to that."

"You make it a point to get to know everything about the people and businesses you plan to partner with, or take over."

"Our partnership will supersede all others. Of course, I will know everything about you."

She liked hearing that, even if it wasn't exactly true. "But you didn't know I was seeing Dr. MacKenzie."

"No." He sounded chagrined.

Maddie laughed. "Even you are not infallible, Vik."

"Miss Grayson knew."

"She's my best friend."

"What am I?"

"The man I'm going to marry. The man I'm falling in love with all over again." There, she'd said it.

What he did with that knowledge was up to him. But one thing she knew, it was time he met Maddie Grace.

Silence stretched between them.

"Vik?"

"I am…honored."

"Good." That was better than thinking she was a fool for believing in the emotion.

"You…I…" For the first time in memory, Vik didn't sound in complete control of his words or his thoughts.

"I don't expect you to say it back."

"Good." The relief in his tone was not complimentary, but she wasn't surprised by it, either.

"You'll never lie to me," she said, as if just making that revelation.

But maybe she understood the depth of his commitment to honesty between them fully for the first time.

"No, I will not."

That included not claiming to love her when he didn't, but it also meant that his promises? Were written in concrete as far as Viktor Beck was concerned.

CHAPTER NINE

MADDIE WAS SHOCKED when her father called and asked her to come to dinner. Alone.

They ate in the formal dining room. Even with the leaves removed from the table, it would easily seat six.

Maddie sat to her father's left and swirled her soup with her spoon, pretending to eat.

Her father didn't seem any more at ease than she felt.

Finally she gave in and asked, "Why am I here?"

"It's been a long time since we had a family dinner."

"There's a two-page magazine spread to prove otherwise."

He shook his head, an expression she couldn't quite decipher on his familiar features. "That is not the same."

"I'm not sure what you mean then."

"You and me. Family."

"We stopped being a family when Mom died." She didn't say it with accusation, or even anger.

He could thank the therapist he didn't know about for that, but it was still the truth.

"It was never my intention for that to happen."

She couldn't hold back a small scoffing sound. "You sent me to boarding school within months of her death. I'd say your intentions were pretty clear."

"That was a mistake."

Something inside Maddie cracked at that admission,

but she merely shrugged. What could she say? *Yes, it had been a huge, painful mistake.*

Somehow agreeing didn't seem like the thing to do, though. Not least of which because no acknowledgment now could change the consequences of his choice when she was fifteen.

"I didn't know what to do," he admitted with a candidness rare for Jeremy Archer. "I failed your mother and I was terrified of failing you, so I sent you away, hoping they could do for you at school what I was so clearly not qualified to do at home."

Maddie stared at him as an emotional maelstrom swirled inside her. "Who are you and what have you done with my father?"

It was an old joke, but *man,* was it appropriate.

Her dad barked out a laugh. "I told Viktor this wouldn't be easy."

"He wanted you to talk to me?" Why wasn't she surprised?

"Yes." Jeremy sighed. "Viktor thinks our relationship is salvageable."

"He's an optimist."

"He is."

Giving up on the pretense of eating, she set her spoon down. "You sound surprised by that fact."

"It's not a side of him I noticed before."

"You don't think his business world-domination plans take optimism?" she asked, only partially tongue in cheek.

Her dad laughed again, this time longer and with more real humor. "I suppose they do."

"I guess that makes you something of an optimist, too." Which wasn't something she'd ever acknowledged before.

"Enough of one to believe things could be different for you than Helene." He sounded like he meant it.

"We all have our demons. I'm learning to cope with

mine without jumping out of airplanes." Maddie could give him that at least.

Her father took a ruminative sip of his wine. "I used to think Helene got into trouble just to get my attention. She seemed to take a perverse pleasure in being written up in the media."

"She did."

He looked startled at Maddie's agreement. "But she was a risk taker before we ever met. You know that, don't you?"

"She used to tell me stories over her scrapbooks." It had all sounded so thrilling to a young girl.

Jeremy nodded. "It was one of the things I admired about her."

"You weren't the first important man in her life to ignore her." That was one of the things Maddie had come to realize.

Helene Madison had craved her own father's attention and only managed to get it when she acted out. By the time she married Jeremy Archer, the attention-seeking behavior was an already established coping mechanism.

"You're saying Helene wasn't adventurous by nature, but because her exploits got her father's attention."

"Oh, I think Mom was definitely adventurous, she just discovered that in giving in to that side of her personality, she got something she craved."

"She always said she understood the amount of time I had to give to my company."

"Would you have listened if she said she didn't?" He certainly hadn't responded to Maddie's verbal pleas for his time, or to return home from boarding school.

"Probably not," her father admitted with more honesty than she expected.

"Her death wasn't your fault." It was a truth that had been very hard come by for Maddie.

She'd blamed her dad for so long, but one of the first

breakthroughs she'd made with her therapist was the realization that Helene Archer had been responsible for her
own choices.

"Wasn't it?"

"No."

He didn't look like he agreed.

"Do you think Mom went racing because she didn't
love me enough to want to be around to raise me?" Maddie asked.

Her dad went pale with shock, his eyes dilating, his
mouth going slack for a second before he nearly shouted,
"No, of course not. She adored you, Madison. You must
know that."

"But she still went racing on the water at night."

"Not because of you."

"And not because of you, either."

"But—"

"Mom was an adult woman who suppressed normal
caution for the adrenaline spikes that made her feel alive."
The fact it had the side effect of gaining her the attention
she craved only made her mom's adventures doubly irresistible to her.

"You sound like a psychologist."

"A degree in early childhood development has its share
of psych courses." Maddie wasn't telling Jeremy about her
sessions with a therapist.

She wasn't ashamed of seeing Dr. MacKenzie, but Maddie didn't trust her father enough to share the more private
parts of her life with him. Not even this *new and improved*
Jeremy. She didn't know how deep the changes went or
how long they would last.

Her dad's eyes—the same shade as her own, but without the vulnerability she saw in the mirror when she was
alone—flickered with something between speculation and
curiosity.

"Speaking of your mother," he said in a more familiar tone that revealed no emotion.

"Yes?"

"You and Viktor have chosen her birthday for your wedding date."

"Yes." A month before Maddie turned twenty-five, it had just felt right to speak their vows on a date connected in such a special way to her mom.

"Viktor said you wanted to honor her memory with the date."

"We do." Did her dad find that uncomfortable?

Neither she nor Vik had considered that possibility.

Her father smiled, the expression appearing genuine. "I was hoping you would be willing to honor her memory in another way as well."

"How?" she asked warily.

"Do not worry, I am not going to use your mother's memory to try to guilt you into withdrawing the paperwork giving company shares to Ramona Grayson upon your twenty-fifth birthday."

But he hadn't forgotten it, either.

"It wouldn't work anyway. Mom loved Romi and I personally wouldn't have survived boarding school if her father hadn't sent her there, too."

Maddie had desperately wanted her SBC to come to the school once she'd realized her father wouldn't budge about her going there. However she'd never asked. It wouldn't have been fair. Just like Maddie, Romi had a life in San Francisco.

But Romi had begged her dad to send her and he'd done so.

Jeremy nodded. "He sent her because I offered to pay the tuition and dorm fees."

"No." Wouldn't her father have told her that before this?

"Yes. He told me when Romi came to him and asked to

follow you. He didn't want to send her, but I thought you would both be better off with each other than your fathers."

Maddie's dad was sounding more and more human by the minute. She wasn't sure how she felt about that, but she thought it might be hope.

However, she felt compelled to say, "Mr. Grayson always loved Romi."

"But he was already drinking heavily by then. Do you think he was any more aware of his daughter's needs than I was of yours?"

No, the man who had fallen asleep drunk most nights had not been aware of what Romi needed.

"If she hadn't gone to boarding school, she would have become her dad's caregiver." Jeremy sounded very certain of that. "Romi needed to get away and Gray needed to pour *himself* into bed at night."

"You used to be his friend."

"I still am, as much as you can befriend a man intent on drinking himself into an early grave and his own business into bankruptcy."

Worry creased Maddie's brow. "It's not that bad."

"Yet. But it will be."

"Don't pretend threatening to take his company over was a favor you would do him."

"No, it wouldn't be a favor to Grayson, but it would be to Romi." Her dad sounded very sure of that assertion.

"So you say."

"You don't trust me at all, do you?"

"Not really, no." She couldn't even say that if she thought the welfare of AIH was a given that her dad would put hers next.

She wasn't convinced of that.

Rather than appear upset by her denial, her dad shrugged. "Maybe you are right not to."

"That's not a comforting thing for you to say."

He shrugged. "Would you rather I lied?"

"No, but you would, if you thought it would get you what you wanted."

"That's one of the primary differences between Viktor and I. Our business peers know it, too. If I want another company president to believe something, I make sure he hears it from Viktor."

"Has he ever lied for you unknowingly?" she asked, not sure she wanted to know the answer.

"No. I'm not saying I haven't been tempted, but while I may not feel the same compunction for truth that my successor does, I do recognize that if I did that and Viktor found out about it, he would find another vehicle for his ambition than AIH."

Well, she'd never considered her father to be stupid. "I think you're right."

"I know I am."

"So, about Mom's memory..." Maddie said, ready to get back to the reason for her presence at her father's dinner table.

"She always said she wanted you to wear her wedding dress when you married."

"You still have it?" Maddie couldn't hide the eagerness in her tone.

If she'd been with Vik, she wouldn't have even felt the need to try.

"Of course."

"But you got rid of all her things." Maddie would never forget coming home for the first time from boarding school to find most of the house redecorated and her mother's things gone.

"I kept her wedding dress and her jewelry for you." Her father's tone implied he didn't understand why Maddie wouldn't know that.

"Why? When you got rid of everything else?"

"The dress is a piece of history."

"Not business history." So, why would her dad care?

"Family history. A famous designer created it for your great-grandmother in 1957, the year after he did a similar dress for an actress in one of her more famous roles." Jeremy cleared his throat almost as if talking about this was making him emotional. "Every generation in her direct line has worn it since."

"I know."

"Oh, I thought maybe you'd forgotten. You didn't mention wearing it."

"I thought you'd gotten rid of it."

"I didn't."

"I'm so glad." It was a dream she'd thought would have to die with her mother.

"You're very much of a size with your mother. I doubt it will require much tailoring."

The beautiful ivory strapless gown with embroidery in champagne silk thread around the full skirt and on the bodice required no altering at all.

Though she and Romi agreed Maddie should wear a corset under the embroidered bodice for smooth lines. The champagne lining flipped over the hem as a contrast lay exactly as it was supposed to.

"You look so beautiful," Romi said with suspiciously shiny eyes.

The dress hugged Maddie's breasts and torso, nipping in at her natural waist and then flaring in a full skirt shorter in the front than the back, which had an understated train that swept the floor elegantly behind her.

"I look like my mom."

"But you have your dad's eyes." Romi twisted her mouth comically. "I can't believe he paid for me to attend boarding school with you."

"Me, either." But Mr. Grayson had confirmed Jeremy's claim.

"He loves you, I always said so."

"In his own way," Maddie agreed. "Just not the way I needed."

"Maybe he just didn't know how. From what you've told me about his parents, it doesn't sound like the Archers were a warm family."

Maddie had only a few memories of grandparents who were both dead by the time she turned five, but none of them included a hug, or a kiss, or any other sign of affection.

"You could be right, but Jeremy admitted he'd lie if it got him what he wanted."

"Well, you knew that."

"I did. It was just weird having him admit it. I guess he has his own personal brand of honesty, too."

Romi adjusted the folds of Maddie's skirt just so. "I suppose. I prefer Viktor's."

"Me, too," Maddie said fervently.

Both women laughed, and it felt good.

But then most things felt pretty amazing right now. Maddie was marrying the man she loved and even if he didn't love her, he'd promised a *real* family.

And Vik kept his promises.

Viktor walked down the elementary school's hallway behind an office aide who had agreed to escort him to Miss Jewett's first-grade classroom.

Unlike Madison, Viktor and Maxwell had attended public school, but in an area more affluent than this one. The mix of children and teachers here reflected San Francisco's varied population like the rarified social strata of the Archers did not.

Viktor wasn't sure why Madison had asked him to meet

her here. She'd said something about wanting to talk to him with the help of a visual aid.

He didn't know what that meant. He couldn't see how an overcrowded public school would work as inspiration for her charter school. Unless it was the success they had with their volunteer program.

He'd done a little research before leaving the office on this grade school and discovered that they had a significantly higher than usual rate of parent participation in the classroom as well as other volunteerism.

When he'd arrived at the office, it was to discover that he was expected. So, he was definitely in the right place.

Whatever Madison's reasons for having him there.

He noticed two things immediately after the aide opened the classroom's door—Madison looking very unlike herself and the absolute silence he did not associate with a roomful of children.

Wearing a mousy brown wig, contacts that obscured the Mediterranean blue of her eyes with brown and clothes clearly bought off the rack at a box store, his fiancée sat at a small desk in a circle with six students.

Tattered books with brightly colored pictures, large print and few words were open on the desks in front of the children. Madison held her own copy, a smile frozen on her face as she met his gaze.

Vik allowed one brow to rise in query. "Hello, Madison. It appears you have some friends I haven't met."

Her fixed smile morphed into a genuine grin as she jumped to her feet. "You're early."

He couldn't help noticing the cheap cotton top and denim jeans she wore showed off her curves in ways that affected his libido as surely as her designer dresses.

He didn't like the wig or colored contacts, though.

He shrugged away her comment about his timing. "Introduce me."

"Of course."

Not wanting to intimidate the children with his size, Viktor dropped to one knee and reached to shake hands with each child as Maddie introduced them.

A few returned his greeting with charming politeness. One small girl, clearly Madison's favorite from the way the small girl tucked herself behind his fiancée's legs, ducked her head, but wiggled her fingers in a shy hello.

Viktor met the teacher and the parent volunteer as well.

"Very nice to meet you," he said to Miss Jewett.

"The pleasure is all ours." She smiled, her eyes warm as they lit on Madison. "Your fiancée is a fantastic volunteer. She's so good with the children and could be a teacher with her credentials."

"I am aware." He just hadn't been aware that she volunteered in the public school system.

Did her father know?

Madison clearly didn't want to leave right away, so Viktor stayed, enjoying the time helping six-year-olds with their reading.

They were in his Jaguar and headed toward the other side of the city when she finally pulled off the offensive wig, exposing her red curls crushed in a messy pile. It reminded him of the way she looked after sex, the only time she was completely disheveled—Madison woke looking more tempting than ever.

She rubbed at her scalp and ran her fingers through her hair, causing some curls to bounce up again. "It's always such a relief to get that thing off."

"Why do you wear it?"

"Because *Maddie Grace* is a normal woman with a degree and desire to volunteer with children. She doesn't get written up in the tabloids or followed by the paparazzi."

"And that's important to you?"

"To be normal? It was when I started. Now, it's just

easier. Can you imagine what the media would make of the billionaire heiress as a volunteer teacher's aide?"

"I have a feeling we're going to find out."

"That's what I thought. With our marriage and the vestiges of Perrygate, I kind of figured it was only a matter of time before my secret got exposed."

"Some secret." She was even more wonderful than he'd always known. "How long have you been volunteering like this?"

"It started as a dare with Romi. Trying to attend a political rally incognito. It worked and I got the idea to volunteer at a soup kitchen the next weekend *dressed up*."

"Don't you mean dressed down?"

She laughed, the sound soft and more enticing than he was sure she meant it to be. "I guess."

"It might be a good idea to come clean before some enterprising reporter does it for you."

"I guess," she said again, not sounding nearly as amused or enthusiastic.

"As much as you enjoy being Maddie Grace, Madison Beck will be able to effect more widespread change and influence." Just giving Madison his last name verbally was satisfying in a way Viktor didn't understand or analyze.

"But will she get to teach a first-grader how to read?"

"Yes. That's what the charter school is about, right? Helping children one-on-one."

"It is." He could hear the smile in Madison's voice.

"So Grace for Romi Grayson?"

"No, my grandmother Madison."

"That's right." He'd forgotten.

"You don't mind?"

He pulled into a parking spot on the side of the road, wanting to have this conversation face-to-face. Cutting the engine, he turned to face her.

Brown eyes stared back at him and he frowned. "Can you take those out?"

"What? Oh…" Comprehension dawned.

She pulled a small case from her backpack, so different than the trendy designer bags he usually saw her wear, and proceeded to take out and store away the contacts.

"This persona, she's more you than the famous designer wedding dress?"

"Sometimes. Sometimes I just really love my Chanel, you know?" Madison's pretty bow lips twisted in a wry grimace. "I like to pretend that I couldn't care less about the latest fashions and keep up with them just to be Madison *Archer*, but the truth is? I like both."

He nodded. Not because he understood. He wore tailored designer suits as a sign of power, not because he thought about how they looked. But because he was glad Madison Archer, soon to be Madison Beck, wasn't someone she didn't want to be.

"So, the question was *do I mind*? Yes?"

Madison's beautiful blue eyes shone at him. "Yes."

"Do I mind that I am going to marry a woman who cares so much about helping others she has created an alternate persona so she can do it? No, Madison. I do not mind at all."

Giving in to the urge that seemed to grow with each passing day, Viktor leaned across the console and kissed Madison.

He lifted his mouth to say, "In fact, I think it's amazing."

Madison sighed and leaned back into the kiss, delight radiating off of her and twisting its way around Viktor's heart.

Viktor's *deda* and *babulya* had them over for dinner a couple of days later and dropped their own bombshell.

Stunned at his grandparents' request, Viktor could only ask, "You want us to what?"

"When we moved here, we gave up all the old ways," Misha said. "We changed our last name from Bezukladnikov to Beck—we even changed our baby boy's name from Ivan to Frank. Very American."

"I know all this." It was family history he had shared with Madison years ago.

Her lovely face expressed memory of the event too. Viktor just didn't understand why his *deda* felt the need to rehash those realities now.

"We did not speak Russian in our home. We encouraged our little Ivan to become fully American." *Babulya's* voice broke on his father's original name. "Frank, who spoke without an accent and did all the things the other children at school did."

"You wanted him to embrace and be embraced by his new homeland," Madison offered in understanding while Viktor reeled with alien confusion.

His grandmother smiled appreciatively. "Exactly, but we gave away too much and he became the man he is today."

"A flake. You can say it, *Babulya*." Vik frowned with frustration, really not liking the idea his beloved grandparents were trying to take responsibility for his father's lifetime of selfish and poor choices. "My dad is a deadbeat."

"Do not speak of your father that way," Misha said, but with little heat.

Viktor didn't argue, but he didn't promise not to, either. He couldn't.

Madison looked at him with something far more attractive than compassion. Her eyes glowed that way they did when she called him her white knight. Viktor had no clue what in this particular situation would put that look on her face, but he would not question the obvious lack of the one emotion he hated above all others.

Pity.

His *babulya's* eyes usually filled with a tranquility he'd always relied on, but now shimmered with regret. "We think we let go of too many traditions and he felt himself cast adrift."

"Oh, for..." Viktor clenched his jaw to bite back the first words that came to his mind. "Dad did not become a con artist because he didn't have a traditional Russian wedding. The one right and good thing he did in his life was his marriage to my mom."

"That is not true," Misha said in a deep voice so like Viktor's own. "He fathered you."

Viktor opened his mouth and shut it again without a word.

Madison grinned, a smug glint in her azure eyes. "I told him the same thing."

"You are a very good match for our grandson." His grandmother's answering smile was blinding. "It pleases Misha and me very much that you appreciate our Viktor as we do."

"He's easy to love."

Once again Viktor did not know how to respond to those words, though he liked hearing them. Very much.

But love was not something he had ever considered in the equation of his marriage to Madison and the life they would build together. Was it enough that she felt the emotion, or did she expect him to reciprocate one day?

Could he? Did he even know how?

He had never been in love before. The affection between his grandparents had grown over time and did not look on the surface anything like the passion that burned between Viktor and Madison.

The silence had stretched and it should have been awkward, but the three most important people in the world to him simply observed Viktor with varying degrees of understanding.

It was a strange experience, but not unpleasant.

"Thank you," he finally said to Madison, hoping that once again it was enough.

His grandfather winced, but patted Viktor on the shoulder. Misha didn't say anything, though.

Madison's smile turned soft in a way Viktor did not understand, but liked nonetheless.

His grandmother rolled her eyes. "Viktor, my dear grandson, you have much to learn about romance."

Viktor could not deny it.

She didn't seem to expect an answer. "Is it so much to ask you follow a few of our family's traditions?"

"I'm not answering before you tell me exactly which ones you're talking about." His caution was necessary.

Russian wedding preparations and celebrations could become extremely complicated and involved.

But his grandparents' requests weren't unreasonable, even if they did mean Madison had to spend the night before her wedding at Jeremy's home instead of Viktor's bed.

Five weeks after Perry's exposé, Maddie waited in the drawing room of her father's mansion the morning of her wedding.

She was wearing the gown her mother had worn, and her mother before that and *her* mother before that in 1957.

Her full-length Victorian-era veil of Brussels lace was even older than the dress. Romi had shown up with it a week ago. And it was the exact same ivory as the gown.

Romi adjusted the veil around Maddie's face now. "You are so beautiful."

Maddie couldn't answer. If she tried to talk, her emotions were going to get the best of her.

"Viktor is going to be here any minute. Are you ready?"

Maddie indicated herself with a wave of her hand and forced an even tone. "What do you think?"

"I already told you, beautiful. But, sweetie, that's not what I'm talking about. Are *you* ready?"

"According to Vik, we got married that day we made promises overlooking San Francisco's skyline."

"Pffft." Romi shook her head. "Men."

"Those promises were vows." Of that Maddie was very certain.

"So are the words you're going to speak today."

Maddie nodded. "I'm ready."

"You love him."

"I do." There was no point in denying it. Besides Romi could always tell when Maddie was lying.

"You always have."

Maddie wasn't so sure about that, but she couldn't deny she'd never fallen in love with anyone else.

"Perry didn't stand a chance."

"He didn't want one." Their friendship had never been like that.

"I'm not so sure about that."

"It doesn't matter."

"No," Romi said with finality. "It doesn't."

Maddie grinned at her sister-by-choice. "I'm getting married today."

"You are." Romi grinned back.

Their hug was fierce enough to crush silk and neither of them cared.

The sound of the doorbell came faintly from the hall. Then Vik's voice and Misha's laugh.

Oh, this was real. It was happening. Now.

More laughter and then the door to the drawing room swung in and bounced against the wall.

Her six-foot-two distant cousin James, wearing a dis-

tinctly masculine tuxedo and tulle veil, stumbled in first.
"He figured out I wasn't you, cuz."

Maddie found herself laughing along with the others
as they came in behind him. The first tradition had been
observed. Her father had pretended to offer an alternate
"bride" and Vik had shown his determination to only wed
one.

Misha, looking dapper in his own tux, and Ana, beautiful in her rose-pink suit, came in behind James. Maddie's
father wore a traditional morning coat and ascot, but Vik
was in breath-stealing Armani.

James's parents were there, too, along with the second
cousins who had been at the family engagement dinner.
Vik's aunt, his father's younger sister by ten years, and
her two teenagers had flown in from New York. Frank
hadn't made it.

The cousins from Russia had extended their stay in
California, though, so they were here as well.

Enough family to please Misha and Ana's need for traditions to be observed, Maddie hoped.

But really? As far as she was concerned, no one else
mattered, not when Vik came to stand in front of her, his
expression hungry, approving and supremely satisfied all
at once.

"Ti takAya krasIvaya." Vik reached out to touch her,
but his hand hovered in the air between them, not quite
connecting.

"He is telling you that you are beautiful," Misha informed her.

Maddie nodded her understanding, but couldn't look
away from the intensity in Vik's espresso gaze.

"I have come to ransom my bride," he said in formal
tones clearly meant for her father, but Vik's attention never
strayed from Maddie.

"Your father tried pawning this one off on us," Misha

said, pointing at James. "But my grandson is too observant to be fooled."

Because anyone would have mistaken her tall, *male* cousin for her.

But Maddie laughed because it was supposed to be in fun and she found she enjoyed this Russian tradition very much.

Vik offered an open Tiffany box with a sapphire-studded tiepin and cuff links resting on the cream satin.

Her father accepted it with what sounded like genuine thanks, but then he shook his head. "This is not enough."

And she knew that was part of the ritual Misha and Ana wanted to see observed.

Misha made a production of arguing the merits of the gentlemen's jewelry, but Vik never even cracked a smile. His powerful focus was entirely on Maddie and she felt a connection to him that was more spiritual than humorous.

Finally, Misha came between them, offering her another Tiffany box. This one contained a five-strand pearl necklace and perfectly matched pearl studs in a vintage inspired gold setting.

Her gaze flicked between the pearls and Vik and then to Romi, because Maddie's SBC had convinced her to go without a necklace. "You knew."

Romi nodded, her brilliant smile watery.

Maddie reached up and removed her mother's diamond earrings and handed them to Romi, who she now realized had left her own ears bare just for this. It was right that Romi would be wearing something of Helene's at Maddie's wedding.

Vik helped Maddie put on the earrings and the necklace, the moment unbearably intimate. When he was done, he bent down and placed a barely there kiss against her lips before carefully dropping her veil back into place.

"Now, there can be a wedding," Misha said with hearty satisfaction.

CHAPTER TEN

THEY TOOK TWO limos to the church.

Maddie didn't pay attention to who went where except that she had Vik on one side of her and Romi on the other.

The Holy Virgin Cathedral looked like it had been transplanted right out of Russia, with its cross-topped triple-domed spires and white facade. The inside was awe-inspiring, with its domed ceilings decorated with iconography and the ornate public altar area.

She lost herself in the beauty of the service, but nothing was as moving as the moment before the crowning ceremony when Vik sidestepped tradition and lifted her veil to kiss her again and whisper that now even God knew she was his.

The words might be considered irreverent by some, but they settled in Maddie's soul. He left her veil folded back so that when the crown was placed on her head signifying the sacrament, Maddie felt both bound and freed at the same time.

They skipped the civil ceremony that would have been required to make the wedding legal in Russia because it wasn't necessary in America. Consequently, they broke crystal glasses at the reception in front of a few hundred of her father and Vik's nearest and dearest.

Both glasses shattered into rubble, though there could

be no doubt that Vik threw his with an impressive force beyond what Maddie used. Everyone cheered.

"It will be a long and blessed union," Misha announced loudly.

She was a little surprised to discover the man hired to be toastmaster was a well-known Shakespearean actor, and one of her favorite up-and-coming performers sang for the guest's enjoyment.

They ate, cut the cake and toast after toast was made to the happy couple.

It was all sort of overwhelming and amazing. Nothing about this wedding felt like a business arrangement. When she mentioned that to Vik, he smiled.

"Because this marriage is *not* a business arrangement," he said firmly.

"But—"

"It's a marriage of dreams. Accept that for what it is."

Happier than she had ever been, Maddie nodded and did just that. She wasn't at all surprised when Romi caught her bouquet.

Maddie had been aiming after all.

What was surprising and even a little worrisome, was that Maxwell Black caught the garter. The look he gave Romi would have had Maddie running for the hills, but her friend just blushed. And looked more than a little interested.

Huh. That was something to think about.

After Maddie's own honeymoon.

She smiled so much during the reception that her cheeks hurt by the time the white Rolls-Royce arrived to take them away.

Maddie was surprised when the car pulled up in front of the Ritz-Carlton instead of Parean Hall.

She turned to Vik. "I thought we were going home."

"I like the sound of that."

"Going home?" she asked, confused and not minding a bit.

"Home. *Our home*," he emphasized.

Heat she did not understand crept into Maddie's cheeks. "But we aren't there."

"No, we are here. And this moment the only three people who know that are you, me and the driver." Vik sounded very proud of that fact.

"What about security?"

"Not even them. Not tonight. No friends. No family. No security. *No press.*"

Delight suffused her. "Tonight is ours."

"Yes."

"I like it."

"Good."

He carried her over the threshold of Suite 919, one of the two most luxurious sets of rooms on the club level.

Its beauty was lost on Maddie, though. She was way too focused on Vik to pay attention to marble floors and Chippendale furniture.

"Champagne?" he asked without putting her down.

She shook her head.

"Snack?"

A smile flirted at her mouth as she said primly, "No thank you."

His eyes darkened with primal intent. "Bed then?"

"Oh, yes."

He carried her into the bedroom and lowered her to her feet. "Did I tell you how lovely you are today?"

"You may have mentioned it, yes."

He nodded, as if in serious contemplation. "I can only imagine one circumstance in which you could be more breathtaking."

"Yes?" she asked.

"Let me show you."

"Okay," she breathed out.

He removed her crown and veil with careful, deliberate movements. Then he took off the jewelry he'd helped her put on earlier.

"I don't think I told you. The pearls are exquisite. Thank you."

"They are just little white beads until you are wearing them."

"Oh, wow...I don't know even know how to take some of the things you say."

"As truth. We've established I do not lie to you." He brushed his lips over the back of her neck.

She did nothing to suppress the shiver the small touch elicited. "Or at all, according to Jeremy."

Vik came around and faced her, and then leaned down to press their mouths together softly for only a brief moment. "Or at all." He kissed down her neck and along her bare shoulder.

Each caress of his lips left a trail of goose bumps in its wake and she was trembling with desire by the time he made it around to the back of her dress.

He undid the bodice, trailing kisses down her spine as he did so.

The silk of her corset was no barrier between his lips and her skin. He helped her step out of the dress and then took the time to carry it into the dining room and lay it on the table.

When he came back into the bedroom, she said, "Thank you."

He looked at her questioningly.

"For caring about my dress."

He shrugged as if his consideration wasn't important, or maybe rather that it should be taken for granted. "It is a living memory for your family."

She hoped she never stopped appreciating the big, but especially little things he did to take care of her.

"So, is this what you were talking about?" she asked with a sweeping gesture toward herself with her hand.

Maddie stood before Vik in her corset, panties, sheer silk thigh highs and glittery Jimmy Choo heels, but nothing else.

His smile was predatory when he shook his head. "Almost, but not quite."

She stepped out of her heels.

"Closer." Sensuality oozed through his voice.

She swallowed. They'd made love every night for the past five weeks, so nothing about this one should make her nervous.

But as much as he'd claimed to consider their promises at the Marin Headlands overlook to be enough to bind them, the look of possession in his eyes was about ten times more intense than it had been the past weeks.

She reached down to unhook her stockings, but he put a staying hand. "Let me."

"Okay." She straightened and waited.

With no consideration for the expensive fabric of his tuxedo trousers, Vik knelt in front of her. But rather than undoing the slide button holding her stocking in place, he settled his big hands on her hips and leaned forward to press a kiss between her breasts.

Her breath caught and her knees went weak. "Vik, please."

"Please what?" he asked, his voice dark with passion. "This?"

He nuzzled the slopes of her breasts, his tongue flicking out to taste her skin. Little sparks of pleasure chased the path he took with his mouth.

His hands slid around to cup her bottom and then fingertips teased the exposed skin between the bottom of her panties and the tops of her stockings.

She only realized he'd undone the hooks when the soft silk slid down first one thigh and then another—with a little help from Vik.

Over a month ago, she'd never been touched like this, but now her body knew the delight to be had. She felt empty inside in a way she never had before she'd known what it was like to be filled up.

Her thighs quivered with brush of his fingertips while part of her craved even more. Firmer touch, more intimate caresses.

Her nipples had already drawn tight in anticipation of his attention.

Images of what he'd done before melded with the present to intensify every brush of skin against skin.

Vik reached behind her to undo the corset and she was grateful she'd gone for one with a zipper rather than laces. It parted and came away from her overheated skin in a matter of seconds.

"Mmmm…" he hummed, his expression both pleased and predatory. "Almost there."

There was no surprise when he hooked his fingers in the waistband of her panties and tugged them down. Only a sense of breathless anticipation.

With one final kiss on each of her nipples, he stood. "Now, that is the most beautiful sight I could ever imagine."

Heat suffused her body; she'd lost her ability to suppress her blushes around this man.

None of her defense mechanisms came naturally around Vik anymore.

"You're still dressed." Her voice sounded like a croaking frog.

"Would you like to change that?" he asked, his tone filled with sensual challenge.

In answer, she stepped forward and undid his bow tie.

"I'm starting to understand how you feel about unwrapping gifts," she said as she pulled the tie slowly from the starched collar of his shirt.

"Yes?"

"Oh, yes." She took her time on the buttons as well, leaning forward to inhale his masculine scent and nuzzle the chest hair not covered by his white silk undershirt.

Maddie reveled in each new inch of golden skin revealed, taking her time to touch and kiss as he had done.

Funny how quickly she'd gained the confidence to do this, but then he'd never reacted with anything but all-out enthusiasm to any sexual overture she made. No matter how small.

When she had him completely naked, she stepped forward so their bodies were flush. He was so much bigger than her and yet they fit together like they'd been created as adjoining pieces of a puzzle.

They kissed for several very satisfying minutes, no sense of urgency, just pleasure as they connected as intimately as when he was inside her.

But there was something she wanted to do, something she hadn't yet tried, something that intrigued, but also intimidated her.

What better time to take the plunge but on her wedding night?

She pulled back to break the kiss, but he drew her back in. This happened a few more times before she finally managed to separate their lips and bodies.

"I want to taste you," she told him.

A supernova flared in his eyes. "I'm not about to tell you no."

"I didn't think you would." She dropped to her knees in front of him.

"Wouldn't you be more comfortable on the bed?" he asked, sounding like it really mattered to him.

And she knew it did.

She took his large erection in her hand and caressed up and down. "Maybe, but not yet." Maddie stroked him a second time.

Groaning, Vik swayed.

She loved the velvety smoothness of his skin here and knowing that small touch affected him in such a primal way.

Leaning forward, Maddie took her first real taste of Vik's straining sex. The skin should taste like any other skin on his body, but it was even more addictive to her taste buds.

Drops of preejaculate burst with flavor on her tongue and she thought how she would be the only one who got to experience this. Never again would another woman know him in this way.

Only Maddie.

Vik was hers.

She swirled her tongue around the spongy skin of his head and he made a sound between a growl and a groan. "Please, *milaya moya.*"

He could deny it, but the wedding made a difference to Vik. He'd never spoken in Russian to, or around her, before today. He was bringing her into his inner sanctum.

And that was as alluring as the naked man in front of her.

"What does that mean?" she asked, tipping her head back to see his face.

Their gazes locked, his dark eyes filled with passion.

"My sweet." His hips canted forward, seemingly of their own accord, and the tip of his erection brushed her lips.

She took him into her mouth, bringing forth another deep sound of pleasure from Vik. Hollowing her cheeks, Maddie sucked, moving her mouth forward and backward, but never so far forward she choked.

His hands settled softly against her head, but he made no effort to hold her in place or guide her movements. It was like he was giving her silent approval, as if he thought maybe his sounds of pleasure weren't enough.

It was wonderful, but her jaw got sore faster than she expected and she had to pull back.

"That was amazing," he said with apparent sincerity.

She smiled up at him. "Short, you mean."

He laughed, the sound husky. "Much longer and I would have come."

"You're easy."

"For you? Definitely." Vik pulled her to her feet and right into a mind-numbing kiss.

Not just easy, but *hungry*.

She hadn't known that missing a single night of love-making would make him so impatient, so ravenous for her and the pleasure they created together.

But Vik lost no time backing her up to the bed. He ripped the coverlet and top sheet off with a single, powerful yank and then maneuvered them onto the center of the king-sized mattress.

He guided her legs apart, her knees bent and she expected immediate penetration. What she got was his mouth against her most intimate flesh.

In moments, she was writhing with the need to climax, but an even stronger desire to have him inside her.

"Please, Vik. Make love to me now."

His head came up, eyes nearly black with passion meeting hers. "What do you think I am doing?"

"Not like that."

"Oh, yes, like this."

"But I'm going to come." Desperation overrode her every inhibition.

"Yes, you will," he promised in a sexy growl.

"But—"

"At least once."

Then he went back to what he was doing, taking her to the edge and over, her cries echoing around them in the luxurious bedroom. His tongue laved her gently through aftershocks until her body went boneless, her legs flopping down to the bed.

He pulled the sheet from its tangle with the comforter and wiped his mouth on it before surging up and over her. "Condom, or no condom?" he asked.

They'd been lucky and their first time without protection hadn't resulted in pregnancy. He'd been very careful to use condoms since.

But they were married now and had agreed to start a family right away. Equally important to her, she wanted the intimacy of no barrier between them.

"No birth control."

He nodded, if anything, his expression turning even more feral with a voracious sexual need. His desire came off him in waves and he still managed to enter her carefully, giving her most sensitive flesh a chance to adjust to his granite-hard erection filling her.

After her recent explosive climax and the way he incited aftershocks until she simply couldn't respond anymore, she'd been prepared to share the intimacy with him and revel in the emotional connection. But not much more.

Maddie was not prepared for the way her body reacted to their joining. The physical ecstasy ignited again, as if it had never been banked, burning hotter with every movement of his body in hers. Pleasure that she should be too sated to feel rolled through her, making her womb spasm and the muscles around his hardness contract.

He set a slow, but thoroughly penetrating rhythm that built the ecstasy inside her until she was on the verge of another inconceivable orgasm.

As if he could read her mind, or maybe it was just the clues her body was giving him, Vik sped up, pounding into her, jolts of pleasure going through her on every thrust.

He stared down at her, his face a rictus of sexual ecstasy, his coffee-brown eyes burning with demand. "Come now, *milaya moya*."

And improbably...she did, screaming as rapture sent her body into tremors that could have toppled cities.

He went completely rigid and joined her in the ultimate sexual pleasure, their gazes as connected and intimate as the most passionate kiss.

"If that didn't make a baby..." she said breathlessly.

He pulled her close into his body. "We will keep trying with great delight."

Which they did for the rest of the night, falling into exhausted slumber after the sun lit the morning fog.

He woke her to shower at noon. Not alone. Showering together was one of her recently discovered perks to sharing physical intimacy with Vik.

They came out of the bathroom to find clothing lying across the freshly made bed.

A familiar black-and-white polka-dot set of hard-sided luggage was sitting against the wall beside a black fold over garment bag and matching leather duffel as well.

"How long are we staying here?" she asked as she donned her bra and then tugged on a black silk shell over it.

Vik flicked the suitcases a glance and then met her eyes. "We are checking out in an hour."

"Where are we going?" Not home.

Both their personal possessions had been moved to Parean Hall the day before the wedding. So, there would be no need for luggage.

He pulled on his briefs and then a pair of dark indigo designer jeans. "Palm Springs."

"Why?"

"Our honeymoon."

She stilled in her own efforts to get dressed. "But I thought we weren't going on a honeymoon."

"I do not recall agreeing to that."

"We never talked about it," she pointed out.

He pulled on a black-and-white Armani X polo. "It is traditional."

"Our marriage isn't exactly." The jeans she stepped into were a pair of her favorites.

"I disagree."

She shook her head, knowing he wouldn't budge on his outlook. Vik saw nothing odd in marrying a woman he didn't love so he could build a legacy for the children he most certainly would.

"So, Palm Springs."

His grin was knowing. "I saw little point in an exotic location when we are likely to spend most of our time in the bedroom."

Blushing, she ignored his assertion and shrugged into the burgundy-and-black color-blocked jacket someone had left out for her to wear. "I like Palm Springs."

In fact, the small resort city nestled in the California desert was one of Maddie's all-time favorite places. She used to visit with her mother every winter. There were enough celebrities that vacationed there, the Archers of the world were barely a blip on the media's radar.

Maddie had continued to travel to the desert when she needed to get away from being Madison Archer, notorious heiress.

Somehow, she thought Vik knew that.

He smiled. "It is a good thing you are as intelligent as you are, or the amount of school you missed traveling with your mother would have been a real problem."

"She always brought a tutor along and got my assignments."

Vik's expression turned heated. "I'll be the only tutor you'll need this week."

"After the last five weeks, and particularly last night, I'm pretty sure there isn't much for you to teach me."

"You'll be surprised."

Not "you could be" or "you might be," but "you will be" surprised. The man had no shortage of confidence.

And the following eight days proved how justified he was in that regard.

True to his word, they spent *a lot* of time in the bedroom of their suite at an oasis-style resort outside of the city. However, Vik also insisted on visiting Maddie's favorite spots, taking her to dine at some of the best restaurants in and around the city as well as shopping in the exclusive boutiques of top designers.

Maddie, who had always considered her socialite side something of a necessary evil, enjoyed herself in ways she hadn't in Palm Springs since Helene's death.

Vik was flatteringly enthusiastic about almost every article of clothing Maddie tried on, and even the growls that particularly revealing pieces elicited were flattering in their own way.

They returned to San Francisco to a list of possible properties for the charter school that Vik had his real estate agent compile.

Vik had too many things on his desk no one else could handle after a week's absence to accompany Maddie and Romi when they toured the properties. But he asked detailed questions each evening about what Maddie had seen, proving the sincerity of his interest in the project.

* * *

Friday morning, Maddie got a text from her father's assistant requesting she come to a meeting in his office that afternoon.

She was supposed to do another tour of the property she and Romi had pretty much decided was *the one* for the school. Feeling magnanimous toward the world in general, even her father, Maddie called and rescheduled the tour before texting the PA that she would be at the meeting.

Maddie was shown into her father's office by his secretary, who surprisingly did not stay to take notes. So, it was a personal meeting?

Only, why at his office?

Her dad stood and came around from behind his desk. "Madison. I would like you to meet Dr. Wilson, the director for..." Jeremy named a well-known institution that specialized in psychiatric studies.

It was then she noticed the other man in the room.

Gray-haired and distinguished-looking in a suit of good quality, if not an Italian designer label, Dr. Wilson was sitting in one of the armchairs that sat opposite a matching leather sofa on the other side of her father's office.

He rose now and walked to Maddie, putting his hand out for Maddie to shake. "Madison. It's a pleasure to meet you."

"Thank you. I hope I can say the same." Though she did not have a good feeling about this.

Why did her father have a psychiatrist in his office for their meeting?

"Let's all sit down and get comfortable," Dr. Wilson said, indicating he considered himself a key player in the meeting to come.

The fact that her father followed the doctor's lead without comment indicated he agreed.

Maddie wasn't feeling quite so acquiescent. She remained standing as her father took a position at one end of the sofa and the doctor returned to his leather armchair. "What is this about?"

"Sit down, Madison, so we can discuss this like civilized people."

"Tell me what we are discussing first," she demanded in a chilly tone she hadn't used in weeks.

Her father frowned. "You are being rude."

"And you are being cagey." When it came to her father? Cagey was way worse than rude.

"Do you see what I mean?" Jeremy asked the doctor. "Unreasonably intractable."

"You've asked Dr. Wilson here to evaluate me?" Maddie demanded, emotion cracking through the facade of cool before she reined it in.

Surprisingly, her dad winced, but he nodded. "It has come to my attention that you've been seeing a therapist."

"I did for a few weeks, yes. Half of America has at one time or another." And her choice to do so was a good thing, not a weakness.

"That is actually a bit of an exaggeration," Dr. Wilson said, like he was making note of Maddie's tendency to overstate things. "The number is closer to twenty percent."

"Who told you I was seeing someone?" she asked Jeremy, ignoring the doctor.

Vik wouldn't have told him. He might not love Maddie, but he was her white knight. Vik would never sacrifice her to the king.

"Does Vik know about this meeting?" she demanded.

Her father gave her his game face. "What do you think?"

"That you don't want to answer my question." She pulled out her phone.

"Who are you calling?" Dr. Wilson asked, his tone overly patient.

"My husband."

"You see? Shades of codependency and paranoia," her father said.

Maddie wanted to throw her phone at his head, but didn't want to know what the psychiatrist would make of that. Vik's phone sent her to voice mail.

He must have been in a meeting.

She left a message. "It's me. Jeremy called me in for a meeting with a psychiatrist. I need to talk to you. Call me."

Dr. Wilson was watching her with an indecipherable expression. Her dad's eyes were narrowed, but she wasn't sure if it was with worry or annoyance.

"So, you know I saw a therapist and you've brought Dr. Wilson here to observe me. Why?"

"No one said I was here to observe you," the doctor said.

"No one said you weren't."

Neither the doctor nor her father answered that.

Finally, Jeremy said, "I've told Dr. Wilson my concerns about your increasingly erratic behavior over the years."

"And while I applaud your positive action in seeking help," Dr. Wilson said, as if speaking to a child, or an adult whose reasoning ability was compromised, "I must concur with your father that your actions since your mother's death indicate a spiraling condition."

"I do not have a condition." What she did have was a brain and it was starting to work. "You aren't going to prove me mentally incompetent to sign the paperwork giving Romi half of my shares in AIH. It's not going to work."

Her father's expression said he disagreed.

Even more ominously, the doctor shook his head. "Signing such a document as the one your father described to me in and of itself is hardly a rational action."

"You think not?"

"You think it is?"

"I know it is and I also know what I do with my money

and assets is not your business, Dr. Wilson, or for that matter, Jeremy Archer's."

"You call your father by his first name. That indicates a level of dissociation to those closest to you."

Who was this guy? Popping off with psychobabble on the basis of nothing but her father's obviously biased assertions and a few seconds conversation was not in any way professional.

"I'm closer to my cleaning lady than my father. In fact, I'm closer to *his* housekeeper than I am to him." And that might have been an exaggeration, but she defied either of them to prove differently.

The psychiatrist gave her a concerned look. "Your lack of emotional intimacy with your one remaining parent is certainly something we can explore together."

"Dr. Wilson, you are not and never will be *my* doctor. Now, if you two will excuse me." She turned to leave the office.

"Madison!" her father barked.

She didn't stop. He could leave whatever threat he wanted to make on her voice mail.

CHAPTER ELEVEN

MADDIE WAS IN the parking garage when her phone rang. Vik's ringtone.

She answered. "My father found out I was seeing a therapist."

"I didn't tell him."

"I didn't think you did."

"Good."

"I'm just…" Frustrated. Confused. Upset. "He wants to prove me incompetent to sign the papers giving Romi half my AIH shares."

"I had n—"

"There's something he didn't think of, I bet," she interrupted, not really hearing Vik.

"What is that?" Vik asked, sounding both cautious and concerned.

"If he gets a judge to say I wasn't competent to sign those papers. I wasn't competent to say my vows, either, and *we* aren't married. What will that do his precious plans to marry me off to his heir?" she demanded.

Vik made a sound like a growl. "That is not going to happen."

"I thought things were getting better with him."

"They are."

"If anyone has lost their mind it is him."

"I agree."

She nodded.

"Madison?"

"You're on my side, right?" Vik wouldn't support his mentor and friend in this, would he?

"Of course. You are my wife and you are staying that way."

Because he wanted control of AIH. Because he wanted the future he planned with her. Right that second, Maddie wished desperately there was another, more emotionally compelling reason for Vik to insist their marriage stood in validity.

Love.

She needed her husband's love. More than she wanted her father's acceptance. A lot more.

She couldn't really care less about Jeremy sliding back into old habits. However, suddenly the knowledge that the man she loved more than her own life appreciated her feelings but didn't share them hurt in a way she couldn't ignore.

"I need some time to think."

"What? Madison, where are you? I will come to you."

"No. I just…give me some time, Vik." She ended the call and then turned off her phone.

She didn't want to talk to anyone. Not even Romi.

Maddie got into her hybrid car—not exactly what an heiress might be expected to drive, but it was environmentally responsible—and drove to her favorite coffee shop/bookstore.

How was she going to live the rest of her life in love with her husband and knowing he didn't reciprocate her feelings. She didn't know if it was *couldn't* or *wouldn't*, but it didn't matter.

Maddie hadn't been to the coffee shop since before Perrygate, but she needed time to think and a place to do it in that Vik wouldn't think to look.

She got her usual order and took it to her favorite table positioned between a book stack and the window. Since the lower half of the window was painted with a mural that looked like old leather volumes on bookshelves, no one would see her from the outside.

Not unless they got right up to the window and looked down.

Her thoughts whirled in a mass of contradicting voices and images as her coffee cooled in its cup, but one idea rose to the surface again and again.

Vik *acted* like a man in love.

He couldn't get enough of her sexually. Maddie's happiness was very important to him. Given a choice, he *always* opted to spend time with her rather than away from her. He wanted her to be the mother of his children.

Did the words really matter?

She'd been doing fine without them to this point. But being thrown back into Ruthlessville by her father had undercut Maddie's sense of emotional security.

Did she really need Vik to admit he loved her for her to feel secure in her happiness with him?

She still had no answer to that question when she heard her name spoken in a masculine tone she'd never planned to hear again.

She looked up and frowned. "Go away, Perry."

"You don't take my calls or respond to my texts."

He was surprised? "I blocked your number."

"I figured that out."

"You aren't supposed to be talking to me."

"Nothing in the agreement that bastard you married got me to sign said I couldn't talk *to* you, only about you." Perry sounded really annoyed by that.

"What did you expect?"

He put on the wounded expression that had always gotten to her in the past. "I didn't expect you to dump six years of friendship over one little mistake."

"It wasn't the first time you lied to the media about us." And that sad look wasn't tugging at her heartstrings anymore.

Perry jerked, like he hadn't expected her to have worked that out. "It was all harmless. I needed the money. We aren't all born with the silver spoon of Archer International Holdings to feed off of."

"Telling people I was a sexual addict who couldn't be satisfied with a single partner wasn't harmless. You destroyed my reputation."

"For exactly twenty-four hours. Viktor Beck saw to that."

"Conrad is good at what he does."

"Your dad's media fixer? Yeah, I kind of expected him to get involved, but he's a cuddly kitten compared to that vicious shark you married."

"Vik protected me when *you* fed me to the wolves. I'm not sure I'd label *him* the vicious one."

"You know I didn't mean it." Perry sounded like he really expected her to believe that.

What a jerk. And this man had been one of her dearest friends for *six* years. "I knew you were lying, that's not the same thing as knowing you didn't mean it."

"I needed the money. You knew I did."

"And I refused to give it to you." Which was what it all came down to, wasn't it?

"I asked for a loan. From a *friend*."

"When have you ever paid back even a single dollar of all the money you *borrowed* from me, Perry?" she demanded, the confrontation with her ex-friend unexpectedly bringing her current situation into clear and certain focus.

Perry was that guy. The user. The manipulator. The prevaricator.

Vik was her white knight. Full stop.

He might never say the three little words she most wanted to hear, but she wasn't going to spend the rest of her life lamenting that fact. Not when he gave her so much to rejoice about instead.

"You can't guarantee business investments."

"So now they were business investments." She narrowed her eyes at Perry. "Where are my contracts showing the percentage ownership I had in those business ventures?"

"We don't need contracts between us."

She thought of the agreement Vik had forced Perry to sign. "Apparently, we do."

"Come on, Maddie. Call off your attack dog."

"Vik?"

"Who else?" Perry did his best to look beseeching.

"We aren't friends anymore and we never will be again," she spelled out very carefully.

"This is because of Romi, isn't it? She finally turned you against me."

"*You* turned me against you, Perry. You lied about me and did your best to destroy my reputation."

He'd gone back to looking wounded. "No."

"Yes. And if you'd succeeded, my dreams of starting a charter school would have been dust." At least with her name on any of the paperwork.

Perry shrugged. "San Francisco doesn't need another school."

His ability to dismiss the dreams of her heart so easily took her breath away. "I don't agree."

"Well, it didn't happen."

"No thanks to you."

"Hey, I went public with an apology and a confession that it was all a joke."

Did he expect her to thank him? "But it wasn't a joke.

It was a big ugly lie. Nothing even a tiny bit amusing about that."

"Come on, Maddie. You have to forgive me."

"Yes, for my own sake. I have to let it go."

Triumph flashed in Perry's washed-out blue eyes. "We can be friends again and forget about that agreement Viktor forced me to sign."

"No."

"But—"

"No one forced you to sign anything. You signed that agreement of your own volition because you didn't want to risk being sued by both AIH and the tabloid you sold that story to."

Maddie's head snapped up at Vik's voice. What was he doing here? How had he found her?

He stood like an avenging angel over Perry. "You are not my wife's friend. She's convinced you were at one time, but that time passed long before this latest incident."

"Who do you think you are to—"

"I am the man who will *ruin* you if you come near *my* wife again." His jaw hewn from granite, Vik's eyes burned with dark fury.

Perry put his hands up. "No problem. Look, I just thought we could still be friends, but I can see you're not comfortable with that."

"I'm not comfortable with it," Maddie inserted. "Stop blaming other people for your screwup, Perry. You destroyed our friendship and Vik is right, that started a long time ago."

"But, Maddie…"

She shook her head. "No. We're over. If you see me at a function, walk the other way because I don't want to talk to you anymore."

"We aren't going to be at the same functions," he said bitterly.

Maddie didn't bother to reply. That was Perry's problem, not hers.

"Are you going to leave, or will you force me to call the police to enforce the restraining order we have against you?"

"I'm leaving," Perry said quickly, backing out of the alcove.

"We have a restraining order?" Maddie asked Vik.

"Yes."

"Didn't I have to sign something for it?"

"No. His malicious intent was in the papers for the world to see. We filed for it on behalf of AIH and its primaries, of which you are one."

"Oh."

He looked down at her untouched coffee. "You're not drinking that."

She shook her head. "How did you find me?"

"Are you sure you want to know?"

"Yes."

"The 'find me' function on your phone."

"I turned it off."

"As long as the battery is in it and holds any charge, the GPS function works."

"So, if I want privacy, I have to take out the battery. Good to know."

He had to have looked up her GPS signal right away to have gotten to the coffee shop so quickly. More evidence that she mattered to him in the ways that were truly important.

Her father never would have just dumped his schedule to go running after her mother, or Maddie, certainly.

Vik inhaled, opened his mouth to speak, closed it again and then said, "I would prefer you not do that."

"Okay." It was a matter of safety as well, as much as she might prefer to forget that fact. "You came after me."

"Of course. You were upset. What Jeremy did to you…"

She coughed out a laugh at the rare vulgarity that came out of her husband's mouth.

Vik put his hand out to her. "Will you come *with* me now?"

Maddie didn't hesitate. "Yes."

"Don't you want to know where?" Vik asked as she took his hand and let him lead her from the coffee shop.

"I guess I assumed we'd go someplace private."

Vik's expression turned hard. "Actually, we're going back to AIH to confront your father."

"Together."

"Yes."

Implying Vik and Maddie were on one side and Jeremy Archer the other. Nice. If she'd needed proof that she came first with Vik, her father couldn't have provided a better opportunity.

Which, okay, maybe having the proof *was* nice, but she wasn't about to thank Jeremy.

Her father was in his office when they arrived, Dr. Wilson gone. The PA tried to tell them that Jeremy was in a meeting, but Vik just walked through.

He reached across Jeremy's desk and ended the call, sending Maddie's father surging to his feet as he spluttered with annoyance.

Vik waited until her father had gone silent to speak. "Have you ever known me to lie to you?"

Jeremy shook his head, his expression instantly wary.

"Do I bluff?" Vik asked.

"No," Jeremy said shortly.

"Then you will know I mean every word I say when I tell you that if you attempt to prove Madison incompetent to forestall her giving half her shares to Romi Grayson, I will destroy Archer International Holdings until the very building we are standing in is leveled to the ground."

"You don't mean that," Jeremy said, his voice warbling with emotion for the first time in Maddie's memory.

She hadn't even seen him appear this distraught at her mother's funeral.

There was no give in Vik. Not in his expression. Not in the way he stood, towering over Jeremy's desk. "We have just established that I do."

Definitely not in his tone.

Her dad said something else, but Maddie wasn't listening. Everything inside her had gone still as she had her second major revelation for the day.

"You *do* love me," she said to Vik, ignoring her father completely.

That oh-so-serious espresso gaze fixed on her. "You are mine to protect."

"And to love." Giddy with joy that could not be tempered even by her father's machinations, she could hardly help the delight surfing every syllable.

She didn't even want to try.

Maddie beamed up at the man she'd crushed on since she was fourteen and loved since she was sixteen. "I love you, too, but you know that."

"Do you?" Vik asked. "Even now?"

"Especially now." He wasn't even remotely responsible for her father's actions.

"I meant what I said to your father." He said it like it was a warning.

"I know."

"I am utterly ruthless and without remorse."

She might argue that point, but understood that Vik believed it. And that was okay with her.

He used his powers for good, even if he didn't see it.

She smiled at him, letting her love show in her eyes.

"Your sense of honor is the shiniest and clearest facet of your nature. Everything else about you is filtered through the light it casts."

"I am not a nice guy."

"You just threatened to destroy my company," her dad said with feeling. "You sure as hell are *not* a nice guy."

Maddie's smile morphed into a full grin. "It's all a matter of perspective. I love that you would pull out every stop to slay my dragons."

"I'm not a dragon. I'm your father, damn it."

She flicked him a disgusted glance. "Who threatened to have me declared mentally incompetent."

"You can't believe I wanted things to go down that way, but you're giving away my company." Vik might claim to be remorseless, but Jeremy's expression and tone were soaked with regret.

"Don't exaggerate," she said, dismissing her father's words. "Twelve and a half percent with the voting proxy assigned to Vik and any successor he should formally appoint."

Vik jolted beside her. "I didn't know that."

"I trust you."

His gaze turned soft like she'd never expected to see. "You do."

"You knew that."

"I told myself you did."

"And me." He'd told her when she'd still been denying it to herself.

"Apparently it is different coming from you."

Her dad sighed. "You know, your mother and I never felt the need to talk our emotions to death."

Finally, Maddie gave Jeremy her attention. "Maybe if you had, things would have been different."

"I cannot change the past," he said with a pained expression.

"You spend enough time screwing up with your daughter in the present, the past is hardly what you need to be worried about," Vik told her father.

"I am sorry for ambushing you with Dr. Wilson, Madison." Jeremy looked at her with appeal. "It probably makes no difference to you, but I told Dr. Wilson I wouldn't be needing his services immediately after you left my office."

"That's hard to believe." Her father didn't back down once he'd set a course of action in motion.

He just didn't. And he *did* lie.

Jeremy said, "Call him. He'll tell you."

Bluffing or truth?

"He's telling the truth," Vik told her.

Maddie looked up at her husband. "How can you tell?"

"His eyes shift to the left when he's lying about something important."

"And this is important to him?" she asked with suspicion.

"It involves you and his company. There is nothing more important to him."

That she believed. At least the part about the company.

"Why did you tell Dr. Wilson to back off?" she asked.

Jeremy shifted uncomfortably in his chair. "I knew that if I followed through with my plan, you would never forgive me."

"Are you sure it wasn't because you realized that my marriage to Vik would be invalidated if I was deemed unfit to make legal decisions?"

Her father's eyes widened, his skin going pale. A reaction he could not fake. He *hadn't* thought of that. "No wonder Vik pulled out the rocket launchers."

"He wants to be married to me more than he wants to be president of AIH." Just saying the words gave her emotional satisfaction to the very depths of her being.

Jeremy nodded, his expression more vulnerable than

she'd ever seen it. "I hope you've worked out that I want to be your dad more than I want control of those shares."

It was her turn to nod, but maybe with not as much conviction.

"It might benefit you both if your father attended some sessions with you and Dr. MacKenzie," Vik said.

Maddie waited to see her father's reaction to that piece of advice before offering her own.

Jeremy Archer shocked her to the very marrow of his bones when he said, "I would like that very much. Are you willing, Madison?"

"I don't know." What if he used the time they had together with the therapist to compile ammunition against her?

"Do you believe Vik will destroy Archer International Holdings if I attempt to have you declared mentally incompetent?"

"Yes." There was not a single atom in her body that did not trust Vik to do just that.

"Then you have nothing to fear," her father said, showing he'd guessed correctly what had her hesitating.

"I'll talk to Dr. MacKenzie. If she thinks it's a good idea, we'll arrange the sessions."

Her dad startled her again, getting up from his desk and coming around to kiss her on the cheek and shake Vik's hand. "Thank you for watching out for her better than I ever have."

"I always will." It was another Viktor Beck promise.

And the places still cold inside from Maddie's unexpected meetings with her father, the psychiatrist and then Perry, warmed. "And I will watch out for Vik."

Starting with taking him home and teaching him how to say three all-important words.

"I believe you. You have your mother's loyalty and my stubbornness. He couldn't be in better hands."

Maddie surprised herself, accepting the compliment with the warmth it was intended. "Thank you."

Vik slid his arm around her waist. "It's time for us to go home, I think."

"What about your afternoon meetings?" she asked, not really wanting him to go back to work.

But now that she knew he loved her, Maddie could wait for the evening to hear him say it. Maybe.

"I canceled everything after your phone call."

"Because nothing is more important to you than I am," she said with satisfaction.

Vik could have shrugged. He could have tried to deny it. He could have grimaced in unhappy acknowledgment.

He did none of those things.

What he did was turn his big body to face her, blocking out her view of her dad and his office.

Vik cupped Maddie's cheeks, his hands trembling against her skin. "Exactly."

Oh, man. She was going to melt right there.

"Take me home, please," she said, her voice low with fervency.

Vik made a sound like something had broken inside him and then leaned down and kissed her. His mouth claimed hers with undeniable need. She gave in to it without hesitation.

Maddie didn't know how long the kiss lasted, but when her father's voice finally penetrated, she was pressed against Vik, his arms tight bands around her.

"Sheesh, you two need to go home."

"Kicking us out?" Vik asked with no evidence of embarrassment at what they were doing.

Her dad, on the other hand, had a definite ruddy cast to his cheeks. "What's coming next is not going to happen in my office."

Maddie's own cheeks heated at the implication of his words. He was absolutely right. It was time to leave.

The trip home happened in a haze for her and Maddie was glad Vik drove.

He surprised her by pulling her into the morning room, the shabby chic so like her former apartment and cheery lemon-yellow accents barely registering as he pulled her to sit with him on the deep sofa.

"I thought we were going upstairs." To make love.

That's certainly where their kiss in her father's office had been leading.

"We're going to talk." Vik winced as if the words pained him. "About the emotional stuff."

"Can't we do that later?" Knowing he loved her was making her desire for the physical proof overwhelming.

"No."

"Why not?" She wasn't whining.

She wasn't, but so far, her day had sort of sucked. Making love with her husband? Now, after learning he was in love with her, that would take this one into the "best days ever" category.

"Because maybe things would have been different for Helene and Jeremy if they had," Vik said, quoting her own words back at her.

"That was them. We aren't my parents."

"No, we aren't." Vik took a deep breath and let it out, his complexion just a little green. "I love you, Madison."

She didn't tease him for nearly being sick with stress over the admission, though the temptation was great. But she appreciated how hard this had to be for her usually single-minded, alpha business tycoon.

"Maddie."

"What?" he asked, like she'd strayed from the script.

"You love me. I love you. You call me Maddie, like Romi does."

"Perry, too." And Vik didn't appear happy about that.

"Not anymore. Perry doesn't get to call me anything. You saw to that."

"The restraining order lasts two years, but we'll renew it."

She shook her head. "I don't need the restraining order. Trust me, you're enough, Vik."

"He approached you."

"So, I'll stop going to that coffee shop."

"That won't be necessary. I'll buy it and have him banned."

"Can you say overkill here, Vik?"

"Nothing is too much to protect you."

"Oh, man." She saw a lifetime ahead of her of reining in Vik's impulses to keep even the hint of harm from her and the children they would have.

Honestly? The image had a pretty rosy glow.

"Do you want me to leave AIH?" he asked.

"What? No!" It was her turn to reach out and cup his face, meeting his eyes with an expression as sincere as she could make it. "I do not need you to give up your dreams to believe you love me."

Though knowing he was willing to heal wounds in her heart from twenty-four years as Jeremy Archer's daughter.

"I do. I did six years ago, but…"

"You didn't recognize what the feeling was," she guessed.

"No. I'd never been in love."

"I'm glad." The thought she could have lost him before she ever had the chance to catch his eye sent cold tremors through her.

"I didn't think I needed love."

"We all need love."

Vik frowned. "I'm not sure that is true."

He sounded so uncertain, so very unlike the man she was used to. But this was not his area of expertise.

Emotions were almost as foreign to Vik as they were to her dad.

"It's okay, Vik. We love each other and we are going to be very happy."

"Aren't we happy right now?"

Giving in to the urge, she threw herself into his arms with a laugh. "Yes, my darling, wonderful husband. We are very happy."

He caught her to him, responding to her kiss and holding her tight.

Oh, yes, *very* happy.

They made love, right there on the sofa, and practiced saying those three little words to each other.

EPILOGUE

Vik agreed with Maddie and Romi on the property they picked out for the charter school. Declaring it the perfect location, he insisted on putting an offer in on it immediately.

Afterward, he took her and Romi out for champagne to celebrate.

"Isn't this a bit premature?" Romi asked as they clinked glasses. "The offer hasn't been accepted yet."

Maddie just laughed. "The sellers could be a business consortium of questionable pedigree and they wouldn't have a chance against Vik."

"We'll get the property," Vik said as if there simply wasn't another option.

Maddie was pretty sure with her tycoon on the case, there wasn't.

Romi grinned, lifting her glass toward Vik. "To business shark negotiators and dreams coming true."

They didn't go straight home after, but Vik took Maddie back up to the overlook at Marin Headlands. She didn't ask what they were doing there.

Maddie just held his hand as they traversed the path to what many considered the best place for viewing San Francisco's skyline.

He stopped in the same spot he'd proposed. "We forgot some promises when we were here before."

"Did we?"

He nodded. "You forgot to promise not to leave your security detail behind anymore."

That wasn't what she was expecting him to say, but it was so in line with Vik and his priorities that she grinned. "Duly noted."

"Promise."

She put her hand over her heart. "I promise to keep my security detail with me."

"Your days of volunteering anonymously are over." He leaned down and kissed her. "I'm sorry."

"It's okay. You'll just have to find me a detail that likes children."

"I think that can be arranged."

Suddenly she realized why they were dealing with this now. "If my detail had been with me when I went to the coffee shop, Perry wouldn't have gotten within ten feet of me."

"If that."

"Right."

Vik shrugged. "Do you think Romi would allow me to assign a detail to her as well?"

"What? Why?"

"She is your sister-by-choice."

"I didn't know you were aware of that."

"Your mother considered her another daughter."

"She did." Maddie smiled in memory. "But I'm not sure Romi needs security because I consider her my sister."

"In a few weeks, she will own twelve and a half percent of a multibillion-dollar company."

"No one but us will know that."

"You know better than that."

She did. "I don't know if we can convince her."

"Tell her security comes with the shares."

"She's not going to be happy."

Vik didn't look too worried about that reality. "She's part of my family now. She'll get used to it."

Maddie wasn't sure she agreed, but she loved the sentiment.

Vik pulled Maddie close, but kept eye contact. "I love you."

It didn't matter that he'd said it before, that she knew it to be true—saying the words here made them a vow for him.

Maddie's throat constricted, moisture burning hot behind her eyes and all she could do was nod.

"I will love you always," he promised.

She took a steadying breath. "Me, too."

"We *will* say the important stuff."

"Yes."

"We'll talk about the emotional stuff often." He still looked a little green around the gills at the idea, but he was making the promise.

And Maddie knew Vik would keep it.

"With our children, too," Maddie vowed.

Vik nodded. "When I forget, you'll remind me."

"Yes." Not that she was convinced he would ever forget the important things.

When Vik set his mind to something, he succeeded.

He looked like he had something he wanted to say, so she waited for him to say it. "Your father…"

"Yes?"

"I could have been him."

"No. You're different."

"I am, but I could have been. He never got that love and family made having the power and the business matter, not the other way around."

"But you do."

"I do." The absolute conviction in Vik's tone touched her to the core.

"Perry really played into your hands, didn't he?"

Vik shrugged. "We would have married, one way, or another."

"Because you loved me and could not imagine your life without me."

Vik's smile was brighter than the sun in the height of summer. "Exactly."

"Ditto."

Their shared laughter floated over the bay as their bodies pressed together in the most basic promise of all.

Shared love for a lifetime.

* * * * *

WHO'S CALLING
THE SHOTS?

JENNIFER RAE

To my sisters from other misters: Sonja Screpis, Carla Poole, Tiffany Steel and Julie Whittington. Without you I'd understand nothing and laugh a lot less. Massive love my beautiful friends. x

CHAPTER ONE

TWELVE PAIRS OF long eyelashes blinked at Jack Douglas. Some of the women were smiling, and some looked as if they were about to burst into a blubbering mess of tears. It was time.

'Congratulations, ladies. You've all made it.'

Squeals, screams and loud relieved sighs followed his announcement.

This day had started like the previous seven. A hundred women at his door, all wanting the same thing. A chance to meet their *Perfect Match*.

'Excuse me.'

The squeals were subsiding and being replaced by excited chatter. Jack watched as the women—virtual strangers this morning—hugged each other. How did women *do* that? Go from open disdain to long-lost best friends in hours? He had known people for years without knowing their last name, let alone throwing his arms around them.

One of the lip-chewing women was in front of him, not hugging anyone. She was standing too close. He looked down. She was a petite woman—tiny, actually. So small he could possibly pick her up and carry her under one arm. Pretty. With a hopeful look in her big green eyes. He swallowed and gave himself a mental uppercut. *Not your problem.*

'Yes?'

He waited for it—the feeling of her tiny little arms around him. He took a step back. She stepped closer. Not only was she going to touch him without permission, she was a close talker. He folded his arms and lifted his chin. Message couldn't be clearer.

'I think there's been a mistake. I shouldn't be here. I should be in one of the other rooms, with the losers.'

She batted her long eyelashes and pulled her lips back into a thin line. She had a wide mouth with full lips, so it looked strange all puckered like that. Jack let his forehead furrow.

'There's no mistake. You've been chosen as a contestant. You're one of the lucky ones.' He smiled, hoping that would satisfy her and she'd step away.

She smiled and a deep dimple formed in her cheek.

'The thing is, I only came here for my sister. She was the one who wanted to get on the show. I'm only here for…support. You should probably check your list. Her name is Madeline Wright—not Brooke Wright.'

Her hands waved as she spoke, and because she was so close the hand holding her phone hit him on the arm. He flinched, but refrained from letting it show on his face.

'The names are correct. Everyone in this room is a winner.'

'But I don't want to *be* here!'

Jack's eyebrows shot up at her fierce announcement. She didn't want to be here? Jack let his eyes run the length of her body. She was dressed in a crisp white shirt and a black skirt to her knees. Clearly she was trying to look professional, but her slightly messy hair and killer body made her look anything but. She looked sexy. Tanned and athletic. As if she didn't belong in those constricting clothes but outside in the sunshine.

Which was where he'd rather be right now. But he was here, trying to get this show off the ground. He wished he was more excited about it. He needed to be—this show was his ticket out—but something was niggling at him. Something he couldn't put his finger on.

It wasn't the format: twelve women competing in a number of challenges in order to win the chance to go on a date with one of the twelve men who had been chosen to match them perfectly. The more challenges they won the more dates they went on. By the end the audience would find out if the man chosen to be their match was the man who had been pegged as their *Perfect Match*. It was fun and interesting and fairly straightforward.

And it wasn't the contestants that bothered him. He'd hand-chosen them all. Even this one. The woman who didn't want to be here. He remembered her audition tape. She'd seemed funny and smart, and he remembered her eyes. A strange dark green. He remembered choosing her. Her eyes had attracted him, but it was her smile that he remembered. A smile that was definitely not present on her face now.

'Did you sign the contract that all the ladies signed before being interviewed by our producers?'

'Well…yes.' The dimple disappeared and colour slashed across her cheeks. 'But…'

'Then you're on the show. We start filming the day after tomorrow.'

Jack pushed a foot back. She was too close and he didn't like close. But she was quick. She reached out and grabbed at his forearm. He stilled. His whole body stiffened. She was touching him and it felt intimate. Wrong. Too personal. His body remained still as the warmth from her fingers spread across his forearm and up past

his elbow. Warm and soft, with a firm grip. The back of
his neck prickled with heat.

'No,' she said, those eyes of hers narrowing. 'There's
been a mistake. I can't go on the show. I'm only here as
a reserve. I would be hopeless. I'm not even looking for
a husband. I'm marriage-averse. Like, *really* averse. I'd
rather chew my own arm off than walk down the aisle.'

Jack tried to move, but her arm was still on his arm
and it was all he could think about. He forced his mind
into gear. Slowly, carefully, he reached over and gripped
her hand. It was as small as the rest of her. Dainty. Slight.
But her grip was firm. He prised her fingers clear of his
arm and relief swam across his shoulders immediately.

Her eyes opened wide. She was clearly not appreciating being manhandled. But he pushed her hand away and
stepped back. Her big green eyes stared at him. Her head
cocked to one side and something in her gaze changed.
First to confusion, then something else. Something more
smug.

'Is my hand bothering you?'

'No.' He smiled. *Charm.* Time to turn on the charm.
It always worked. 'As much as I appreciate a beautiful
woman touching me, I'm afraid I'm going to have to leave
you for your perfect match. After all—that's what you're
here for. *Perfect Match*—the only show on TV where we
make sure the man you marry is the man of your dreams!'

His marketing team would be proud of that speech.

Jack pulled his face into a wide grin flashing the set
of teeth his father had paid thousands of dollars to fix.
And reminded him about frequently.

Her hands folded tightly across her chest. 'Look…
Jack, is it?'

He nodded tightly. They were definitely not on a first-name basis, but he had to keep the peace here. Nothing could go wrong this time.

'Jack…' Her smile changed. Dimples formed in her cheeks and she fluttered her eyelashes.

She was good. But she wasn't that good. She was trying to use her looks and her charm to get her own way—that much was obvious. Little did this twittering sparrow know that he'd written the book on that game.

'I understand that it's probably a pain to change things now, but I have to tell you I really can't do this. I'm not great around cameras and I'm quite shy—and to be honest there's not really much interesting about me. I'm dull. I'll send your viewers to sleep. Wouldn't it be better to give the spot to someone more exciting? My sister Maddy ticks all those boxes. Seriously—you really should reconsider.'

Jack blinked. Her speech had been a passionate one. His mind wandered back to that audition tape. She'd made fun of herself, pulled faces, clearly not taking it too seriously. She'd smiled that amazing smile a lot on the tape, but she wasn't smiling today.

Mick had said no to her straight up—said she'd be trouble. But there had been something about her…something that had caught his eye. Something that had made him keep watching. She said the viewers wouldn't want to watch her, that she was dull, but he couldn't disagree more. Those eyes, that smile…that body. She'd make perfect viewing. Especially now he knew she didn't want to be here. People out of their comfort zone always made excellent reality TV.

'Our decisions have been made and I don't think you give yourself enough credit. You don't seem dull at all. A little pushy—but definitely not dull.'

Her brows furrowed. 'Pushy? I'm not *pushy*. I'm just telling you the facts.'

'Then let me tell you some facts. You're on the show. You signed a contract. We'll see you back here at nine a.m. the day after tomorrow.'

She didn't say anything, but he watched her chest rise and fall as she breathed deeply.

'I don't think you understand—I can't go on this show.'

'Then perhaps you should have thought of that before you applied.' Her eyes were big and her shoulders slumped. He felt himself falter. *No.* He couldn't do that again. He couldn't feel sorry for her. This was her problem—not his. His job was to make this show a success—not to get her out of the hole she'd dug for herself.

'Think of this as an opportunity. What do you need? Publicity? Money? Hell—you may even meet your perfect match. What woman doesn't want that?'

As soon as he'd said it he knew it had been the wrong thing to say. Her cheeks pinked. Her mouth opened, then closed. Her arms unfolded and she stood with feet shoulder-width apart, fists clenched.

'That's not what I'm here for,' she said tightly, clearly trying to stay controlled. 'I don't want to be here. My sister can take my place; she's the one who wants to be here. She's the one who's looking for love. She's wanted to marry since she was five years old. Trust me, you don't want me. Like I said before—I would *not* make very good viewing.'

'You're making good viewing right now, beautiful.'

Jack let his eyes sweep over her. A compliment always calmed the savage beast. Compliments rolled off his tongue easily, but this time there was a bit of truth in his hollow words. She was a beautiful woman. A nice heart-shaped face, and those perfectly placed big green eyes. She looked healthy, tanned and fun, and she was making his body stand still and take notice. Their male audience would love her.

He shifted his feet. Something grabbed at him. A strange, quiet pull inside him that he recognised immediately but pushed aside. No. He couldn't feel anything. Not for her or anyone else. He couldn't think of any of these women as different from each other. They were all the same. And none of them was anything to him—nor would they ever be. Especially not her.

The way she looked up at him was starting to make something else shift. She stepped forward until her breasts were almost touching his still folded arms. Heat radiated from her but he didn't step back. The scent of her perfume touched his nose and kept him still. Something rumbled inside him. He pushed it down. *No.* Not his problem. Not his anything.

'I'm not here for your viewing pleasure. I'm not here for *anyone's* viewing pleasure. And I'm not going on your stupid show.'

Jack felt his smile falter; she was getting serious now and it was time he did too. She needed to know the rules of this game, and she needed to play by those rules.

'Let me tell you a little about the TV business, darlin'.'

She flinched when he called her *darlin'*, just as he'd thought she would. She didn't like to be patronised— that much was clear. Smart woman. Smart women were much harder to deal with, but he'd done it before. He could deal with her.

'When you sign a contract, your soul belongs to me.' That was a lesson he'd learned years ago. When he'd first sold his own soul.

'I beg your pardon?'

Her voice changed. It became clipped, professional. The voice of a woman who could turn herself into someone else quickly. She straightened her spine and ran a hand over her hair, smoothing it as if trying to take the mess out of it and make it look neater and more business-like. It didn't work. She still looked young and fun and as if she belonged on a beach somewhere in a skimpy bikini.

Jack's producer's mind kicked in. The beach. Perfect for the first episode. And no wetsuits—he'd make the girls dress in bikinis—what a first great ep. He'd open with a faux *Baywatch* running sequence. The girls running along the beach…chasing the men! Gold! It would rate its butt off.

Her voice brought him back to the moment. It was tight and high and way too loud.

'My soul does not—nor will it ever—belong to you. I signed a contract, yes. But now I choose to break that contract. What do I need to do? Pay you some money? Fine. But don't assume that you own me—or that I won't fight you to get what I want.'

Jack's cheeks heated. Her fire was surprisingly sexy. She'd gone from twittering sparrow to swooping eagle in seconds, but those green eyes remained the same. Strong, wide, green as an open ocean and beautiful.

Jack shook it off. He couldn't think of her as beautiful. He couldn't think about her at all. That was when things got complicated and he got into trouble. This woman was definitely one who could cause trouble. Too smart. Too pretty. And she knew what she was worth, which made her dangerous. He didn't need dangerous. He needed this show to be a hit.

Maybe Mick was right and she would be too much trouble. But, then again, that was exactly what the show needed. She was perfect. Bad-tempered, unwilling and impossible to control. That was what this show was lacking. He knew she was a risk, but he needed to take some risks. If he didn't he'd continue to be the man who'd got his job through nepotism rather than because he deserved it. He should leave. Get a job as a garbage man. Far away from his father and far away from all the talk of him not deserving his job. But the truth was this station—and by extension his father—owned him. Until he proved he could finally produce a hit show he was stuck. And so was she. And as long as he didn't get sucked in to her sob story he was out of danger.

She stepped forward and he stepped back—away from her—but she managed to step forward again.

'Don't you run away from me. I need this sorted. I cannot stay.'

Jack felt the air thicken and his breath shorten. Her eyes sparked and he felt it deep in his core. Her pretty eyes were ready for a fight. She might be small, but this one didn't need his protection. She was doing a good job of protecting herself.

He let out a breath and sucked in another big one. He could read the way she felt on her face. *Trapped*. He knew the feeling well. But, like him, she would have to figure it out for herself. Like him, she was on her own. A strange feeling of solidarity with this woman crept over him. Two independent souls. Two people who could take care of themselves. Two people who came up swinging no matter how many times they were knocked down.

'I'm afraid you have no choice, Ms Wright. You are now a lucky contestant on *Perfect Match*!'

'Are you kidding me? This is *great* news!'

Brooke stared at her boss, who was also her sister. Her mad sister. Who had convinced her to join in with this ridiculous, absurd scheme. A scheme that was so bonkers Brooke wondered if she'd actually lost all sense of reality for a moment.

'Brooky—it's perfect. I wanted to go on the show because I'm sick of meeting losers. I wanted to meet Mr Right—someone who's been interviewed and vetted so I didn't have to do all the hard work. Which, when you think about it, is a silly reason to go on the show. Interviewing and vetting men is the fun part! But you—you're not there to find love. You're there with your head screwed on—which makes you an even better candidate than me.'

'Maddy—I really don't think it's a great idea...'

Caution shot through Brooke. Maddy always made sense. She was the eldest of the Wright clan, and the most sensible sister. Brooke looked to Maddy whenever she needed advice. But right now Maddy was acting more like Melody, the youngest and loopiest sister.

This scheme to gain promotion for their business was mad. It had been mad when Maddy had thought it up a month ago. It had been mad when Maddy had suggested she come along as 'back-up', and it was even madder now that Brooke was going to have to make a fool of herself in front of the entire country just to sell some gym gear.

'It makes perfect sense, Brooky! I would have been too emotional. I would have been distracted. But you will be perfect! Sensible, straightforward, practical Brooky.' Maddy's animated face softened and she came out from behind her desk to put her arms out. 'Think about it. How much would we have to pay to advertise on prime time TV every night for three months?'

Brooke didn't care about the free advertising this show would expose their gym gear to. She couldn't think about marketing opportunities and how well-known their brand might be if she managed to get their products on the screen. All she could think of was the potential humiliation. When all those millions of people watching realised how bad she was at relationships and love and flirting and all the other rubbish that was sure to happen on this ridiculous show.

Brooke breathed in, then out. That familiar feeling crept over her. She knew what it was and she breathed through it, just as Maddy had taught her all those years ago. She wasn't going to get angry. She was going to explain herself rationally and clearly. Brooke released the fist her hand had formed. Her palm hurt where her fingernails had dug in.

'Thousands, Brooky!'

Maddy threw her arms around her sister and hugged her hard. The hug helped. Brooke felt her sister's love as she let go and held on to Brooke's shoulders.

'You know that because we checked. And we checked because the brand needs help, Brooke. *Major* help. Think about how many people will be watching you. Think about all those lonely, desperate women out there, watching you night after night as a handsome man falls in love with you. They'll be listening to every word you say—and looking at everything you wear. *Everything.* Including your clothes. They'll want to be like you, work out like you, dress like you so they can find the man of their dreams too.'

Maddy was doing what she always did to calm Brooke down. Giving her rational arguments. Explaining things. Talking to her until Brooke started to breathe normally again.

'Maddy…' Brooke started, her voice normal again. 'You're crazy. That's an awfully long shot.'

'It's perfect PR—you even said it yourself at the marketing pow-wow last month. You don't have to tell anyone to buy our products—you just show them how fabulous they look and how well they work and be your amazing self and they will sell themselves.'

Maddy was really working overtime. Brooke could tell she was passionate about this, and she could also tell her sister was working hard to get her excited. But Brooke wasn't buying it.

'Maddy! Listen to yourself. This is ridiculous!'

'No, it's not.' Maddy said, her voice calm, strong and matter-of-fact. 'It's genius. *I'm* a genius. Wright Sports is poised for world domination, little sister.'

'You're not a genius—you're a madwoman. First of all, if you want someone to model the clothes to make women aspire to be like them, you should have chosen Melissa. She's the long-legged, big-boobed beauty in the family. Or even Melody—she's cute and perky and blonde and fun! I'm short and I have a forgettable face and my mouth is too wide.'

Maddy attempted to interject but Brooke held up a hand.

'I don't need you to compliment me, Maddy, which I know you were going to do. I'm just stating facts here. And reason number two why this plan is absolutely bonkers: women will only aspire to be like me if I successfully seduce a man. Which I won't. I can't flirt, I'm awkward and boring, and I am *really* bad at competing. I'm the only one in this family who hasn't won a gold medal in something. And even if I don't fail every challenge I'm sure my appointed "perfect match" will probably kill me in my sleep. You've got the wrong girl, Maddy. Me being me will do more damage to the brand than good.'

'Why do you do that, Brooky?' Maddy asked gently.

Brook bristled. 'I'm not doing anything besides telling you what a terrible idea this is.'

'Brooke, you're beautiful and talented and fabulous. You'll win every challenge and your perfect match will fall for you—just like the entire country will when they see you on the telly. You're exactly the right girl. I *knew* you'd get it—why do you think I made you come along with me?'

'Maddy, I don't need any of your motivational nonsense right now.'

'It's not motivational nonsense. As a matter of fact…' Maddy moved away to go back behind her desk. She drew herself up to her full five foot nine and stared straight at her little sister. 'I think this will be good for you. You need to put yourself out there. It's time you got yourself a man.'

Brooke rolled her eyes. This wasn't the first time she'd heard this lecture. Her four sisters were always telling her she needed to go out more, be more social—meet new people. But the truth was she liked being alone. It was safer that way. She liked her quiet nights in and she didn't need a man bothering her with his opinions and demands…and his lies and broken promises.

'I don't want a man, Maddy.'

'Brooke. It's time you got over Mitch. It's been twelve months.'

Brooke felt the familiar burn of tears in the backs of her eyes. *Mitch*. Even the sound of his name felt like sandpaper rubbing on foam.

'I'm over him, Maddy.' She heard her voice go quiet. She wished it hadn't. She didn't want her sisters to worry about her. She was over Mitch. Of course she was. Why wouldn't she be? Like Maddy said—it had been twelve months.

Something caught in Brooke's throat. Twelve months since she'd decided not to put up with another one of his lies. Twelve months of thinking about all the things she'd say to him if she ever saw him. Something hurt in Brooke's chest. She wasn't in love with Mitch any more, but the anger about what he'd done was still there. She'd tried everything—yoga, meditation, drinking some disgusting concoction Melody called 'calm juice'—but the feeling was still there. A hard ball of anger she couldn't seem to shake.

'It's clear you're not, Brooke. You don't go out; you don't want to meet anyone new. You just sit at home listening to sad music or working out like a demon. Honestly, babe, we're worried about you. You need this. More than me. More than the brand. You need to do something to break you out of this rut.'

Brooke breathed out heavily. She *was* in a rut. It was true. But she was happy in her rut. Happy to push herself to her limits at the family-owned gym and happy to work herself ragged as marketing manager for her family's company.

She excelled at her job. It was the only time she'd ever been close to competing with her sisters. Micky, the second oldest, was the country's leading female equestrian at only twenty, Melody was in line to join their sister Melissa at the next Commonwealth Games, while Maddy, the most successful of all, was a former gold medallist.

Brooke had just achieved her personal best number of pull-ups in a row at the gym. Five. Pathetic. At only four foot nine, and barely fifty-two kilograms, Brooke was smaller, weaker and so much less remarkable than her sisters. But she was very good at data and statistics and predicting trends.

Since leaving school six years ago she'd managed to

help Maddy take their company from a fledgling gym and activewear business to an award-winning national brand, with seventeen retail stores across the country and a dozen new lines ranging from home workout gear to protein powders. But times were tough. Money was tight. And to move to the next level—which they'd all decided it was time for—they needed to up their game.

Publicity. Recognition. That was what they needed. Brooke knew it. But they'd planned for *Maddy* to get on to this stupid TV programme—Brooke had gone there for moral support and some sort of pathetic back-up on the off-chance Maddy didn't get it. Brooke hadn't doubted for a second that Maddy would get in. Maddy always won everything… Except this time.

And now, in some cruel, unexpected twist of fate, Brooke was expected to expose herself on a reality show based on the ridiculous premise that there was a *Perfect Match* out there for everyone. But Brooke knew what she had to do. She had no choice. This was her family's future and it was in her hands. Every team she'd ever been on had dumped her, due to her pathetic athletic ability, but her sisters never had. They'd always been there for her. From that first day.

'OK, I'll do it.'

Maddy came around the desk to throw herself at Brooke, but Brooke held her back with an arm.

'I'm going to hate every second, I'm going to regret this with every atom in my tiny body, but I'll do it. For you. And Micky and M'Liss and Melody.'

Maddy smiled her brilliant white smile and pulled her in for a giant hug. 'You might be surprised, little sister— you might end up loving every minute.'

Brooke pulled her face into a massive frown as she was squashed into Maddy's chest, knowing deep, deep down that there was no way in hell she was going to enjoy *any* minute of this humiliating and utterly absurd experience.

CHAPTER TWO

JACK SCHOOLED HIS features into something more gen-
tlemanly. His father's face beamed at him from the big
screen TV.

'He's a quality unit, Jack. He can make a hit out of
anything. I want you to do anything you can to help him
out.'

The hairs on the back of Jack's neck stood erect. It
was happening again. Just like last time. Just like every
damn time. And, just like last time, he wanted to hit
someone. Preferably his father. But since his father was
on the screen, not there in person, he'd do more damage
to himself and probably have to fork out for a new TV.
Not smart.

'I've got it sorted, Max. I don't need any help.' He kept
his tone low and calm.

'Now, don't go getting your knickers in a knot, Jacko.
Rob Gunn is not there to take over. He's a hit-maker—
you should be relieved he's coming on board.'

His father never kept his voice low and calm. When
Jack was younger, he'd thought of his father as some
kind of god-like Santa Claus. He was big and loud and
jolly, and he would fly back home laden with gifts for
his only child. He hadn't seen him often, so when he had
Jack would hang on every word and lap up any attention

he could get. But Jack wasn't a child any more, and he could see his father for what he was. And he no longer believed in Santa Claus.

'Mick and I have this under control. Anyone else joining would just make it messy...'

Jack's father held up a big, beefy sun-reddened hand. 'Like you and Mick had it "under control" last time? We can't afford another stuff-up like that, Jack. I've told you—'

Jack knew his father hated being interrupted. It was one of the few things they had in common. Which was why Jack did it. That, and the fact that his father was moving into uncomfortable territory.

'Max, I told *you* it's under control. I don't need your hotshot. What happened last time won't happen again. Trust me.'

Jack watched as his father's face turned redder, which made his grey hair burn even brighter. Not for the first time during this conversation Jack noticed how old his father was looking. His normally round cheeks were drooping, his fleshy nose was covered in purple veins and his hair looked even thinner and greyer than normal. Jack felt an unusual flash of sympathy for the man. Something he hadn't felt in a long time. Not since he'd grown up and realised that this loud, full-of-life man was an overbearing bully. Jack shook it off. If his father had taught him anything it was to eradicate any emotions when you were talking business.

'You listen to me, boy. I've lined this bloke up to help you. It's all about *you*. Like everything I do—trying to keep your head above water. Trying to keep you afloat. Do you have any idea how much your last little mistake cost our company?'

Jack knew exactly how much it had cost. He'd been

at every meeting. He'd gone through every figure with the accountants and he'd earned back every penny. But there was no use telling his father that. From the look on his face Jack knew the steam train had already left the station. The old man was about to blow and Jack was going to cop it—big-time.

'I started from nothing to build this company, boy. *Nothing*. You have no idea of the things I did to make this company what it is today. And I did it for you. So you would be left with something rather than nothing—like I was.'

Jack leaned back in his chair. He was going to be there a long time. He'd heard this story so many times he could predict what his father was going to say next.

'And what have you done to repay me? Drugs. Women. Wild parties. Deadbeat mates. You haven't appreciated *anything*. I gave you the best of everything—the greatest opportunities. Any kid would gnaw off their right arm to be handed the position of Executive Producer for all our media, the way you were, and what have you done to repay me?'

Jack mouthed the words along with him, knowing full well his father was too blind with his own indignation to notice.

'You've produced a string of reality shows that have ended in fights and lawsuits and disaster. I can tell you now, boy, that's *not* going to happen again. Not on my watch. This time you'd better get it right or you can kiss your inheritance goodbye.'

Jack sighed. 'Like I've said to you a thousand times, Dad—I don't want your money. I don't need your money.'

His father's heavy breaths could be heard through the speakers. Jack saw him knock against the computer he was speaking into, losing his balance a little. Max's lips pursed and released, then pursed and released again. He was thinking. Jack could practically see the old man's mind ticking behind his eyes.

'Maybe not, Jacko. Maybe you would be able to make a few measly bucks on your own. But how 'bout your mother? What would happen to *her*, Jack, if I were to shut up shop, take my money and run?'

And there was the stinger. It pierced Jack's gut and lodged there. Jack's father only had one weapon left to use against Jack. His mother. Who was still in love with his father, for some reason Jack couldn't understand. His mother—who would be devastated if she found out how much Max *didn't* care for her any more.

Jack knew exactly what his father meant. At the moment everything Max had—everything he knew about, anyway—was fifty per cent owned by Jack's mother. But when Jack had discovered his father was having an affair fifteen years ago and threatened to tell his mother Max had told him he'd leave his mother with nothing if he did. He'd made Jack realise how powerless he was and then produced a contract saying he had to stay with the media arm of his father's company until he earned enough money to buy his way out of it.

At nineteen, he'd thought it would be easy. But after station cutbacks, a fall in the economy and a cultural shift towards reality TV, Jack had barely covered costs each year. *Perfect Match* was his chance. It had trialled well in market research and the time was right. Dating shows were rating through the roof, and he'd already had a few bites to syndicate it in the US, the UK and India. This show was his ticket out of here—away from his father and the hold he had over him. But until then his father owned him, and he knew it.

'What's that, Jack? Your smart mouth can't come up with anything intelligent to say?'

Jack's blood sizzled but he held his face steady. He was getting too old for this. He needed to take control—one way or another. He needed to get his father out of his life, and today was going to be the start.

'I'm running this company. I'm in charge. Not you. Goodbye, Max.'

Jack pressed the button that would end the video call. His father's face disappeared. This show would be a hit. And when it was he'd pay his father his money and he'd never look back. And when he'd made his own money his mother wouldn't need his father either. They could both escape from his cage.

'Mick, I need you in here, my friend.' Jack spoke into his phone, his voice back to its low, calm tone.

Mick didn't need to know about that conversation. The crew were jumpy enough as it was, with all the rumours flying around about Max pulling their funding. He didn't need them thinking there would be any changes in management. He needed to keep this ship sailing steady.

'How'd it go with Max, boss?' Mick was a man of few words, but he had an eye for entertainment and was one of the best editors in the business. For a man of such little drama, he knew how to produce one.

'Excellent. Couldn't have gone better,' Jack lied. 'But I've been thinking about the format for the show. I know we were going to introduce the men later in the show, once the girls have had a chance to get to know each other, but I think we should move it forward.'

Mick remained silent.

'Bring the men in and have them decide what challenges they want the girls to do. Have them call the shots so they can decide which girls they want to take on dates.

And I think we should cut it back to only four men. That way the girls will have to fight for a chance to meet their perfect match.'

Mick looked thoughtful. He stood still, moving only his head to stare out of the window behind Jack. Jack was used to him by now. He knew what he was doing. Thinking. He gave him a few minutes.

'Female audience are not gonna like it,' Mick finally said in his quiet voice.

'Exactly. They'll hate it. They'll rage and be indignant and it'll be all over social media. It's a genius idea.'

Jack knew the female audience would hate it. He wasn't even sure if it was a great idea. But he needed this show to be a hit. He needed it to work and work quickly—he couldn't afford for anything to happen like last time. This time he was going to be brutal. He was going to call the shots. He was going to create a drama-filled show that had people tuning in every week. This show was about ratings—not about the people on the show. He had to remember that.

Slowly Mick faced Jack and a stern furrow formed on his weathered forehead. 'They'll kill you.'

They would. They'd slam him in the media. They'd call him a misogynist pig. He wondered how the contestants would react to the change. It was within his rights to change the format. He'd written it into the contract. Reality TV was like that—it needed to be fluid and reactive.

And the girls might not understand—they might have questions. He'd go and see them after this. He was sure he'd be able to win them over—he'd deliberately chosen women he could mould and shape. Except *that* one. Ms Wright. She hadn't seemed very malleable. Gorgeous. Great mouth. Insane body. But not malleable. No, if anyone was going to jack up about this new twist it would be her.

'That little firecracker won't like it,' Jack admitted.

Mick grunted. 'I told you not to put her on the show. I knew she'd be trouble.'

Brooke Wright was the only contestant Mick had objected to. He'd said she'd be trouble, would cause problems and make their job harder. And he had been right. She'd protested from the beginning—not wanting to be on the show, then grumbling when he'd informed them they wouldn't have any contact with their friends and families during the entire six weeks of taping. But she was nothing he couldn't handle. He had learned how to charm women years ago. His father had been his mentor.

'Tell 'em what they want to hear,' his father would say. 'Then do whatever the hell you want anyway!'

He'd always laugh after that. Jack never had. Not when it came to his mother. But after a few awkward 'falling in love with a girl who didn't love him' moments back in high school he'd started to use his father's tactics. And it had worked. Since then he'd been able to get women to do what he wanted—mostly.

Ms Wright, however, might prove to be a bit of a challenge. She tended to get into his personal space. She was a little too confrontational. To be honest, she made him a little uncomfortable. But she wasn't there for him. She was there for the show—to make it a hit. Maybe this would be perfect. This new twist would send her into a new flutter and he'd catch it all on camera. It would be just what he needed.

He pushed down the small flutter of guilt that settled in his chest. He needed to work out the details and amend their choice of men. But first he had to supervise the taping of the first challenge. This time he was going to be

there for everything. All the on-camera highlights as well
as the off-camera drama. This time he wasn't missing a
thing—because this time was his last.

'Tell Gaz to bring the car around, Mick—we're going
to see the ladies.'

She could do this. She knew she could do this. It was
like lifting heavy weights. Ninety per cent mental, ten
per cent physical. All she had to do was believe she could
paddle out past the crashing waves, stand up on a thin
piece of timber and balance while avoiding sharks and
the tumble of the constantly moving water, all the while
making sure she kept a smile on her face and her bikini
top up—because at least eight cameras were set up on the
beach and on jet skis to capture every fall, every failure
and every embarrassing facial expression.

Yep, she could do this. For sure. Absolutely. Brooke
hitched up the strap of her candy-red Wright Sports bikini and pushed a large ball of nervous energy back down
her throat.

She'd never been surfing. It seemed like just another
sport to fail at, and her balance wasn't great even on
solid ground, so she'd never been tempted to try. But
now she had to go out there. Because her crazy sisters
thought her coming on this show was their most cun-
ning scheme ever.

'It'll be so good for you, Brooky.'

'It'll help you come out of your shell.'

'People will love you.'

'Imagine what it will do for the brand!'

And the last and most irritating comment of all: 'You
might meet your Mr Right.'

She wasn't interested in meeting Mr Right. Or Mr
Wrong. She was interested in meeting this month's sales

targets. And besides, if Mr Right were out there she was pretty sure he wouldn't be on a surfboard. She had always been more into quiet, sensitive, musician-types. They *got* her. Those carefree athletic types were way too into themselves even to attempt to get her.

'OK, ladies. On your boards.'

The tall, broad-shouldered instructor was hurling instructions at the twelve women lined up on the beach. At least *he* got to wear a wetsuit. Brooke pulled the skimpy fabric to cover up more of her breasts. She'd already argued with the producer over this. Why were they lined up like sheep at a sale yard? Why couldn't they wear wetsuits? Wright Sports made an amazing one, lined with the highest quality Neoprene.

But the producer, Jack Douglas, had done what he always did. Smiled. Turned on his deep, calm voice. His 'you're crazy and I need to calm you down' voice. Stepped back, away from her, and brushed her off.

She was sure she'd got a little red-faced when she'd argued with him about it, but he'd ignored her concerns. Told her that viewers wanted the full beach scene. And then he'd had the hide to tell her she had an amazing body and she should be proud to show it off. Which was totally not the point.

But arguing had been useless. Before too much longer he'd pulled out the old 'you're under contract, sweetheart' card and walked away. So she'd lost. Again. And now she was lined up like a horse in the ring at the Melbourne Cup, awkwardly turning away every time she noticed a camera swivelling towards her butt cheeks.

Most of the other girls didn't seem to care a fig. They were on their boards, laughing, joking—jumping up and down so their bountiful breasts bounced in the sunlight. Brooke's breasts didn't bounce—they were way too small for that—but she did try to smile. For her sisters. For the brand. For her family's business. For the most important people in her life.

That was why she was here, she reminded herself as she heaved the huge board up under her arm and wrapped her fingers tightly around the edge.

Brooke grimaced to the girl on her left—Katy, she remembered. Katy the Lawyer, with her long shiny dark hair and big soulful eyes.

'Let's hope the lifeguards are on duty,' she quipped.

Katy smiled back. 'Hopefully they'll be cute, because I'm sure I'll end up face-down in the sand.'

Brooke felt her shoulders relax. At least most of the other girls were friendly. Something about having to go through this all together had bonded them. That and the fact that the annoying producer had forced them to all live together in a Manly penthouse. As if they were a bevy of pets from the seventies and he was hoping for a little girl-on-girl action.

Brooke felt the steam rise again. At the fact that she was being filmed in a bikini on the beach, doing something she knew she was going to fail at. At the idea of being forced to compete with other women for the chance to go on a date with a man she hadn't even met yet and was sure she wouldn't like anyway. But mostly she fumed at the producer. Jack Douglas.

She knew all about Jack Douglas. After their first disastrous meeting she'd looked him up. The man had only got where he was because of his dear old dad. Although, to be honest, she was in *her* job because of her family, too. But that was different. Jack Douglas was, by all accounts, a womaniser, a publicity whore, a charming pig. And from what she'd seen all of that was true.

Because—seriously—what type of man encouraged this type of sexist, voyeuristic television?

But what annoyed her the most about Jack Douglas was that every time she looked at him she moved. Inside. Deep down. Where she didn't want to move. Especially not for him. But his jaw was so square and his eyes were so dark, and when he crossed his arms he stood tall and strong and so incredibly sexy…it moved her. And she couldn't control it. And that annoyed her. She was so good at controlling herself. She'd taught herself how to control her temper a long time ago. She was now quiet and easygoing and Zen. But Jack Douglas was doing his best to upset her Zen.

'Ladies! Looking beautiful, as always.'

And there he was. Tall, athletic, self-centred, small-minded. The exact opposite of her type. Brooke hadn't had a drink all day, but right then she felt drunk. Drunk on her own indignation. Drunk on humiliation and drunk on the idea that there was no way she was getting out of this mess now she was in it.

'We look stupid. We should be in wetsuits,' Brooke fumed. *Zen*, she reminded herself, breathing deeply the way Maddy had taught her when she was young. *Stay Zen.*

Jack stopped and turned to her, looking at her as if he was surprised she was even there. Arrogant. Self-important. And he still managed to move her…*again*. Annoying.

'Nonsense. It's a beautiful, summer's day in Manly. What you're wearing is perfect. And you all look so good—why would you want to cover that up?'

Jack's eyes were almost black in the sun. His hair was thick, with a slight wave at the front where it swept over as if he'd just run a hand through it. His cheekbones were high and his jaw was strong, but that wasn't what made him sexy. It was the way he looked at her. His chin tilted up, his eyebrows slightly furrowed, his full lips together. Arrogant. Entitled. Confident. As if he was thinking about having sex with her right now.

He stood like a man who was aware of his own presence. He was physically intimidating and he knew it. And he was using that now. Despite the various…*annoying*… movements in her core, Brooke was aware of what he was doing and she wasn't buying into it. He could stand there, all pouty and sexy and as manly as he wanted, but right now all Brooke saw was a snout and two piggy eyes.

'Are you serious? I mean—did you actually *say* that?' Heat rose up the back of Brooke's neck and fizzed in her ears. She turned to the cameraman who was now getting closer to Katy's breasts. 'Did you get that? I mean—on film? Did you get that sexist, disgusting comment on tape?'

She turned back to Jack, who was standing with his hands in his pockets, his face blankly staring at her as if he had no idea what she was talking about.

'Because that's what the Australian public need to see. The extent of this man's sexism and arrogance and…and piggishness.'

Her voice was getting higher. Her fists were in balls. She wasn't even sure what she was saying. But a thought was forming in her head. *That's it!* That was all she had to do! He wouldn't put her on the telly if she was insulting and rude and…and honest! But then if he didn't put her on the telly where would that leave Wright Sports?

Brooke tried to breathe. She tried to think. But her tongue had other ideas. 'This whole show is a vulgar attempt to make women appear shallow and stupid and competitive. A way to prove this man's theory that women are second-class citizens. Well—I won't do it!'

Brooke dropped her surfboard and it made a satisfying thud in the sand.

'And nor will anyone else. Will we, girls?'

Brooke turned to her fellow contestants. Her peeps. Her sisters from other misters. She expected them to crowd around her, fists raised, a cry of *I am woman, hear me roar* on their lips. Just as her real sisters would have. But instead eleven sets of long eyelashes blinked. A seagull swooped and made Contestant Number Four swat above her head. Someone coughed.

'Right, girls?'

The girls were still blinking at her.

'C'mon. We're not going to let him get away with this, are we?'

Someone shuffled in the sand. Katy moved her surfboard from one side to the other.

'We aren't here to be ogled...' Katy said quietly, hesitantly.

'Yes! Exactly!' Brooke let out a yell and pointed at Katy before turning back to Jack. 'We're not here to be ogled. Our *Perfect Match* won't care what we look like. Not if he's truly our perfect match. He won't be attracted to big boobs or a small bum or be interested in the size of our thigh-gap. Love is more chemical than that. Love is more intuitive than that. Our perfect match will see through all that. He'll be attracted to us because of our thoughts, our opinions... That's what we should be showing. Our minds—not our butt cheeks.'

Jack nodded slowly. He pushed his lips together and his mouth turned down at the corners.

'Is that right?' He raised his eyebrows.

'Yes!'

Brooke left her position to move and throw an arm around Katy. Katy was quite a bit taller than Brooke, so putting her arm around her was a little awkward, but they were banding together for a common good. There was nothing awkward about that.

'That's right—isn't it, Katy?'

Katy didn't speak, but she nodded. Slowly. Tentatively. But she definitely nodded.

Brooke squeezed her shoulder. 'We won't be paraded like cattle,' Brooke said firmly.

'Actually…'

Brooke's head swivelled to face Alissa, a blonde-haired, big-boobed beauty who stood behind her.

'I don't mind being in a bikini. I mean—yes—I want my perfect match to want me for who I am, but I mean—a man's got to have a little incentive.' Alissa jiggled her boobs and giggled. 'He *is* a man, after all.'

Brooke watched as the evolution of woman stepped back at least forty years.

'She's right…' another big-bosomed beauty piped up. 'We have to use what we have to attract them in the first place.'

'You don't want a man who's attracted to you just for your looks!' Brooke insisted.

'No,' said someone else. 'But men are men, Brooke. They're visual creatures. They have to like what they see.'

'You're missing the point.' Brooke was feeling hot, and she knew she should probably stop but she couldn't. She needed to say what she had to say. 'Your perfect match will be attracted to *you*. To *your* face and *your* body and *your* eyes—and *your* bum. Not because it's perfect, and not because it's out on display. Think about it—when you're attracted to someone you just *are*. You can't help it. And it doesn't matter if they have a crooked nose or thinning hair. When that chemical attraction takes hold all their imperfections are gorgeous. They make them who they are. You don't see them as negatives—you see everything about them as gorgeous.'

'That's true, Brooke, and I'm not saying we're all perfect. I'm saying that it doesn't hurt to introduce the men to some of our…imperfections.'

Alissa smiled, but Brooke didn't. She turned back to smug Jack Douglas and realised her mistake immediately. He was rocking on his heels with his hands in his pockets. Satisfied. Triumphant.

'And, *cut*!'

Horrified, Brooke turned to face the camera now on her face. Jack sauntered towards her and came in closer than he ever had before, the heat of his skin making her cheeks burn.

'Ratings gold.'

That deep, calm voice didn't calm her this time. But it did make her whole body break out in a rash.

'Good Job, Ms Wright.'

Then he moved back, smiled wide, turned and walked away—while eleven girls stood silently behind her and a lone camera beeped to indicate that it was back on and recording.

CHAPTER THREE

JACK'S HEAD WAS beating incessantly. Over and over. It had started with a throbbing in the back of his head and had now moved to right behind his temple. He resisted the urge to rub at it. All eyes were on him. Now wasn't the time to show any weakness.

'Keep rolling.'

'But, Jack…'

'Keep rolling.'

Jack's calm was slipping. As a matter of fact it was now sliding right out of him and creeping into the ocean, where Contestant Number Three was being hauled up into a lifeboat by three lifeguards. She couldn't swim. A fact she'd failed to mention when they'd told the women they'd be surfing today. So desperate to find her 'perfect match', the crazy woman would rather drown than lose the opportunity to go on a date with a man she'd never met.

Jack tried to relax. The lifeguards had this. But his shoulders stayed tense. He wasn't sure why he was so anxious. Maybe it was the fact that these twelve women were his responsibility. All of them. For the entire six weeks of taping. No matter how much he wanted to stay out of it, the truth was he had to make sure they were safe, make sure they were happy, and make sure they all stayed right where he needed them—in front of the cameras.

Most of them were proving to be easy to manage—except Stephanie Rice, out there, and Ms Wright. The petite blonde. The fiery woman with the sparkling eyes. The woman he couldn't get out of his mind and he suspected the reason his shoulders remained tight even as the lifeguard pulled the flailing contestant out of the water.

Her rousing speech kept going through his mind. Her pink cheeks, her clenched fists. She hadn't just been spouting words back there—she'd felt it. *'When you're attracted to someone you just* are. *You can't help it.'*

He didn't want her to be right about that. She *couldn't* be right about that. It was his responsibility to find perfect matches for these women. But what if she was right?

Attraction *didn't* make sense. It *wasn't* logical. A questionnaire could tell you about likes and dislikes, but it couldn't predict that physical blow right in your chest when you met someone and they blew you away. Not just because of their body or their looks, but because of something else. Something you couldn't explain. Something he was becoming very afraid he felt when he looked at Brooke Wright.

She was a beautiful woman, that was obvious—but it wasn't her beauty that made his heart beat faster when she was around. It was something else. A look she gave him when she was standing up for what she believed in. Attraction was purely physical, wasn't it? Why couldn't he just think about one of the other women? They were beautiful. And they all looked magnificent in a bikini.

But every time he tried to think of another woman his thoughts wandered back to Brooke. To *her* body in that tiny red bikini. To the way she'd tried to rouse the girls. To the way her eyes had glowed brighter and her hair had moved as she'd bounced around, encouraging the girls to fight. Holding her sword aloft against the fire-breathing dragon to protect her people. She was brave and strong and smart and perfect.

But of course she wasn't perfect. She was argumentative and difficult—and if he was honest her mouth was too wide for her face. But somehow that just made him want to look at her even more. He wanted to stare at her and he had to force himself to look away. He was sure he was becoming obvious.

Sex. Lust. That was all it was. Physical attraction. It wasn't as if he hadn't felt it before. He just had to push the feeling down. Easy. He did it all the time. It was just a stupid crush. But somehow it felt different, and that irritated him. She *wasn't* different. She'd be like all the others—after something. His money, his influence, his name. He'd not met anyone yet who liked him for *him*. It was what his father had always warned him about and unfortunately the old man had been right. Every damn time.

He couldn't trust anyone—he knew that. And he definitely couldn't trust Brooke Wright. And not just because he hadn't figured her angle out yet—because she was beginning to occupy his mind a little more than he was comfortable with. And right now he needed to focus on the show. On his father's threats and the executive producer his father was pushing him to take on. And on the contestant they were now struggling to get on an inflatable rescue boat.

He needed to concentrate on how he was going to introduce more twists and turns to keep viewers tuned in. But every time he thought of something he also thought of Brooke's reaction and what she would say. And he wasn't sure why. Why did it even *matter* what she said or did? He barely knew her. She was just another contestant. But the way she'd spoken about the way the show was representing women stuck in his chest. It forced him to think of his mother and the way his father treated her. How he lied to her, cheated on her, threatened her, bullied her. He hated it. He hated seeing the look in her eyes when his father said something cruel or thoughtless or failed to turn up again.

This was nothing like that. This was just a game—just a TV show—surely she could see that? It wasn't real.

But Brooke had no idea. She was too sincere. Too ethical.

Jack ran a hand through his hair. Nothing came easy. Between ensuring this show became a hit, protecting his mother from the truth about his father and trying to earn enough money to buy himself out of his contact, he was wondering when it would let up. When he'd get a break. And now Brooke Wright had come along and embedded herself under his skin. Questioned him. Argued with him. He didn't need that, and he definitely didn't need to feel attracted to her.

He wondered for a minute how someone so small could be so much trouble. And *why* was she so much trouble? The woman seemed constantly angry. Why?

He'd thought he knew all about her. Just as he'd had all the other contestants researched, he'd had *her* researched. Marketing Manager of a family-owned company, one of five sisters. Seemed to have had a comfortable upbringing. Seemed to get along with everyone. No enemies anyone could find. No psycho ex-boyfriends. Currently single. Financially stable.

She had every reason to be perfectly happy, yet clearly she wasn't. At least she wasn't when he was around. Maybe something about *him* made her mad? Maybe he reminded her of an ex-boyfriend or someone else who had annoyed her?

From experience he knew that the way people reacted to each other almost never reflected how they felt about that person—it was more about what was happening in their head. The story they'd made up or the conclusion they'd come to almost never had any bearing on reality. Women were experts at it.

He made a conscious effort to work with facts. Not to read too far into things, to take each moment for what it was. *Don't look forward and don't look back*. So far that approach was working for him, and every time he found himself reflecting or looking forward to something he pushed those feelings right back down where they belonged. Out of sight and out of mind.

Some people called him cold. Distant. One particularly upset woman had called him soulless. But that wasn't true. The truth was everyone had an ulterior motive and you couldn't trust anyone. He was just protecting himself.

The lifeguards' boat had reached the woman in the waves. She was still afloat, waving her arms. Her calls could be heard faintly billowing on the wind as it blew towards shore. His shoulders hurt from holding them so tight but he didn't move his eyes. They had to keep rolling.

He had their number—these women on the show. He knew the ones who were doing it just to get famous, the ones who were looking for true love and the ones who were hoping it would change their lives.

His mind turned back to the Tiny Terror. He wasn't sure what her angle was yet. She seemed sincere when she spoke, but she could just be a very good actress— most women were. She also seemed determined not to spend too much time on-camera. She'd come in, see the camera, smile awkwardly and move towards it, then she'd seem to change her mind and hightail it out of the room, or—more often—give him a tongue-lashing and then leave.

He hadn't figured her out yet, but he would. He always did. Everyone had an angle, and sooner or later they slipped up—giving him the perfect opportunity to see them for what they really were.

'Aren't you going to do anything?'

Jack turned to see the woman he'd just been thinking of. Dripping wet in that small red bikini. It was a *very* small bikini. A bikini that was in danger of exposing even more than it already was. He stood, transfixed. Not by her face but by her body. Her petite but muscular body. It was perfect. It curved in where it should and was soft where there should be softness. But where there was no softness it was hard, glistening with sea water when the sun hit her. His throat went dry and his eyebrows felt heavy.

'She's drowning!'

Her manic cry snapped his head back up to her face. Her forehead creased and her wide mouth was hanging open. He watched as she drew her bottom lip in and held it against her teeth. His already tense shoulders seized up. She was angry again. Getting ready to tell him off. But rather than annoying him right then it was turning him on.

Not many women argued with him. Not many people in general argued with him. And when they did he could normally talk them down, make a joke and defuse the situation, but she seemed determined to disagree with him. It should annoy the hell out of him, but it didn't. Nothing about her was turning him off right now.

Lust. Physical attraction. That was all this was.

'What?' he asked absently as her lip bounced out from between her teeth again.

'Alissa! She's drowning out there and all you can do is stand and watch.'

Jack's face moved back to the ocean. He remembered Contestant Number Three and the action that was unfolding out on the sapphire-blue water among the white tips of the waves that were crashing relentlessly to the shore.

'She's fine. The lifeguards have her.'

No point panicking. She was in good hands. He hoped she hadn't swallowed too much water. She was a long way out but he could see her moving into the boat. She was flailing about a lot. So much so that one of the lifeguards had just received a nice hefty slap up the side of his head. She was fine.

His shoulders relaxed a little and he allowed a smile to lift one side of his mouth.

'You think this is *funny*?'

Jack felt Brooke move closer. He didn't move a muscle.

'This isn't funny! She could have drowned. She could have died. All for the chance to meet some man she doesn't even know if she's going to like! Don't you see how crazy this is?'

She'd moved now and was standing in front of him. He wished she wasn't. She was angry—that was obvious. He wanted to listen to her and calm her down, but it was hard when she stood dripping in front of him. Her breasts peeped out of her brief bikini top—so much so he was sure that if she just moved a little more he'd be able to see the darkness of her nipple.

'Are you looking at my breasts?'

Busted.

'Yes.' He met her eyes. No point in lying. She'd caught him—and why *wouldn't* he look? They were lovely, and she wasn't exactly trying to cover them up. For someone who had spent an hour arguing about why they should be wearing wetsuits instead of bikinis earlier that morning, she'd chosen herself one of the briefest and sexiest ones he'd ever seen.

'You make me sick.'

'Well, clearly I make you *something*...' He nodded towards her breasts, where her nipples now stood to attention. She was either excited or cold and he didn't mind which. There was something incredibly hot about hard nipples showing through a bikini.

She folded her arms across her chest. 'That—' her voice was practically a hiss '—was caused by extreme anger. At you and your disgusting attitude.'

'In my experience that reaction is usually due to excitement—not anger.'

Her eyes opened wide at that comment, as he'd expected them to do. He was finding annoying her strangely pleasant.

'I can assure you that you *don't* excite me. Quite the opposite. You make me feel...'

She paused and he cocked his head, removing his hands from his pockets to fold them across his chest. How *did* he make her feel? He wanted to know—because right now she was making *him* feel something he hadn't felt in a long time: playful. And interested in what she had to say next.

'I make you feel...what?'

'You make me feel...' Her lips moved as if she was about to say something but nothing came out. 'You make me feel....indignant.'

'Indignant?'

'Yes. And offended and outraged and angry and... and...furious.'

'You seem to be quite an angry person. What's the matter—some old boyfriend do you wrong?'

He could practically light a cigarette with the steam coming out of her ears.

'I am *not* an angry person. I'm actually quite calm and quiet. But you have a way of ruining my Zen.'

'Zen is about inner peace. You need to be at peace with *yourself* to have Zen. It shouldn't matter what other people say and do—other people can't ruin your Zen… only you can do that.'

'Well, apparently you can.'

'I'd love to know what it is exactly that you find so offensive about me. It can't be my looks—I've been told I'm unusually handsome.'

She sniffed and folded her arms, which just resulted in him getting a better view of her breasts. He shifted his eyes quickly.

'And it can't be my personality because—let's face it—I'm charming.' He smiled. She'd laugh at that. Surely? He hadn't seen her laugh and something inside him ached to see her laugh.

But she didn't.

'I find you offensive because you're an insensitive bully who couldn't give a toss about what anyone else thinks.'

For some reason that comment caught in his chest. She'd called him a bully. He *wasn't* a bully. His father was a bully. He wasn't.

'Well, you're an opinionated troublemaker who speaks before thinking. What's the matter—didn't get a say when you were a kid? Picked on by your sisters? Left out? There's got to be a reason you feel this need to stand up for everyone.'

To his surprise, she stopped. Her big eyes widened.

He recognised that look immediately and a foul taste rose in his mouth.

'You really *are* a piece of work, Jack Douglas. You don't care about anyone but yourself, do you? Alissa could have drowned out there and all you can do is stand here on the sand and pass judgement on me when you have no idea who I am.'

Jack sucked in a breath and swallowed.

That look. That was the look his mother's face had when his father let rip with one of his insults. He knew that look and he'd never thought he'd be the one to cause it. He wanted to take it back. He wanted to rewind the tape and start again. But he couldn't, and she was standing there all hurt and confused.

What had he done?

'Brooke…I'm…'

'No.' She stepped back. 'Forget it. I shouldn't have said anything about anything. I shouldn't have expected you of all people to understand what I was trying to say.'

He wanted to stop her from leaving, explain himself, but they were hauling Alissa onto the sand and all he could do was follow Brooke to where the woman lay.

Brooke's body buzzed. Jack Douglas was standing closer to her than he ever had before. Tall and big and confrontational. He was behind her and her breath was coming in short bursts.

What the hell was she *doing*? Why was she getting so emotional? She barely knew this man, but for some reason everything he said seemed to touch her deep down. She wasn't sure what the hell was going on with her lately. She didn't have a bad temper. Not any more. Not for years. Not since she'd been loved and felt loved and had come to realise what it meant to care about people.

She certainly didn't normally lecture people. She was usually the one who stayed well in the background, forced herself to stay in the background—but since she'd been here and since she'd met him she'd felt compelled to stand up. For herself, for the other women, and strangely for all of womankind.

Brooke classed herself as a feminist—surely all self-respecting women did. She believed in equality and didn't appreciate women being treated badly. But she'd never so aggressively attacked someone about their sexism before. But then, she'd never met anyone quite like Jack Douglas. Charming, handsome. A man who took no prisoners. Who used people and spat them out.

Her internet research had proved her suspicions that Jack Douglas was a womanising, partying, poor little rich boy. He worked for his father—had done since leaving his exclusive private school. But what she hadn't found out was any private information. There were plenty of photos of Jack at parties, standing with yet another glamorous woman, but as far as friends or pastimes went the man was impenetrable. It seemed as if he lived alone and was close to no one.

She hated him—she was sure of that. Hated everything he stood for. There really was nothing to like about him. But for some reason her stupid body and her ridiculous mind and her outrageously misinformed heart wouldn't listen.

Lust. Sex. Physical attraction. That was all this was, she reminded herself. Nothing else. He wasn't different from any other handsome man. But somehow it felt different. Awful, dangerous…*different*.

'Ohhh, help me!'

The moan from Alissa brought Brooke back to the moment.

Alissa was coughing and crying and calling out. Her hair was plastered to her face and her bikini was barely staying on her body. She was trying to get up out of the boat, clinging to the shoulders of a lifeguard who was trying to get an oxygen mask on her. But she wouldn't let him.

'I went under...I was drowning...' Her tears were manic, which was clearly making breathing more difficult. She gasped for air and the lifeguard tried to haul her backwards, but she was strong and fought him off, her arms reaching for Jack as he moved past Brooke and knelt at Alissa's side.

'I was going to die out there. I couldn't breathe. I didn't know how to get up!'

Her eyes were wide and tracks of red made them look almost mad. Her hands clawed at Jack's shoulders, soaking his shirt. Brooke saw Jack tense. Something about people touching him clearly made Jack uncomfortable. But he didn't move. He was solid, allowing Alissa to claw at him.

Brooke heard the deep tenor of his voice before she heard his words. Alissa was looking straight into his face, her eyes not moving but her hands still clawing at his shirt.

'You're safe now, Alissa, we have you. You're OK.'

Jack's words were delivered calmly and they reverberated with a sincerity Brooke hadn't heard before.

'C'mon, now, love—you need to lie back. We have to put the mask on.'

'No! No!' Alissa started to move again, away from the lifeguard and closer to Jack and his deep voice.

'It's all right, Alissa. We have you. *I* have you. Just look at me. Look at *me*.'

Alissa turned at his voice and stared into his eyes

again, her gaze shifting from one of his eyes to the other. 'I couldn't breathe.' Tears were falling fast down her face.

Jack let his hand rub from her forehead down the back of her head. 'You're OK now, Alissa. You're safe.'

His calm, steady voice and the way he stroked her head over and over again as his other hand held hers on his shoulder was clearly making Alissa breathe deeply and more steadily. He kept repeating himself, reassuring her, letting her hands claw him until they stilled and her head fell onto his shoulder.

Again Jack tensed. Brooke watched the muscles in his back through the now wet shirt. He didn't move from where he was perched on the sand in front of Alissa. His eyes never left her face.

This was a Jack Brooke hadn't seen before. She hadn't expected it. She hadn't expected the calm with which he handled the situation or the tenderness as he stroked Alissa's head. Jack didn't seem to her to be a sympathetic man. She wondered if he was doing it just for the cameras, but when she looked around the cameras were switched off. This wasn't for TV— this was just him. Calming Alissa down. Making her feel safe.

But of course he was. Anyone would do that in this situation. No one could see a panicked woman and ignore her. He wasn't special. He wasn't doing anything a normal person wouldn't do. Not that she thought him a normal person. But right now, on the beach in the sand, with a woman who'd thought she was going to die, Brooke saw a man. Just a man. Trying to help.

She shook her head. He was the enemy. The man who was trying to make her look like a fool. The man who didn't care about the women on this show. She was just shocked that he was a normal human being, that was all. He definitely wasn't different.

The lifeguard managed to lie Alissa down with Jack's help, but she wouldn't let Jack's hand go. He had to walk to the ambulance with her.

'Please come with me,' begged Alissa, her eyes still red and her chest still heaving.

An ample chest, Brooke noticed. Alissa's breasts were spilling out of her bikini top. Brooke managed to locate a blanket and threw it over Alissa. To keep her warm and protect her modesty. Definitely not because she didn't want Jack to see her breasts. She didn't care whose breasts Jack ogled.

'Of course I will. Brooke—you jump in too.' Jack turned to her for the first time since they'd met Alissa on the beach.

'Me? What for? There's not enough room.' It wasn't that she didn't want to go with Alissa. She just didn't like to be ordered about by him. And she noticed the cameras had been turned on again.

'Because I shouldn't be in the shots and she needs someone to be with her the whole time. You'll have to sit next to her so it looks like you're taking her to the hospital.'

Brooke wanted to argue. She wanted to tell him that it wasn't reality TV if he dictated who went where and sat where and said what—where was the reality in that? But the truth was she was worried about Alissa and she knew Alissa wouldn't let him go. And she knew he'd keep insisting and she just wanted to fix this.

So she hauled herself up into the ambulance, knowing the camera was on her face and knowing it would look as if she was the one who was comforting Alissa when it was really Jack.

But then she remembered her tiny red bikini. And how good it would look if she were the heroine, helping someone in her Wright Sports bikini. And she thought of her sisters, and she sat in the ambulance and held Alissa's hand while Jack sat on the other side, just out of camera view, doing all the comforting work.

CHAPTER FOUR

THE OXYGEN AND whatever else the lifeguards and the paramedics had mixed into Alissa's mask was calming her down. They'd checked her out and there didn't seem to be anything very wrong with her. Her lungs had taken in a lot of water and she was in shock, but otherwise she was well. No cuts or bruises or dangerous internal injuries.

Alissa's hand relaxed in Brooke's. Her eyes rolled back and forth between Brooke and Jack.

'You saved me,' she said to Jack, who was off-camera.

He smiled at her. Brooke watched his face as the sincere smile softened it. Lines appeared at his eyes. He looked older, gentler. More real. He didn't say anything but flicked his eyes suddenly to Brooke and raised his eyebrows—nodding as if to tell her to say something in response because he wasn't supposed to be there.

'Oh, you're...you're safe now, Alissa.'

Alissa's head lolled back to Brooke. 'Brooke, you're here too?' She was smiling.

Brooke smiled back and squeezed the spaced-out Alissa's hand. 'I'm here too.'

'You're here... You're always here. Fighting for us and sticking up for us and not taking any crap from anyone. Our big sister.'

Alissa squeezed Brooke's hand and tried to get up. Brooke rested her hand on Alissa's shoulder. Jack did the same on his side.

'You're so little, but you're so big—y'know? Angry. Loud. Opinionated.'

Alissa smiled at her and Brooke smiled tightly back. Brooke knew Alissa's drugs were starting to kick in, but her words had still managed to freeze Brooke's heart. Angry? Loud? Opinionated? *Her?* Was that what they thought of her? That *so* wasn't her. Quiet. Predictable. Dull. Easy. That was her. Happy. Alissa was just pumped up on something. She didn't know what she was talking about.

'I'm not loud...' Brooke's eyes flicked to Jack's and they met. He smiled with one side of his mouth and she understood. She was *always* loud with him. And angry and argumentative. This was bad. This show was changing her. She was becoming someone she wasn't and she didn't like it.

'We've been worried about you, Brooke...' Alissa was talking again—all slurred and sleepy. 'Who's going to be your perfect match? What man will want you? You'll frighten them all away with your angry women's lib speeches and all those little muscles you have. So *hard*, Brooke...' Alissa reached out and squeezed Brooke's bicep. 'Hard and angry.'

Brooke's smile froze. That was what the others thought of her? That wasn't her. She wasn't hard or angry. It was these cameras and Jack. Brooke looked up. *Him*. It was him who brought this out in her. This side of her personality she thought she'd buried years ago.

'You're pretty, though. You have a lovely smile. You should smile more. You'd look prettier. And you have some amazing clothes!' Alissa turned to Jack. 'She's pretty and nice and has nice clothes. You like her, don't you, Jack? *He* likes you Brooke. Can't stop looking at you. Can you, Jack? Maybe *he's* your perfect match!'

Brooke knew it was the drugs talking. She knew Alissa had no idea what she was saying. But still her words made her stop still. Jack *looked* at her? No, he didn't. Not like that. He thought she was a troublemaker. Someone who spoke without thinking. He didn't like her.

A lump caught in Brooke's chest. She'd thought her temper was gone. Her sisters had made sure of that. They'd loved her despite her temper. But her parents hadn't been able to tolerate it. She hadn't been good enough for them.

The thought flew into her head unexpectedly. She hadn't thought like that in years. Her sisters had made sure those thoughts stayed out of her head. But her sisters weren't here. She hadn't seen them or talked to them in almost a week and she just wasn't herself without them. She was angry and volatile and now she was pathetic and feeling sorry for herself.

Right now, as she held Alissa's hand and let the drugged woman's words swirl in her head, all she wanted to do was call her sisters. But Jack's rules stated that there was to be no contact with the outside world. The only people they could talk to were people on the show.

Jack had provided counsellors, and a couple of the girls had already spoken to them. But Brooke just wanted her sisters. The women who loved her and cared about her and wanted the best for her. The people who would tell her when she was being difficult, let her know when her dress was too short and hold her when everything got too much. But they weren't here and the cameras were rolling and Alissa was still going on to Jack about how much he looked at Brooke.

'No one is looking at me, Alissa. You're right. I'm too loud and angry. But I'm not worried about me right now—how are *you* feeling?'

Alissa moved sluggishly. 'Oh, darling, you're not angry at me, are you?' Alissa turned to Jack. 'She's always angry at something and someone. Mainly you. Why is she so angry at you all the time? What have you done? Have you hurt her?' Alissa tried to get up again. 'Don't you hurt her—because she sticks up for us and she's good and kind and lovely and I don't *want* you to hurt her.'

Brooke's cheeks burned. Alissa's words were making it more and more awkward by the second. Her insistence that Jack felt something for her was ridiculous. And her insistence that Brooke was an angry person was even more humiliating. Angry was something she never wanted to be again.

Brooke couldn't look at Jack. She knew what she'd see. Horror. Denial. She had to get Alissa to stop talking about her because the cameras were rolling and she wouldn't shut up and she didn't want everyone in Australia hearing about all this stuff.

'You need to rest, Alissa. Stop talking and rest.'

Finally she looked at Jack. She dreaded his smug and patronising face. Or, worse, his pathetic sad face, feeling sorry for her. But when she looked at him his face was none of those things. He was looking at her, his eyes steady and his jaw set. He looked as if he wanted to say something, but he didn't. He just held her eyes as he held Alissa's hand.

Alissa spoke again, this time to Jack, but Brooke didn't hear. All she could focus on was Jack's direct look. It spoke of comfort and understanding and resolution. She wasn't sure why, but he was holding her gaze steady.

Brooke felt the thumping in her chest caused by Alissa's words starting to recede. Alissa was talking about something else now. Something about a zoo and the animals escaping. Her words made Brooke break Jack's gaze and she looked back just in time to see Alissa start to doze off.

The paramedics came then and checked her over, so Brooke moved away to the front of the ambulance. She watched as the camera followed the movements of the paramedics and Alissa, and didn't notice that Jack had moved and was now sitting next to her.

'I think she'll be OK.'

He didn't say anything about what Alissa had said. Good. She didn't want him to.

'You look at me?' *No, don't say that.*

'I…'

'You hate me.'

'I don't hate you, Brooke.'

'You said I was a troublemaker.'

'You are.'

'Then why do you look at me?' Brooke faced him, her fingers hurting as she gripped the seat. She really shouldn't be talking—shouldn't be asking him this. Why couldn't she just shut up?

His dark eyes held hers. Brooke's heart thumped. They weren't close. They weren't touching. But she could feel him. Feel him breathing and feel him near her. Big and strong and solid. She held her breath.

'I look at you because I find it hard to turn away.'

Brooke sat silently. She had nothing to say. No words formed on her tongue or in her head. Nothing.

Alissa started to talk again and the ambulance bounced heavily on the road. Brooke felt Jack's leg press against hers. Deliberately. It didn't move with the bumps. The muscles in his thigh were tense. He was keeping his leg right next to hers.

Again, he'd surprised her. What the hell was going on and why was her heart beating so fast? What did she care if he looked at her? If he couldn't turn away? She didn't want his attention. She didn't want *him*. So why did his words seep so quickly and violently into her dry, parched heart?

'I'm not normally angry. Or opinionated.'

Why had she said that? She didn't have to justify herself to him.

'It's OK to be angry sometimes. If you don't like something you should speak up. This situation you're in would make anyone angry.'

'I'm not me right now. You don't even know me.'

He smiled and the ambulance moved again, rocking her sideways. Although she wasn't entirely sure the ambulance had moved…

'You're right. I don't know you. But I do know you're more than angry. You're loyal and passionate and…you're gorgeous.'

'Gorgeous?'

She kept her eyes on him and his eyes remained on her. He held steady with every bump and every turn and she involuntarily leaned a little closer, mesmerised by the way he held her still.

'Stunning.'

His words were sincere and his voice was deep, and the way he said it—not looking away as his body held against her still—made something shake inside her. A feeling she knew lay dormant—something she didn't want to wake—stirred. She pushed it down, but it rattled her as he looked at her.

'What's so stunning about me?'

Her voice was quiet but she wanted to know. She really wanted to know what he could possibly find stunning about her. She wasn't that pretty. And since she'd met him she'd abused him and caused him trouble and been mean and rude and difficult and so angry. How did he find *that* stunning?

She waited for his answer. Not breathing, not moving—allowing the moment to last.

'Everything.'

His answer came just as the ambulance pulled up at the hospital. A mad rush meant everyone was pulled out of the ambulance and the cameras rushed to film their responses. Brooke was whisked away by one of the production staff and Jack remained at the ambulance.

Brooke's heart beat hard and fast. Adrenalin rushed through her. *Everything.* That was what he'd said. Everything? How could he say that? What did he mean? He didn't even know her. And what he did know wasn't very good. Why had he said that? Was it a line? He'd seemed so sincere.

Confusion rattled her brain and made her reactions slow.

'We've got to get you to the emergency beds, Brooke. We want you to go see Alissa.'

The production team rushed her to Alissa's side. Jack didn't reappear.

Brooke spent the afternoon getting ice and water and food for Alissa. She didn't see Jack again but she did think about him. *A lot.* He'd said that everything about her was stunning. Was that what he really thought?

Confusion made her tired. Alissa's demands made her tired. Until eventually she fell asleep on a hospital chair, dressed in nothing but a bikini and dreaming of drowning in a sea of crashing waves.

CHAPTER FIVE

BOTH THE GIRLS were asleep. Heavy breathing and the occasional snore coming from under the covers in the bed assured Jack that Alissa was sleeping soundly, and Brooke was on an armchair, her head bent right over to the arm, her legs twisted.

She looked uncomfortable, but she was asleep too. Deep, steady breaths came from her tiny body. She was still and quiet—two things he'd never associated with her. Brooke was a fireball of energy and opinions. She made him tense, but yesterday in the ambulance he'd seen something else in her. A vulnerability he'd not noticed before.

Alissa's words had shocked and upset her and he'd known exactly what Brooke was feeling. She hadn't had to tell him—he'd been able to see it in the way her shoulders had fallen forward. In the way her eyes had opened and she'd sucked the edge of her bottom lip in. Alissa had hurt her.

For a moment Brooke hadn't looked like a confident woman. She'd looked like a little girl bullied in the schoolyard. Unsure how to react. That was why he'd felt the need to come to her rescue. Feeling alone and picked on was a feeling he knew too well. He didn't deserve to feel that way and neither did Brooke.

He'd wanted to tell her that Alissa didn't know what she was talking about. He'd wanted her to know that having cameras pointed in her face and feeling out of control was normal—and so was her reaction. Getting angry wasn't a weakness—sometimes it was the right thing to do. But clearly she wasn't comfortable with that side of her personality. Something about losing control upset Brooke, and he wanted to find out why. He wanted to know more.

But he shouldn't have said what he had. Brooke might think things. She might imagine he wanted something he didn't and he didn't want her to do that. Because he didn't want anything. He couldn't allow anything to happen—and not only for the sake of the show. He knew that if he let Brooke in he would hurt her for sure.

Brooke was the kind of woman who threw herself into things. A defender of the universe. A superwoman. Strong and kind. But she was still a woman. She still got hurt. Alissa had hurt her. And he knew he would hurt her too. At the beach, he'd said things he didn't mean. As much as he tried to keep it at bay he knew deep down he was just like his father. A selfish bastard who was only out for himself.

Today he'd fix it. He'd let her know what he'd meant. She *was* gorgeous, of course—she was passionate and interesting and argumentative and challenging and a breath of fresh air. She'd be special to someone one day. Someone would see her and sweep her off her feet and they'd deserve her. But it wouldn't be him.

Brooke moved and moaned and shifted, and sleepily she opened her eyes. Rubbing them, she ran her fingers through her hair and yawned wide as she sat up, looking around. He could see she was a little confused and unsure where she was.

'Good morning, Sleeping Beauty.' Best to keep it light and flirty.

She turned to him with a start. 'Jack! What are you doing here?'

'Just checking on the patient.'

Her eyes darted behind him. They opened wide and narrowed. 'You brought the cameras?'

'Of course.' Brooke seemed constantly surprised by the appearance of the cameras. Didn't she know what she'd signed up for?

'Jack, Alissa is going to wake up and feel terrible. She's going to *look* terrible. She's not going to want the cameras here.'

Brooke was sitting up now. All quiet and peace was fast evaporating. Jack's shoulders tensed. Ready for a fight. Brooke liked to fight with him, it seemed. She did it so often. He wondered for a moment what she'd be like if she didn't want to fight. All soft and loving, lying in his bed after a wild session.

His mind wandered…he grew hard. Taming Brooke would be a fun task. She was certainly hot—and he was sure she'd be the type to demand she received her own pleasure in bed. He wasn't into those girls who just lay there—waiting for him to take what he wanted. He liked a bit of spit and fire in the bedroom. He liked a fight—it made the winning so much sweeter.

What he *didn't* like was the cuddling afterwards. Most women liked to cuddle—they wanted to snuggle and touch. But he liked to get up and away. Not because he didn't feel affection for the women but because touching seemed a little too personal, a little too close. He wasn't into close. And he suspected Brooke was the kind of woman who needed close.

'Jack.'

Brooke's angry tone brought him back to the hospital room. Brooke's long-sleeved shirt was open, revealing a tight white singlet. He'd had someone go to the house and get some clothes for the girls last night. They couldn't stay in their swimsuits. Jack's mind wandered back to Brooke's red bikini. It hadn't left much to the imagination. And her body was perfect. Small, tight and athletic. Strong. He imagined how athletic she'd be in bed.

'Jack.'

Again her voice brought him back and his eyes turned to hers. She was angry now. Clearly she didn't like being ignored. 'You need to send the cameras away until she wakes and fixes herself up.'

No. He didn't. The whole point was to see real reactions. The audience would love to see these two, just woken up after a night in hospital. But Brooke was right—no one would want a camera in their face right after they woke.

'This is what you both signed up for, Brooke—Alissa knows that.'

'Alissa had no idea she was going to end up in hospital. I'm sure she didn't sign up for *that*.'

'The cameras are staying.'

He was done arguing. The more she talked, the more sense she made—and he didn't want to change his mind. He knew what would rate best and he needed this show to work, so he didn't want her changing his mind. He couldn't modify this show—not for her or anyone else. It had to be raw and real and make people sit up and take notice.

'What do you care, anyway? You look great. And it'll make you look good to be here when she wakes up—people will love you.'

He knew he'd said the wrong thing even before he'd

finished his sentence. She stood up. White-hot rage seeped through her eyeballs at him. Her fists clenched and her shirt slipped off her shoulder but she was too mad to fix it. His eyes moved to the golden tan of her shoulder. Smooth, with a smattering of freckles from too much time in the sun.

'I don't care how people see me, Jack. This isn't about me—or you, for that matter. This is about Alissa and the fact that she almost died yesterday. Do you even *get* that? Or do you just think about ratings and audiences and everything else that doesn't matter?'

'That's *all* that matters right now, Brooke.'

Didn't she get that? Why couldn't she understand that this wasn't about her or Alissa? This was about making good TV.

'No, it's not what matters. You're so caught up in what people think that you forget what this is really about. Twelve women so disillusioned with love that they think coming on some badly conceived TV show will help them find it. I don't care what you think—that's what these girls are here for—to find love. Not be made fools of in front of the nation.'

'These girls are here to get their heads on the TV. If they weren't they'd find some other way to find love.'

'No. The problem is people like you, Jack. People who perpetrate the myth that men fall in love with looks. But they don't. There's plenty of beautiful women out there, but true love is not about what you look like on the telly or on Instagram or on Facebook. It's not about what people think about you, it's about who you actually are. It's about the type of person you are and the little things that someone notices. People aren't attracted to a perfect nose or the right shade of blonde in your hair. It's not that specific. You can't explain why you're attracted to some people but not others. These women think that if they look hot and do some cool things they'll be desirable, but that kind of attention attracts meat-heads and pathetic, insecure men who don't want a real women—they want the image of a woman. And those are the men these girls should be staying away from.'

She was right. This *wasn't* the place to find a decent bloke. This was a television show. Even though it was called reality it wasn't—you didn't live your life on a TV screen. But right now she seemed to be blaming him for the wrongs of the world. Putting everything that was wrong with society and modern dating on him. It wasn't his responsibility to make these women see themselves as more than just images. It was his job to deliver a TV show that would achieve high ratings. That was it. The end of his responsibility.

'They're all over eighteen—they can make their own minds up.'

'You have no idea, do you? Have you ever stopped to think of what goes on in the lives of these women outside this show? Do you even know anything about them? They could have no support. They could have a group of family and friends who make them feel less than they are. Have you ever thought about the reasons they're here?'

'No!'

That had come out louder than he'd wanted. But she was making him feel things he didn't want to feel. Like guilt. Why should he feel guilty? He hadn't begged these women to come on the show. He wasn't responsible. He couldn't be responsible. That just led to trouble and he couldn't afford trouble. Not this time.

CHAPTER SIX

BROOKE HAD STOPPED talking. She was clearly surprised by his violent outburst. Good. He needed her to be quiet. He needed to think. Or not think in this case. He just needed this to happen.

'Mick, get the boys in here. We need to start taping.' Alissa was waking. He needed her reaction. He needed to get out of the way so the scene could get shot.

He stepped back, away from Brooke and out of the way, but Brooke stepped forward.

'Don't you leave. You want people to see the real re-actions then you need to be here. You need to take responsibility. You were a big part of this—you sent Alissa into the ocean, you calmed her down, and I suspect you were the one to send all the clothes and supplies for us. Now you're here. You need to be in this, too.'

No, he didn't. 'I'm not on the show—you are. Now turn around and talk to your friend.'

He was sure that order would send her into a fit. He was sure that would make great TV and he was sure he only felt a slight twitch at the thought of that. But she didn't have a fit. She smiled. She looked at him, direct and hot in the eye. Then she turned and went to Alissa.

It took half an hour of Brooke talking to remind Alissa of where she was and what had happened. Alissa delivered a magnificent performance, forgetting where she was and then crying over the accident before declaring that she hoped her perfect match was worth the trouble. Perfect line. Perfect TV. But for some reason it didn't make Jack feel good. It made him feel old and jaded and uncomfortable. Uncomfortable because he knew he'd just done something his father would have been proud of.

The food in the hospital was terrible. Brooke pushed the plate away and it scraped noisily, echoing in the empty space. Brooke's neck ached and her shoulders hurt. A night spent sleeping upright in a chair had taken its toll. Especially after a day surfing and hours consoling Alissa, who was clearly OK but still sore and unsteady.

And the cameras wouldn't go away. They captured every word and every movement and Brooke was sure she looked about as cute as she did after a particularly hard workout. All she wanted to do was go home and have a shower and sleep. But she couldn't. Because Jack always wanted another shot, and the cameramen were always wanting her to sit and look this way or that.

The more Brooke saw of it, the more she realised there *was* no reality in reality TV. The reality was behind the camera. The reality was Jack. The man who said she was stunning. The man she couldn't stop thinking about.

What had he meant yesterday? Why had he told her everything about her was stunning? It made it so hard to stay angry with him. He made bad choices. He did things for the wrong reasons. But this show wasn't her responsibility and neither were the other eleven women. All she had to do was wear Wright Sports gear and get Wright Sports products on prime-time TV.

She needed to calm down. Maybe it was just the lack of sleep and the fact that it had been almost eight days since she'd had any contact with her sisters that was making her so angry. Brooke breathed deeply. Where the hell was her Zen?

'Here you are.'

Jack. Again. Brooke searched for the cameras. She was sick of them. Sick of watching what she said and thinking about how she looked. She just wanted a minute to herself—which was why she was down here in the hospital canteen.

'Jack. Seriously. I can't do this right now. I'm exhausted. I can't do cameras.' She was too tired to fight. She just needed him and his annoying cameras to go away.

'There are no cameras.'

Brooke looked up in surprise.

'I wanted to talk to you in private.'

In private? Jack never did anything in private. He was all about the show. Brooke was immediately nervous. He wasn't going to say she was stunning again, was he? Because she didn't know what he meant by that…and it was probably just a line…and he was probably lying to get his own way…and that would make her angry and she really didn't want to get angry again.

'What about?'

'About before.' Jack scraped back a plastic chair and the noise reverberated across the vacant canteen.

'Before?'

'Before. In Alissa's room.'

'Jack. I can't fight right now. I'm too tired.'

She *was* tired. Tired of Alissa's complaining and tired of being constantly watched and tired of this bad, bitter coffee. She put the cup down and made to stand, but Jack's arm on hers stopped her. That made her still. Jack rarely touched her. Not voluntarily. She'd noticed that about him. He didn't touch anyone and he stood well away from people. The couple of times she'd accidentally touched him he'd actually flinched.

'I'm not here to fight, Brooke. I'm here to apologise.'

That stopped her. Jack? Apologising? That just didn't seem right. Something about it didn't compute.

'You are?'

'I was an ass before. I made you do something you didn't want to do. I should have waited until you girls were awake and ready before I brought those cameras in there.'

Brooke sat heavily. Jack's apology stilled her tongue. She didn't know what to say. She'd never heard him say he was sorry—he didn't seem the type of person ever to apologise. This man had a real knack for confusing her.

'Brooke?'

'You're saying sorry?'

'Yes.'

'You're saying I was right?'

He paused. His mouth went tight, then his dark eyes set on hers. 'Yes.'

Yes. He was admitting she was right.

The shock was too much. She was tired and surprised and Brooke didn't know what else to do so she leaned forward and rested her head on her hands.

'Brooke?'

She felt Jack's hand on her arm. It was warm and he squeezed her firmly. She sat up quickly and grabbed his hand, squeezing back. Jack's face registered shock and he tried to pull away, but she didn't let him. He wasn't getting away that easily.

'You're sorry? You think I'm right? You're taking responsibility?'

'Yes.'

Brooke let her fingers lace between his and he tried to pull away again. Again she didn't let him. She just pulled her light plastic chair closer to him. So close their knees were touching.

'Where is Jack? What have you done with him?' she teased.

She knew he wanted to pull away, she knew she was making him uncomfortable, and she liked the power she had over him. But he didn't pull away. He actually smiled at her joke and leaned in closer. Brooke noticed his skin. It was dark and smooth and a sprinkling of hairs spread across his jaw, as if he hadn't shaved that morning. He looked a little dishevelled. He looked a little less than the put-together, in control Jack she knew. She liked it. It made him more real somehow.

She leaned closer, taking in his eyes, dark and dancing. His mouth had turned up at the edges. She watched it, then watched his eyes again. They were exploring her face. She suspected he was trying to figure out what she was doing and what she was thinking. She pulled on his hand, letting it rest on her chest. She liked it there. She liked this Jack. The Jack without the Instagram filter.

'I've got him locked up somewhere you'll never find him.'

'Good!' She laughed. 'Keep him there—I prefer this Jack.'

'Why?'

'Because he's real. He feels things. He touches me.'

Jack's smile disappeared. She felt his fingers tighten over hers. 'You like it when I touch you?'

'Yes. Very much. I like your hands. I like your fingers.'

She squeezed his fingers again, before letting go and allowing her own fingers to trail over his palm. When she looked up he was watching her fingers. Brooke's breathing became shallow. In this moment this wasn't Jack. In her sleep-deprived, hungry state this seemed to be someone else. Someone sincere and real whose warm hands she wanted to feel on her skin. Someone who thought she was stunning.

Jack's eyes met hers. Their stare was unbroken—both were having trouble breathing. Brooke wasn't sure if it was the lack of sleep or the gratefulness she felt for his physical touch, but that was what she blamed when she leaned forward and let her lips rest gently on his.

Jack didn't move. He didn't react. He let her press her lips to his and sat still, clinging to her fingers. Brooke opened her eyes, instantly regretting what she'd done. He still didn't move. Except his eyes. They darted from one of hers to the other, but he didn't pull away. Did he want her to do it again? His hand still clung to hers. Should she kiss him again?

She didn't know what to do so she kissed him again. And this time he did react. He pushed closer. He kissed her back, his tongue pushing on her lips till they opened, letting him in. He still didn't let go of her hand and it was hot in hers. His lips were hot too as he tilted his head so his kisses could deepen.

Brooke's heart pounded in her chest. The kiss felt wrong and forbidden. It was over in seconds, and it left her breathless and a little shocked and a lot embarrassed. She let go of his hand and sat back. She blinked, unsure as to why the hell she'd done that.

Brooke couldn't speak but she looked at his face, wondering what he was thinking. He looked back at her blankly before a slow smile spread over his face. A slow, knowing smile that made Brooke's heart drop.

'Nice kiss.'

Brooke shut her eyes tight. *Nice kiss*. That was all it was. He didn't feel anything. He'd just taken the opportunity. He hadn't been kissing her back. He'd just been kissing whoever kissed him. She was right about him—a total player. Incapable of real feelings. Despite his apology. Despite his 'stunning' comment. Of *course* he didn't really think she was someone special. She needed to stop doing that. Stop thinking that people meant what they said and that their actions meant anything. All that kiss meant was that she was tired and he would kiss anyone, anywhere.

Totally disappointed in herself, and extremely over it, Brooke stood.

'That was a bad idea.'

Jack stood as well, his smile now gone. 'Was it?'

'Yes. Very bad. I need to go.'

'Wait.'

Brooke turned back, stupid hope lifting her heart. 'What?'

'I came down here to talk to you. I wanted to ask you something.'

So that was it. He was only apologising because he wanted something. She was so naïve sometimes.

'What?'

'Meet me tonight at Lottie's, near the apartment. For a drink.'

Jack sat back, his eyes blank and his jaw tight again. Gone was friendly, affectionate Jack from moments back. Uncaring, unfeeling, business Jack had escaped from his ropes and was back. He wanted something. Not just a drink—something else. Brooke was sure of it. A hot rash spread up Brooke's neck and into her cheeks. Embarrassment—that was what she felt right now. She was embarrassed that she'd managed to let herself be played by a man she knew was a player. God, she must be tired!

'I'm not sure that's a good idea.'

Jack paused. He sat back even further.

'I mean, clearly we just broke some kind of contestant/producer ethical code or something. I shouldn't have done that.'

A slight vulnerability shadowed his dark eyes. Brooke's heart saw it before her eyes did. Did he actually *want* to take her for a drink? No. *No.* He wanted something. Information. Maybe he wanted to tape her getting sloshed. He definitely didn't want to take her for a drink because he felt something, otherwise he would have said something other than 'nice kiss'.

Brooke's stomach swirled and her head hurt. She wanted him to take her for a drink because he felt the attraction she did. She wanted him to take her for a drink so they could get to know each other, without the cameras and the lights and the direction. She wanted him to feel something—but she wasn't sure he was capable of that. Not with his aversion to closeness and his playboy reputation.

Brooke wanted to get out—away from him and his knowing eyes and his expert lips and the way he was making her move again. Move violently. She didn't want to feel for him. She just wanted to go home and sleep and forget about her recent lapse in judgement.

'But you did, and we should probably talk about it.'

'No, we shouldn't.' Brooke stood to leave.

'Brooke, I know why you're here. For your family's business. I've noticed that you wear Wright Sports clothing most of the time.'

Brooke watched his face. Was he angry? Did that mean he wanted her off the show? For some reason that didn't make her as happy as she'd thought it would. She didn't like the way this show was changing her, the fact that it was making her angry and aggressive, but she liked the other girls. And who would stand up for them against Jack and his outrageous demands if she wasn't there? He'd apologised to her just minutes ago—maybe she was getting through to him. What if she left and he just went back to his old ways?

'What…what are you going to do about it?'

'Nothing. If you come and have a drink with me.'

Brooke wanted to have a drink with him. She wanted to be alone with him. But she wasn't sure if that was such a great idea. Maddy had said this show would be good for her, that it would take her out of her comfort zone. Having a drink with bad-boy Jack Douglas was certainly that. Maybe she should do it.

'Will the cameras be there?'

'No!' he answered emphatically. 'No. It'll just be me and you.'

Her and him. And a drink. In a dark bar. This was dangerous, and so out of her comfort zone. But she wanted to do it. That kiss had made her feel something she hadn't felt in so long. Alive. Excited. No longer numb. Maybe this was just what she needed.

'I'll send someone to pick you up. You might get lost.'

'I don't need an escort and I never get lost.'

Brooke still wasn't sure if this was a good idea. She still didn't know what he wanted or how he felt, and she certainly didn't want any witnesses. No cameras, no one else. Just him and her.

'No, I bet a good girl like you always checks Google Maps.'

'That's right. I'm good, but when people screw with me I can get very bad.' She wasn't sure of that, but it annoyed her that he'd pegged her as a good girl. She'd been bad before. He had no idea.

Another lazy smile spread across his face. He slipped his hands into his pockets. 'Good girl gone bad? I'm looking forward to that.'

Brooke didn't say anything. He didn't deserve any more of her time and he looked too hot right now, all crumpled and lazily sexy, so she turned and left. Before any more bad thoughts could creep their way into her good head.

CHAPTER SEVEN

THE NIGHT WAS hot and still. Laughs rang out from the restaurants that lined the footpath. The smell of the sea lingered in the air and Brooke breathed it in.

Brooke had spent almost her whole life living in Sydney, but she'd never spent much time in Manly. Her family lived in the inner west and she worked in the city and there just weren't that many reasons to cross the bridge. But she liked it. She liked the laidback, casual charm of the coastal suburb. She liked the feeling that it was trapped in holiday mode. No one seemed to work in Manly—they just went to the beach and jogged with their dogs.

But she was missing her sisters and she was missing her work. The *Perfect Match* contract said they were to have no contact with anyone other than each other for the six weeks of taping. No internet, no smartphone. Which was harder than it sounded.

Although Brooke got along with the girls, she missed the comfortable ease of having her sisters on hand. It had been eight days now that they'd been holed up in the penthouse and, although the days had been filled with briefings and hair and make-up sessions and various staged tapings, Brooke was starting to feel very anxious and a little lost without her sisters.

Lottie's was one of those new Sydney bars. One of those discreet hole-in-the-wall places with almost no signage at the front—because signage was, like, *so* five years ago. It took Brooke a few laps around the Corso to find it. She almost wished she'd taken Jack up on his offer of an escort, but the more she thought about it the more she thought the escort would have been a spy.

She didn't know what to make of Jack. He was so confusing and he made her so angry. All she wanted to do was go back to the way things had been. Predictable. Easy. Dull. *Dull?* Where had *that* thought sprung from? Her life wasn't dull. She had her sisters and her friends and she had fun.

But as her heels clicked on the cobblestones she was remembering how she'd felt before she'd come on this hideous show. Numb. But she didn't feel numb any more. She felt anything but numb. She was on some mad, out-of-control rollercoaster and she was sure she wanted to get off. She had to concentrate on not letting her emotions get away from her and on not getting angry. And she had to concentrate very hard on not letting Jack get under her skin.

But as she slipped through the heavy wooden door and spotted Jack in the corner, sipping on a short glass of something dark, her focus went out of the window.

In the darkness of the bar, with the slow sexy beat of the music in the background, Jack was looking…delicious. There was no other word. This wasn't work Jack—this was night-time Jack. And all those rumours about all those women suddenly became so much more believable. He had on a dark shirt, open at the neck but not too far so as to seem sleazy. As she got closer she noticed his black pants were pulled tight at his knees to expose some very nicely developed vastus lateralis muscles. She'd been trying to develop those muscles for two years, but her knees were still knobbly and the muscles there pathetically small. His were anything but small. Hard, muscular thighs.

He saw her and smiled and she steeled herself against the anxious flutter in her chest.

Don't look at his smile, look at his teeth. White, straight—perfect. *No, not helping. Look away*.

His hair. Look up. It looked thick and wavy and he was holding it up over his forehead. Very nice hair. *Don't look at his hair*.

His eyes. Dark and velvety. Chocolaty. Sexy. Bedroom eyes. *Definitely don't look there*. Especially not now he'd said she was gorgeous. Stunning. She remembered the way he'd said it. The word had rolled off his tongue like a thick, sticky liquor and she'd become stuck in it. Even now the word stuck in her head and wouldn't get out.

A lazy layer of dark stubble sat on his jaw. Good— she preferred clean-shaven. Except on him… She liked the stubble. She didn't want to but she did. It made him look a little rougher, a little more manly—maybe even a little dirty.

Oh, crap.

Movement rattled her core. Annoying hot, sexual movement. She tried to force it away but it swelled and intensified—as did her confusion about Jack and what she was feeling about him. She wasn't into all that He-Man stuff. Sensitive. Caring. That was what she liked. Stubble was not her thing. *He* was not her thing.

Focus on something else. His hands. They were resting on his knees as he sat in that wildly confident way some men did. Knees apart. On show. Boasting. *No! Don't look there*.

Concentrate. His hands. His fingers were long and his

hands looked solid. As if they'd never let go. She imagined he'd have a great grip for rope climbs. She wondered if he worked out. He raised his hand to wave and his shirt pulled at his shoulder. Yep. Definitely worked out. So definitely not her type.

Brooke swallowed hard and pulled at the collar of her shirt. She'd undone a few buttons so her bra just peeked out. She'd wanted to look sophisticated, in charge and in control. But now all she felt was exposed. She tried to cover herself up a little before pushing her lips into a wide smile and attempting to saunter towards him.

He didn't get up. Bad, *bad* man. He just smiled and said, 'You look incredibly sexy tonight. Hot date?'

Thank God it was dark, because a hot blush spread up Brooke's neck and into her cheeks. Of *course* he'd think she'd dressed provocatively for him. For him to enjoy. But that wasn't why she'd done it. She'd wanted to look like a woman in charge—she'd wanted to look stunning.

'No. I'm meeting an arrogant player who thinks he can win me over with a few free drinks.'

He smiled. Slow and sexy. And lust licked up around Brooke's body.

'Well, if I see him I'll get rid of him, because I want you all to myself tonight.'

Brooke stopped. What was *that*? A line? She didn't want a line. Anger mingled with the lust and her lust for him made her angry. Brooke felt her emotions bubble to the surface again. Nope. Zen didn't exist when she was around Jack. She needed to fix this. She needed to find out why he made her so angry. Tonight. She had to stop this and go back to the way things had been. However dull that was. She couldn't keep getting angry. Anger never solved anything.

'Jack, why am I here? What do you want?'

He turned his head and smiled at her. One of his fake smiles she was so used to.

'Why do you assume I want something?'

'You think it's amateur hour? I know all about you. I know the kinds of things you get up to.'

'Sounds like you Googled me. You're someone who graduated with a high distinction in marketing and business management—I would have thought your research abilities were better than that.'

'I can do more than use Google, Jack. You'd be surprised at the things I manage to dig up about people.'

'Would I? You graduated in the top ten per cent of the state six years ago, then studied at uni by distance because you started working for the family business the day after you left school. One of five highly competitive and athletic sisters. Mother Mandy, a former Commonwealth hurdler, and father Mark, head coach at the Australian Institute of Sport. You run marketing for the company, which has a current annual turnover of almost a million dollars—a turnover that is mostly due to your sisters' bravery and your marketing skills. Your favourite restaurant is La Galleria on Norton Street and your favourite bar is Tio's Tequila Bar in Surry Hills. You drink green tea, never coffee, and your cup size is thirty-two B.'

Brooke knew her mouth was open but she couldn't shut it. He was good. *Very* good. But clearly he didn't know everything. Although he did know her cup size? *Really?* How had he found that out?

'The internet does *not* give out information on cup sizes.'

'No…' Jack's eyes moved to her chest. 'That one I figured out by myself.'

Heat. More heat. Spreading across her chest and up her neck. She suddenly wondered if he liked small breasts.

What was she thinking? Jack Douglas would like *all* breasts.

'Fine. You know all my secrets. Time to tell me yours—why am I here, Jack?'

The waitress arrived back with her drink and made a show of setting up a napkin and making sure the straw was facing the right way. She was taking an awfully long time.

'Thank you.' Brooke looked up into two very large breasts. Definitely not thirty-two B. The waitress was leaning forward, her eyes fixed on Jack. Brooke turned to see Jack smile back at her. Right. Sleazebag. *So* not her type. She needed to get this over with.

When the waitress finally moved away, swaying her hips ridiculously as she walked, Brooke spoke. 'When you're finished lining up your next conquest, I'd like to know what you want from me.'

'You're a pushy little thing, aren't you?'

She hated being called little even more than she hated being called pushy. Even though she knew she was. But it was condescending and rude, and coming from Jack after the way he'd just ogled their waitress it made her even angrier.

'Yes, I'm pushy. Because I'm suspicious. I'm suspicious about why I'm here and what your motives are. But don't worry, Jack, it's not you. I'm pushy and suspicious with everyone.'

She'd always been that way. Sometimes she wished she was more trusting and easygoing, like her little sister Melody. She wished she could put on rose-coloured glasses and expect people to treat her with respect and be gentle. But people weren't like that. They were selfish. And most of the time they were too concerned with what was happening in their own little bubble to worry about hurting the feelings of those around them.

Jack smiled slowly. He leaned back, putting the heel of his shoe up to his knee. His muscles bulged. Brooke looked away. Muscles meant nothing to her. She spent hours in the gym with muscle-heads, and most of them had less between their ears than she had numbers in her little black book. Although she wasn't sure Jack was one of those guys who spent the hours they worked out taking selfies of their muscles. Jack seemed a little more worldly—a little more aware. Which made him infinitely more dangerous.

'That's interesting. Tell me more.'

Brooke smiled. 'Why would you think I'd tell you anything?'

'Because you're alone and you miss your sisters. Because you're feeling abandoned and you're angry and you need someone to talk to.'

Brooke opened her mouth to deny it but she couldn't. He knew exactly how she felt. How did he do that?

'Maybe I should be more like you and talk to no one about anything? Totally independent. An island.'

Jack's eyes hardened. 'No man is an island—haven't you heard?'

'*You* are.'

'That's where you're wrong, Brooke.'

Something in his tone stilled her. Something was different. *He* was different. As if he wanted to say something he wasn't saying. As if he wanted her to know something but couldn't tell her.

'Why can't you stand being touched?'

'What?'

'It's fairly obvious. Your eyes get all shifty whenever someone gets too close to you. You cross your arms and step back, and if anyone touches you I can practically see the hairs on your arms stand on end.'

Jack shifted, moving his leg back down. He moved forward, then back, before reaching for his drink again. When he'd sculled the last of it he motioned to the waitress. 'We're going to need a bottle of tequila, some lemon and some salt. And beers. Lots of beers.'

'I'm not drinking.'

'Yes, you are. You and I are getting ridiculously drunk tonight.'

'Why?'

'Because, Brooke, you make me uncomfortable. And the only way I can tell you what I want to tell you is if my brain is swimming in tequila.'

That statement sounded almost honest and it took Brooke aback a little that he'd admitted a vulnerability. A weakness. It seemed so off for Mr Cool to admit he was uncomfortable. Which was probably why she threw back two shots with him as soon as the tequila arrived a few minutes later.

After a long sip of beer Jack shifted back and Brooke shifted with him, resting her head on the cool leather cushioning of the bench seat. She turned her head to watch the side of his face.

'So are you going to tell me why I'm here? What you want from me?'

'I know why you're here, Brooke. I know you're trying to promote your family business.'

'So you mentioned.'

'Every person on this show has an agenda. Most are fame junkies, some are attention–seekers, and I suspect there are one or two who really are looking for love. But your motivation took me a little longer. Until that day on the beach and the red bikini. Which you looked unbeliev-ably hot in, by the way.'

'I'm too skinny.'

'Your body is perfect. Strong. Healthy. Athletic.'

'I have no boobs.'

Jack turned to look at her breasts. He stared at them. Brooke felt heat rise up her throat as he studied her chest. His head moved and his eyes narrowed. Then—to her surprise—he lifted a finger and used it to pull her shirt aside. She slapped his hand away and shot him a hor-rified, disgusted look which he held. Steady. Her eyes against his.

No words were spoken but a conversation went on regardless.

How dare you touch me without permission?

You wanted an honest opinion on your breasts. I have to see them to give you one.

But I don't even know you and I definitely don't trust you. It's weird.

It's not weird.

Don't touch my skin.

I won't.

Don't check me out...sexually.

I will. But I won't touch your skin.

Brooke sighed, which meant, *Do it.*

So he did it, and even though he didn't touch her skin every cell on her body throbbed. Small bumps formed on her skin as the fabric slid away from her body. She felt the heat of his finger as it slowly traced her shirt, open-ing it wider so he could look inside. She watched his eyes—they were so close now. Dark and mysteriously unreadable. Then his lips parted slightly and her core throbbed even harder.

She wished he'd touch her skin. Accidentally. His

closeness reminded her of how long it had been since she'd been with someone. Since Mitch. Almost twelve months. Twelve months since a man's hands had made their way over her skin. Twelve months since she'd felt a man's lips on the back of her neck. Too long.

Jack's bottom lip stuck out and he moved his head from side to side before letting his finger drop from her shirt. But he didn't say anything.

'What's that supposed to mean?' she asked, anxiety bubbling in her chest. What the hell did that movement mean? Did he not like her breasts? What was wrong with them?

'Eh…' He shrugged and poured another two shots before settling back onto the leather seat to throw one back.

'Eh? *Eh?* That's what you have to say about my breasts? Eh? What the hell does *eh* mean?' He thought her breasts were *eh*? They were small, yes. But they were better than *eh*. Pig. Sexist pig. Knuckle-dragging, Neanderthal pig.

Brooke grabbed a shot and flung it back, enjoying the burn as it flew down her throat and into her stomach. Her head shifted. She hadn't been drinking much lately as she'd been focussing on training and the booze was going to her head. *Good.* She'd be able to say what she was thinking.

'Want to know what I think about *you*?' She was leaning forward now—too close for him to be comfortable, she knew, but she didn't care. Indignation burned at her temples.

'Not really, Brooke. You see—I'm not like you. I don't need people. I don't need their approval and I don't need anyone to like me.'

'Clearly. Is there actually anyone that you treat well?

Do you have any friends? What about your family? Are you as mean to them as you are to me?'

'I'm not mean to you, Brooke, I'm honest. There's a difference.'

'Yeah, there's a difference. It's called tact. If you were being honest you'd have some. Without tact you're just mean.'

Brooke was angry. Somehow this man always made her angry. Which was why the fact that she found him physically attractive was so annoying. And right now the way he was leaning back, all relaxed and comfortable, his dark hair sitting perfectly and a layer of stubble swathed across his jaw, he looked even more attractive than he ever had.

Brooke reached for the tequila bottle and poured two more shots. 'How about I employ your brand of tactless honesty? See how you like it?'

'Go ahead.'

He turned to smile at her and Brooke wondered how the hell he could look so boyishly gorgeous at the same time as looking like sex on a stick. It truly was a gift.

'I think you're lonely. I think you have Daddy issues. I think you have no friends because you have no idea how to treat people. I think you're mean and you're bad and you use your looks and your money to make friends and bed women. You're a bad person, Jack Douglas. Bad and mean.'

Brooke sucked back her tequila, not taking her eyes off him.

There was a pause before Jack lifted his head, held her eyes and spoke—in that deep, calm voice of his. '"Bed women"? Do people actually *say* that?'

'What? Yes. They do. Bed women. That's what you do.'

'Pretty sure I have sex with them. Sometimes I kiss them too.'

He smiled and Brooke felt it all across her body. The way he said sex. The way his eyes held her steady when he talked. The way his smile said *good boy* and his eyes said *badass sex god*. Brooke knew her breath was becoming shallower. She could hear herself breathing heavily and she wanted to stop it but she couldn't.

Slowly he reached for the bottle and topped up her shot glass before topping up his own. Then he drank and so did Brooke.

He placed his glass on the table and leaned in closer, his voice now dark and dangerous and way too deep to be legal. 'Sometimes I go down on them—and if they're very bad I might even spank them. *Bed* them hardly seems to say enough, does it?'

'No.' Brooke heard her voice squeak a little. 'It doesn't.'

Brooke leaned back. Away from his voice and his eyes and his provocative scent and those hands and those arms and his muscles and tattoos and everything else that was making the tequila rush to her head much too fast. No, no, *no*. Not this man. No.

'Jack.' There was a slight wobble to her voice so Brooke sucked in a breath. 'Why am I here?'

Thankfully Jack leaned back, too. But not before pouring another tequila and handing it to her. Brooke paused. Getting drunk was not a good idea. Not when thoughts such as what those vastus lateralis muscles looked like in the flesh kept pushing into her mind. She put the glass down and picked up her mineral water. She was here for business, not pleasure. He wanted something from her. Maybe if she gave it to him she could get the publicity she needed. But how much was that going to cost her? she wondered.

The pause after she spoke seemed to last a very long time. Jack looked down at his drink, then back up, then at her.

'I like you.'

'You *like* me?' Brooke was confused. What was he saying? The tequila was making her a little dizzy. 'What do you mean?'

'What do you think I mean?'

He looked away and stared into his drink again. What *did* he mean?

'I don't understand?' She felt anxiety coiled, poised. Ready to strike when he delivered his blow.

'I mean I like you. I like how you tell me things I don't want to hear. I like that you argue with me and fight with me and stop me from turning into...well, stop me from making bad choices. I want you and I to be...friends.'

He liked her. He wanted to be friends. Her friend. Not her lover?

She didn't want to be his friend. She wanted to kiss him and sleep with him and have him go down on her and spank her and all those other bad things he said he did. She didn't want to be friends. She wanted more and he didn't.

His rejection hurt. Just as Mitch's had hurt twelve months ago. Just as it had hurt when her parents had rejected her. It hurt and he wasn't getting away with it. Not this time. This time she was going to take it.

'No.'

'What?' Jack turned to her, clearly surprised.

'I said no.'

'No? No, I don't like you?' Now *he* looked confused,

as if he'd never heard the word *no*, let alone had anyone say it to him.

'No. You *do* like me. And I like you. But I don't want to be friends.'

'You don't?' He still looked confused as he turned the glass around in his hand. 'You don't want to be friends?'

'Stop saying that word.'

'What word? Friend?'

'Yes. *Friend.* I'm not your friend. Nor will I ever be your friend. I have enough friends. Real friends. Friends I actually like. I don't need any more friends.'

The silence that followed dragged out for what seemed like hours. Jack spun the glass in his hand. His right leg shook as he tapped his foot on the ground.

'Right. OK…' was all he said.

The silence stretched out for too many minutes. Jack didn't speak and neither did Brooke. But she didn't want to leave either.

'We need more tequila.'

Jack's eyes hit hers hard. She took him in—his dark eyes, the stubble on his jaw, his full lips. Her eyes trailed down his chest to the dark hairs that whispered at his neckline. She wanted him. She wanted to put her hands on him and her lips on him. She wanted him to feel something for her. She wanted him to stay.

Jack breathed in, long and hard. She waited for him to refuse her, for him to get up and leave. But he didn't.

'Hit me.'

CHAPTER EIGHT

THE TEQUILA WENT down fast. As it did so Brooke found her shoulders relaxing. She also found herself moving closer to Jack. Drunk Jack was a lot more entertaining that sober Jack. When he smiled at her Brooke noticed the crinkles at his eyes. Sexy. He was *so* sexy when he smiled.

'Tell me about you, Brooke. What were you like as a teenager? Wait—let me guess? Straighty-one-eighty, Miss Goody Two-Shoes, I-didn't-lose-my-virginity-until-I-was-eighteen?'

Brooke tried to be indignant but it was true. 'Nineteen, actually, and, yes, I was a good girl. Still am.'

'Good girls make the best bad girls,' he teased, his arm resting close to her shoulder but still not touching. Never touching.

Brooke felt her body heat. Mitch had never made her stomach flip and the heat curl low in her belly the way Jack did. 'Good girls make terrible bad girls. We think too much.'

'That's what makes you so good at being bad. You know what you're doing. When you decide to let yourself go you do it completely and without any hesitation. Confidence and knowing what you want is incredibly sexy.'

Brooke knew where this conversation was headed.

She really should stop it but the tequila said no. 'Sounds like you've had plenty of experience.'

'I have. But that's not a bad thing. It means you don't have to worry when you're with me. I'd satisfy you. I wouldn't give up until I did.'

'Ha! You wish.'

'I do wish, Brooke. I *do* wish.'

It was the sincerity in his tone that did it. It was the way he seemed really to mean what he said. Her brain knew that he didn't, but her stupid, needy, desperate tequila-laced heart wanted to believe he did.

Which was why she leaned in. Which was why she stared at his lips. And which was why, when the hotness of his lips met hers, she let herself go. Completely.

Jack pulled her bottom lip in between his teeth. This was what he'd been wanting to feel all night. Her. Close to him. So close he could taste her. And right now she tasted like lemon and salt and warmth and comfort and it was just what he needed. Especially after his terrific failure at actually trying to be honest with her earlier.

He'd struggled in the past few days. He'd thought about her so much. About the way she exposed his faults. The way she made him want to be better. He realised now it wasn't just lust. He liked her. Who she was. He wanted to let her in.

And then she'd arrived in her sexy shirt, almost open to the waist, and she hadn't let him get away with anything. She'd made him accountable, and she'd made him want to actually *talk*. She'd told him what she thought of him. That was unusual. People usually told him what he wanted to hear. He was surrounded by people too scared to annoy him, but she seemed to have no problem with it. Which was why he wanted more with her. But she'd refused. She'd said she had enough friends. *Real* friends.

But now she was moving her soft lips against his and exploring his mouth with her tongue—and it felt very friendly. And he wanted her close. Her hands snaked up his chest. He grabbed her wrists and held them back. She leaned against him, trying to press her skin to his, but he held her away. Her mouth he wanted close, but not her skin.

'Jack, what's wrong?'

'Nothing,' he murmured as his kisses moved from her mouth and down her neck.

She made a little mewling noise in the back of her throat and he knew he'd found her spot. It was at the base of her neck, and as she arched her back he kissed it again, letting his tongue flick the spot and his teeth tease her skin before soothing it with a hard kiss. She said she didn't want to be friends. He wanted more. Not just sex. *More*. But she didn't want that. He had to hold back. He couldn't fall. He couldn't get too close. He needed to protect himself.

'Jack…let me touch you,' she whispered as she pushed against his hands.

He had them held still. No, she couldn't touch him.

'Relax. Let me touch you.'

When he felt her wrists stop fighting against his hold he lifted a hand to cup her jaw and moved his mouth back to hers. Taking her lips, kissing her deeply, allowing her bad girl every excuse to escape. She was proving to be a wonderful bad girl. Responsive. Passionate. The noises she was making were making him even harder. The way she tried to push herself into him made his body heat and his brain blur. But not enough to stop him keeping her wrists held so she knew not to touch.

Slowly, carefully, he let his hand explore her skin. Down her jaw and neck and further down still, till he hit the soft mounds of her breasts. They *were* small, but perfect, and when he'd pulled her shirt away earlier he'd glimpsed a flash of dark pink. He wanted to feel her nipple now. Twist it between his fingers before licking at its hardness.

He moved his head and she seemed to encourage him as he kissed down her chest, but a loud cough to his right brought him back to reality. They were still in the bar. There were people either side of him. Public displays of affection were not his thing. He hadn't kissed a girl in a bar in years—too many camera phones had stopped that habit. But the combination of Brooke and tequila was making him do some very stupid things.

Like trying to get her naked right here in front of everyone. Like sleeping with a contestant. Like wanting more from her. That was a monumental mistake. Even through the tequila he knew that was wrong.

Quickly and efficiently he pulled her shirt back to where it was supposed to be and sat up. Brooke's eyes opened wide, as if she were coming out of a daze, and she rubbed the back of her hand across her mouth.

What the hell was he thinking? He'd become too carried away. She was so easy to talk to and she laughed in all the right places. It was as if he'd reverted back to his sixteen-year-old self for a second. Thinking that this girl was different. Thinking he could actually trust her. Of course he couldn't. The only reason she was here was to get publicity for her business, and the only reason she'd agreed to meet him tonight was because he'd forced her. Bullied her into getting what he wanted.

No, that wasn't him. He wasn't going to be like his father and make people do what he wanted even when they didn't want to. If she was going to be with him it would be because she wanted to. He had to pull back.

'Wow. I think we got a bit carried away.' A shy smile spread across Brooke's face and she lifted her eyes to his.

Jack's body tensed when he looked at her. Her hair was loose and curling round her shoulders, her lips dark red and her green eyes glowing in the low light. He wanted her even more than ever but he couldn't do anything about it. He had to stop. He could easily throw himself at her in here, but he wasn't going to do that. He liked her too much and that meant it would cut him too much when she left.

'We did. My mistake.'

No more tequila, Jack decided. Time for a real drink. He picked up the discarded Scotch on the table and took a sip. He hated the taste. He hated the burn. And he hated the way it reminded him of his father. Wouldn't his father celebrate if he could see him now? *Another mistake, Jacko? I knew you'd slip up.*

Jack sipped again—before almost spitting it out when he felt Brooke's hand on his thigh.

'What if it wasn't a mistake? What if it's what we both need?'

Jack felt his chest rise and fall. Something about Brooke made him uncomfortable. Not in a bad way but a confrontational way. She made him feel things he didn't want to and think things he wished he didn't have to. But he'd been handling it fine because she always delivered her messages with spit and fire. Now she was touching him, and her smile had gone sexy, and her lashes blinked. His eyes slipped to her breasts again. He wanted to touch them. He wanted to feel her body beneath him. And she wanted him—that was clear. But maybe it was just the tequila talking.

'What I need to do is take you home.'

Brooke's mouth drooped a little at the edges and he didn't like it that he'd done that. He liked it when he made her laugh. She had a wide smile and deep dimples, and when she flashed her white teeth she looked carefree and fun and everything he wished he could be.

'What's the matter? Are you scared?'

'Not scared. Sensible. You're a contestant. It's unethical.'

'What do you care about ethics?'

She had a point. 'I don't like messy.'

'Messy?'

Her eyebrows shot down and her hand moved away. Strangely, he missed it.

'It wasn't "messy" when you wanted to be friends— why would this be messy?'

'Because one of us would want more.'

Her smile was back. Wide and gorgeous.

'More? From you? I know better than to expect anything more from *you*.'

There it was. The reason she didn't want more. He wasn't good enough for her. Well, maybe he wasn't. But she didn't know that. She assumed she knew him. Had read about him in the papers, heard the rumours. But she didn't know him. She thought he just wanted sex. Well, he might as well live up to his reputation—she was determined not to like him anyway.

'Well, seeing as you expect the worst—let's go.'

She stared at him but didn't move. Just as he'd suspected. She hadn't meant what she'd said. She didn't want anything from him. He'd had enough. He wanted to go to bed. The tequila had given him a headache and with a staff meeting scheduled for tomorrow he was in for a big

day. This woman was doing his head in. She was complicated and confusing and he wasn't in the mood any more.

'OK.'

It was so quiet he thought he'd misheard, but then she
repeated herself.

'OK. Let's go.'

At those three words, Jack's whole body fired up.
She'd said OK. She wanted to go home with him. The
woman he wanted actually wanted him. But he shouldn't.
She was a contestant and she was fiery and she could
make trouble. *Sensible*. That was what he had to be.

But her hand was back on his thigh and she massaged
the muscle just above his knee. Then he watched as her
hand slid up his leg, closer and closer to his groin. Her
pink-painted nails glowed against the lighting in the bar.
He couldn't believe he wasn't throwing her hand off. He
didn't want her to touch him. He never wanted anyone
to touch him. But her hand was firm and confident—as
if she knew what she wanted. Good girl gone bad. They
were hard to find, but when you found one…

Brooke's hand expertly cupped him and he felt as if
he was going to explode. He wanted to stop what she was
doing but her hand moved again, up past his buckle and
over his chest. As if she was feeling every inch of him.
He didn't want her hands all over him but he couldn't stop
her. He was mesmerised by her fingernails.

When her hands hit the skin of his neck he finally
looked into her eyes. He saw lust and something else.
Something deeper. She lowered her chin and her mouth
was close again. He wanted to throw her back and kiss
her. He wanted to have his hands all over her. But he
held steady. He still couldn't figure out why he felt so
much for her. It was almost chemical—like a magnet attracted to iron. He couldn't stop thinking about her and

his mind refused to let him forget about her. Even though the logical part of his mind knew he shouldn't like her— the rest of him didn't care. He liked her. He wanted her. He had to have her.

Slowly, seductively, she leaned forward, and he felt her words on his ear before he heard them.

'Take me home, Jack, and make love to me.'

Jack didn't care if she was playing games. He wanted her and tonight she wanted him. He leaned in, catching a glimpse of her breasts, and touched his cheek to hers, wanting to feel her skin on his but needing to tell her what she needed to know. Needing to warn her.

'I want you *bad.*'

CHAPTER NINE

BROOKE LOST IT. She dropped her glass and it clattered onto the hardwood floor. She felt the breaths in her chest come way too fast. She needed air. She needed to breathe. But most of all she needed Jack Douglas. Tonight.

She didn't care what he meant about being friends. She didn't care that he was the producer. And she didn't care that soon she was supposed to meet her 'perfect match'. All she cared about was her skin being right next to his skin and his tongue sucking on her '*eh*' breasts.

'We need to leave.'

She didn't want to wait for the tequila to wear off or for herself to change her mind. Jack was bad and mean and no good. Perfect for one night of hot sex—which was exactly what she needed. No wonder she'd been so angry lately. Sex. That would fix it. After she had hot, hot sex with this very bad man she'd go back to being her normal, calm, sweet self. She could finish this stupid show and get the hell out of here.

'Leave?'

'Right now. We need to go.'

Brooke stood. If she didn't take him home right now the waitress would, and tonight *she* wanted him. She wanted to have sex with someone who knew what the hell they were doing. It had been too long. She'd been good for too long. Her sisters were right, she needed to do something mental to bust her out of the rut she was in. And Jack Douglas was certainly mental.

'Now.'

She didn't touch him but she gave him a look that she hoped left him in no doubt of her intentions. And if he was as bad as she suspected, and—let's face it—she knew he was, he'd follow her. He'd take her home and give her a seeing-to until she couldn't stand straight. Which was just what she needed, she'd decided. Or maybe the te-quila had decided for her. Either way—it was happening.

Brooke walked out through the door with only a sliver of doubt that he'd follow. The doubt disappeared as soon as she felt the warm breeze hit her outside. She felt him behind her, heard his footsteps on the cobbles.

'Where are we going?'

Brooke turned, stopping but not touching him. 'Your place, obviously. There are eleven other women at my place.'

He smiled but didn't say anything. He didn't have to. She knew what he was thinking.

'I'm sure twelve women at once is a mild night for you, but tonight I want you all to myself. Just you and me—and you know what?'

'What's that, Brooke?'

She didn't miss the satisfaction in his voice.

'You're going to enjoy it. And you're going to make me enjoy it. You're going to pull out every trick you have in that bag of yours because I haven't had sex in twelve months and I need unbelievable sex tonight. Not good. Not even great. Un-freaking-believable. And, Jack? We're not friends. Can you do that?'

'I can try.'

'There's no *try*.'

Brooke turned to walk again. She wasn't sure where he lived, or where he was staying, but she wasn't about to stop and ask because if she did she might change her mind. She might think about tomorrow and how awkward it would be. She might also think about how she would probably enjoy it and might want to do it again, but he wouldn't, and then she'd get mad and offended and probably say something to him, and then he'd think she liked him and she'd try and explain that she didn't, and then he'd think she *really* liked him, and then she'd get really angry and start thinking about it and obsessing, and then she'd probably convince herself she actually wanted to see him again, and then he'd break her heart. *Sigh.*

Brooke stopped. This was going to end in tears, wasn't it?

'Something wrong?'

He was so close behind her but still not touching her. She wished he would touch her. Something to encourage her. Something to stop her from thinking and to remind her that this was about a bad boy and a night of fun.

Brooke breathed in a big gulp of muggy sea air. The tequila swam in her head. It was telling her things. Telling her to say things she didn't want to. But the tequila was strong.

'I haven't had a boyfriend in almost a year.'

Don't say that!

'Then you're well overdue for some attention.'

'My boyfriend left me.'

No! Not sexy.

'Your ex sounds like a jerk.'

'He's not. He wasn't. He was perfectly lovely and we were perfectly happy. One day he just didn't call. And he didn't answer my calls. And he was never home, and I couldn't get hold of him, and his friends kept feeding me excuses. I didn't know what the hell was going on until I saw a Facebook post a few weeks later. It was a picture of him and "his love". That's what he called her.'

Brooke didn't cry. She'd shed so many tears over Mitch that there were none left, but somewhere deep in her heart something twisted.

'He left me. Then he got someone else and posted it all over social media. Didn't even have the balls to tell me. Couldn't even give me a heads-up. Just humiliated me.'

Jack was silent behind her and she knew what he was thinking. She'd said too much. He didn't want to know. He didn't want heavy. He was a bad boy—he wanted light, fluffy bimbo. Not feelings. Bad boys didn't *do* feelings.

Bloody tequila!

Brooke started to walk before she thought about what she'd said and before he could say anything to her. She'd blown it. There'd be no hot sex with Jack tonight. She'd been humiliated by a man in the past—why the hell would she want to do something that was sure to lead to more humiliation?

Brooke's feet started to move faster and so did her anger. It escalated as she remembered every sexist, horrible thing Jack Douglas had done to her. It escalated when she thought of the girls back at the penthouse. All believing they were going to find their perfect match on the show. All believing that there was a man out there who was going to make them happy.

It seemed only she knew the truth. Men didn't make you happy—they made you miserable. The only person you could count on was yourself.

Brooke's feet stopped and a massive lump caught fiercely in her throat. Then why had she been so miserable since Mitch left? Why had she let her happiness depend on him being around? Mitch. Who had left her for no reason. Who hadn't even said goodbye. Who hadn't even had the decency to tell her it was over to her face.

He'd left her a message. A very public, very humiliating Facebook message on her wall. Everyone had known he'd left her. *Breathe in, breathe out.* She'd been humiliated. Exposed. Which was exactly what she was going to feel in a few weeks, when this show aired. When the men arrived tomorrow and she failed all the challenges and didn't get to meet anyone. When it was her time to fail, like Alissa had at the beach. *Keep moving. Keep walking.* She started to walk again.

'Brooke. Stop.'

Jack's deep voice was close behind her. Only a few steps away. The sound of it made her move. Quickly. But his long legs against her short ones meant he was keeping up. So she walked faster and faster, until both her feet were off the ground and she was jogging. But he was still keeping up.

'You can't outrun me, you know.'

Challenge accepted.

Brooke paused to slip off her heels and broke into a run. An all-out pelt up the Corso and across the road to the beach. The sand would slow him down. But it didn't. Once she reached the bottom of the stairs and her heels started to dig into the sand he was right beside her, arms pumping.

'Faster Brooke, faster!' She heard her father's voice ringing in her head.

She ran faster. Faster and faster towards the water. Wanting to get away. Wanting to forget. Wanting not to think, just to breathe and pump her legs.

When her feet hit the water it was cold and she braced herself as she dived in. She dipped her head, allowing the noises of the ocean to take all her thoughts and worries and anxieties and humiliations away. She swam and stood and dived and swam until her lungs burned. Then she stopped. She was a long way out. Past the breaking waves. The water was black and everything around her was black. She was alone, and the exhilaration she'd been feeling as she swam was quickly replaced with fear.

When Jack's arms grabbed her from behind her first feeling was an irrational terror that it was a shark. When she turned and looked at his face she realised he was a shark. He was beautiful. Wet and dripping, his face shadowed, his eyes hooded. He had his shirt off and he was panting and his eyes were fixed on her lips.

'I know you're angry, Brooke.'

His voice was low and deep and Brooke felt it rumble through her chest.

'I can make you feel better.'

Jack Douglas was a bad man. A man who partied hard, broke hearts and didn't care about anyone or anything. He *was* a shark.

'I want to make you feel better.'

Right now he was telling her exactly what she wanted to hear. He knew what he was doing. *She* knew what he was doing. But for some reason she couldn't stop pressing her lips to his and kissing him as if it was her last day on earth.

Brooke's body felt as good as it looked. Her skin was smooth where his hands explored her wet flesh. Jack pushed the fabric of her shirt out of the way so he could come into contact with her skin. His aversion to touching was forgotten as his other hand came up to cup her chin. She was beautiful—but here in the ocean, all wet and frantic, she was out of this world.

Her eyes closed as he let his mouth press to her lips. He pushed in hard and she met him. Her kisses weren't soft or tender, and her passion was turning him on. She wanted him badly and he felt exactly the same. Their tongues explored and her hands were moving as wildly as her lips, touching everywhere. He didn't mind. He wanted her close.

He pushed and she pushed, and while his legs paddled wildly to keep them afloat he pressed closer, making sure they were as close as two people could be. He wanted her close. He wanted to hold her up and keep her afloat. He wanted to take her anger away, make her forget.

Brooke wrapped her legs around his waist. She clearly wanted to get closer to him, and her desire was unexpected and all the more sweet because of it. He suspected that right now she was hurting and wanted to hurt him as well. She wanted to make him feel how angry she was.

Her teeth bit at his lip and he growled a little. He tasted the salt on her skin as he kissed past her lips to her ear, then down the milky column of her neck. She threw her head back and moaned wildly as his kisses made their way down her chest.

He needed more traction. He wanted to do more with this beautiful mermaid. He wanted to lay her in the sand and kiss her all over. He wanted to take her anger until she wasn't angry any more—just wild with passion. For him. And only him.

Jack pulled back quickly. What was he doing? She wouldn't want to be with him. Not when she met her perfect match. Not when she realised he wasn't good at communication and feelings and all the other things that went on in relationships.

'Don't stop.' Her voice was soft and demanding.

'We should go back to shore.'

'No!'

Her legs tightened around his waist, making his erection painfully hard.

'I want to stay here. With you.'

She kissed him again and he felt as if he were drowning in it. Every thought and reason flew from his head. All he could concentrate on was the way his heart was beating faster and how he wanted to get close, closer to her and her skin, and her mouth and her hands. Her small body clung to him and he wrapped his arms around her, holding her close, wanting this to be something that it wasn't. He knew what this was. A fleeting moment of lust. He had to stop it before he got in too deep.

Pulling her arms from around his neck, he met her eyes. 'Brooke, we have to go back.'

She understood. He saw her eyes searching his. She was thinking, but he didn't know what.

When she let him go he felt cold and bare and he hated that he felt it. This was why you couldn't get close. The confusion and the wondering what the other person was thinking. He'd not had a relationship yet that was honest and he was sure it would be the same with Brooke. She confused the hell out of him already, with her arguing and fighting and then her unexpected kisses.

He watched as she took skilful strokes through the water to the shore. He wasn't a strong swimmer. He hoped she didn't turn around when she reached the sand to watch him. She was athletic—good at everything. He wondered how she did that. And she was smart and hot. She was stunning and special.

But not *his* special, he reminded himself as his feet finally hit the sand and he was able to stand and step over the gently rolling waves to the shore. His breathing was heavy. He hadn't been to the gym in three months. Ever since work on this show had started.

He missed it. He missed seeing his workout on the board and thinking there was no way he'd complete it in time, then the satisfaction when he did. He felt unfit right now, and he was sure Brooke would want someone fit. She was so fit herself. Women like her put value on health and fitness and he caught himself wishing he were fitter. Wishing he could impress her—because so far he hadn't been able to, and that was starting to bother him.

When he made it past the water she was waiting for him. Soaking wet. Her hair was pulled back and her face was shining in the moonlight. He'd never wanted to kiss anyone more, but he didn't. He couldn't. This would never work. She'd get hurt, and something deep inside him knew he didn't want to hurt her.

But she didn't give up that easily. She stepped forward, wrapped her arms around his waist and leaned her head on his chest. That was all. Just quietly stood there, hugging him tight. It was an intimate feeling and he wanted to push her away. Explain that he didn't *do* intimate. But right then it seemed as if she needed him and he liked it. She needed comfort and warmth and understanding and he wanted to give it to her.

He let his arms envelop her. Maybe he couldn't give her a lifetime of happiness, but he could give her a moment. He could make her feel better for now. As his arms tightened she looked up. The smile she gave him was relaxed and grateful and he was so glad he'd done that. He liked to make her smile even more than he liked to fire her up. Which was why he leaned down to kiss her.

But the comforting kiss soon turned into something more. Her hands explored his chest, her tongue eager and exploring. He let his hands rest on either side of her face, keeping her still, keeping her there—not letting her go. Something wild and frantic built inside him. He wanted her. He needed her. He had to have her. Here. *Now*. Carefully and quickly he wrapped one arm behind her back and let her fall to the sand.

Brooke wasn't angry any more. The emotion she was feeling now was something else. Something much more desperate. She wasn't sure if it was still the tequila doing the thinking, but right now she felt something from Jack she hadn't felt in a long time. He wanted to please her. He wanted to comfort her. And she was grateful—because she was lonely and sad and angry and his comfort was exactly what she needed.

When he pushed her back into the sand Brooke felt strangely safe. He was strong and he was leading her to where she needed to be. She didn't have to think—all she had to do was feel.

'Are you sure you want to do this? With me?'

When she looked at him she was surprised at the uncertainty in his eyes. She'd never seen that look before. She hadn't ever considered he'd be insecure. Didn't he realise how much she wanted him?

'Yes. I want this. I want *you*.'

He didn't smile, but he held her eyes before kissing her. His soft lips soothed her and Brooke's head swam. She thought of nothing but him, and the weight of him on top of her, and the feeling of his hands running over her body.

Keeping one hand on her waist, with the other he pulled at her shirt. Moved the wet fabric aside, as well as the bra underneath, to expose her thirty-two B breasts. His tongue laved at her nipple and any residual anger in Brooke's head gave way to something else. A pleasure that made thinking impossible. That made reason vanish. She just wanted more. More of his mouth and more of his tongue and more of *him*.

The cool night air hit her nipples and they hardened. He took them in his mouth again before allowing his lips to trail further down her stomach. With a tug he managed to get her wet jeans off. He threw them in a heap on the sand and Brooke clawed at him, trying to get him back up to kiss her again. But he didn't. He stayed where he was.

'You're beautiful,' he murmured as his tongue licked around her lower stomach.

Brooke lay still in anticipation of his touch. Of his tongue. His kisses moved lower and she opened her legs, allowing his head to get closer. She watched him. Watched the way his eyes eagerly drank her in. She watched his hands as they stroked her thighs, and then she watched as he trailed one finger through her wetness.

'So wet… So hot…' he murmured, before allowing his face to fall and his tongue to push in, searching for her clit.

Brooke arched her back in delight. She moaned, grabbed at the sand, trying to get some traction—but there was none so she reached for his shoulders instead. Looking down, she watched him as ripples of pleasure shuddered through her. She pushed her pelvis up, wanting to get closer, needing him to go deeper, and he obliged. His tongue worked like magic and he sucked gently, making her groan even louder.

This was what she needed. Pure release. With a man who knew what he was doing. Mitch had never done this properly and he'd certainly never been this enthusiastic.

Jack's head moved a little from side to side and Brooke almost screamed. That slight movement had his tongue hitting every G-spot she had. She wanted more…she needed more. She was building fast.

'Don't stop,' she moaned, pushing herself closer and closer to him.

He didn't stop. His movements became more frantic. His tongue started to move in and out and up and down and then he made a low, growling noise that she felt reverberate through her whole body.

That did it.

The orgasm started down low but once it took hold Brooke couldn't stop it. It grew inside her like a werewolf howling at the moon till she felt it burn through her veins, up her stomach and into her arms. Her whole body shook and still he didn't stop. She felt him suck and the orgasm shot through her again, even more powerful than before.

'Stop, stop! You have to stop.'

She pushed on his shoulders, trying to get him to release her. She was swollen and sensitive and her brain felt as if it were about to burst.

With one last tender kiss, Jack moved. He looked up, his face flushed and his eyes glowing.

Brooke didn't move. She couldn't. Her body lay in satisfied pleasure.

'That was…that was…' She couldn't speak. She couldn't explain how good she felt.

Then she felt him next to her. His arms weren't on her, but he lay next to her. His skin was still wet but she was hot so it felt good.

Brooke lay panting for a few more minutes before she turned in the sand to look at him. He had one hand behind his head and was staring up to the moon, but he turned when she looked at him. A slow smile spread across his face.

'Feeling better?'

'Much better.'

Brooke shifted and spread an arm across his chest. She felt him immediately stiffen beneath her so she withdrew her arm. Even after what had happened he still didn't want her to touch him. She should have been offended, but she was too relaxed and relieved to feel anything but curiosity.

'Why don't you like being touched?'

'I do. I was enjoying you touching me earlier.'

He was smiling, but she wasn't fooled.

'That's different. You don't like anyone hugging you or putting their hands on you. You get nervous when I touch you. Like right now—you went stiff when I tried to cuddle you. And today, in the hospital, you hated that I was holding your hand.'

He was quiet and Brooke turned to face the moon, wondering if he'd answer.

'I don't like insincerity.'

'Touching is insincere?'

'It is when you hardly know someone. I just don't understand why you would want someone that close to you.'

'Because it feels good. Because everyone needs physical touch. Because people like to feel loved and cherished and they want people to show them.'

'I just don't like lies.'

That made Brooke turn. 'That's hilarious, coming from you.'

His eyes met hers. They were hard and challenging. 'I may be an emotionless, indifferent, unfeeling, apathetic bastard—but I'm not a liar.'

Brooke laughed. She couldn't help it. There clearly was no one who could abuse Jack better than he could himself. 'You're a bit hard on yourself, lover.'

Jack propped himself up on his hand and looked at her, his smile back. 'Lover? Is *that* what I am?'

'Yes. You are. If you think we're not going to do that again you're wrong. That was…you were…magnificent. And I *don't* think you're emotionless and indifferent and unfeeling and—what was the other thing?'

'Apathetic.'

'Right. Apathetic. I think you're passionate and thoughtful and you care more than you think you do.'

Jack didn't take his eyes off her. He watched her watching him and Brooke started to feel an uncomfortable feeling settle over her. As if she was thinking too much about him and wanting too much of him. But then she felt the warmth of his hand on her shoulder. Brooke held her breath as his hand slid down her arm to her waist, where it rested. She knew what this was. Jack's form of post-sex snuggling.

Brooke sucked her core in tight. She didn't know what it meant, but it made her nervous. Something was happening and she was very afraid it was another thing she wouldn't be able to control.

CHAPTER TEN

TODAY THE MEN were arriving. The tone of the show was about to change. Testosterone was about to be introduced, meaning more aggression, more competition and even more drama. Perfect. Just what the show needed.

Jack sat watching the reel Mick had edited so far. It had the lot. Dramatic scenes, backstabbing, lots of flesh and a few tears. His blood was running hot. He was sure this time he'd have a hit. He'd managed to find that perfect combination of personalities and format. This show would be a success and then he could get out. For good. Away from this lifestyle, away from these people and away from the rumours.

But Jack's shoulders were still tense and tight. This wasn't over yet. But—surprisingly—he wasn't worried. Far from it—he was excited. He was fired up. He kept shooting questions and suggestions at Mick. He wanted to watch the reels again and again. He felt buzzed, as if he'd spent the night drinking coffee. But he hadn't. He'd spent the night alone in his bed. Not sleeping, but being kept wide awake by the memory of two green eyes, a petite body and a pair of thirty-two B breasts.

Brooke Wright shouldn't be stuck in his head. But she was. The way she tasted when he kissed her salty skin. The way her frantic kisses made him feel bigger, stronger and needed. She was desperate for him, angry and crazy, and he shouldn't even be thinking twice about her, or that kiss, but it was stuck in his head. *She* was stuck in his head and he couldn't shake her. And somewhere in the night he'd had an epiphany.

'It's good, Jack, but...'

'But what?'

'The female audience are not going to like the men calling the shots.'

'No, they're not. Which is why we're switching it up. The women are going to determine the challenges.'

Mick didn't move. He was waiting.

'We've been concentrating too much on drama for getting our ratings, Mick, but we were wrong.'

'We were?' Mick asked quietly.

'We were. We need to focus on emotions. On relationships. We need the drama to come from the way the women *feel*. If we leave it up to the men this will all be about ridiculous and demeaning challenges. That's surface stuff. We're going to dig deeper—and who better to dig deeper and get to the core of something than a woman?'

Mick stayed silent.

'The women will determine the challenges—they'll make the men work for them. They'll force the men to talk and to feel and to try harder. That's good TV.'

Mick breathed in through his nose quickly, then released it slowly. 'It's risky, Jack. It's harder to capture emotion on tape. It's harder to edit. It'll take longer, and it'll cost more.'

'But it will make better TV and that's the point.'

Jack waited. If Mick didn't agree he wasn't sure what he'd do. He respected Mick. His opinion was like gold in this industry. He'd been around for ever, had seen everything. He knew what worked and what didn't. And Jack wanted this to work. Not just because he believed in it but because it was the right thing to do. He'd forgotten what TV shows were about as he searched for ratings and audiences and advertising dollars. Storytelling. Emotions. Human reactions. And that was what he needed to get back.

'Let's give it a go.'

Jack breathed out and slapped Mick on the back. Today was a good day.

Jack paced his office floor one more time. The sound of Brooke's heavy breathing in his ear rang through his brain. He thought of the feel of her skin under his hands, smooth and wet. His chest actually hurt, thinking about her. He was seventeen again and finding it very hard to control himself. He'd tried not to think about her, tried to distract himself as he sorted out the last of the male contestants and rewrote the format. But it wasn't working.

He found himself reaching for his car key, determined to drive over there and find out what she was thinking and if she'd changed her mind about being friends. But he stopped himself. She didn't want more. If she did she'd have contacted him. She'd have let him know. But she didn't. He had to get that through his thick head.

With the editing done it was time to get to the penthouse and start getting the girls ready for the big scene later on today. Meeting the men. And letting them know that *they*—the women—were now determining the challenges. He was looking forward to it, but more than that he was looking forward to seeing Brooke again. Which he knew he shouldn't be.

Ever since they'd met he'd known there was something between them. A little spark of sexual energy that he'd thought would go nowhere. She had seemed too up-tight to do anything like she had the other night. And the other night she had been anything but uptight. No—stop. He had to shake this off. He needed to go for a work-out, a run—or maybe go and have sex with a beautiful stranger. Anything to get Brooke and her green eyes out of his head.

But he didn't want to have sex with anyone else. He wanted to finish what he'd started with her.

He drove silently through the city and back over the bridge to Manly. The sun was out and burning even brighter today. A perfect Sydney Sunday. Jack hadn't felt this fired up in years. Today's shoot was a big one. The girls were spending most of the day in hair and make-up—getting styled for the big meet-and-greet this after-noon. The men were being bussed in at three. This scene was important. He needed to make sure there was enough sex in the air to make it spicy and enough tension to have everyone almost wetting themselves in anticipation.

He didn't usually get this involved in the day-to-day of any show. But this time he was determined to be there every step of the way. This time there would be no mis-takes like last time.

A flashback of the fight scene ran through his mind. If he had been there he would have stopped it from get-ting out of control. The scene had rated well, but the com-plaints afterwards had seen the show pulled off the air and millions go down the drain. His father hadn't been impressed. Jack had dreaded the call from his house in Italy.

'How the hell did you let that happen, Jack?'

Useless, stupid idiot...should have known better than to leave you in charge...

It had been his father at his worst.

The names and jibes hadn't bothered him. He'd already heard everything his father could possibly call him throughout his life. But the way he'd felt afterwards had. He'd been used. Manipulated. He'd assumed someone needed him and they hadn't. He should have known not to get so close. But he'd been younger then. Filled with ridiculous heroic tendencies. Now he was older and knew that getting too close always ended in disaster. You couldn't trust anyone.

He could see some of the girls up on the balcony as soon as he pulled up. He'd collected twelve of the most beautiful women in Australia for this show. Blonde, brunette, redhead—they were all gorgeous. But none was more stunning that the woman he was now trying to forget.

Brooke's chest hurt from the rapid beating of her heart and her dry throat itched. She checked the clock. Ten minutes till Jack Douglas arrived. Ten minutes till he walked through that door, all smiles and cockiness, and ten minutes till all her pride disappeared. Her entire insides felt as if they were going to come up out her throat.

Why the hell had she done that the other night? Why the hell had she let her emotions turn into something she really didn't want? Before, Jack Douglas had been a player, but she had had his number. She'd been driving the bus. But now she'd kissed him. She'd opened her legs for him and pushed her nipples wantonly into his mouth. Now *he* was driving the goddamn bus and she wanted to get off.

It had been three days since they'd had fun in the sand. He'd taken her home. Kissed her goodnight, then left. She'd waited to hear from him—sure he'd felt something. But clearly he hadn't. She hadn't seen him or heard from him and now she felt stupid. He'd been drunk on tequila that night. He hadn't really wanted to do that and he didn't want any more. He'd made no promises, but she'd assumed. She'd assumed he wanted as much as she did. And now here she was—disappointed and angry and feeling like a fool.

Breathe. Deep breaths. That was what she needed.

Around her nervous excitement was almost making a fog in the air. The other girls were sipping champagne and their voices were getting higher and higher. The men were arriving today. Their competition on the beach had been a warm-up. A prelude to the *real* competition. She suspected the producers—or Jack Douglas—had wanted the girls to bond and make friends before the men arrived. That way, when they started getting their hearts broken and getting rejected, their responses would be even more dramatic.

She knew what he wanted. A few 'That-Bitch-Stole-My-Man' moments. Great TV. But an awful, awful thing to create. Did the man have no shame? No. Of course not. He didn't even *know* her. He'd known she'd had too much to drink. He'd known she was angry and upset and he'd taken advantage of her. He had no morals. No idea of consequences. Just as she'd assumed, Jack Douglas was a take-whatever-he-wanted kind of guy.

And in ten…no, *eight* minutes he was going to walk through that door, throw her a knowing wink and shatter her confidence. Which was something she didn't really need. Not now the men were arriving. Twelve tall, handsome men. Twelve men and one perfect match. Twelve men she wouldn't even get a look-in with. Because she would only be able to go on dates with them if she won the challenges—and she never won anything.

If there was ever a time she'd needed to talk to her

sisters it was now. She needed Maddy to calm her down, Melissa to tell her she was awesome, and Melody to... Well, Melody would just ignore Brooke's problems and talk about her own. But that would be fine! At least Brooke wouldn't have to talk about her own problems then. She'd be distracted and she wouldn't keep checking the clock...

Seven minutes. She started to pace. She joined a small circle of three women in the lounge. She needed to find her Zen. Jack could throw whatever he wanted at her, but she was going to remain Zen. *Breathe.*

'I wonder if they'll be hot?' Katy looked at the other girls anxiously.

'Of course they'll be hot. They don't put *fuglies* on a show like this. Who wants to watch fuglies?' Alissa was back to her normal self and completely over her near-drowning experience.

'I don't care what they look like. I'm after a man with a good heart,' another girl said.

'What about you, Brooke? What are you hoping for?'

Brooke almost spat out her sip of water—she didn't trust herself around alcohol any more.

'What?'

'What are you hoping these men are like? What's your perfect match?'

Her perfect match? Jack's face swam in front of her eyes. His muscled body and those tattoos that skipped all the way down his arm to his wrist. She remembered how good it had felt when he'd finally let his palm run over her arm to her waist. Then, when it had travelled back up and his thumb had rested on her bottom lip, he had kissed her. Long and hard and deep.

Everything in Brooke's core suddenly went hot and heavy. He wasn't her perfect match. He was careless and thoughtless and he hadn't called in three days. She *hated* him.

Brooke shifted her eyes, aware of the cameras all around them. There were even more than normal here tonight. Set up right in their faces. Waiting for every word. Brooke smoothed down her skirt and shifted. She was wearing a Wright Sports watch tonight. She moved her hand, trying to get it into the shot. That was what she was here for, she reminded herself—not to meet her perfect match!

Everyone was waiting for her response. She checked her watch. Three minutes. What was she going to say? What would her sisters want her to say? What would be the best thing to say for the sake of the business? What could she say that wouldn't make her look like a fool in front of the man who was now making her armpits feel like the inside of a Swedish sauna?

'My perfect match is a nice cup of tea and a piece of chocolate cake.' She smiled.

The women laughed. Except for Katy.

'No, really, Brooke—what are you looking for?'

Brooke glanced at her. Katy *knew*. She knew Brooke was avoiding the subject. She wanted the truth.

Katy had been up when she'd got home the other night, and even though Brooke hadn't told her what had happened Katy had known something was wrong. She'd been asking her for days if she was OK.

'It was a joke, Katy.'

'You're so funny, Brooky,' said Alissa, giving her an embrace.

Katy didn't say any more. Brooke's shoulders relaxed. She still missed her sisters, but somehow these women had become her temporary family. She wasn't even as angry any more. The girls had begun to recognise when she was firing up and now they helped her calm down. Backed off. Gave her food. Told her a joke. She'd even started to enjoy herself.

Until she saw a camera and realised that none of it was real. Just as the other night hadn't been real. Nothing Jack had said or done had been real.

Except that orgasm.

Brooke folded her legs tighter as heat surged there. That had been real—and unbelievable—and the most stunning orgasm she'd ever had. And, although it annoyed her, she wished she could feel it again. But she knew she couldn't. That was over.

Brooke's thoughts were interrupted by a flurry of activity at the door. More cameras had arrived. Producers had started to make their way through the door and Brooke held her breath, waiting for her first glimpse of the man she'd decided she'd never wanted to see ever, ever again.

Jack's eyes scanned the room from outside the door. He looked at each of the faces of the twelve women assembled but saw none of them except the one face he couldn't get out of his mind. Brooke—like the rest of the women—looked angry and shocked.

Something about her look made his stomach drop. What had happened *now*? He wanted to go to her. He wanted to put his arms around her, make her laugh—take her anger away. But he couldn't Not here.

'Jack, we've got problems.'

Mick was at his side and his quiet voice sounded anxious. Mick was never anxious—which put Jack immediately on alert.

'What's happened?' Jack looked around. Some of the

women looked noticeably shaken. A couple were on the couch, comforting each other.

'Rob Gunn was here before you.'

'What?' Rob Gunn? His father's hotshot producer? What the hell had *he* been here for?

'The format is staying as it is, Jack. The men are determining the challenges. Rob announced it all to the girls—said they had to fight for their places. Told them to consider their friends their enemies and reminded them this is a competition. It wasn't good, Jack.'

Jack's blood burned red. His father had done this. His father had sent Rob here. He'd known it was a mistake to have told him about the revised format. He'd known he should have done this on his own.

'Where is he now?'

'Gone. But he showed me his contract, Jack. Signed by your father. It's legit. He's in charge now.'

Anger burned white-hot in Jack's ears. Not this time. Jack was in charge and his father wasn't calling the shots here. *He* was. He'd had enough—enough of playing his father's game, enough of putting up with his father's demands and enough of not getting angry. Tonight he was taking control of his life.

'Get him on the phone, Mick. This ends now.'

'This is ridiculous.'

When the door had opened and the stranger had appeared Brooke had known immediately that something was up. Where was Jack? Who was this new man? And when the perpetually happy man who'd said his name was Rob Gunn had announced that the men would be setting the challenges, and that there would only be four men, Brooke's anger had fired up again. It was bad enough she had to compete in challenges, but challenges chosen by four men who all seemed as if they shared half a brain between them was quite another thing.

'Since when do the men get to choose the challenges? The original format said we'd complete challenges set by the producers and we'd get to choose the men. What's going on?'

Rob Gunn had left now, but Mick had just come back into the room. He didn't appear to have much to say.

'Where's Jack? Does he know about this?'

'Look, ladies, I don't know what's going on right now. This was Jack's original idea but...'

This was *Jack's* idea? Of course it was. He was a sexist pig, she reminded herself. No matter how good he was at convincing her that he wasn't. No matter how talented he was with his tongue.

'This is embarrassing and demeaning. You can't make a major change like that without telling us.'

Mick stood. He rushed over to her and the cameras fell back.

'No, Mick!' Brooke's voice was getting louder. 'It's not right. Do you mean to tell me that now only four women will have the chance to meet their perfect match? That now we'll have to fight each other for the chance? This is silly.'

Mick was trying to calm her down, but she didn't want to be calmed down. This was outrageous.

'Calm down, there, love. All you girls have an equal chance of getting to meet us. There's no need to get your knickers in a knot—*you* might be one of the lucky ones.'

One of the four men Rob Gunn had introduced earlier spoke up.

Brooke turned slowly. She stared at him. 'My knickers are none of your business—*love*. And I can tell you right now I would be anything *but* lucky if I ended up with *you*.'

'Brooke, calm down. Jack will be here soon. I'll talk to him. We'll get this sorted. Just wait. Sit. Wait. I'll talk to Jack.'

'You'd better.'

She knew this wasn't Mick's fault, but her blood was boiling and her bones were shaking. She *wouldn't* fight the other women for these men. She *wouldn't* pit herself against women she'd become friends with. And if Jack thought he was going to make her he clearly didn't realise how angry she could get.

CHAPTER ELEVEN

JACK'S ANGER HAD subsided. A little. He'd managed to gain back a little control. He'd finally tracked down Rob Gunn, who was hiding in a luxury apartment owned by Jack's father. Jack had laid down the law. Told him to stay the hell away from the set *and* the girls.

Rob Gunn had reached for his phone, but Jack had reached for his as well. He'd done his research. He knew about the formal complaints of sexual harassment brought against Gunn in his last job. He knew Gunn wouldn't want that made public.

It had been enough to get rid of Gunn, but not his father. His father was adamant the format stayed the same, determined that the men would be calling the shots. Jack knew that was suicide. Women would hate it and they were the ones watching. It would turn them off. There'd be no chance of a spin-off. And, more important than that, it wasn't the right thing to do. Brooke had made him realise that.

The next person he wanted to see was his mother. He wanted to make sure his father didn't get to her first.

But he was too late. When he got to his mother's house her eyes were bloodshot and her normally perfect hair was in a mess.

'I yelled at him, Jacky...'

Jack remembered the way his mother's eyes had used to look. Soft and blue and wrinkled at the sides. Now she used Botox. It kept the wrinkles at bay. She didn't need it. He preferred the way she looked without it.

'It's all right, Mum, you don't have to worry about it. I have it under control.'

His mother had been pouring herself a drink and Jack jumped as he heard the glass smash against the wall. Quickly he went to his mother. It wasn't like her to lose her temper. His father must have really rattled her, Jack fumed. Right then he made his mind up to get on a plane to Italy and sort that man out once and for all.

'No, Jack, I *do* have to worry. I don't want you to fight for me. You're my son—not my protector. It's time I fought for myself.'

Jack stilled. His mother's voice was raised. She never raised her voice. She was always cool. Always calm.

'Mum, what's wrong? What did he say to you?'

'Nothing! Nothing more than what he usually says. It's not him that's making me angry now, Jack, it's *you.*'

'Me?' He'd done everything to try and fix this.

'Yes—you. When are you going to learn? When are you going to grow up? When are you going to realise that you can't control your father? He's the type of man who does whatever he wants.'

'I know who he is, Mum, but that doesn't mean he can treat you like he does.'

'Oh, Jack…' His mother poured the drink and fell into a nearby armchair. She lifted her arms, took her earrings out and placed them on the table next to her. 'Honey, sit down. It's time we talked.'

So Jack sat. And he listened.

'Your father is a passionate man. He throws himself headfirst into things. That's his charm. That's what I fell for. When we met he chased me. He pursued me and made me feel I was the only girl in the world. I felt like the most important person in the world. I thought that meant he loved me. But I was just something he wanted. After he had me the novelty wore off. He moved on. I could have left. I considered it. But you were so young and you loved him—he was so good to you then. He'd take you everywhere with him and lavish you with presents and attention.'

'And then he'd leave.'

'Yes, then he'd leave. But you have to realise that people don't always stay. People like your father have a full tank of love but they use it up quickly and madly. Then they need to leave and go and fill that tank again.'

'That just sounds like an excuse for him to do whatever the hell he wants.'

'I could have left, Jack, but what would have been the point? I loved your father. I wanted him so badly I was willing to put up with him going elsewhere because I knew he'd come back. He always came back.'

'You *knew*?' Jack felt the blood drain from his face.

He reached for his mother's hand but she pulled it away. His mother didn't like touching either.

'Of course I knew, Jacky.'

She knew. He'd been trying to protect her, but she knew. And she didn't look sad—just exhausted.

'I should have ended it years ago. I should have been more angry. I should have yelled and screamed and demanded he stay with me. But I didn't. I shut up and I put up.'

Jack finally really saw his mother. For the first time. Not as someone who needed his protection, but someone who needed his love. His mother had lived for thirty years with little affection. Always feeling second-best. He saw how lonely she was. She was right: she should have got angry years ago. Just as he was angry now.

'Never again.' When she looked at him determination lit his mother's eyes. 'Your father will be back—when this affair is over—but this time I won't be there. I'm tired, Jack, and I'm lonely. I need to find someone who cares about me. I need to be happy and it's taken getting angry for me to be able to do that.'

'Do you love him?'

'Do I *love* him? I have no idea—I'm not sure I even know what love is any more. Or if I'll ever meet anyone I love as much as your father. But the truth is all you can really hope is that you'll meet people to spend a few moments of your life with. Share some good times. Make some wonderful memories. I don't know if I'll love again, Jack, but it doesn't matter because I have you. I love you, and you love me, and our love is stronger and more real than any love I'll ever have with a lover.'

Jack stared out of the window as he approached the bridge. He'd spent so many years worrying about his mother, thinking she needed his protection. But that wasn't what she needed. She just needed *him*. Being there and making her laugh when she needed it. Letting her know that she was loved when she'd spent so much time feeling unloved.

He wished his mother had got angry years ago. He wished she'd realised years ago that his father was never coming back. But she was angry now and Jack was pleased for it.

The girls looked nervous when he arrived for the challenge. They were being kitted out in climbing suits and ropes. He wasn't sure if Brooke looked nervous or not because he didn't want to look at her. He remembered the sadness in his mother's eyes. Loving someone who didn't love you back was pointless. He wasn't going to make the same mistake his mother had made.

'OK, ladies. You're all ready—it's time to climb the magnificent Harbour Bridge!'

The girls tittered and giggled and they set off, led up the stairs by the climb leader. Only one woman remained behind.

'Come on, Brooke, we have to stick together—we're all joined.'

Finally Jack looked at Brooke's face. This wasn't just nerves. Real fear spread across her features. Brooke was scared and he couldn't just stand back and watch. Not when he knew how brave and strong she normally was.

'Brooke, what's wrong?'

Brooke didn't look at him. Her face had gone white and she was gripping the rails on either side of her.

'Nothing.'

'Brooke, it's OK. It's safe. You're connected by ropes. You can't fall.'

Brooke finally met his eyes. 'Yes, I *can* fall. It's too high. I can't do this,' she whispered.

Jack had never seen Brooke like this. She was genuinely frightened. He wanted to tell her not to do the challenge. He wanted to take her away and make her feel better, But he couldn't. The cameras were rolling. He shouldn't even be talking to her. But he couldn't leave her. He knew no one else would be able to help.

'You won't fall. I'll come with you. I'll stand right behind you.'

He could see in her eyes that she wanted to say no. She wanted to tell him she could do this on her own but the fear was clearly too much. She took one hand off the rail and grabbed his forearm, holding him tight. He reached out and held her arm, not once wanting to throw her hand off.

It had been over a week since he'd touched her. Over a week since he'd felt her skin. He missed it. He missed her. But he had to push all that away.

'Don't let me fall.'

Jack held on tight and let his gaze fix hard on hers.

'I won't.'

The view from the top was not what Brooke was expecting. She'd expected to open her eyes, look down and see death swirling beneath her. But when she opened her eyes she didn't see death—or near-death. She saw sky. Wide, blue sky. She felt the wind as it picked up her hair and the breeze as it tickled behind her ears, cooling her body.

'Just breathe it in.'

Jack's voice was calming her. Like it always did. But it shouldn't. His voice should mean danger and warnings and everything that was bad. But it didn't.

'Don't look down. There's nothing interesting there. Look up. Out there—past the city.'

Brooke looked up and saw the clouds as they moved slowly. She couldn't hear anything but Jack's voice, and the hum of the traffic below muffled the squeals and giggles and conversations around her. Jack moved a little closer. Not close enough to touch—he'd never do that. But close enough that she could feel him. Big and strong and solid. If she fell he'd reach out and stop her.

Brooke breathed in deeply. The air was different up here. Cleaner, crisper—but thinner. She needed to breathe again and again just to stop her heart beating so fast. She was angry with him for not calling. For forgetting about her. But the emotion running through her right now wasn't anger—it was fear.

'It's different to what I thought it would be.'

The city didn't look real from up here. It looked like an animation. A pretend city you'd see in a boy's train set.

'Everything looks different when you conquer something you thought you couldn't.'

'Wow.' Brooke whipped her head round to face Jack. 'Those are wise words from a self-confessed emotionless, indifferent, unfeeling, apathetic bastard.'

Jack blinked at her and twisted his mouth into a half-smile before looking out to sea, then back at her. 'Is that what I said?'

'Word for word.'

'You have a good memory.'

'Sometimes. When I know someone is saying something untrue and I want to use it against them later.'

'I should have known you had an ulterior motive.'

'Well, at least I put my motives on the table.'

'I think I've made *my* motives pretty clear.'

'You're right—your motives *are* clear.'

Jack blinked in the wind, his hair blowing across his forehead. His eyes were dark and set on her, making her feel unable to move. She wanted to reach for him, wanted to feel him hold her, but he just wanted to be friends. She didn't need a friend.

'I don't have motives, Brooke. I just want to get through the next few weeks of taping. That's all.'

That's all. That was all this had ever been about. The show. Ratings.

'That's right—you don't think, do you? It's all about you and what you want.'

His eyes didn't leave hers. 'Is that what you think of me?'

She was angry. She could feel it burning at her. But this time she wasn't going to let it out. She wasn't going to show it. She would find her Zen if it killed her.

Brooke gripped the rails and looked up. 'I don't think about you, Jack.'

It was a lie. A terrible, awful lie. But she had to lie because if she let the words she wanted to say out of her mouth she wasn't sure she'd be able to stop.

'Yes, you do. I know you do.'

'I don't.'

She looked at him then, straight into his eyes, refusing to believe that when her stomach flipped it was from anything but hunger. Refusing to believe that she could possibly smell him as she thought she could. They were hundreds of feet up and the wind was blowing. She couldn't smell *anything*. It must just be the memory of his scent. Because his scent had been all around her the other night and hadn't left her mind for the past three days.

Brooke thought of the other night. Again. She was hot now, and heavy, and she knew what she wanted. But she didn't want to remember his scent.

'You're nothing to me.'

Good. Cool. Nice response. He would have no idea what she was thinking. And that was a relief, because right now she was realising what it was about bad boys that women found so attractive.

It wasn't just their muscles and their tattoos and the dirty way they spoke, or the passionate, almost disrespectful way they pushed you down to kiss you. It was a pathetic female need to believe that inside every bad man was a *good* little boy, waiting for the right girl to find him. Which was complete rubbish. Jack wasn't good. He was bad. *Very* bad. She just needed to remember that—not his incredible sexy smell.

He didn't answer her and he didn't move.

'What's supposed to happen now?' Brooke moved away, still gripping the rail in front of her. 'Are we supposed to say how beautiful Sydney is? How much is Sydney Tourism paying you for this segment, Jack?'

She knew she was being cynical and flippant and rude but she had to be—because if she didn't she'd tell him what she really thought. And she wasn't going to do that. She wanted to get away from the memory of his smell and the flashing reminders of the way he'd kissed her and the words he'd growled into her ear that night. Of the way he'd made her feel as if she was the only woman he thought about and the only one he wanted.

No. She pulled her core in tight to stop the heat there from spreading. She needed to get the hell away from here. *Right now.*

'They're paying plenty. So you should take some photos, enjoy the view. Make it look as if you're having fun. You may as well settle in—we'll be here for another twenty minutes.'

'Then don't let me hold you up—I'm sure you have work to do.'

Jack leaned back to peer behind her. 'Nope, I'm good. Looks like Mick's got everything under control there.' There was a new anger in his voice now. As if he was holding back too.

Maybe if she didn't say anything he'd walk away.

'It's better up here, don't you think?' he said.

No, she didn't think that at all. Up here was beginning to feel a lot like torture. 'Mmm...'

'Nothing matters for a few minutes. You can just stop and breathe, you know...and think.'

She heard something in his voice. He was trying to tell her something but she had no idea what and she feared it was something she didn't want to hear. Some pathetic excuse. Some patronising brush-off.

Brooke breathed in. He was right. They were so far up and so far removed from anything it really *did* feel as if they were somewhere else and nothing else mattered. She had to calm down. She didn't want to hear what he had to say. She could tell he was angry too. Anger only got you into trouble.

Talk about something else. That would stop him from saying whatever it was he was going to say.

'When I was little I used to hide in a cupboard. It was dark and quiet and no one could find me. It was the only place I felt safe. That's what this feels like. Like I'm in the middle of everything but hidden away.'

'You hid in a cupboard?'

Crap. She shouldn't have said that. She needed to think of something else.

'Only a couple of times.'

'Why? I thought you and your sisters were best friends—why would you want to get away from them?'

Brooke licked her lips and lifted her hands to her hair, pulling it to one side. The anger was still there and it was starting to build again. 'We were…the cupboard-hiding business was…'

What was she *saying*? She needed to zip it.

'Was what?'

He was looking at her now. Intently. She could feel his dark eyes boring into her. Brooke tossed her hair, then gripped it again, pulling it into a ponytail at the back of her head.

'Well, it was…before.'

'Before?'

'Before I met my sisters.'

'You hid in a cupboard before you met your sisters?

Maybe it *is* time to go down, Brooke—clearly the air is too thin for you up here.'

He thought she was crazy. She knew she wasn't making any sense. But she didn't want him to think she was crazy—or angry.

Still pulling at her hair, she turned away from him. 'I didn't meet my sisters till I was six. I was adopted.'

The words came out soft, her lips barely moving. Her anger evaporated in an instant and was replaced with another emotion she hated even more. Sadness. Being adopted wasn't something she was ashamed of—it was just something she didn't like to talk about. People always asked questions. and she didn't like the answers she had to give.

But Jack was silent. He didn't ask any questions.

Brooke turned back. 'Did you hear me?'

'Yes.' He was still looking at her. His eyes dark, his long lashes still.

'Aren't you going to ask me about it?'

'No. Not unless you want me to.'

Not unless she wanted him to.

He *wasn't* considerate and lovely and thoughtful. Even though he'd taken away her anger in the sand the other night. Even though he'd helped her get up this damn bridge. Even though he was still here, talking to her, when she was saying things he didn't like. No, he was selfish and self-centred and he only wanted to be friends and didn't call. She was angry with him.

Brooke's mouth clamped shut and she turned back to the sky, resting her hands on the rail. Jack moved next to her, his elbows on the rail, fingers clasped—looking out at she wasn't sure what. They stood like that for a while. Not talking, not touching. Just looking.

Brooke wanted to tell him. She wanted to confide in

him. She missed her sisters, and she was lonely, and he was paying her attention so she wanted to tell him. She wanted to have this moment with him even if it was the only moment they'd ever have. Possibly *because* it was the only moment they'd ever have. After this was all over he'd be gone. It was safe to tell him.

'My birth parents put me up for adoption when I was five. I had to go to a foster home. I don't remember much—except that I would sit in a cupboard for hours. The old lady who was looking after me—Mrs Edwards, her name was—tried to get me to come out, but I didn't like her. I don't know why—looking back I'm pretty sure she was perfectly nice, but I hated her. So I hid in the cupboard.'

Jack still didn't say anything, but he turned to face her, one elbow still on the rail.

Brooke didn't look at him. She kept staring out to the ocean. 'One day she asked me if I wanted carrots with my dinner and I screamed and screamed at her, saying, *No! I don't want carrots!* That's all I remember saying— *I don't want carrots!* I was so angry.'

Brooke tried to smile. It sounded ridiculous now. But the smile kept disappearing, no matter how she forced her lips to move upwards. It wasn't funny. Not even now.

Brooke stopped and took a breath, pushing down the hard lump that was in danger of moving up from her chest into her throat. That had happened a long time ago. All that anger…all that hate. Brooke stared into the black water of the harbour below. When she spoke again her voice was quieter.

'She had all these porcelain cats everywhere and I started picking them up and throwing them. Smashing them. She grabbed me and tried to cuddle me but I fought her off. I threw the cats at her and they hit her in the head.

She was bleeding. There was so much blood. I remember all the blood.'

Still Jack remained silent. His silence was somehow comforting. She needed it. Slowly Brooke turned her body towards him. She still couldn't look at him, though, so she looked over his shoulder instead.

'I got moved then—to a house with two boys. I can't even remember their names. They didn't want me there. They would go off on their bikes super-fast so I couldn't catch up. They called me names. Sooky Brooky...The Girl That No One Wanted.'

Brooke felt Jack stand a little taller, his eyes still on her. She still couldn't look at him.

'One day I got angry because they were throwing rocks at me. I picked up the biggest one I could find and threw it back at them.'

Brooke pushed at her lips again and one of them managed to tip up half-heartedly. She looked down at her hands and picked at her nails. Something she hadn't done since she was a child.

'It hit one of them and he fell. He ended up in hospital.'

Brooke's heart stilled. Those boys had hated her. They'd told her that her father had got rid of her because she was too ugly and her mother hadn't wanted her because she couldn't do anything. But they didn't deserve what she had done. All because she'd got angry.

'Brooke...'

When Jack finally spoke his voice was deep and soft. As soon as she heard him say her name she wished he hadn't. It wasn't emotionless and indifferent and unfeeling at all.

She didn't look at him. She remembered those boys. She remembered the way they'd left her out and the way they'd only played boys' games and wouldn't let her join in. She remembered the boy splayed out in the dust. She'd thought she'd killed him. She remembered running away as fast as she could. They'd come and taken her away that night. She'd been so scared and so angry.

'Brooke. You were just a little kid.'

Brooke shook her head. She'd been a kid but she'd known what she was doing. She'd wanted to hurt them. The way she had hurt. Still hurt. The lump rose and Brooke choked it back down. She swallowed hard, trying desperately to stop the sob from falling out. She wasn't going to cry. Not about that. Not now—and not in front of Jack.

'Brooke.'

When his hands touched hers the sob stuck in her chest. He wasn't touching her the way he had the other night. It wasn't fast and hard and fleeting. It was firm, but tender. His fingers wrapped around hers, stopping her from picking at her nails. The air stilled for a moment and breathing became difficult. When Brooke looked up she met Jack's eyes. Dark and soft and full of concern. But almost as quickly as he came he went away. He pulled his hands back and shoved them in his pockets, breaking his gaze and searching the ocean for something.

'It's natural for someone to get angry when they're hurt.'

Brooke's heart jumped and started beating again. That small intimate moment had made the sob disappear. Somehow that second of recognition behind his eyes, the very small show of concern she hadn't been expecting, had given her whatever it was she'd needed to become unstuck from that memory and move on to another one.

'Getting angry doesn't solve anything.'

The burning behind Brooke's eyes stopped. She kept her eyes on him. On his nose and the way it jutted from his face. On the way he tilted his chin up almost defiantly. But mostly she watched the way his jaw was working... up and down and up and down... As if he was thinking and trying to hold back his own emotion. The idea that Jack could get emotional made her focus. Jack...? Emotional...?

'I hurt them because I was angry.'

'You were angry because they hurt you. I'm not saying you should have thrown things or made people bleed...'

He turned his dark eyes to her and held them steady. They were almost black. She didn't know him well enough to know what he was thinking, but he was definitely thinking *something*. What she'd said had affected him in some way and it surprised her.

'But sometimes you need to get angry. You need to let people know that you've had enough and you won't be treated like that. Sometimes you need to get angry so people know you're hurting and that you need help. And just think—if you hadn't got angry and done those things you never would have ended up with your sisters.'

The words of those boys still rang through her ears every now and again. So did visions of the old lady bleeding or the little boy lying in the dust. When something bad happened or when she was sad or lonely. But mostly they were drowned out by the things her sisters had said to her since. The good things and the happy things, the sweet things and the encouraging things. She knew how lucky she was to have her sisters. She'd seen what it was like to live without love, and the chaos and bickering she'd grown up with from her sisters was infinitely better. Without a doubt.

'Anger isn't always bad. It's just something we need to feel sometimes so we know what we don't want. Just like we need to feel sad so we can appreciate when we feel happy. You shouldn't be scared of how you feel.'

Jack was looking at her. For too long. His hands were still in his pockets and his eyes were on her. He was not touching, not coming close, just watching—almost warily.

'But *you* get scared, Jack. Maybe not of anger or sadness, but you're scared of getting close. Of being happy.'

There was something Jack wasn't saying. She needed to tread carefully here. If she was going to get him to reveal anything she'd need to be gentle.

Jack watched her, his eyes not leaving hers. She was right. He *was* scared of getting close. Scared of being happy. Because happiness never lasted. He'd known moments of it. Short, hard, fast moments of happiness that would disappear into puffs of smoke. It never lasted.

'Getting close means getting hurt.'

'Is that why you didn't call?'

Her face had changed. Her eyes dipped, then met his again. They widened, then she turned to look out at the water again. She was upset—he could see that. He hadn't meant to upset her. He'd meant to give her space. That time in the sand had just been comfort. She hadn't wanted more. He hadn't called because she didn't want more.

'What would I have said if I *had* called?'

Her head whipped back and she faced him, her green eyes bright and narrowed. She crossed her arms over her small body and stared at him, anger obviously simmering on the surface. 'How about, *How are you?* How about, *I'm thinking of you*? How about, *That meant something to me*?'

Her cheeks pinkened and her eyes challenged him. She looked beautiful. Petite and defenceless but Amazonian and capable all at once. He liked that about her. He liked her contrasts so much it made his chest ache. He wanted to know more—he wanted to reach out and touch her hot cheeks, he wanted to kiss her. But he didn't because he had no idea what she wanted. She was confusing and beautiful and it made his head spin.

Jack clung to the rail, planting his feet so he wouldn't sway. He had to just tell her. He had to just let her know what he was thinking. If his parents had taught him anything with their messed up fallacy of a marriage it was that he needed to say what he was thinking.

'*You* mean something to me.'

Brooke opened her mouth, then closed it. A line creased her forehead between her eyes. She opened her mouth again and closed it again. Her eyes remained on his, searching.

'What?'

'I think about you all the time. I think about your eyes and your smile, and I think about your gorgeous body and how it moved in the sand when I was kissing you.'

Brooke sucked in a deep breath.

He needed to stop. He had no idea what she was thinking, but he couldn't stop. Not now he'd started.

'I think about how you fight with me about everything and how you don't let me get away with anything. I think about that dimple in your left cheek.'

She let out a little puff of air and that dimple appeared. It swelled his brain. He had to keep going.

'I think about how you always say what you think, even when you know it'll probably get you into trouble. But the thing is—mostly I just think about *you*. Just you.'

Brooke stared. Then her hands flew to her eyes and she rubbed them, before taking them away and staring at him again.

'But you didn't call.'

'No. I didn't call. Because I didn't think you wanted me to.'

There—she had it all. It was on the table and now it was her turn. The idea filled him with a fear that made him go cold. He *never* gave his power away. He never gave anyone the ammunition to hurt him. But he'd given it to her. She'd give him the speech now. The 'let's be friends' speech. He hadn't heard that in years, because he'd always been the one giving it.

His stomach ached and his head hurt. He gripped the rail hard and held his breath.

Slowly, carefully, she moved her hand. It rested on his forearm and he shivered. Then she let her fingers trail down to his and he watched their journey. Her touch wasn't uncomfortable. It made his skin tingle. It made the hairs on the back of his hand stand up. But it wasn't uncomfortable. Exciting, erotic, electric—but not un-comfortable.

'I wanted you to call.'

'You didn't want to just be friends the other night?'

'No.'

Finally her fingers met his hand and she looped them underneath his palm. Relief coursed through his body.

'I didn't want to be friends. I wanted to be more than friends.'

More than friends? 'How much more?'

Her fingers moved until they were holding his hand tight. She stepped in closer and he felt her, warm and soft against his chest. He carefully moved his other hand till it was behind her neck. He pushed and she came closer. His body was hard and he wanted her there. Close and soft and pressing up against him. He moved forward until the whole length of him was pushed up against the whole length of her. Her free hand moved to his waist and curled around his back. She moved even closer, her breasts pushing against him and her hand pushing on his back.

Everything in his body screamed at the contact but he ignored it. He wanted her close, he needed to feel her, and he needed to feel the way she wanted him back. *More.* He could give her more. He could give her anything she wanted.

Her chin tilted up to him and her hair fell off her shoulders, tumbling down her back. He let his fingers thread though it—soft and fragrant. He leaned down to bury his face in her hair before finding her hot neck with his lips and kissing her. Tenderly, softly, and with a passionate reverence he hoped she'd be able to feel.

The low moan that escaped her lips was enough. His whole body fired to attention and the kisses on her neck became harder and faster and more desperate, until he'd kissed his way up to her mouth and was taking her in. Desperately kissing and moving to get as close as he could.

And then he realised she was doing the same.

CHAPTER TWELVE

'What I remember...'

Max Douglas's voice boomed off the screen. This was Max at his bullying best. The veins in his forehead bulged through his reddened skin. Jack knew his own veins looked exactly the same.

'...is that you let your heart rule your head—even after everything I taught you. You let some woman manipulate you and change all the rules to suit *her*. And what happened in the end, Jack? She lied to you. She didn't want you. She wanted that other tosser. All that happened was that you caused an on-air fight that got us chucked off the air.'

Jack tried to breathe. Once again his father had got it wrong. No matter how many times Jack told him what had happened his father always preferred his own version of events. Jack hadn't been in love with Kayla. But she'd been young, and had seemed innocent and frightened and unsure what to do. So he'd helped her.

She'd said she was frightened of one of the other contestants—said he intimidated her when the cameras weren't there. Jack hadn't been able to have him thrown off the show so he'd adjusted the editing to 'out' the man, ensuring he would be voted off because of his bullying. What he hadn't known was that Kayla was in love with the bully and he'd rejected her advances. He'd made her feel small and unworthy. And then he'd started something with her on-screen best friend.

Jack should have known what a woman scorned in love was like. But he'd believed her. He'd wanted to protect her.

When the new edits had been shown the truth had come out: Kayla wanted her best friend's man. She'd lied and manipulated until she'd managed to get the man in bed and had waited till the cameras had caught them. She'd wanted her best friend's man and she'd got him—with Jack's help.

The other contestants had got involved—people had started taking sides—and when the punches and the hair-pulling had started things had got ugly. And it had all been caught on camera. Jack had thrown Kayla off the show but it had been too late—the TV authorities had shut the programme down, the company had lost millions, and Jack's father had nearly come through the phone line.

That had been five years ago. Jack had learnt his lesson. He'd learnt to keep everyone at a distance—that way he couldn't get sucked into any of their lies. Except now he'd let Brooke in. Was his thinking screwed up because of her? Were his father and Rob Gunn right? *Should* he let the men choose? He didn't know—and that made him angry.

But what made him angrier was his father on the line—telling him what to do. Overriding his decisions and making everything so much harder.

'This is *my* show, Max. I came up with the concept, I wrote the format, I got all the funding together and I handpicked the team. You're not going to take over.'

'I couldn't care less what you've done, Jack. You're wrong. I'm right. Gunn stays.'

'No. *You're* wrong. Gunn is banned from the set. If I see him again I'll have him escorted from the building and there's nothing you can do about it—unless you come here yourself, and we both know you won't do that.'

His father had been living in Italy for over four years now. He'd been home maybe five times. He'd told Jack's mother he was setting up a new company. Jack knew he was living with his mistress.

'I still own this company, Jack, and the last time I checked you were on my payroll. The format stays as is. The men choose the competitions. The men choose the women. The men control the show. The women are there for decoration and drama and if you don't like it you know where the door is. Be prepared to pay me back every cent. And don't think I won't come after your mother for it if *you* can't deliver.'

Jack's blood steamed. Not only was his father at his intimidating, bullying best, he was pointing out the very reason Jack couldn't leave. His father would target his mother if he did. But, he reminded himself, his mother could take care of herself. Or could she? And what would happen to Brooke and the others if he walked off the show?

No, he had to stay. He had to stay and try and protect Brooke and the others as well as he could. At least from within he could do something—if he left he would be powerless, and right now he was angry and he wanted to fight. For his mother, for Brooke, and against the man whose voice made him feel as if his hands were squeezing tight around his throat.

'You win, Max. You have me where you want me. I'll stay.'

* * *

When the girls received the envelope explaining the next challenge Brooke's heart sank. A cheer-off. Of all the demeaning, humiliating things…

The men had demanded they dress in skimpy cheerleader outfits and dance and sing and run around like chooks with their heads cut off. All for their amusement. How this determined who was their perfect match she had no idea. But she wasn't calling the shots—Jack was. The man who confused her more than anyone ever had.

After their mind-blowing kiss on the bridge they'd said goodbye with smiles full of meaning. He'd called the apartment the next day. Said he was thinking of her. She'd clung to the receiver so it wouldn't fall. Her heart had beat so fast she was sure the other girls would be able to see it.

Their conversation had been short—she hadn't been able to talk anyway, with the other girls listening in— and then she'd got mad, because she'd realised he was able to shift her emotions so severely. As if she had no control over them. She didn't want him to be able to control her like that but he did—and that made her angry. Except it was hard to be angry when she thought of his mouth and his kisses and the way he'd told her she meant something to him.

And now she gripped the envelope in her hand and her stomach rose to her throat as she thought about Jack making them do this. He surely knew how much she'd hate it? Did he not consider her feelings? Or were her feelings second to the ratings?

But one thing she'd learnt over the past few weeks was not to assume anything, and the moment she saw Jack she was going to sort this out. There was no way she and the other girls were going to endure a series of embarrassing challenges only to be chosen or rejected by four meat-heads who hadn't even taken the time to get to know them.

The night they'd been introduced the men had zeroed in on the women they'd clearly thought were the hottest, then got bored and spent the night talking to each other and drinking before disappearing. Probably to visit some seedy strip club and talk about what a sweet deal they had.

Heat rose from Brooke's legs up to her head. How *dared* they do this? How *dared* they assume that the twelve of them would just sit back and accept this new twist? If her sisters had taught her anything it was to respect herself and make her own choices. She wasn't about to let four strangers make her feel rejected or less than she was. And as she looked at the other women, still talking about the cheerleading challenge, she knew she wasn't going to let those strangers do it to these girls either.

Some of these women were vulnerable and shy and didn't have a lot of confidence to begin with. She wasn't going to let their confidence be shattered by a few bad men with perverted control fantasies. Jack had once said that anger could be a good thing, that you should speak up for what you believed in. She'd never thought about that before. She'd thought that anger always got you into trouble. That was why she'd spent years trying to keep her anger tucked away. Now she realised that anger could be good.

But instead of lashing out, and providing Jack with 'great TV', she needed to channel that anger into something much more productive. Like forming a plan to let these men—*and* Jack—know exactly what she and the other girls thought of their challenge. A plan to let them know who was really calling the shots on this show.

Brooke's body buzzed with the anger that flowed through her veins. She needed to release it—that was the only way she was going to survive this.

'Jack, it's humiliating!'

'Brooke. Listen to me—'

'No! You listen to *me*. We're not here to be humiliated and made to feel like pieces of meat. We won't do this.'

This time the girls were behind her. She'd spoken to them. They hated the idea of there being only four men. How were they supposed to meet their perfect match when there were only four men to choose from? They were united. They weren't going to take it. The girls were ready to rebel—they were just waiting for their fearless leader to give the word.

'You *have* to do this. Trust me—it could be a lot worse.'

'Worse? How? How could it be *worse*? We'll be on national television with our butts hanging out, dancing and chanting with no idea what we're doing! What are you hoping for—that we'll all fall and break our necks? That would be great TV, wouldn't it!'

Brooke stood up. She needed to be above him. She couldn't look into his calm eyes any longer. He wasn't getting roused at all. He wasn't even getting defensive. He was just sitting and watching her. She knew what he was doing—trying to calm her down. Well, she didn't want to be calm. He'd told her getting angry was good, so she was getting angry. She was going to test his theory. She had a plan.

She wasn't going to tell him about it, though. She had a plan to turn the tables on the men and let them know what the women all thought of their 'challenge' and the new rules. But that wasn't what was making her angry right now. It was Jack.

Was this who he really was? Where was the sensitive man on the bridge? Or the comforting man in the sand? This emotionless, unfeeling Jack infuriated her. She didn't want him.

'Brooke, I know you're angry, but you have to trust me.'

'Trust you? How can I trust you? What are you *doing*, Jack? This is ridiculous—and awful. How can you think this is OK?'

How can you think this is OK to do to me? She didn't say it, but she was thinking it—oh, was she thinking it!

'I *don't* think this is OK.'

'Then why are you letting it happen?'

'I have to. I have no choice. You have to trust me, Brooke—the first suggestion was a lot worse than this...'

'What do you mean, you have no choice? You're the producer!'

He didn't move. She watched him still, and then he retreated. His eyes blanked. He turned away.

'Jack. Tell me what's going on.'

'Just trust me, Brooke.'

He didn't reach for her. His hands stayed where they were. She knew what that meant. He wasn't touching her because he was feeling out of control. Keeping her at a distance was his way of regaining it. But this couldn't be about control. If they had a chance of working Jack had to realise that they were a team. He didn't have to do this on his own.

So she sat back down—this time next to him—and reached for his stiff hand. She curled her small fingers through his and didn't let go, even when he didn't squeeze back. She just moved closer.

'What's going on, Jack? Tell me.'

* * *

When Jack looked into Brooke's eyes he saw something he'd never seen before. Someone who wanted to know what was wrong with him. Someone who was concerned with what he was going through. Someone who was shattering his walls and wanting to see the man behind.

It made his chest ache. He felt exposed and uncomfortable, but he wanted her to keep looking at him like that. He wanted to feel her warm hand in his and he wanted her to smile again and then kiss him. So he told her. *Everything*. About his father and his mother and the deal he'd made when he was nineteen.

Brooke didn't speak. She just held his hand and listened as no one had ever listened before. When he'd finished he felt sick and completely exhausted. As if everything that he'd been keeping to himself was physically weighing down on him. He looked into her eyes, worried he'd said too much. Worried that she wouldn't understand.

But he shouldn't have worried. The fierce little nymph sitting next to him moved closer, her perfect breasts brushing his arm, her dimple getting deeper as she smiled, moving in closer to his ear. And when he felt the warmth of her breath on his ear as she whispered his whole body stood to attention.

'Sounds like it's time you got angry, Jack.'

The girls were buzzing. They'd been up half the night working out their routine, chanting the words and practising the lifts. For most it was hard work. Many of these women hadn't ever done anything more strenuous than running on a treadmill.

Despite being the least athletic in her family, Brooke excelled at the cheerleading routine. She was strong, so she could throw the other girls in the air and catch them with ease. She was also agile enough to flip when she was thrown up herself. She supposed that all those years of training had achieved something. Perhaps comparing herself to her sisters was not the best idea—they were freakishly good, after all—but compared with the rest of the population Brooke realised that her persistence and dedication had actually paid off. She was *good*.

They were all dressed in ridiculously brief outfits—although Brooke *had* managed to convince the wardrobe consultant to purchase everything from Wright Sports. Maddy was going to flip when she saw it all on screen.

For a moment Brooke wondered if her plan would perhaps show the brand in a bad light. But how could it? Standing up for themselves and turning the tables on men could never be bad. And if some people didn't like it then Brooke didn't care. She didn't want them as customers anyway.

One of the goals of Wright Sports was to promote women in sport. As professionals who demanded as much respect and money as their male counterparts. Her little cheer today would only help their cause. No—this was the right thing to do. Channelling her anger into a well-thought-out plan was a *good* idea. And Brooke couldn't wait for this thing to start.

The crowd at the football game was pumped. It was a big game—a fierce battle. Screams and whoops echoed around them as the girls stood waiting in the tunnel and the ground's announcer started to talk.

'Make some noise, everyone—we have over eighty-five thousand fans in the stadium tonight and we want to hear each and every one of you!'

The crowd howled in delight. Excitement turned to

flutterings in Brooke's stomach. She turned to the other girls and knew they were feeling the same.

Katy was looking a little green. She reached for her hand. 'We're going to nail this, Katy,'

'Do you think we're doing the right thing?'

'Yes, absolutely. One hundred per cent.'

Katy's eyes flickered with doubt. 'But what if one of those men actually is my perfect match?'

'Katy—look at me.'

Katy's big brown eyes stared into hers. Brooke saw her fear. She saw her doubt. She saw twenty-seven years of wondering if she was good enough. Wondering if she'd ever meet 'the one'. Wondering what she'd done every time it went wrong. Wondering if one of the men she'd let go because he'd treated her badly should have received a second chance.

'Your perfect match doesn't exist. That's not what it's about. It's about meeting someone who helps you on your journey. Who heals your heart and sees through your pain—who sees who you are and loves you anyway. Who holds you when you're sad and celebrates with you when you're happy. You'll meet that person when the time is right. And it may not last with that person, but then you'll meet someone else. And if you don't—it's OK. You'll have family and friends and people who love you and you'll be happy. Love isn't perfect, Katy—it gets messy and complicated because *people* are messy and complicated and we're all just muddling through together. There's no destination to get to. And there's no guarantee that finding the perfect man will make you happy. But I'll tell you something…'

Brooke reached up high to put her hands on Katy's shoulders before pulling her into a hug and whispering in her ear.

'The next five minutes *will* make you happy.' Brooke smiled. 'I promise.'

The loud voice of the announcer boomed across the field and into the tunnel. It was time. They were supposed to go out there, dance and cheer, and let four men they didn't even know assess their abilities and choose which one of them he wanted to go on a date with.

Brooke couldn't wait to see their faces. And she couldn't wait to see Jack's.

The girls rushed onto the podium in a hurry. Brooke called out to them to get ready. She looked each of them in the eye. They looked back. It was time. They were ready.

With a whoop and a cheer they began their chant while simultaneously flipping each other up and around.

You might be good at cricket
You might be good at that
But when it comes to football
You might as well step back
Might as well step back
Say what?

The crowd roared in appreciation and started to clap along. Brooke smiled as she flew into the air. They shouted louder this time.

You might as well step back
Cause we ain't gonna play no more
No, we ain't gonna play your way
Cause we're the girls of Perfect Match
And we're about to say
Say what?
We're about to say...

The girls stopped flipping. They formed a line. Their voices boomed through the microphones attached to their tiny crop tops.

You can take your silly cheering comp
Cause we think it's corrupt
Say what?
We hate to disappoint you
We hate to interrupt
But this is what we think of you
It's time you all got...

They turned, flipped up their skirts and bent over. An audible gasp filled the stadium and the clapping stopped. No one moved. Then suddenly there was a flurry of activity as photographers rushed from the sidelines to take photos of the girls butts. They stayed where they were.

Brooke turned her head. 'Done!' she called, and they stood up, turned around and faced the crowd, who had started to twitter.

They called out, then clapped, and finally they roared and cheered. Relief rushed through Brooke's body. They *got* it. They understood.

Brooke clasped the hands of the girls either side of her and squeezed and then, holding their hands aloft, the girls took their bows before bouncing offstage as if they'd just been fed a truckload of red frogs.

The conversation Jack was having with his father that afternoon wasn't pretty. His father was roaring. He wanted to know who had organised it. He wanted heads to roll and blood to be spilled. He blamed Jack, of course, and Jack was taking great pleasure in the rant his father was giving him.

'Which one was it?' his father demanded, the angry purple veins in his neck popping. 'It was the little one, wasn't it? Tell me! It was her, wasn't it? She's been causing trouble from the beginning. You need to get rid of her!'

Jack's throat closed. His father couldn't get wind of Brooke's having anything to do with this. The thought of his father saying anything to her made his body fill with a rage he hadn't felt in years. Not since he'd found out about his father's first girlfriend.

'The girls were never going to put up with this, Max, you had to expect rebellion.'

'If I find out it was her she'll be sorry she ever opened her stupid little mouth…'

'That's enough, Max.'

Jack's blood pumped. *Calm.* He had to stay calm. He couldn't let his father know how he felt about Brooke. If he knew Brooke would pay…big-time.

'It's not enough. That small-titted little troublemaker had better watch herself. I can make her life miserable— you tell her that.'

Jack stood up. White spots danced before his eyes. 'First of all, you don't speak about her like that. And second—if you hurt her in any way I will hunt you down, Max, and you'll be the one who's sorry.'

As soon as the words left his mouth he regretted them.

'Geez, Jack, don't tell me you're having a fling with her? Is *that* what this is about? You've let *another* woman manipulate you?'

'I'm not having a fling with anyone.' That was true. Brooke was not a fling. 'But you're not going to threaten *any* of the contestants like that. I'm still in charge here.'

'If I find out you've become involved with this girl…'

Jack had to dig himself out. He couldn't let his father

know—couldn't let his father turn his anger and hatred on Brooke. That wasn't going to happen.

'I'm not. Do you think I'd send her on a date with the biggest jerk on the show if I was involved with her?'

Jack was thinking on his feet. He wasn't sure if he was doing the right thing, but right now he just had to steer his father off-course.

'Brent?'

'Yes. I've teed it up for Brent to choose her. She'll hate it. It'll make great TV.'

It would. But what would make greater TV was what she was going to say to him after that date. Brent was the most stupid, sexist loser Jack had ever met. All muscles, no substance. Brooke would hate him. And hate Jack for setting them up. But he had to get his father off the trail. He wouldn't be able to stand what would happen to her if he didn't.

'Nothing had better go wrong this time, Jack. Get it together. I'll pull it off the air myself if *anyone*—including that troublemaker—does anything to jeopardise our ratings or the show's future. Do you understand?'

Jack understood. He understood that he'd had enough. He was getting out. He'd pay his father back any way he could, but after this show was done and Brooke was safe—he was out.

'I choose Samantha Draper.'

'I choose Dimity Lee.'

'I choose Brooke Wright.'

The whole room fell silent. In their wisdom, the powers-that-be had decided that the dates would be doled out on a boat in Sydney Harbour. Brooke suspected it was so no one could run.

They were dressed in full formal regalia. They'd been

in make-up for hours, getting their hair to sit just right and creating the perfect winged eyeliner. Brooke had never felt less like herself. When she looked in the mirror a stranger stared back. A beautiful stranger—but some-one Brooke didn't recognise. False eyelashes hovered over her eyes—she longed to rip them off.

Someone shifted. The women were standing in a row on the top deck of the boat, their backs to the magnifi-cent Harbour Bridge. The four men stood before them, smiling in their suits. One leered at her. He'd just called out her name.

A gust of wind blew a strand of hair into Brooke's open mouth. Someone had chosen *her*? Why? He was smiling at her. Big and muscly, clearly a bodybuilder. *So* not her type. He was dressed in baggy jeans and he had a flat cap on his head. Clearly he was trying to look younger than he was—she was sure he was bald under-neath that cap he never took off.

He held out a brawny hand to her and she took it, won-dering what this meat-head saw in her. His eyes trailed over her body and she knew.

'You looked hot out there today, Brooke.'

Brooke didn't answer him. She turned back to the other girls, who offered a few sympathetic smiles.

What the hell had she got herself into?

The date started badly. His name was Brent and he was thirty. Although he dressed as if he was twenty-one. He laughed a lot, but conversation clearly wasn't one of his strengths. His biceps bulged out of his too-small shirt. A faint smell of fake tan lingered around him.

'Your arse looks hot in that dress.'

Brooke gulped down the water she'd just taken a swig of. He'd chosen an oceanside bar for their date. It was

packed, but the producers had managed to set up a se-
cluded set of stools for them so they could tape without
too much noise. Brooke had a headache from the thumping music and her patience was incredibly thin as she
watched this thick-head eye up every woman who walked
past in a short skirt.

'Thank you. Your biceps look ridiculous in that shirt.'

He laughed uncertainly, clearly not sure if she was
joking. She wasn't.

'What do you want to eat? This mob are payin', so
order as much as you want.' He smiled.

The man was attractive—she'd give him that. Nice
teeth. A wide jaw. He was manly-looking. Big and handsome. But it was his personality she was struggling with.
Or rather she was struggling to find one.

'What do you do, Brent?'

Brent's head turned as another pretty young thing
walked past.

'I'm a project manager.'

Brooke rolled her eyes. If she had a dollar...

'So you're a tradie?'

'Ah...yeah, I s'pose you could say that. I'm a sparkie.'

An electrician. Good job. Steady. Reliable work. OK—
one good thing.

'And where do you live?'

'Bondi.'

Brooke smiled, waiting. But the silence was long-last-
ing. He sipped on his drink and pulled out his phone.
Brooke waited while he checked it, quietly annoyed that
he was able to have contact with the outside world while
she couldn't.

'What made you come on this show?'

'What is this? A police interview? Just relax, darl, and
enjoy your drink.'

Brooke felt frustration swell in her chest. So he didn't want to talk… What the hell were they going to do till the food arrived?

'I'm in marketing.'

He didn't look up but he grunted a little. The waitress came to take their order and he finally put his phone away, slipping it into his back pocket. Brooke was actually in pain now. This was without doubt her number one worst date *ever*.

'Are you looking for love, Brent?'

'Geez, slow down. You're pushy!' Brent took another sip of his drink and pulled out his phone again.

Brooke felt heat rise in her head. She could hear it fizzing in her ears. 'Look, mate. I don't know why you asked me on this date. You don't want to talk—you just want to check your phone and every girl who walks past. Clearly I'm not your "perfect match", so what are we doing here?'

Brent looked up and for the first time looked into her eyes. 'Jack said so.'

A breath expelled from Brooke's chest. *Jack?*

'What do you mean? I thought you chose me?'

'You're hot and all that, babe, but Jack told me to pick you. He said we'd be a perfect match. Look…' He leaned in to whisper in her ear. 'I have a girlfriend, but I'd be willing to forget her for one night if you want to have some fun.'

Brooke closed her eyes. She breathed deeply. *Don't go off,* she coached herself. *Don't go off.* This is what Jack wants. *Great TV.* Brooke going off about something else. Brooke being humiliated on national TV. *Don't go off— that's exactly what he wants.*

Every time she thought she had him figured out— every time she thought she'd got through to him—he did something else to make her anger flare her.

'Thank you for the lovely date, Brent, but I have to go.'

'Not yet! We haven't even eaten! I'm starving!'

'You stay, tiger. Eat all you want. I have somewhere I need to be.'

Brooke moved fast. Her feet barely hit the ground.

She grabbed the cameraman by the arm. 'Turn it off. *Now*. And take me to Jack.'

She was mad. A white rage had made spots appear before her eyes.

The cameraman didn't argue. He put down the camera and took her to his car.

CHAPTER THIRTEEN

SHE WAS HERE and she was angry—that much he could tell. And he knew *why* she was here. The unwatched footage sat leering at him on the computer screen. Mick had just emailed it over. Mick's promise of it being a great scene rang in his ears.

He wanted to watch. Not for the scene. Not for the drama. But he wanted to know. How had her date gone? Somewhere in his jealous heart he was worried that she might have enjoyed her date with that meat-head.

'Open the door, Jack. I'm not going anywhere until you do.'

Definitely angry.

Jack's heart leapt ridiculously. Maybe the date hadn't gone well. Maybe she'd realised the man was a jerk and she'd given him a serve and now she was here to declare her feelings for him.

Jack stepped back. No, she was angry. He knew what she was here for. To tell him off for forcing her to go on a date with Brent. She'd hate him. She wouldn't want 'more' from him now. But he'd had to do it—it was the only way Jack's father would leave her alone.

Reaching the video entry system, he swiped the screen to allow her face to show. 'What's wrong, Brooke—what are you doing here?'

Her face turned to the camera. 'Let. Me. In.'

She was mad. Madder than ever. And he knew he had to let her in. He *wanted* to let her in. She was angry and she needed to yell at him and, strangely, he wanted her to. He wanted her to take her anger out on him—as if he could absorb it for her and ease her pain.

Two short minutes later Jack opened the door to reveal Brooke. Dressed in a body-hugging black dress and pushing her way past him.

'This is *it*, Jack. The very end. I'm not putting up with this any longer. You've had your fun—I want out.'

'Brooke—'

Her arms were folded tight across her chest, making her breasts rise up and peep out from the top of the dress. Her cheeks were flushed and her hair was pulling free from the tight style she had it in. She looked angry and beautiful all at once.

'Don't "Brooke" me. I *know* what you did. I know why you chose Brent. You wanted the exact type of man that would annoy me the most. A misogynistic, stupid man-slut who has no self-worth and absolutely no idea how stupid he is.'

'Are you talking about your date, Brooke?'

'Yes, I'm talking about my date! The big knuckle-dragging caveman *you* set me up with. He spent all night checking out every other woman in the place. Then he suggested we go back to his place after they finished the taping because his girlfriend was away. You couldn't have found a more repulsive man and you know it.'

'I didn't know he had a girlfriend.'

'But you *did* know he was a pig? You told me that you wanted the best for us. That you really cared about us finding our perfect match. But you don't, do you? You just want to make entertaining TV.'

'I thought you liked the bodybuilder type.'

'Since when do I go for the stupid bodybuilder type? Since when do I seem like the type of woman who puts up with a man who thinks monogamy is a pizza topping? You don't know me at all and neither does anyone on your team. Do you even know what you're doing? Maybe your father was right and they *should* have brought in that hotshot producer. Maybe *he* would have found a man who was even close to being my type.'

'I thought you didn't want to find a man? I thought this was all about your family's business?'

'It is…' She hesitated, looking away.

She wanted a man. She was *disappointed*. Something burned hot in his gut and he knew what it was: jealousy. Stupid, worthless jealousy—for a man who wasn't even worth her notice.

'Is that the problem, Brooke. Did you get all excited when you saw Mr Muscles and hope he was the one for you? What happened?'

Brooke's eyes were wide and to his horror they were filling quickly with tears. He'd hit a nerve and he knew it, and he wished he could take back the stupid thing he'd just said.

'He has a girlfriend. He just wants to have some fun. He told me you told him to choose me, so I left.'

'Good.' *Good.* He felt better, but his chest was still pumping with blood. 'That's what you should have done.'

'He was a pig, Jack. He was mean and thoughtless and stupid and completely out of touch with the real world— and you sent him to me. You chose him for me.'

He had. She was right. He'd known they wouldn't go well together. He'd known she would hate him and he'd sent him to her. He shouldn't have done that. He should have found another way. Because now she was upset and it was his fault and he felt as big as an ant.

'Brooke, that's not what I—'

'Not what you *what*? Meant to do? You didn't mean to hurt me? Well, you did. You humiliated me and you treated me like any contestant on the show and you've never done that before. You treated me like I was a puppet to be manipulated and you made me feel used and dirty and stupid—and now I can't trust you.'

But that was what she'd signed up for. She knew that. She had to expect that. She *was* a contestant. This *was* a TV show. So why did he feel so small?

His chest with heaving with the heavy breaths he was taking. She wasn't just mad at him—she hated him. He could see it in her eyes, in the way she didn't come anywhere near him. Brooke always wanted to touch, she always came too close, but right now she was as far away from him as she could be and it made him feel cold and desperate. Desperate because he'd pushed her too far.

And the desperation that was prickling like a cold heat all over his body was a feeling a lot like something he hadn't felt in a long time. *Love.* He saw it in a flashing instant. He loved her. He wanted to protect her because he loved her. And that thought scared the hell out of him.

'You *are* a contestant, Brooke. That's what you're here for.'

The look she flashed him made his whole body go cold. *Hate.* Hate and disappointment and utter repulsion. The breath stopped in his throat. He sucked in air through his nose.

Time ticked by slowly. She stared at him, her eyes darting around his face as if trying to read him. Then they were still, and the mouth that had been held in a tight white line moments earlier opened.

'That's good, Jack. I needed to hear that. I needed to know what I am to you and how you really feel about me. I needed to be reminded what a selfish, narcissistic man you are before I started believing that you were actually one of the good guys. But you're not, are you? You're just as bad as the knuckle-dragger. No—you're worse. At least *he* was obvious about it. He let me know what a pig he was up-front. But you're stealthy, aren't you? You come across all sympathetic and kind and thoughtful, make me think you actually feel something for me—but it's just lies. You are a *liar*, Jack.'

Brooke had felt her body shake as she delivered her speech. She watched his face—unmoving and unemotional—as she spewed out her feelings. As she put everything out on the floor, waiting to see what he would pick up. But he didn't move. He just stood there. As if she were a stranger in the street. As if they hadn't shared the moments they had and as if they hadn't…

She'd wanted more from him—but not now. Now she was glad she hadn't let herself get carried away, because she knew if they'd gone further she would have let herself fall and she'd be feeling even worse than she was already.

'I told you before. I'm bad news.'

He delivered his statement so quietly she almost didn't hear him.

She wanted to walk out. His coldness and the way he wasn't even trying to apologise or salvage anything was hurting her physically. She wound her arms tighter to her body, pinching herself under her arms.

'So that's it? You just absolve yourself from any responsibility by saying you're bad news? You warned me so it's *my* fault when I get hurt? There's low, Jack—and then there's you. For you to deliberately hurt me—deliberately want to humiliate me—makes me think you're so much more than bad news.'

She wasn't sure how she could hurt him as much as he had hurt her but she wanted to. She wanted that frozen look on his face to change. To something. *Anything*. Anger, even—she didn't care. She just wanted him to react—to acknowledge that he'd hurt her.

She let out a little huff of ironic laughter, searching for the most hurtful words she could find. Her mind was blank. She could only tell him how she felt—it was all she had left right now.

'You're worse than your father. You are possibly the most horrible person I've ever met. No. Not possibly. You *are*.'

His face didn't move. She waited for his reaction—his anger—but there was none.

She opened her mouth again. 'You're disgusting. I know why you're single now, Jack—you're a horrible, horrible person and I hate you.'

The words came without her thinking. She didn't even mean them any more, but a blinding need to hurt him had taken over her brain and her mouth.

'I feel sorry for the people who work for you and I feel sorry for your family and anyone who has to put up with you. You're cold and mean and a terrible person. I hate you and I wish I'd never met you and I *definitely* wish I'd never kissed you and I'm glad we didn't become friends or anything else. You make me sick.'

Finally Brooke took a breath. The fog cleared and she tried to remember what she'd said. Still Jack stood before her, starting at her. Unmoving. Her heart hurt. Her arms hurt where she was pinching them. Everything hurt and nothing she was saying was working. She needed to leave. *Now.* She wanted to see her sisters and not to feel like this any more.

But just as she unfolded her arms to move she felt him. He moved quickly and he was in front of her, not touching, but standing so close she couldn't move. When she looked up his face was still hard, his mouth turned down at the edges, but his eyes were different. They were hot and angry and set on hers.

'Are you finished?' he asked, his voice a low, threatening growl.

He was too close and he stood over her. She didn't feel scared of *him* but she did feel scared. She'd wanted this reaction. She'd finally made him feel something—that was what she'd wanted. He felt…what? Anger? Something… This was just what she'd wanted but right now she wasn't sure if she'd done the right thing. Her mind flicked back to what she'd said. She couldn't be sure of every word but she knew she hadn't meant most of it. She'd just wanted him to react and now he had.

'You're angry, Brooke. *Good.* Get angry. Get angry at that jerk who didn't deserve you—get angry at me.'

Her breathing was now so heavy her breasts were moving up and down against his chest. She didn't answer him right away—she'd used up all her words and she just wanted to look at him. She wanted to watch his reaction. She wanted to know if he was as angry as she was.

The answer came seconds later when she felt his mouth, hot and hard against hers. His tongue pushed against her lips violently. His teeth nipped and he pushed at her, his arms coming around her back to pull her closer. Brooke pulled back, shocked, but he didn't let her go. For a second their eyes met, and she saw the anger in them before he closed them and set about kissing her again. Even harder. Even more passionately.

They weren't nice, loving kisses. They were genuine I-hate-you kisses. She felt his hate and his anger and his need to hurt her. She felt it in his lips and in the way he flicked his tongue as if the pleasure was all his. She wanted to push him away. She hated him even more. He had hurt her and she didn't want him to think she wanted this. But for some perverted reason she did. She wanted him pushing against her and kissing her and her stupid brain wouldn't let her pull away.

She pushed her lips closer, pushed her hips and her breasts and everything she had closer to him, snaking her hands up to his big shoulders and gripping them tightly, digging her fingernails in hard. His free hand moved up to her cheek and he cupped it as he kissed her, deeper and deeper, pushing her back further and further, till she was against the wall.

Before her brain could even register what was going on her body had reacted and she'd hoisted herself up, straddling his waist, which made him push her even harder into the wall. She felt him, long and hard against her, and moved her hand down till she felt him through his jeans. A deep growl escaped from his mouth and he left her lips for a second so he could kiss her neck, underneath her ear and further down. But these weren't gentle kisses either. They were hard, and he sucked as he went, his hands expertly moving behind her back to unclip the clasp on her bra.

There was no stopping now. She knew that. She accepted that. She didn't want to stop. She needed him close. She wanted to hurt him—to make him feel the violence of her kisses. When his face moved back up to hers she didn't give him time to look into her eyes. She kissed him again, biting his bottom lip and sucking it in, letting him know that she hated him as much as he hated her.

'I know you don't hate me, Brooke.'

His voice murmured in her ear as he kissed her neck. Brooke's blood was running hot and heavy. She *did* hate him. So much.

'I do hate you.'

'You don't hate me.'

He didn't stop kissing as he spoke. His hands explored her body and she responded with a loud moan as she arched into his touch.

'I do. You won't give me what I want.'

'What *do* you want?'

Jack pushed her skirt up and out of the way. His fingers explored beneath her underwear. She felt him gently sliding against her wetness.

'That—I want that.'

She wanted that. She wanted him. She wanted comfort. She wanted everything he had to offer.

Brooke kissed him hard. She bit his lower lip and he responded by pushing her against the wall. Her legs clung to him. She pushed into him. Angry and sad that she couldn't get what she wanted. Annoyed that she even wanted it. She should have known better than to fall for the wrong man.

Jack kissed her back, just as hard, and with the strength she knew he had lifted her up against the wall. She clawed frantically at his buttons. She needed to feel his skin. And when her hands found what they were looking for relief rushed to her head. She let her hands wander across his muscles and up to his shoulders as his large palms wrapped around her thighs and pulled her closer to him.

Their mouths didn't stop. Not for a second. When he wasn't kissing her mouth he was kissing her eyelids, or her neck, or her jaw, and she threw her head back to allow him access to every part of her. The only sound was the heavy breaths they took and her groan of pleasure as he finally removed her underwear.

Finally they paused. Made eye contact. This wasn't just sex. Couldn't be just sex. She wanted more, and when she looked at him she knew it *was* more.

He lifted a hand, dragged his thumb across her bottom lip, then kissed her. Long and hard and deep. Brooke forgot to breathe. She kissed him back, forgetting the sex, forgetting everything else except that kiss and the way they seemed to be drinking each other in, taking away each other's anger and leaving themselves with something more pure. Something much deeper.

By the time he pulled back she was ready. She had to have him. With a quick movement he was naked from the waist down and pushing on her, asking for permission. Which she gave, with a push and a long, hard slide.

Brooke couldn't help it. Her head flew back and the moan was out of her mouth before she could even think to stop it. His noises were much deeper, much more guttural, and they came from the back of his throat.

She focussed on the noise, on the way he was sliding up and down, and then on how he was using one finger to circle her clit before plunging into her again. She kissed his neck, now clammy with sweat, kissed his jaw, until finally she put her mouth over his and let her kisses match his strokes, faster and faster and deeper and deeper, until she felt it burst and shatter and she had to tell him to stop.

He stilled. He wasn't done. He hadn't finished and he wasn't going anywhere. He shifted as she shook and she held tight, not *wanting* him to go anywhere.

'Is that what you needed?' he growled into her ear.

'Yes. That. *Again.*'

She moved to allow the sparks to subside and then

start all over again. She was sensitive, and her orgasm sat right at the surface, so when he started to slide again she felt herself shudder and shake. But he didn't stop. He kept going. Pushing and going deeper, pausing to look down—clearly turned on by what he was seeing. She looked too, and watched as he slid in and out. Her fire sparked again. So close to the surface. But she didn't have time for release because it was his turn and he pushed into her with a force she wasn't expecting, banging her head on the wall behind her.

'Ouch!'

'Sorry...sorry!' His eyes were glazed but his hand came up to cradle the back of her head.

She felt his legs buckle a little, but he held her up. She lifted a hand to cover his on the back of her head. Warm, big... She put her small hand over his and he met her eyes.

'I'm sorry,' he whispered, his voice deep and hoarse.

'I know,' she whispered back, waiting for him to let her drop. But he didn't let her go. He wrapped his big arms around her and she buried her face in his warm skin, breathing in his scent and placing soft, tender kisses on his biceps.

They stood naked and silent for minutes before Brooke pulled away, brushing the hair from his forehead where it had fallen. She lifted herself up onto her toes and kissed his lips. This kiss was different. Soft and tender. He'd taken away her anger. He'd let her rage and allowed her to release herself without judgement. Without argument. And she was grateful for that. She'd needed that. She'd needed *him*.

'That was a bad thing you did, Jack.'

'I know.'

His voice was soft and she felt it travel through his chest and into hers.

'Are you going to tell me why you did it?'

She watched him, watched his eyes, sure he was going to tell her. That he had a plan. That sending her on that disastrous date had a hidden meaning she didn't know about. Maybe hoping that he'd sent her on a date with that dope so she wouldn't fall for anyone else. Because he wanted her to himself.

It couldn't be for ratings and great TV. She understood him now. She knew about his father and what he was making him do. All she wanted was to know that they were in this together. But he didn't say anything. He just shook his head.

'No?'

He still didn't say anything. Just lifted a hand to her hair and pushed it back, away from her face. It was a tender movement that didn't make any sense when he still wasn't letting her in. Brooke felt she was on a rollercoaster. Up and down, frightened and happy, exhilarated and angry—and right then, after what had happened, she just couldn't take it.

Brooke pushed against him till he released her. As she righted her clothes and retrieved her handbag from the floor a weakening sadness spread over her. Would Jack ever give her what she needed? Would he ever really get rid of that wall he'd built up in front of himself and let her in? Trust her?

'Brooke. Don't go yet.'

He didn't reach for her, just stood with his hands by his sides. Brooke looked into his eyes. More sadness. He was sad too. But, as much as he was sad, he wasn't offering her any more.

'I have to, Jack. I'm afraid my broken old heart can't

handle this. I don't know why you're holding back, and I don't know why you don't trust me, but you don't. I don't think you ever will. And I can't just have meaningless sex with you—I like you too much.'

'I can't tell you what's going on, Brooke.'

'Yes, you can. But you won't. And if I'm not on your team, Jack, I'm on the other side.'

She didn't wait for his reaction. She just turned, took a deep breath and walked out through the door.

CHAPTER FOURTEEN

WHEN THEY FINALLY reached the peak Brooke was panting. Sweat dripped down her neck and between her shoulder blades. It had to be almost forty degrees. Everything on her was hot and she needed a drink. The girls around her were sighing and breathing heavily too. They were exhausted.

The last day had come. The last challenge was over. And Brooke was so relieved she almost felt like crying. But she didn't have time to cry, because in the distance was a table laden with food and drinks, and standing around the table were some men.

Brooke counted them. Twelve. One for each woman. Who *were* these men? The girls started to twitter in excitement. Brooke felt an arm loop through hers and her stomach started to swirl as well. What was going on? Weren't they done?

After last night's party Mick had come to see them. He'd said they only had one more challenge left. He'd said the men would then make their choice. The challenge was supposed to be a hike to the top of the Curl Curl peninsula. Mick had said nothing about anyone else being there.

Brooke couldn't ask Jack. She wasn't even sure where Jack was. Typically, Jack hadn't been in contact. She

missed him. She wanted to know how he was and what
the hell was going on. But, as usual when it came to Jack,
she was left in the dark. And now there was a crowd of
people waiting for them.

What was going on *now*?

Brooke was exhausted. Physically and mentally. She
was confused and starting to feel angry again. Angry
that Jack was leaving her in the dark and frustrated that
she was so close to seeing her sisters again but still so
far away.

As they walked closer the girls' steps started getting
faster. Excitement was starting to build. There were about
ten cameras facing them as they climbed the last of the
slope and came to the table and the strange men.

'Oh, no.'

Someone stopped.

'You can't be serious.'

Brooke looked around. Some of the girls had gone
white. They didn't look happy. Brooke turned back to the
table and squinted in the sun. She scanned the faces of
the men until finally one of the faces registered. Brooke's
blood rushed cold in her veins. Pinpricks touched her
skin in a rush. *That face*. That wasn't a strange man. That
was the man she'd hoped never to see ever again. *Mitch*.
Standing behind the table. Smiling. At her.

Brooke wanted to run. She wanted to get the hell out of
here and away from that face. But she couldn't. The cameras were close now, and all but two of the women had
stopped. Those two had rushed to the table and embraced
two of the men waiting. But the other women didn't.

Brooke realised what this was. Everyone's exes were
here. *Great TV.* What better finale than forcing the
women to come face to face with the men who had led

them even to come on this ridiculous show? The drama
was sure to be top level.

As she finally reached the table Mitch smiled at her.
A smile that had once been so familiar and dear to her.
Now it just seemed as if he was mocking her.

'Brooke. You look great!'

He was talking to her. How *dared* he talk to her?
Around her, things were not going well. Someone was
crying. There was shouting at one end of the table. Most
of them were stiff and unsure.

'What the hell is going on? Why are you here, Mitch?'

'It's all about moving on, Brooky. I'm here to release
you, so you can move on.'

Brooke's ears burned and she gripped the chair in front
of her. 'Excuse me?'

'They thought it would be a good idea if you faced
your demons. If you met up with the men you'd loved the
most and had the chance to talk.'

'*They?* Who is they?'

Mitch's eyebrows furrowed. 'The people in charge—
I don't know.'

Jack. Jack was in charge. Jack had arranged this.

Brooke didn't want to believe it. As she listened to the
words coming out of Mitch's mouth she thought maybe
it had been Mick's idea. Or even Jack's father's. But it
hadn't. Jack had done this. Jack had sent Mitch back to
her. *Jack.* Who knew what Mitch had done. Who knew
how Mitch had made her feel. Why would he do this?

A woman's voice boomed out across the table.

'Ladies and gentlemen, it's time to sit. Today is all
about breaking bread with someone from your past who
has caused you pain. The aim is to get everything out
in the open so you're able to move on to your own *Perfect Match*.'

People started to sit, but Brooke didn't want to sit. She wanted to leave. But then she saw the cameras. She wasn't going to make a scene. That was exactly what Jack wanted. That was exactly what Mitch wanted.

Why would Jack do this? How had she got him so wrong? How had she thought he was different? He *wasn't* different. This was all about ratings to him. And it didn't even matter if the show did end—Jack would always put success above her. She realised that now. This dirty trick had shown her the truth. Jack wasn't true and sincere. Jack would do anything to get what he wanted. Right now—he wanted a reaction. Well, Jack could go jump.

Brooke sat down and piled food on to her plate. Her appetite was gone but she was determined to eat and smile and pretend that none of this mattered.

'How have you been, Brooky?'

Mitch's voice had a high-pitched twang to it that she never noticed before. It irritated her. She shoved a piece of bread in her mouth and chewed.

'Don't talk to me, Mitch. Don't make polite conversation,' she hissed through the food and through her teeth. 'Just sit there and shut up.'

Mitch stopped eating. 'You know, Brooke, that was always the problem with you. You were always telling me what to do.'

What? The man had a hide. She'd never told him what to do. Perhaps she should have. He might have treated her better. Brooke remained silent. She didn't want to fight. She didn't want any reason for the camera to come her way.

'Still cold, Brooke? Still not letting anyone in?'

Brooke told herself to breathe. Cold? Her? She'd given Mitch *everything.* All of her. She'd been there for him when he was down. She'd pumped him up when his ego was low. She spent all her time and all her energy on him and then he'd left. As if she hadn't mattered. He'd replaced her and moved on.

'You know, Brooke, if you talked to me instead of projecting all this anger we might be able to work things out. I still care about you, you know.'

The spots of anger were back in front of Brooke's eyes. Her breathing was shallow. She sucked in a breath and chewed the remains of her bread.

'If your sisters butt out, that is.'

Brooke put her hands to her eyes and rubbed. She knew what she was about to do and she couldn't stop herself. She'd had enough.

Brooke stood up and banged her hands on the table. 'Ladies, this is *enough*. We've gone through enough. We don't have to sit here with these…men. These people who didn't understand us, didn't care about us. We are the authors of our own stories—not these sad excuses for men here at the table.'

'You're right, Brooke. I don't want to eat with you, Grant. I don't even want to look at you. I don't like you. I don't think I ever did.'

'And I won't sit across from *you*, knowing how many times you cheated on me. How many times you lied to me, Patrick.'

Alisssa's voice rang out across the table. 'And you know what, Matthew? I *did* cheat on you. You want to know why? Because you're bad in bed!'

Another woman stood and said her piece, then another, and another. Then it was Brooke's turn.

'You listen to me, Mitch, you little weasel. My sisters *knew* what a lying, cheating arse you are. They tried to warn me but I didn't listen to them. I believed *you*. And you betrayed me. You took everything I gave you, sucked up all my goodness, and then you walked away. You humiliated me and you treated me like I meant nothing. You are low, Mitch. Lower than low. But you're not my demon. You're nothing to me now. I don't even think about you, except to think how lucky I was to get away from you. I don't like you, I don't love you, and I've realised I never did. You were what I needed at that time in my life. But I don't need you any more. I don't need *any* man. I deserve to be treated with respect. I deserve a man who isn't afraid to love me madly and deeply. And I am way too good for you. I won't sit with you, Mitch. You don't deserve my time.'

By now she knew all the cameras were on her and she didn't care. Mitch needed to know that she wouldn't be treated like this. He needed to know that she was angry and that she was done. Done with bad men and bad relationships. And right now she needed to tell another man that too, because she was angry and she was worth it and *she* was calling the shots around here.

CHAPTER FIFTEEN

JACK GRABBED HIS bag and headed for the door. The taxi was here. He had waited as long as he could. He knew they were still taping the last scene. He'd tried to tell himself to stay away but he couldn't. He couldn't stand the thought of Brooke being there—without him. The need to protect her was too strong. He couldn't just leave it.

He'd just called his father and informed him that he would not be screening the last two scenes and the show was finished. All he wanted to do now was go and see Brooke and tell her how he felt—even though he knew she probably hated him. Even though he knew she wouldn't want anything to do with him. He wanted to be there after she'd faced that dirt-bag of an ex of hers.

The buzzer went again. The taxi driver was impatient and so was he. With a click of the door, Jack left. He took the stairs two at a time. His stomach was still lodged in his throat, but it dropped quickly when he saw who was at the door.

Brooke.

Standing next to four tall blondes. Somehow, even among that bevy of beautiful Amazonian women, Brooke stood out. To him she always did. Her eyes. Her dimples. Her body. It all made sense to him. It was as if someone had reached into the depths of his mind and pulled out everything he'd ever wanted in a woman and now she was here.

She looked calm. His heart leapt into his throat. Brooke didn't do calm. Something was really up.

The tall blonde standing next to Brooke spoke up. 'Are you Jack Douglas?'

He turned to her and nodded. He didn't want to talk to her—he wanted to talk to Brooke. He wanted to calm her down. Had she seen her ex yet?

'Then I have something to say to you.'

'Maddy, wait…'

Jack turned eagerly towards Brooke's voice. It was quiet and soft and so unlike her that he wanted to step forward and take her in his arms. He wanted her to be his. But he had no idea what she was feeling. Calm Brooke was not someone he'd experienced.

He gripped the strap of his bag hard. 'Brooke. Are you all right?'

'No, she's *not* all right. How could she be all right after what you did?'

'Melissa, stop.'

There it was. Tough Brooke. *His* Brooke.

'I can handle this. Go and wait in the car.'

'We're not leaving you.'

'Go.'

Her voice had become louder. He saw her spark again. His body went tense in anticipation. She was going to tell him off. He hadn't realised till now how much he missed that.

The tall blondes each threw him a look of disdain but they stalked off one by one—the last one putting her fingers to her eyes and then pointing to his before finally leaving him alone with Brooke.

'Jack. We need to talk. Not because I want you back. Don't think that's what I'm here for.'

Jack's heart sank and he had to suck in a few deep breaths. She didn't want him. Now he knew.

'I'm here to ask why? Why you did it?'

'Why I did what?'

She made a sniffing noise and looked away, folding her arms across her chest. When she looked back there were tears in her eyes. She was sad. Angry he could do—but not sad.

Jack stepped forward.

Brooke stepped back. She tried to harden her heart, to keep her emotions in check. It had been easier with her sisters standing beside her, but here alone with him she felt herself waver.

'No. Don't touch me. Don't think you can touch me and make this OK. I want to know why you used what I said against me. Why you lied to me. Why you made me feel like we had something and then threw it all away. For ratings? Or was it for fun? Why would you *do* that? Why would you make me feel like that?'

'Brooke, I did the wrong thing. I thought I was protecting you. I thought that by staying in the background and preventing my father from doing even worse things I was helping you.'

'How did they find out about Mitch? Did *you* tell them?'

This was the question she wanted to know the answer to the most. Had he used the information she'd given to him when she was upset against her? She wanted to hear him say no. She wanted to believe he was good deep down inside.

'Yes, I did.'

Brooke's heart shattered and she stumbled, her act of bravery forgotten for a few seconds.

'But if I hadn't they would have found out some other way. It was going to be worse, Brooke—a lot worse. My father came up with a scheme to trick you all into revealing your feelings about your exes before having them appear. You have no idea how much I fought him on that.'

'You should have fought harder.'

She understood now that he had been trying to help her, but it wasn't enough. He'd let her fall.

'I know I should have. But I realised that too late.'

The tears that threatened Brooke's eyes leapt to the surface. She'd wanted him to fix this. She'd wanted him to be the one. But he wasn't.

'I realise now I'm on my own, Jack. There's no prince coming to rescue me. There's no perfect match for me. I'm going to have to save myself.'

'We all have to save ourselves, Brooke.'

The first teardrop fell. That wasn't what she'd wanted to hear. As much as she knew that she was in this on her own, and that there wasn't a perfect match out there for her, she hadn't wanted it to be true. But it was.

'But that doesn't mean you have to do it on your own.'

Sobs threatened Brooke's chest. She didn't want to listen to him any more. She just wanted to be back with her sisters and hear their comforting words.

'Sometimes you have to be taken out of your comfort zone and be thrown into a completely new situation to see if you sink or swim. And you, Brooke—you're a swimmer. You fought the whole way. For yourself, for the other girls—for women everywhere. There's no doubt in anyone's mind that you are the bravest, toughest woman in Australia right now.'

She *was* brave—he was right. She was tough. But she was still sad that she was alone.

'But no one will ever know how tough you are because I'm not letting the last two episodes go to air. I've cancelled the show. It's over. Everything beyond the football match will never be seen.'

'What?'

Brooke stared at him. What was he saying?

'I told my father to stick it. He can sue me, but those episodes will never see the light of day.'

Brooke's heart leaped. That rollercoaster rocked into view. 'You did that? For me?'

'Of course. I'd do anything for you, Brooke. Because—well, quite frankly, I'd be too frightened of what you'd do to me if I didn't.'

His smile was shy and quiet and genuine. She felt his arms around her, his lips landing on her forehead, her eyelids and her mouth.

'And because...'

Jack stepped forward, but Brooke stepped back again, into the gutter on the street. She was now even tinier. He moved swiftly and grabbed her arms. He wasn't letting her go—not until he'd told her how he felt. She had to know. Everything he'd done was because of her. Because he wanted to protect her. And maybe he was an idiot, and maybe he'd gone about it the wrong way, like he had with his mother, but he wasn't making the mistake of not letting her know how he felt. Not this time.

'I love you.'

Brooke didn't want to cry but she couldn't stop. She was confused and frightened and angry. And Jack was here, telling her what she wanted to hear, and it seemed too good to be true.

'Brooke—listen to me.'

His hands were hot on her arms. He was so close she could smell his scent and it was making her weak. She wanted to fall against him, have him tell her everything was OK, but she wasn't sure. Was this real? Was he telling her that he actually loved her?

'You don't love me, Jack. If you did you wouldn't have let me go so easily.'

Brooke gasped when she felt Jack's arms around her. He lifted her up until her face was level with his.

'Let me tell you something, Brooke. You have no idea how hard it's been for me to let you go. I thought that was what you wanted. I thought you hated me—that you were too angry with me to ever want to be with me again. I thought you didn't want me.'

'I *did* want you.'

She was looking into his eyes now and she saw something. Hurt. Pain. Loneliness. And she knew that was what he could see in hers.

'Do you still want me?'

He was unsure. Big, bold confident Jack was unsure. Brooke's broken little heart started to beat again. Maybe he was telling the truth. Maybe he did love her.

'Yes.' The word came out as a whisper. 'Yes. I still want you.'

The kiss landed on her lips with a force she hadn't been expecting, but he held her steady. Strong and steady. He wanted her. It wasn't over. He hadn't betrayed her. Brooke kissed him back. Hard and furious. She was angry he'd let it come to this and she needed him to know. His kisses trailed down her neck.

'I know you're angry, Brooke. I can feel it.' His lips moved back up to hers. 'And I hope to spend my life making you angry so we can constantly enjoy making up.'

Brooke punched his arm with her fist. Then she kissed him again. Hard.

'Then you need to know one thing, Jack Douglas.' Brooke drank in his smile, his eyes, and the feel of his arms wrapped around her. '*I'm* calling the shots around here.'

* * * * *

A TANGLED AFFAIR

FIONA BRAND

"The kingdom of heaven is like a
merchant in search of fine pearls."
Mathew 13:45

One

The vibration of Lucas Atraeus's cell phone disrupted the measured bunch and slide of muscle as he smoothly bench-pressed his own weight.

Gray sweatpants clinging low on narrow hips, broad shoulders bronzed by the early morning light that flooded his private gym, he flowed up from the weight bench and checked the screen of his cell. Few people had his private number; of those only two dared interrupt his early morning workout.

"Si." His voice was curt as he picked up the call.

The conversation with his older brother, Constantine, the CEO of The Atraeus Group, a family-owned multibillion-dollar network of companies, was brief. When he terminated the call, Lucas was grimly aware that within the space of a few seconds a great many things had changed.

Constantine intended to marry in less than a fortnight's

time and, in so doing, he had irretrievably complicated Lucas's life.

The bride, Sienna Ambrosi, was the head of a Sydney-based company, Ambrosi Pearls. She also happened to be the sister of the woman with whom Lucas was currently involved. Although *involved* was an inadequate word to describe the passionate, addictive attraction that had held him in reluctant thrall for the past two years.

The phone vibrated again. Lucas didn't need to see the number to know who the second caller was; his gut reaction was enough. Carla Ambrosi. Long, luscious dark hair, honey-tanned skin, light blue eyes and the kind of taut, curvy body that regularly disrupted traffic and stopped him in his tracks.

Desire kicked, raw and powerful, almost overturning the rigid discipline he had instilled in himself after his girl-friend had plunged to her death in a car accident almost five years ago. Ever since Sophie's death he had pledged not to be ruled by passion or fall into such a destructive relationship ever again.

Lately, a whole two years lately, he had been breaking that rule on a regular basis.

But not anymore.

With an effort of will he resisted the almost overwhelming urge to pick up the call. Seconds later, to his intense relief, the phone fell silent.

Shoving damp, jet-black hair back from his face, he strolled across the pale marble floor to the shower with the loose-limbed power of a natural athlete. In centuries past, his build and physical prowess would have made him a formidable warrior. These days, however, Medinian battle was fought across boardroom tables with extensive share portfolios and gold mined from the arid backbone of the main island.

In the corporate arena, Lucas was undefeated. Relationships, however, had proved somewhat less straightforward.

All benefit from the workout burned away by tension and the fierce, unwanted jolt of desire, he stripped off his clothes, flicked the shower controls and stepped beneath a stream of icy water.

If he did nothing and continued an affair that had become increasingly irresistible and risky, he would find himself engaged to a woman who was the exact opposite of the kind of wife he needed.

A second fatal attraction. A second Sophie.

His only honorable course now was to step away from the emotion and the desire and use the ruthless streak he had hammered into himself when dealing with business acquisitions. He had to form a strategy to end a relationship that had always been destined for disaster, for both of their sakes.

He had tried to finish with Carla once before and failed. This time he would make sure of it.

It was over.

Lucas was finally going to propose.

The glow of a full moon flooded the Mediterranean island of Medinos as Carla Ambrosi brought her rented sports car to a halt outside the forbidding gates of Castello Atraeus.

Giddy delight coupled with nervous tension zinged through her as the paparazzi, on Medinos for her sister's wedding to Constantine Atraeus tomorrow, converged on the tiny sky-blue car. So much for arriving deliberately late and under cover of darkness.

A security guard tapped on her window. She wound the glass down a bare two inches and handed him the cream-colored, embossed invitation to the prewedding dinner.

With a curt nod, he slid the card back through the narrow gap and waved her on.

A flash temporarily blinded her as she inched the tiny rental through the crush, making her wish she had ignored the impulse that had seized her and chosen a sensible, solid four-door sedan instead of opting for a low-slung fun and flimsy sports car. But she had wanted to look breezy and casual, as if she didn't have a care in the world—

A sharp rap on her passenger-side window jerked her head around.

"Ms. Ambrosi, are you aware that Lucas Atraeus arrived in Medinos this morning?"

A heady jolt of anticipation momentarily turned her bones to liquid. She had seen Lucas's arrival on the breakfast news. Minutes later, she had glimpsed what she was sure must be his car as she had strolled along the waterfront to buy coffee and rolls for breakfast.

Flanked by security, the limousine had been hard to miss but, frustratingly, the darkly tinted windows had hidden the occupants from sight. Breakfast forgotten, she had both called and texted Lucas. They had arranged to meet but, frustratingly, a late interview request from a popular American TV talk-show host had taken that time slot. With Ambrosi's new collection due for release in under a week, the opportunity to use the publicity surrounding Sienna's wedding to showcase their range and mainstream Ambrosi's brand had been pure gold. Carla had hated canceling but she had known that Lucas, with his clinical approach to business, would understand. Besides, she was seeing him tonight.

Another camera flash made the tension headache she had been fighting since midafternoon spike out of control. The headache was a sharp reminder that she needed to slow down, chill out, de-stress. Difficult to do with the type A personality her doctor had diagnosed just over two years ago, along with a stomach ulcer.

The doctor, who also happened to be a girlfriend, had

advised her to lose her controlling, perfectionist streak, to stop micromanaging every detail of her life including her slavish need to color coordinate her wardrobe and plan her outfits a week in advance. Her approach to relationships was a case in point. Her current system of spreadsheet appraisal was hopelessly punitive. How could she find Mr. Right if no one ever qualified for a second date? Stress was a killer. She needed to loosen up, have some fun, maybe even consider actually sleeping with someone, before she ended up with even worse medical complications.

Carla had taken Jennifer at her word. A week later she had met Lucas Atraeus.

"Ms. Ambrosi, now that your sister is marrying Constantine, is there any chance of resurrecting your relationship with Lucas?"

Jaw tight, Carla continued to inch forward, her heart pounding at the reporter's intrusive question, which had been fired at her like a hot bullet.

And which had been eating at her ever since Sienna had broken the news two weeks ago that she had agreed to marry Constantine.

Tonight, though, she was determined not to resent the questions or the attention. After two years of avoiding being publicly linked with Lucas after the one night the press claimed they had spent together, she was now finally free to come clean about the relationship.

The financial feud that had torn the Atraeus and Ambrosi families apart, and the grief of her sister's first broken engagement to Constantine, were now in the past. Sienna and Constantine had their happy ending. Now, tonight, she and Lucas could finally have theirs.

A throaty rumble presaged the glare of headlights as a gleaming, muscular black car glided in behind her.

Lucas.

Her heart slammed against the wall of her chest. He was staying at the *castello,* which meant he had probably been at a meeting in town and was just returning. Or he could have driven to the small town house she and Sienna and their mother were renting in order to collect her. The possibility of the second option filled her with relieved pleasure.

A split second later the way ahead was clear as the media deserted her in favor of clustering around Lucas's Maserati. Automatically, Carla's foot depressed the accelerator, sending her small sports car rocketing up the steep, winding slope. Scant minutes later, she rounded a sweeping bend and the spare lines of the *castello* she had only ever seen in magazine articles jumped into full view.

The headlights of the Maserati pinned her as she parked on the smooth sweep of gravel fronting the colonnaded entrance. Feeling suddenly, absurdly vulnerable, she retrieved the flame-red silk clutch that matched her dress and got out of the car.

The Maserati's lights winked out, plunging her into comparative darkness as she closed her door and locked the car.

She started toward the Maserati, still battling the after-effects of the bright halogen lights. The sensitivity of her eyes was uncomfortably close to a symptom she had experienced two months ago when she had contracted a virus while holidaying with Lucas in Thailand.

Instead of the romantic interlude she had so carefully planned and which would have generated the proposal she wanted, Lucas had been forced into the role of nursemaid. On her return home, when she had continued to feel off-color, further tests had revealed that the stomach ulcer she thought she had beaten had flared up again.

The driver's side door of the car swung open. Her pulse rate rocketed off the charts. Finally, after a day of anxious waiting, they would meet.

Meet.

Her mouth went dry at a euphemism that couldn't begin to describe the explosive encounters that, over the past year, had become increasingly intense.

The reporter at the gate had put his finger on an increasingly tender and painful pulse. Resurrect her relationship with Lucas?

Technically, she was not certain they had ever had anything as balanced as a relationship. Her attempt to create a relaxed, fun atmosphere with no stressful strings had not succeeded. Lucas had seemed content with brief, crazily passionate interludes, but she was not. As hard as she had tried to suppress her type A tendencies and play the glamorous, carefree lover, she had failed. Passion was wonderful, but she *liked* to be in control, to personally dot every *i* and cross every *t*. For Carla, leaving things "open" had created even more stress.

Heart pounding, she started toward the car. The gown she had bought with Lucas in mind was unashamedly spectacular and clung where it touched. Split down one side, it revealed the long, tanned length of her legs. The draped neckline added a sensual Grecian touch to the swell of her breasts and also hid the fact that she had lost weight over the past few weeks.

Her chest squeezed tight as Lucas climbed out of the car with a fluid muscularity she would always recognize.

She drank in midnight eyes veiled by inky lashes, taut cheekbones, the faintly battered nose, courtesy of two seasons playing professional rugby; his strong jaw and firm, well-cut mouth. Despite the sleek designer suit and the ebony seal ring that gleamed on one finger, Lucas looked somewhat less than civilized. A graphic image of him naked and in her bed, his shoulders muscled and broad, his skin dark against crisp white sheets, made her stomach clench.

His gaze captured hers and the idea that they could keep the chemistry that exploded between them a secret until after the wedding died a fiery death. She wanted him. She had waited two years, hamstrung by Sienna's grief at losing Constantine. She loved her sister and was fiercely loyal. Dating the younger and spectacularly better looking Atraeus brother when Sienna had been publicly dumped by Constantine would have been an unconscionable betrayal.

Tonight, she and Lucas could publicly acknowledge their desire to be together. Not in a heavy-handed, possessive way that would hint at the secretive liaison that had disrupted both of their lives for the past two years, but with a low-key assurance that would hint at the future.

As Ambrosi's public relations "face," she understood exactly how this would be handled. There would be no return to the turgid headlines that had followed their first passionate night together. There would be no announcements, no fanfare…at least, not until after tomorrow's wedding.

Despite the fact that her strappy high heels, a perfect color match for the dress, made her more than a little unstable on the gravel, she jogged the last few yards and flung herself into Lucas's arms.

The clean scent that was definitively Lucas, mingled with the masculine, faintly exotic undernote of sandalwood, filled her nostrils, making her head spin. Or maybe it was the delight of simply touching him again after a separation that had run into two long months.

The cool sea breeze whipped long silky coils of hair across her face as she lifted up on her toes. Her arms looped around his neck, her body slid against his, instantly responding to his heat, the utter familiarity of broad shoulders and sleek, hard-packed muscle. His sudden intake of breath, the unmistakable feel of him hardening against the soft contours of her belly filled her with mindless relief.

Ridiculous tears blurred her vision. This was so *not* playing it cool, but it had been two months since she had touched,
kissed, made love to her man. Endless days while she had
waited for the annoying, debilitating ulcer—clear evidence
that she had not coped with her unresolved emotional situation—to heal. Long weeks while she had battled the niggling
anxiety that had its roots in the disastrous bout of illness in
Thailand, as if she was waiting for the next shoe to drop.

She realized that one of the reasons she had not told Lucas
about the complications following the virus was that she had
been afraid of the outcome. Over the years he had dated a
string of gorgeous, glamorous women so she usually took
great care that he only ever saw her at her very best. There
had been nothing pretty or romantic about the fever that had
gripped her in Thailand. There had been even less glamour
surrounding her hospital stay in Sydney.

Lucas's arms closed around her, his jaw brushed her cheek
sending a sensual shiver the length of her spine. Automatically, she leaned into him and lifted her mouth to his, but
instead of kissing her, he straightened and unlooped her
arms from his neck. Cold air filled the space between them.

When she moved to close the frustrating distance he
gripped her upper arms.

"Carla." His voice was clipped, the Medinian accent
smoothed out by the more cosmopolitan overtones of the
States, but still dark and sexy enough to send another shiver
down her spine. "I tried to ring you. Why didn't you pick
up the call?"

The mundane question, the edged tone pulled her back to
earth with a thump. "I switched my phone off while I was
being interviewed then I put it on charge."

But it had only been that way for about an hour. When
she had left the private villa she was sharing with her mother
and Sienna, she had grabbed the phone and dropped it in her

purse. His hands fell away from her arms, leaving a palpable chill in place of the warm imprint of his palms. Extracting the phone from her clutch, she checked the screen and saw that, in her hurry, she had forgotten to turn it on.

She activated the phone, and instantly the missed calls registered on the screen. "Sorry," she said coolly. "Looks like I forgot to turn it back on."

She frowned at his lack of response. With an effort of will, she controlled the unruly emotions that had had the temerity to explode out of their carefully contained box and dropped the phone back in her clutch. So, okay, this was subtext for "let's play it cool."

Fine. Cool she could do, but not doormat. "I'm sorry I missed meeting you earlier but you've been here most of the day. If you'd wanted we could have met for lunch."

A discreet thunk snapped Carla's head around. Automatically, she tracked the unexpected sound and movement as the passenger door of the Maserati swing open.

Not male. Which ruled out her first thought, that the second occupant of the Maserati, hidden from her view by darkly tinted windows, was one of the security personnel who sometimes accompanied Lucas.

Not male. Female.

Out of nowhere her heart started to hammer. A series of freeze frames flickered: silky dark hair caught in a perfect chignon; a smooth, elegant body encased in shimmering, pale pearlized silk.

She went hot then cold, then hot again. She had the abrupt sensation that she was caught in a dream. A *bad* dream.

She and Lucas had had an agreement whereby they could date others in order to distract the press and preserve the privacy she had insisted upon. But not here, not now.

Jerkily, Carla completed the movement she realized Lucas wanted from her: she stepped back.

She focused on his face, for the first time fully absorbing the remoteness of his dark gaze. It was the same cool neutrality she had seen on the odd occasion when they had been together and he'd had to take a work call.

The throbbing in her head increased, intensified by a shivery sensitivity that swept her spine. Her fingers tightened on her clutch as she resisted the sudden, childish urge to hug away the chill.

She drew an impeded breath. Another woman? She had not seen that coming.

Her mind worked frantically. No. It couldn't be.

But, if she hadn't felt that moment of heated response she *could* almost think that Lucas—

Emotion flickered in his gaze, gone almost before she registered it. "I believe you've met Lilah."

Recognition followed as Lilah turned and the light from the portico illuminated delicate cheekbones and exotic eyes. "Of course." She acknowledged Ambrosi's spectacularly talented head designer with a stiff nod.

Of course she knew Lilah, and Lilah knew her.

And all about her situation with Lucas, if she correctly interpreted the sympathy in Lilah's eyes.

Confusion rocked her again. How dare Lucas confide their secret to anyone without her permission? And Lilah Cole wasn't just anyone. The Coles had worked for Ambrosi's for as long as Carla could remember. Carla's grandfather, Sebastien, had employed Lilah's mother in Broome. Lilah, herself, had worked for Ambrosi for the past five years, the last two as their head designer, creating some of their most exquisite jewelry.

Lilah's smile and polite greeting were more than a little wary as she closed the door of the Maserati and strolled around the front of the car to join them.

The sudden uncomfortable silence was broken as the front

door of the *castello* was pushed wide. Light flared across the smooth expanse of gravel, the soft strains of classical music filtered through the haze of shock that still held Carla immobile.

A narrow, well-dressed man Carla recognized as Tomas, Constantine's personal assistant, spoke briefly in Medinian and motioned them all inside.

With a curt nod, Lucas indicated that both Carla and Lilah precede him. Feeling like an automaton, Carla walked toward the broad steps, no longer caring that the gravel was ruining her shoes. Exquisite confections she had chosen with Lucas in mind—along with every other item of jewelry and clothing she was wearing tonight, including her lingerie.

With each step she could feel the distance between them, a mystifying cold impersonality, growing by the second. When his hand landed in the small of Lilah's back, steadying her as she hitched up her gown with a poised, unutterably graceful movement, Carla's heart squeezed on a pang of misery. In those few seconds she finally acknowledged the insidious fear that had coexisted with her need to be with Lucas for almost two years.

She knew how dangerous Lucas was in business. As Constantine's right hand, by necessity he had to be coldly ruthless.

The other shoe had finally dropped. She had just been smoothly, ruthlessly dumped.

Two

Tucking a glossy strand of dark hair behind her ear—hair that suddenly seemed too lush and unruly for a formal family occasion—Carla stepped into the disorienting center of what felt like a crowd.

In reality there were only a handful of people present in the elegant reception room: Tomas and members of the Atraeus family including Constantine, his younger brother, Zane, and Lucas's mother, Maria Therese. To one side, Sienna was chatting with their mother, Margaret Ambrosi.

Sienna, wearing a sleek ivory dress and already looking distinctly bridal, was the first to greet her. The quick hug, the moment of warmth, despite the fact that they had spent most of the morning going over the details of the wedding together, made Carla's throat lock.

Sienna gripped her hands, frowning. "Are you okay? You look a little pale."

"I'm fine, just a little rushed and I didn't expect the media ambush at the gates." Carla forced a bright smile. "You know me. I do thrive on publicity, but the reporters were like a pack of wolves."

Constantine, tall and imposing, greeted her with a brief hug, the gesture conveying her new status as a soon-to-be member of Medinos's most wealthy, powerful family. He frowned as he released her. "Security should have kept them at bay."

His expression was remote, his light gray gaze controlled, belying the primitive fact that he had used financial coercion and had even gone so far as kidnapping Sienna to get his former fiancée back.

"The security was good." Carla hugged her mother, fighting the ridiculous urge to cling like a child. If she did that she would cry, and she refused to cry in front of Lucas.

A waiter offered champagne. As she lifted the flute from the tray her gaze clashed with Lucas's. Her fingers tightened reflexively on the delicate stem. The message in his dark eyes was clear.

Don't talk. Don't make trouble.

She took a long swallow of the champagne. "Unfortunately, the line of questioning the press took was disconcerting. Although I'm sure that when Lucas arrived with Lilah any misconceptions were cleared up."

Sienna's expression clouded. "Don't tell me they're trying to resurrect that old story about you and Lucas?"

Carla controlled her wince reflex at the use of the word *resurrect*. "I guess it's predictable that now that you and Constantine have your happy ending, the media are looking to generate something out of nothing."

Sienna lifted a brow. "So, do they need a medic down at the gates?"

"Not this time." Lucas frowned as Carla took another

long swallow of champagne. "Don't forget I was the original target two years ago, not the media."

And suddenly the past was alive between them, vibrating with hurtful accusations and misunderstandings she thought they had dealt with long ago. The first night of unplanned and irresistible passion they'd shared, followed by the revelation of the financial deal her father had leveraged on the basis of Sienna's engagement to Constantine. Lucas's accusation that Carla was more interested in publicity and her career than she had been in him.

Carla forced herself to loosen her grip on the stem of her glass. "But then the media are so very fascinated by your private life, aren't they?"

A muscle pulsed along the side of his jaw. "Only when someone decides to feed them information."

The flat statement, correct as it was, stung. Two years ago, hurt by his comments, she had reacted by publicly stating that she had absolutely no interest in being pursued by Lucas. The story had sparked weeks of uncomfortable conjecture for them both.

Sienna left them to greet more arrivals. Her anger under control, Carla examined the elegant proportions of the reception room, the exquisite marble floors and rich, Italianate decor. "And does that thought keep you awake at night?"

Lucas's gaze flared at her deliberate reference to the restless passion for her that he had once claimed kept him awake at nights. "I'm well used to dealing with the media."

"A shame there isn't a story. It could have benefited Ambrosi's upcoming product launch." She forced a brilliant smile. "You know what they say, any publicity is good publicity. Although in this case, I'm sure the story wouldn't be worth the effort, especially when it would involve dragging *my* private life through the mud."

Lucas's expression shuttered, the fire abruptly gone. "Then I suggest you sleep easy. *I* don't kiss and tell."

The sense of disorientation she had felt the past few minutes evaporated in a rush of anger. "Or commit to relationships."

"You were the one who set the ground rules."

Suddenly Lucas seemed a lot closer. "You know I had no other option."

His expression was grim. "The truth is always an option."

Her chin jerked up. "I was protecting Sienna and my family. What was I supposed to do? Turn up with you at Mom and Dad's house for Sunday dinner and admit that I was—"

"Sleeping with me?"

The soft register of his voice made her heart pound. Every nerve in her body jangled at his closeness, the knowledge that he was just as aware of her as she was of him. "I was about to say dating an Atraeus."

Sienna returned from her hostess duties to step neatly between them. "Time out, children."

Lucas lifted a brow, his mouth quirking in the wry half smile that regularly made women go weak at the knees. "My apologies."

As Constantine joined them, Lucas drew Lilah into the circle. "I know I don't need to introduce Lilah."

There was a moment of polite acknowledgment and brief handshakes as Lilah was accepted unconditionally into the Atraeus fold. The process of meeting Maria Therese was more formal and underlined a salient and well-publicized fact. Atraeus men didn't take their women home to meet their families on a casual basis. To her best knowledge, until now, Lucas had never taken a girlfriend home to meet his mother.

Lucas's *girlfriend*.

Lilah was smiling, her expression contained but lit with an unmistakable glow.

A second salient fact made Carla stiffen. A few months ago, while stuck overnight together at a sales expo in Europe, she and Lilah had discussed the subject of relationships. At age twenty-nine, despite possessing the kind of sensual dark-haired, white-skinned beauty that riveted male attention, Lilah was determinedly single.

She had told Carla a little of her background, which included a single mother, a solo grandmother and ongoing financial hardship. Born illegitimate, Lilah had early on given herself a rule. No sex before marriage. There was no way she was going to be left holding a baby.

While Carla had stressed about finding Mr. Right, Lilah was calmly focused on marrying him, her approach methodical and systematic. She had moved on a step from Carla's idea of a spreadsheet and had developed a list of qualifying attributes as precise and unwavering as an employment contract. Also, unlike Carla, Lilah had *saved* herself for marriage. She was that twenty-first century paragon: a virgin.

The simple fact that she was on Medinos with Lucas, thousands of miles from her Sydney apartment and rigorous work schedule, spoke volumes.

Lilah did not date. Carla knew that she occasionally accompanied a gay neighbor to his professional dinners and had him escort her to charity functions she supported. But their relationship was purely friendship, which suited them both. That was all.

Carla took another gulp of champagne. Her stomach clenched because the situation was suddenly blindingly obvious.

Lilah was dating Lucas because she had chosen him. He was her intended husband.

Anger churned in Carla's stomach and stiffened her spine. She and Lucas had conducted their relationship based on a set of rules that was the complete opposite of everything that

Lilah was holding out for: no strings, strictly casual and, because of the family feud, in secrecy.

An enticing, convenient arrangement for a man who clearly had never had any intention of offering *her* marriage.

Waiters served more chilled champagne and trays of tiny, exquisite canapés. Carla forced herself to eat a tiny pastry case filled with a delicate seafood mousse. She continued to sip her way through the champagne, which loosened the tightness of her throat but couldn't wash away the deepening sense of hurt.

Lilah Cole was beautiful, elegant and likable, but nothing could change the fact that Lilah's easy acceptance into the Atraeus fold should have been *her* moment.

The party swelled as more family and friends arrived. Abandoning her champagne flute on a nearby sideboard, Carla joined the movement out onto a large stone balcony overlooking the sea.

Feeling awkward and isolated amidst the crowd, she threaded her way through the revelers to the parapet and stared out at the expansive view. The breeze gusted, laced with the scent of the sea, sending coils of hair across her cheeks and teasing at the flimsy silk of her dress, briefly exposing more leg than she had planned.

Lucas's gaze burned over her, filled with censure, not the desire that had sizzled between them for the past two years.

Cheeks burning, she snapped her dress back into place, her mood plummeting further as Lilah joined Lucas. Despite the breeze, Lilah's hair was neat and perfect, her dress subtly sensual with a classic pureness of line that suddenly made Carla feel cheap and brassy, all sex and dazzle against Lilah's demure elegance. Her cheeks grew hotter as she considered what she was wearing under the red silk. Again, nothing with any degree of subtlety. Every flimsy stitch was designed to entice.

She had taken a crazy risk in dressing so flamboyantly, practically begging for the continuation of their relationship. After the distance of the past two months she should have had more sense than to wear her heart on her sleeve. Jerking her gaze away, she tried to concentrate on the moon sliding up over the horizon, the churning floodlit water below the *castello*.

A cool gust of wind sent more hair whipping around her cheeks. Temporarily blinded, she snatched at her billowing hemline. Strong fingers gripped her elbow, steadying her. Heart-stoppingly familiar dark eyes clashed with hers. Not Lucas, Zane Atraeus.

"Steady. I've got you. Come over here, out of the wind before we lose you over the side."

Zane's voice was deep, mild and low-key, more American than Medinian, thanks to his Californian mother and upbringing. With his checkered, illegitimate past and lady-killer reputation, Zane was, of the three brothers, definitely the most approachable and she wondered a little desperately why she hadn't been able to fall for him instead of Lucas. "Thanks for the rescue."

He sent her an enigmatic look. "Damsels in distress are always my business."

The warmth in her cheeks flared a little brighter. The suspicion that Zane wasn't just talking about the wind, that he knew about her affair with Lucas, coalesced into certainty.

He positioned her in the lee of a stone wall festooned with ivy. "Can I get you a drink?"

A reckless impulse seized Carla as she glanced across at Lucas. "Why not?"

With his arm draped casually across the stone parapet behind Lilah, his stance was male and protective, openly claiming Lilah as his, although he wasn't touching her in any way.

Unbidden, a small kernel of hope flared to life at that

small, polite distance. Ten minutes ago, Carla had been certain they were an established couple; that to be here, at a family wedding, Lucas would have had to have slept with Lilah. Now she was abruptly certain they had not yet progressed to the bedroom. There was a definite air of restraint underpinning the glow on Lilah's face, and despite his possessive stance, Lucas was preserving a definite distance.

A waiter swung by. Zane handed her a flute of champagne. "Do you think they've slept together?"

Carla's hand jerked at the question. Champagne splashed over her fingers. She dragged her gaze from the clean line of Lucas's profile and glanced at Zane. His expression was oddly grim, his jaw set. "I don't know why you're asking me that question."

Zane, who hadn't bothered with champagne, gave her a steady look, and humiliation curled through her. He knew.

Carla wondered a little wildly how he had found out and if everyone on the balcony knew that she was Lucas's ditched ex.

Zane's expression was dismissive. "Don't worry, it was a lucky guess."

Relief flooded her as she swallowed a mouthful of champagne. A few seconds later her head began to spin and she resolved not to drink any more.

Zane's attention was no longer on her; it was riveted on Lilah and realization hit. She wasn't the only one struggling here. "You want Lilah."

The grim anger she had glimpsed winked out of existence. "If I was in the market for marriage, maybe."

"Which, I take it, you're not."

Zane's dark gaze zeroed in on hers, but Carla realized he still barely logged her presence. "No. Are you interested in art?"

Carla blinked at the sudden change of subject. "Yes."

"If you want out of this wind, I'll be happy to show you the rogue's gallery."

She had glimpsed the broad gallery that housed the Atraeus family portraits, some painted by acknowledged masters, but hadn't had time to view them. "I would love to take a closer look at the family portraits."

Anything to get her off the balcony. "Just do me one favor. Put your arm around my waist."

"And make it look good?"

Carla's chin jerked up a fraction. "If you don't mind."

The unflattering lack of reaction to her suggestion should have rubbed salt into the wound, but Carla was beyond caring. She was dying by inches but she was determined not to be any more tragic than she had to be.

Lucas's gaze burned over her as she handed her drink to a waiter then allowed Zane's arm to settle around her waist. As they strolled past Lucas, she was forcibly struck by the notion that he was jealous.

Confusion rocked her. She hadn't consciously set out to make Lucas jealous; her main concern from the moment she had realized that Lucas and Lilah were together had been self-preservation. Lucas being jealous made no sense unless he still wanted her, and how could that be when he had already chosen another woman?

Carla was relieved when Zane dropped his arm the second they were out of sight of the balcony. After a short walk through flagged corridors, they entered the gallery. Along one wall, arched windows provided spectacular views of the moonlit sea. The opposite wall was softly lit and lined with exquisite paintings.

The tingling sense of alarm, as if at some level she was aware of Lucas's displeasure, continued as they strolled past rank after rank of gorgeous rich oils. Most had been painted pre-1900s, before the once wealthy and noble Atraeus family had fallen on hard times. Lucas's grandfather, after discovering an obscenely rich gold mine, had since purchased most of the paintings back from private collections and museums.

The men were clearly of the Atraeus bloodline, with strong jaws and aquiline profiles. The women, almost without exception, looked like Botticelli angels: beautiful, demure, virginal.

Zane paused beside a vibrant painting of an Atraeus ancestor who looked more like a pirate than a noble lord. His lady was a serene, quiet dove with a steely glint in her eye. With her long, slanting eyes and delicate bones, the woman bore an uncanny resemblance to Lilah. "As you can see it's a mixture of sinners and saints. It seemed that the more dissolute and marauding the Atraeus male, the more powerful his desire for a saint."

Carla heard the measured tread of footsteps. Her heart sped up because she was almost sure it was Lucas. "And is that what Atraeus men are searching for today?"

Zane shrugged. "I can't speak for my brothers. I'm not your typical Atraeus male."

Her jaw tightened. "But the idea of a pure, untouched bride still has a certain appeal."

"Maybe." He sent her a flashing grin that made him look startlingly like the Atraeus pirate in the painting. "Although, I'm always willing to be convinced that a sinner is the way to go."

"Because that generally means no commitment, right?"

Zane's dark brows jerked together. "How did we get on to commitment?"

Carla registered the abrupt silence as if whoever had just entered the gallery had seen them and stopped.

Her heart slammed in her chest as she caught Lucas's reflection in one of the windows. On impulse, she stepped close to Zane and tilted her head back, the move flirtatious and openly provocative. She was playing with fire, because Zane had a reputation that scorched.

Lucas would be furious with her. If he *was* jealous, her behavior would probably kill any feelings he had left for her, but she was beyond caring. He had hurt her too badly for her to pull back now. "If that's an invitation, the answer is yes."

Zane's gaze registered unflattering surprise.

Minor detail, because Lucas was now walking toward them. Gritting her teeth, she wound her finger in Zane's tie, applying just enough pressure that his head lowered until his mouth was mere inches from hers.

His gaze was disarmingly neutral. "I know what you're up to."

"You could at least be tempted."

"I'm trying."

"Try harder."

"Damn, you're type A. No wonder he went for Lilah."

Carla's fingers tightened on his tie. "Is it that obvious?"

"Only to me. And that's because I'm a control freak myself."

"I am *not* a control freak."

He unwound her fingers from his tie. "Whatever you say."

Cut adrift by Zane's calm patience, Carla had no choice but to step back and in so doing almost caromed into Lucas.

She flinched at the fiery trail of his gaze over the shadow of her cleavage, her mouth, the impression of heat and desire. If Zane hadn't been there she was almost certain he would have pulled her close and kissed her.

Lucas's expression was shuttered. "What are you up to?"

Carla didn't try to keep the bitterness out of her voice. "*I'm* not up to anything. Zane was showing me the paintings."

"Careful," Zane intervened, his gaze on Lucas. "Or I

might think you have a personal interest in Carla, and that couldn't possibly be, since you're dating the lovely Lilah."

A sharp pang went through Carla at the tension vibrating between the brothers, shifting undercurrents she didn't understand.

Spine rigid, she kept her gaze firmly on Zane's jaw. She hadn't liked behaving like that, but at least she had proved that Lucas did still want her. Although the knowledge was a bitter pill, because his reaction repeated a pattern that was depressingly familiar. In establishing a stress-free liaison with him based on her rules, she had somehow negotiated herself out of the very things she needed most: love, companionship and commitment.

Lucas had wanted her for two years, but that was all. The relationship had struggled to progress out of the bedroom. Even when she had finally gotten him to Thailand for a whole four-day minibreak, the longest period of time they had ever spent together, the plan had crashed and burned because she had gotten sick.

She wondered in what way she was lacking that Lucas didn't want a full relationship with her? That instead of allowing them to grow closer, he had kept her at an emotional arm's length and gone to Lilah for the very things that Carla needed from him.

She glanced apologetically at Zane in an effort to defuse the tension. "It's okay, Lucas and I are old news. If there was anything more we would be together now."

"Whereas marriage *is* Lilah's focus," Zane said softly.

Lucas frowned. "Back off, Zane."

Confusion gripped Carla along with another renegade glimmer of hope at Lucas's reaction. She was tired of thinking about everything that had gone wrong, but despite that, her mind grabbed on to the notion that maybe all he was doing *was* dating Lilah on a casual basis. Just because Lilah wanted marriage didn't necessarily mean she would get what she wanted.

Grimly, she forced herself to study the Atraeus bride in the painting again. It was the perfect reality check.

Her pale, demure gown was the epitome of all things virginal and pure. Nothing like Carla's flaming red silk dress, with its enticing glimpse of cleavage and leg. The serene eighteenth-century bride was no doubt every man's secret dream. A perfect wife, without a flirty bone in her body. Or a stress condition.

Lucas's gaze sliced back to Carla. "I'll take you back to the party. Dinner will be served in about fifteen minutes."

He *was* jealous.

The thought reverberated through her, but for the first time in two years what Lucas wanted wasn't a priority. *Her* rules had just changed. From now on it was commitment or nothing.

Her chin firmed. "No. I have an escort. Zane will take me back to the party."

For a long, tension-filled moment Carla thought Lucas would argue, but then the demanding, possessive gleam was replaced by a familiar control. He nodded curtly then sent Zane a long, cold look that conveyed a hands-off message that left Carla feeling doubly confused. Lucas didn't want her, but neither did he want Zane anywhere near her.

And if Lucas no longer wanted her, if they really were finished, why had he bothered to search her out?

Three

Lucas Atraeus strode into his private quarters and snapped the door closed behind him. Opening a set of French doors, he stepped out onto his balcony. The wind buffeted the weathered stone parapet and whipped night-dark hair around the obdurate line of his jaw. He tried to focus on the steady roar of the waves pounding the cliff face beneath and the stream of damp, salty air, while he waited for the self-destructive desire to reclaim Carla to dissolve.

The vibration of his cell phone drew him back inside. Sliding the phone out of his pocket, he checked the screen. Lilah. No doubt wondering where he was.

Jaw clenched, he allowed the call to go through to his voice mail. He couldn't stomach talking to Lilah right at that moment with his emotions still raw and his thoughts on another woman. Besides, with a relationship based on a few phone calls and a couple of conversations, most of them purely work based, they literally had nothing to say to each other.

The call terminated. Lucas found himself staring at a newspaper he had tossed down on the coffee table, the one he had read on the night flight from New York to Medinos. The paper was open at the society pages and a grainy shot of Carla in her capacity as the "face" of Ambrosi Pearls, twined intimately close with a rival millionaire businessman.

Picking up the newspaper, he reread the caption that hinted at a hot affair.

He had been away for two months but by all accounts she had not missed him.

Tossing the newspaper down on the coffee table, he strode back out onto the balcony. Before he could stop himself, he had punched in her number on his phone.

Calling her now made no kind of sense.

He held the sleek phone pressed to his ear and forced himself to remember the one overriding reason he should never have touched Carla Ambrosi.

Grimly, he noted that the hit of old grief and sharp-enough-to-taste guilt still wasn't powerful enough to bury the impulse to involve himself even more deeply in yet another fatal attraction.

When he had met Carla, somehow he had stepped away from the rigid discipline he had instilled in himself after Sophie's death.

The car accident hadn't been his fault, but he was still haunted by the argument that had instigated Sophie's head-long dash in her sports car after he had found out that she had aborted his child.

Sophie had been beautiful, headstrong and adept at winding him around her little finger. He should have stopped her, taken the car keys. He should have controlled the situation. It had been his responsibility to protect her, and he had failed.

They should never have been together in the first place.

They had been all wrong for each other. He had been disciplined, work focused and family orientated. Sophie had skimmed along the surface of life, thriving on bright lights, parties and media attention. Even the manner in which Sophie had died had garnered publicity and had been perceived in certain quarters as glamorous.

The ring tone continued. His fingers tightened on the cell. Carla had her phone with her; she should have picked up by now.

Unless she was otherwise occupied. *With Zane*.

His stomach clenched at the image of Carla, mouthwateringly gorgeous in red, her fingers twined in Zane's tie, poised for a kiss he had interrupted.

He didn't trust Zane. His younger brother had a reputation with women that literally burned.

The call went through to voice mail. Carla's voice filled his ear.

Despite the annoyance that gripped him that Carla had decided to ignore his call, Lucas was riveted by the velvet-cool sound of the recorded message. The brisk, businesslike tone so at odds with Carla's ultrasexy, ultrafeminine appearance and which never failed to fascinate.

During the two months he had been in the States he had refrained from contacting Carla. He had needed to distance himself from a relationship that during an intense few days in Thailand had suddenly stepped over an invisible boundary and become too gut-wrenchingly intimate. Too like his relationship with Sophie.

Carla, who was surprisingly businesslike and controlled when it came to communication, had left only one text and a single phone message to which he had replied. A few weeks ago he had seen her briefly, from a distance, at her father's funeral, but they hadn't spoken.

That was reason number two not to become involved with Carla.

The ground rules for their relationship had been based on what she had wanted: a no-strings fun fling, carried out in secret because of the financial scandal that had erupted between their two families.

Secrecy was not Lucas's thing, but since he had never planned on permanency he hadn't seen any harm in going along with Carla's plan. He had been based in the States, Carla was in Sydney. A relationship wasn't possible even if he had wanted one.

The line hummed expectantly.

Irritated with himself for not having done it sooner, Lucas terminated the call.

Grimly, he stared at the endless expanse of sea, the faint curve of the horizon. Carla not picking up the call was the best-case scenario. If she had, he was by no means certain he could have maintained his ruthless facade.

The problem was that, as tough and successful as he was in business, when it came to women his track record was patchy.

As an Atraeus he was expected to be coolly dominant. Despite the years he had spent trying to mold himself into the strong silent type who routinely got his way, he had not achieved Constantine's effortless self-possession. Little kids and fluffy dogs still targeted him; women of all ages gravitated to him as if they had no clue about his reputation as The Atraeus Group's key hatchet man.

Despite the long list of companies he had streamlined or clinically dismantled, he couldn't forget that he had not been able to establish any degree of control over his relationship with Sophie.

Jaw taut, Lucas padded inside. He barely noticed the

warm glow of lamplight, the richness of exquisite antiques and jewel-bright carpets.

His gaze zeroed in on the newspaper article again. A hot pulse of jealously burned through him as he studied the Greek millionaire who had his arm around Carla's waist.

Alex Panopoulos, an archrival across the boardroom table and a well-known playboy.

Given the limited basis of Lucas's relationship with Carla, they had agreed it had to be open; they were both free to date others. Like Lucas, Carla regularly dated as part of her career, although so far Lucas had not been able to bring himself to include another woman in his life on more than a strictly platonic basis.

Panopoulos was a guest at the wedding tomorrow.

Walking through to the kitchen, he tossed the paper into the trash. His jaw tightened at the thought that he would have fend off the Greek, as well.

He guessed he should be glad that it was Zane Carla seemed to be attracted to and not Panopoulos.

Zane had been controllable, so far. And if he stepped over the line, there was always the option that they could settle the issue in the old-fashioned way, down on the beach and without an audience.

Dinner passed in a polite, superficial haze. Carla made conversation, smiled on cue, and avoided looking at Lucas. Unfortunately, because he was seated almost directly opposite her, she was burningly aware of him through each course.

Dessert was served. Still caught between the raw misery that threatened to drag her under, and the need to maintain the appearance of normality, Carla ate. She had reached the dessert course when she registered how much wine she had drunk.

A small sharp shock went through her. She wasn't drunk, but alcohol and some of the foods she was eating did not mix happily with an ulcer. Strictly speaking, after the episode with the virus and the ulcer, she wasn't supposed to drink at all.

Setting her spoon down, she picked up her clutch and excused herself from the table. She asked one of the waitstaff to direct her to the nearest bathroom. Unfortunately, since her grasp of Medinian was far from perfect, she somehow managed to take a wrong turn.

After traversing a long corridor and opening a number of doors, one of which seemed to be the entrance to a private set of rooms, complete with a kitchenette, she opened a door and found herself on a terrace overlooking the sea. Shrugging, because the terrace would do as well as a bathroom since all she required was privacy to take the small cocktail of pills her doctor had prescribed, she walked to the stone parapet and studied the view.

The stiff sea breeze that had been blowing earlier had dropped away, leaving the night still, the air balmy and heavily scented with the pine and rosemary that grew wild on the hills. A huge full moon glowed a rich, buttery gold on the horizon.

Setting her handbag down on the stone pavers, she extracted the MediPACK of pills she had brought with her, tore open the plastic seal and swallowed them dry.

Dropping the plastic waste into her handbag, she straightened just as the door onto the terrace popped open. Her chest tightened when she recognized Lucas.

"I hope you weren't expecting Zane?"

"If I was, it wouldn't be any of your business."

"Zane won't give you what you want."

Carla swallowed to try and clear the dry bitterness in her

mouth. "A loving relationship? The kind of relationship I thought we could have had?"

He ignored the questions. "You should return to the dining room."

The flatness of Lucas's voice startled her. Lucas had always been exciting and difficult to pin down, but he had also been funny and unexpectedly tender. This was the first time she had ever seen this side of him. "Not yet. I have a...headache, I need some air." Which was no lie, because the headache was there, throbbing steadily at her temples.

She pretended to be absorbed by the spectacular view of the crystal-clear night and the vast expanse of sea gleaming like polished bronze beneath the moon. Just off the coast of Medinos, the island of Ambrus loomed, tonight seemingly almost close enough to touch. One of the more substantial islands in the Medinos group, Ambrus was intimately familiar to her because her family had once owned a chunk of it.

"How did you know these are my rooms?"

She spun, shocked at Lucas's closeness and what he'd just said. "I didn't. I was looking for a bathroom. I must have taken a wrong turn."

The coolness of his glance informed her that he didn't quite believe her. Any idea that Lucas would tell her that he had made a mistake and that he desperately wanted her back died a quick death.

A throb of grief hit her at the animosity that seemed to be growing by the second and she pulled herself up sharply. She had run the gamut of shock and anger. She was not going to wallow in self-pity.

It was clear Lucas wasn't going to leave until she did, so she picked up her bag and started toward the door.

Instead of moving aside, Lucas moved to block her path. "I'm sorry you found out this way. I did try to meet with you before dinner."

Her heart suddenly pounding off the register, she stared rigidly at his shoulder. "You could have told me when I called to cancel and given me some time. Even a text would have helped."

His dark brows jerked together. "I'm not in the habit of breaking off relationships over the phone or by text. I wanted to tell you face-to-face."

Her jaw tightened. It didn't help that his gaze was direct, that he was clearly intent on softening the blow. The last thing she wanted from Lucas was pity. "Did Lilah fly in with you?"

"She arrived this afternoon."

Relief made her feel faintly unsteady. So, Lilah hadn't been with Lucas in the limousine.

As insignificant as that detail was, it mattered, because when she had seen the limousine she had been crazily, sappily fantasizing about Lucas and the life they could now share. Although she should have known he hadn't arrived with Lilah, because there hadn't been any media reports that he had arrived at the airport with a female companion.

Lucas's gaze connected with hers. "Before you go back inside, I need to know if you intend to go to the press with a story about our affair."

Affair.

Her chin jerked up. For two years she had considered they had been involved in a relationship. "I'm here for Sienna's wedding. It's her day, and I don't intend to spoil it."

"Good. Because if you try to force my hand by going public with this, take it from me, I'm not playing."

Comprehension hit. She had been so absorbed with the publicity for Ambrosi's latest collection and the crazy rush to organize Sienna's wedding that she had barely had time to sleep, let alone think. When Sienna married Constantine, Carla would be inextricably bound to the Atraeus family.

The Atraeus family were traditionalists. If it were discovered that she and Lucas had been seeing each other secretly for two years, he would come under intense pressure from his family to marry her.

Now the comment about her looking for his rooms made sense.

What better way to force a commitment than to arrange for them both to be found together in his rooms at the *castello?* Anger and a burning sense of shame that he should think she would stoop that low sliced through her. "I hadn't considered that angle."

Why would she when she had assumed Lucas wanted her?

He ignored her statement. "If it's marriage you want, you won't get it by pressuring me."

Which meant he really had thought about the different ways she could force him to the altar. She took a deep breath against a sharp spasm of hurt. "At what point did I ever say I was after marriage?"

His gaze bored into hers, as fierce and obdurate as the dark stone from which the fortress was built. "Then we have an understanding?"

"Oh, I think so." She forced a bright smile. "I wouldn't marry you if you tied me up and dragged me down the aisle. Tell me," she said before she could gag her mouth and instruct her brain to never utter anything that would inform Lucas just how weak and vulnerable she really was. "Did you ever come close to loving me?"

He went still. "What we had wasn't exactly about love."

No. Silly her.

"There's something else we need to talk about."

"In that case, it'll have to wait. Now I really do have a headache." She fumbled in her clutch, searching for the painkillers she'd slipped in before she'd left the villa, just in case. In her haste the foil pack slipped out of her fingers and dropped to the terrace.

Lucas retrieved the pills before she could. "What are these?"

He held the foil pack out of her reach while he read the label. "Since when have you suffered from headaches?"

She snatched the pills from his grasp. "They're a left-over from the virus I caught in Thailand. I don't get them very often."

She ripped the foil open and swallowed two pills dry, grimacing at the extra wave of bitterness in her mouth when one of the pills lodged in her throat. She badly needed a glass of water.

Lucas frowned. "I didn't know you were still having problems."

She shoved the foil pack back in her clutch. "But then you never bothered to ask."

And the last thing she had wanted to do was let him know that she had been so stressed by the unresolved nature of their relationship that she had given herself an even worse stomach ulcer than she had started with two years ago.

After the growing distance between them in Thailand, she hadn't wanted to further undermine their relationship or give him an excuse to break up with her. Keeping silent had been a constant strain because she had wanted the comfort of his presence, had *needed* him near, but now she was glad she hadn't revealed how sick she really had been. It was one small corner of her life that he hadn't invaded, one small batch of memories that didn't contain him.

She felt like kicking herself for being so stupid over the past couple of months. If Lucas had wanted to be with her he would have arranged time together. Once, he had flown into Sydney with only a four-hour window before he'd had to fly out again. They had spent every available second of those four hours locked together in bed.

Cold settled in her stomach. In retrospect, their relationship had foundered in Thailand. Lucas hadn't liked crossing the line into caring; he had simply wanted a pretty, adoring lover and uncomplicated sex.

Lucas was still blocking her path. "You're pale and your eyes are dilated. I'll take you home."

"No." She stepped neatly around him and made a beeline for the open door. Her heart sped up when she realized he was close behind her. "I can drive myself. The last thing I want is to spend any more time with you."

"Too bad." His hand curled around her upper arm, sending a hot, tingling shock straight to the pit of her stomach as he propelled her into the hall. "You've had a couple of glasses of wine, and now a strong painkiller. The last thing you should do is get behind the wheel of that little sports car."

She shot him a coolly assessing look. "Or talk to the paparazzi at the gate."

"Right now it's the hairpin bends on the road back to the villa that worry me."

Something snapped inside her at the calm, matter-of-fact tone of his voice, as if he was conducting damage control in one of his business takeovers. "What do you think I'm going to do, Lucas? Drive off one of your cliffs into the sea?"

Unexpectedly his grip loosened. Twisting free, she grasped the handle of the door to the suite she had briefly checked out before, thinking it could be a bathroom. It was Lucas's suite, apparently. Forbidden territory.

Flinging the door wide, she stepped inside. She was about to prove that at least one of Lucas's fears was justified.

She was going to be her control-freak, ticked-off, stressed-out self for just a few minutes.

She was going to behave badly.

Four

The paralyzing fear that had gripped Lucas at the thought of Carla driving her sports car on Medinos's narrow roads turned to frustration as she stepped inside his suite.

Grimly, he wondered what had happened to the dominance and control with which he had started the evening.

Across boardroom tables, he was aware that his very presence often inspired actual fear. His own people jumped to do his bidding.

Unfortunately, when it came to Carla Ambrosi, concepts like power, control and discipline crashed and burned.

He closed the door behind him. "What do you think you're doing?"

Carla halted by an ebony cabinet that held a selection of bottles, a jug of ice water and a tray of glasses. "I need a drink."

Glass clinked on glass, liquid splashed. His frustration deepened. Carla seldom drank and when she did it had always been in moderation. Tonight he knew she'd had champagne, then wine with dinner. He had kept a watch on her intake, specifically so he could intervene if he thought she was in danger of drinking too much then making a scene. He had been looking for an opportunity to speak to her alone when she had walked out halfway through dessert. Until now he had been certain she wasn't drunk.

He reached her in two long strides and gripped her wrist. "How much have you had?"

Liquid splashed the front of her dress. He jerked his gaze away from the way the wet silk clung to the curve of her breasts.

Her gaze narrowed. A split second later cold liquid cascaded down his chest, soaking through to the skin.

Water, not alcohol.

Time seemed to slow, stop as he stared at her narrowed gaze, delicately molded cheekbones and firm jaw, the rapid pulse at her throat.

The thud of the glass hitting the thick kilim barely registered as she curled her fingers in the lapel of his jacket.

"What do you think you're doing?" His voice was husky, the question automatic as he stared at her face.

"Conducting an experiment."

Her arms slid around his neck; she lifted up onto her toes. Automatically, his head bent. The second his mouth touched hers he knew it was a mistake. Relief shuddered through him as her breasts flattened against his chest and the soft curve of her abdomen cradled his instant arousal.

His hands settled at her waist as he deepened the kiss. The soft, exotic perfume she wore rose up, beguiling him, and the fierce clamp of desire intensified. Two months. As intent as he had been on finishing with Carla, he didn't know how he had stayed away.

No one else did this to him; no one came close. To say he

made love with Carla didn't cover the fierceness of his need or the undisciplined emotion that grabbed at him every time he weakened and allowed himself the "fix" of a small window of time in her bed.

Following the tragedy with Sophie, he had kept his liaisons clear-cut and controlled, as disciplined as his heavy work schedule and workout routines. He had been too shell-shocked to do anything else. Carla was the antithesis of the sophisticated, emotionally secure women he usually chose. Women who didn't demand or do anything flamboyant or off-the-wall.

He dragged his mouth free, shrugged out of his jacket then sank back into the softness of her mouth. He felt her fingers dragging at the buttons of his shirt, the tactile pleasure of her palms sliding over his skin.

Long, drugging minutes passed as he simply kissed her, relearning her touch, her taste. When she moved restlessly against him, he smoothed his hands up over her back, knowing instinctively that if she was going to withdraw, this would be the moment.

Her gaze clashed with his and he logged her assent. It occurred to Lucas that if he had been a true gentleman, he would have eased away, slowed things down. Instead he gave into temptation, cupped her breasts through the flimsy silk of bodice and bra. She arched against him with a small cry. Heat jerked through him when he realized she had climaxed.

Every muscle taut, he swept her into his arms and carried her to the couch. Her arms wound around his neck as she pulled him down with her. At some point his shirt disappeared and Carla shimmied against him, lifting up the few centimeters he needed so he could peel away the flimsy scrap of silk and lace that served as underwear.

He felt her fingers tearing at the fastening of his trousers. In some distant part of his mind the fact that he didn't have a condom registered. A split second later her hands closed around him and he ceased to think.

Desire shivered and burned through Carla as Lucas's hands framed her hips. Still dazed by the unexpected power of her climax, she automatically tilted her hips, allowing him access. Shock reverberated through her when she registered that there was no condom.

She hadn't thought; he hadn't asked. In retrospect she hadn't wanted to ask. She had been drowning in sensation, caught and held by the sudden powerful conviction that if she walked away from Lucas now, everything they had shared, everything they had been to each other would be lost. She would never touch him, kiss him, make love with him again, and that thought was acutely painful.

It was wrong, crazily wrong, on a whole lot of levels. Lucas had broken up with her. He had chosen someone else.

His gaze locked with hers and the steady, focused heat, so utterly familiar—as if she really was the only woman in the world for him—steadied her.

Emotion squeezed her chest as the shattering intensity gripped her again, linking her more intensely with Lucas. She should pull back, disengage. Making love did not compute, and especially not without a condom, but the concept of stopping now was growing progressively more blurred and distant.

She didn't want distance. She loved making love with Lucas. She loved his scent, the satiny texture of skin, the masculine beauty of sleek, hard muscle. The tender way he touched her, kissed her, made love to her was indescribably singular and intimate. She had never made love with another man, and when they were together, for those moments, he was *hers*.

Sharp awareness flickered in his gaze. He muttered something in rapid, husky Medinian, an apology for his loss of control, and a wild sliver of hope made her tense. If Lucas had wanted her badly enough that he hadn't been able to stop long enough to take care of protection, then there had to be a future for them.

With a raw groan he tangled his fingers in her hair, a glint of rueful humor charming her as he bent and softly kissed her. Something small and hurt inside her relaxed. She wound her arms around his neck, holding him tight against her and the hot night shivered and dissolved around them.

For long minutes Carla lay locked beneath Lucas on the couch. She registered the warm internal tingle of lovemaking. It had been two months since they had last been together, and she took a moment to wallow in the sheer pleasure of his heat and scent, the uncomplicated sensuality of his weight pressing her down.

She rubbed her palms down his back and felt his instant response.

Lucas's head lifted up from its resting place on her shoulder. The abrupt wariness in his gaze reflected her own thoughts. They'd had unprotected sex once. Were they really going to repeat the mistake?

A sharp rap at the door completed the moment of separation.

"Wait," Lucas said softly.

She felt the cool flutter as he draped her dress over her thighs. Feeling dazed and guilty, Carla clambered to her feet, snatched up her panties and her bag and found her shoes.

"The bathroom is the second on the left."

Her head jerked up at the husky note in his voice, but Lucas's expression was back to closed, his gaze neutral.

He was already dressed. With his shirt buttoned, his jacket on, he looked smoothly powerful and unruffled, exactly as he had before they had made love. Somewhere inside her the sliver of hope that had flared to life when they had been making love died a sudden death.

Nothing had changed. How many times had she seen him distance himself from her in just that way when he had left her apartment, as if he had already separated himself from her emotionally?

As if what they had shared was already filed firmly in the past and she had no place in his everyday life.

The moment was chilling, a reality check that was long overdue. "Don't worry, I'll find it. I don't want anyone to know I was here, either." Her own voice was husky but steady. Despite the hurt she felt oddly distant and remote.

She stepped into the cool, tiled sanctuary of the bathroom and locked the door. After freshening up she set about fixing her makeup. A sharp rap on the door made her jerk, smearing her mascara.

"When you're ready, I'll take you home."

"Five minutes. And I'll take myself home."

She stared at her reflection, her too pale skin, the curious blankness in her eyes as if, like a turtle retreating into its shell, the hurt inner part of her had already withdrawn. With automatic movements, she cleaned away the smear and reapplied the mascara.

When she stepped out of the bathroom the sitting room was empty. For the first time she noticed the fine antiques and jewel-bright rugs, the art that decorated the walls and which was lit by glowing pools of light.

Lucas stepped in from the terrace, through an elegant set of French doors.

She met his gaze squarely. "Who was at the door?"

"Lilah."

Oh, good. Her life had just officially gone to hell in a handbasket. "Did she see me?"

"Unfortunately."

Lucas's choice of word finally succeeded in dissolving the curious blankness and suddenly she was fiercely angry. "What if I'm pregnant?"

A pulse worked in his jaw. "If you're pregnant, that changes things—we'll talk. Until you have confirmation, we forget this happened."

When Carla woke in the morning, the headache was still nagging, and she was definitely off-color. She stepped into the shower and washed her hair. When she'd soaped herself, she stood beneath the stream of hot water and waited to feel better.

She spread her palm over her flat abdomen, a sense of disorientation gripping her when she considered that she could be pregnant.

A baby.

The thought was as shocking as the fact that she had been weak enough to allow Lucas to make love to her.

If she was pregnant, she decided, there was no way she could terminate. She loved babies, the way they smelled, their downy softness and vulnerability, the gummy smiles—and she would adore her own.

Decision made. If—and it was a big *if*—she was pregnant she would have the child and manage as a single parent. Lucas wouldn't have to be involved. There was no way she would marry him without love, or exist in some kind of twilight state in his life that would allow him discreet access while he married someone else.

Turning off the water, she toweled herself dry, belted on a robe and padded down to breakfast. Her stomach felt vaguely nauseous and she wasn't hungry, but she forced herself to chew one of the sweet Medinian rolls she had enjoyed so much yesterday.

Half an hour later, she checked on Sienna, who was

smothered by attendants, then dressed for the wedding in an exquisite lilac-silk sheath. She sat for the hairdresser, who turned her hair into a glossy confection of curls piled on top of her head, then moved to another room where a cosmetician chatted cheerfully while she did her makeup.

Several hours later, with the wedding formalities finally completed and the dancing under way, she was finally free to leave her seat at the bridal table. Technically, as the maid of honor, her partner for the celebration was Lucas, who was the best man. Mercifully, he was seated to one side of the bride and groom, and she the other, so she had barely seen him all evening.

As she rose from the table and found the strap of her purse, which was looped over the back of her seat, lean brown fingers closed over hers, preventing her from lifting up the bag.

A short, sharp shock ran through her at the pressure. Lucas released his hold on her fingers almost immediately.

He indicated Constantine and Sienna drifting around the dance floor. "I know you probably don't want to dance, but tradition demands that we take the floor next."

She glanced away from the taut planes of his cheekbones and his chiseled jaw, the inky crescents of his lashes. In a morning suit, with its tight waistcoat, he looked even more devastatingly handsome than usual. "And is that what you do?" she said a little bitterly. "Follow tradition?"

Lucas waited patiently for her to acquiesce to the dance. "You know me better than that."

Yes, she did, unfortunately. As wealthy and privileged as Lucas was, he had done a number of unconventional things. One of them was to play professional rugby. Her gaze rested on the faintly battered line of his nose. An automatic tingle of awareness shot through her at the dangerous, sexy edge it added to features that would otherwise have been *GQ* perfect.

His gaze locked on hers and, as suddenly as if a switch had been thrown, the sizzling hum of attraction was intimately, crazily shared.

Her breath came in sharply. Not good.

Aware that they were now under intense scrutiny from guests at a nearby table, including Lilah, Carla placed her hand on Lucas's arm and allowed him to lead her to the dance floor.

Lucas's breath feathered her cheek as he pulled her close. "How likely is it that you are pregnant?"

She stiffened at the sudden hot flood of memory. On cue the music changed, slowing to a sultry waltz. Lucas pulled her into a closer hold. Heat shivered through her as her body automatically responded to his touch. "Not likely."

Since the virus she had caught in Thailand she hadn't had a regular cycle, mostly because, initially, she had lost so much weight. She had regained some of the weight but she hadn't yet had a period. Although she wasn't about to inform Lucas of that fact.

"How soon will you know?"

"I'm not sure. Two weeks, give or take."

"When you find out, one way or the other, I want to be informed, but that shouldn't be a problem. As of next week, I'm Ambrosi's new CEO."

She stumbled, missing a step. Lucas's arm tightened and she found herself briefly pressed against his muscular frame. Jerkily, she straightened, her cheeks burning at the intimate brush of his hips, a stark reminder of their lovemaking last night. "I thought Ben Vitalis was stepping in as CEO."

Lucas's specialty was managing hostile acquisitions. Since her family, embattled by long-term debt, had voluntarily offered The Atraeus Group a majority shareholding of Ambrosi Pearls, the situation was cut-and-dried. Lucas shouldn't have come within a mile of Ambrosi.

Unless he viewed *her* as a problem.

Her chin jerked up as another thought occurred to her. "You told Constantine about us."

His brows jerked together. "No."

Relief flooded her. The thought that Lucas could have revealed their relationship now, when it was over, would have finally succeeded in making her feel cheap and disposable.

She drew in a steadying breath. "When was the decision made?"

"A few weeks ago, when we knew Ambrosi was in trouble."

"It's not necessary for you to come to Sydney. In the unlikely event that there is a baby, I will contact you."

His glance was impatient. "The decision is made."

She drew an impeded breath at the sudden graphic image of herself round and heavy with his child. She didn't think a pregnancy was possible, but clearly Lucas did.

The music wound to a sweeping, romantic halt. There was a smattering of applause. Carla allowed Lucas to complete the formalities by leading her off the dance floor.

The rest of the evening passed in a haze. Carla danced with several men she didn't know, and twice with Alex Panopoulos, an Ambrosi client she'd had extensive dealings with in Sydney. The wealthy owner of a successful chain of high-end retail stores, Alex was a reptile when it came to women. He was also in need of a public relations officer for a new venture and spent the first dance fishing to see if she was available. Halfway through the second dance, Lucas cut in.

His gaze clashed with hers as he spun her into a sweeping turn. "Damn. What are you doing with Panopoulos?"

"Nothing that's any of your business. Why? Do you think

I'm in danger of meeting a man who might actually propose?"

"Alex Panopoulos is a shrewd operator. When he marries, there will be a business connection."

She stared at the clean line of his jaw. "Are you suggesting that all he wants is an affair?"

His grip on her fingers tightened. "I have no idea what Panopoulos wants. All I know is that when it comes to women he doesn't have a very savory reputation."

"I'm surprised you think I need protection."

"Trust me, you don't want to get involved with Panopoulos."

Dragging free of his gaze, she stared at the muscular column of his throat. "Maybe he wanted something from me that has nothing to do with sex? Besides, you're wasting your breath trying to protect me. From now on, who I choose to be with is none of your business."

"It is if you're pregnant."

The flash of possessive heat in his gaze and the tightening of his hold finally succeeded in making her lose her temper. "I might have some say in that."

Five

Lucas leaned against the wall in a dim alcove, arms folded over his chest as he observed the final formality of the wedding, the throwing of the bouquet.

Zane joined him, shifting through the shadows with the fluid ease that was more a by-product of his time spent on the streets of L.A. than of the strict, conventional upbringing he'd received on Medinos. He nodded at Carla, who was part of a cluster of young women gathered on the dance floor. "Not your finest hour. But, if you hadn't rescued her, I was thinking of doing it myself."

"Touch Carla," Lucas said softly, "and you lose your hand."

Zane took a swallow of beer. "Thought so."

Lucas eyed his younger brother with irritation. Four years difference and he felt like Methuselah. "How long have you known?"

"About a year, give or take."

The bouquet arced through the air straight into Carla's hands. Lucas's jaw tightened as she briskly handed it to one of the pretty young flower girls and detached herself from the noisy group. She made a beeline for her table, picked up the lilac clutch that went with her dress, and made her way out of the *castello's* ballroom.

Lucas glanced at Zane. "Do me a favor and look after Lilah for me for the rest of the evening."

Zane's expression registered rare startlement. "Let me get this right, you won't let me near Carla, but with Lilah it's okay?"

Lucas frowned at his turn of phrase, but his attention was focused on the elegant line of Carla's back. "The party's almost over. An hour, max."

"That long."

Impatiently, he studied the now empty hallway. "She'll need a ride back to the villa."

"Not a problem. Aunts at six o'clock." With a jerk of his chin, indicating direction, Zane snagged his beer and made a swift exit.

Pushing away from the wall, Lucas started after Carla, and found himself the recipient of a shrewd glance from his mother and steely speculation from a gaggle of silver-haired great-aunts.

He groaned inwardly, annoyed that he had dropped his guard enough that not only Zane but his mother had become aware of his interest in Carla. The last thing he needed was his mother interfering in his love life.

Seconds later, he traversed the vaulted hallway and stepped outside onto the graveled driveway just as the sound of Constantine and Sienna's departing helicopter cut the air.

The sun was gone, the night thick with stars, but heat still flowed out of the sunbaked soil as he strode toward Carla.

The ambient temperature was still hot enough that he felt uncomfortable in his suit jacket.

A stiff sea breeze was blowing, tugging strands loose from the rich, dark coils piled on top of Carla's head, making her look sexily disheveled. The breeze also plastered her dress against her body, emphasizing just how much weight she had lost.

His frown deepened. A regular gym bunny, Carla had always been fit and toned, with firm but definite curves. The curves were still there but if he didn't miss his guess she had dropped at least a dress size. After the virus she had picked up in Thailand, weight loss was understandable, but she should have regained it by now.

She spun when she heard the crunch of gravel beneath his shoes. A small jolt went through him when he registered the blankness of her gaze.

Carla didn't do sad. She had always been confident, sassy and adept at using her feminine power to the max. For Carla, masculine conquest was as natural as breathing. He had assumed that when their relationship was at an end she would have a lineup of prospective boyfriends eager to fill the gap.

In that moment it hit him forcibly that as similar as Carla was to Sophie with her job and her lifestyle, there were some differences. Sophie had been immature and self-centered, while Carla was fiercely loyal to her sister and her family, to the point of putting her own needs aside so as not to hurt Sienna. Even though that loyalty had clashed with what he had wanted, he had respected it. It also occurred to him that in her own way, Carla had been fiercely loyal to him. She had dated other men, but only ever in a business context for Ambrosi Pearls.

Broodingly, he considered the fact that Carla had been a virgin the first time they had made love, that she had never slept with anyone but him. He realized he had conveniently pushed the knowledge aside because it hadn't fitted the picture of Carla he had wanted to see.

He had been the one who had held back and played it safe, not Carla, and now the sheer intimacy of their situation kept hitting him like a kick to the chest.

He should let her go, but the shattering fact that he could have made her pregnant had changed something vital in his hard drive.

They were linked, at least until he had ascertained whether or not she was carrying his child. Despite his need to end the relationship, he couldn't help but feel relieved about that fact. "The limousines are gone. If you want a lift, I'll drive you."

"That won't be necessary." Carla extracted a cell phone from her clutch. "I'll get a taxi."

"Unless you've prebooked, with all the guests on Medinos for the wedding, you'll have difficulty getting one tonight."

She frowned as she flipped the phone closed and slipped it back in her clutch. "Then I'll ask Constantine."

He jerked his head in the direction of the helicopter, which was rapidly turning into a small dot on the horizon. "Constantine is on honeymoon. I'll take you."

Her glare was pointed. "I don't understand what you're doing out here. Shouldn't you be looking after your new girlfriend?"

"Zane's taking care of Lilah." Before she could argue, he cupped her elbow and steered her in the direction of the *castello's* stable of garages.

She jerked free of his hold. "Why doesn't Zane take me home and you go and take care of Lilah?"

His jaw clamped. "Do you want the lift or not?"

She stared at a point somewhere just left of his shoulder. Enough time passed that his temper began to spiral out of control.

Carla shrugged. "I'll accept a lift because I need one, but please don't touch me again."

"I wasn't trying to 'touch' you."

Her gaze connected with his, shooting blue fire. "I know what you were doing. The same thing you tried to do on the dance floor. Save it for Lilah."

He suppressed the cavemanlike urge to simply pick her up and carry her to the car. "You don't look well. What's wrong with you?"

"Nothing that a good night's sleep won't fix." Her gaze narrowed. "Why don't you say what's really bothering you? That, with all the paparazzi still on the loose, you can't take the risk that I might give them a story? And I think we both know that I could give them quite a story, an exposé of the *real* Lucas—"

Lucas gave in to the caveman urge and picked her up. "Did I mention the paparazzi?"

She thumped his shoulder with her beaded purse. "Let me down!"

Obligingly, he set her down by the passenger door of the Maserati. He jerked the door open. "Get in. If you try to run I'll come after you."

"There has to be a law against this." But she climbed into the sleek leather bucket seat.

"On Medinos?" Despite his temper, Lucas's mouth twitched as he slid behind the wheel and turned the key in the ignition. For the first time in two months he felt oddly content. "Not for an Atraeus."

Carla's tension skyrocketed when, instead of responding to her request and parking out on the street, Lucas drove into the cobbled driveway of the villa. At that point, he insisted on taking the house key from her and unlocked the door. When she attempted to close the door on him, he simply stepped past her and walked into the small, elegant house, switching on lights.

A narky little tension headache throbbing at her temples, Carla made a beeline for the bathroom, filled the glass on the counter with water and took her pills. Refilling the glass, she sat down on the edge of the bath and sipped, waiting to feel better.

A sharp rap on the bathroom door made her temper soar. She had hoped Lucas would take the hint and leave, but apparently he was still in the house. Replacing the glass on the counter, she checked her appearance then unlocked the door and stepped out into the hall.

He was leaning against the wall, arms crossed over his chest. She tried not to notice that, though he was still wearing his jacket, his tie and waistcoat were gone and several buttons of his shirt were undone revealing a mouthwatering slice of bronzed skin. "I'm fine now. You can leave."

She stepped past him and headed for the front door. Her spine tightened as Lucas followed too close behind, and she remembered what had happened the last time they had been alone together.

Note to self, she thought grimly as he peeled off into the sitting room and picked up his tie and waistcoat, *do not allow yourself to be alone with Lucas again.*

Opening the front door, she stood to one side, allowing him plenty of space. "Thank you for the lift."

He paused at the open door, making her aware of his height, the width of his shoulders, the power and vitality that seemed to burn from him. "Maybe you should see a doctor."

"If I need medical help, I'll get it for myself." She glanced pointedly at her wristwatch, resisting the urge to squint because one of the annoying symptoms of the headache now seemed to be that her eyes were ultrasensitive to light.

Not good. Her doctor had warned her that stress could

cause a viral relapse. With her father's funeral, Sienna's wedding and the breakup with Lucas, she was most definitely under stress.

His hand landed on the wall beside her head. Suddenly he was close enough that his heat engulfed her, and his clean, faintly exotic scent filled her nostrils.

Grimly, she resisted the impulse to take the half step needed, wrap her arms around his neck and melt into a goodnight kiss that would very likely turn into something else. "Um, shouldn't you be getting back to Lilah?"

For the briefest of moments he hesitated. His gaze dropped to her mouth and despite the tiredness that pulled at her, she found herself holding her breath, awareness humming through every cell of her being.

He let out a breath. "We can't do this again."

"No." But it had been an effort to say that one little word, and humiliation burned through her that, despite everything, she was still weak enough to want him.

His hand closed into a fist beside her head, then he was gone, the door closing gently behind him.

Carla leaned her forehead against the cool cedar of the door, her face burning.

Darn, darn, darn. Why had she almost given in to him? Like a mindless, trained automaton responding to the merest suggestion that he might kiss her.

After the stern talking-to she had given herself following the episode on the dance floor, she had succeeded in making herself look needy, like a woman who would do anything to get him back into her bed.

The pressure at her temples sharpened. Feeling more unsteady by the second, as if she was coming down with the flu, Carla walked to her bedroom. The acute sensitivity of her eyes was making it difficult to stand being in a lit room. No doubt about it, the virus had taken hold.

Removing her jewelry, she changed into cool cotton drawstring pants and a tank. She pulled on a cotton sweatshirt and cozy slippers against the chill and walked through to the bathroom. After washing and moisturizing her face, she pulled the pins out of her hair, which was an instant relief.

A discreet vibration made her frown. Her cell phone had a musical ring tone, and so did Sienna's. Margaret Ambrosi didn't own a cell, which meant the phone must belong to Lucas.

She padded barefoot into the sitting room in time to see the phone vibrate itself off the coffee table and drop to the carpet. A small pinging sound followed.

Carla picked up the phone. Lucas had missed a call from Lilah; now he had a text message, also from Lilah.

Fingers shaking slightly, she attempted to read the text but was locked out. A message popped up requesting she unlock the phone.

Not a problem, unless Lucas had changed his PIN since the last time they had dated.

Not dated, she corrected, her mood taking another dive. *Slept together.*

The last time he had stayed over at her apartment, before the holiday in Thailand, Lucas had needed to buy a new phone. The PIN he had used had been her birth date. At the time she had been ridiculously happy at his sentimental streak. She had taken it as a definite, positive *sign* that their relationship was progressing in the right direction.

She held her breath as she keyed in the number. The mail menu opened up.

The message was simple and to the point. Lilah was waiting for Lucas to call and would stay up until she heard from him.

The sick feeling in her stomach, the prickling chill she'd felt when he had broken up with her the previous night, came back at her full force. If she'd needed reinforcement of her decision to stay clear of Lucas Atraeus, this was it.

He was involved with someone else. He had *chosen* someone else, and the new woman in his life was waiting for him.

Closing the message, she replaced the phone on the coffee table and walked back to the bathroom. She switched off lights as she went, leaving one lamp burning in the sitting room for her mother when she came home. The relief of semidarkness was immense.

In the space of the past few minutes, she realized, the throbbing in her head had intensified and her skin hurt to touch. She swallowed another headache tablet, washing it down with sips of water. The sound of the doorbell jerked her head up. The sharp movement sent a stab of hot pain through her skull.

Lucas, back for his phone.

Setting the glass down, she walked back out to the hall, which was lit by the glow from the porch light streaming through two frosted sidelight windows. The buzzer sounded again.

"Open up, Carla. All I want is my phone."

That particular request, she decided, was the equivalent of waving a red rag at a bull. "You can have the phone tomorrow."

"I still have the key to this door," he said quietly. "If you don't unlock it, I'll let myself in."

Over her dead body.

"Just a minute." Annoyed with herself for forgetting to reclaim the key, she reached for the chain and tried to engage it. In her haste it slipped from her fingers.

She heard Lucas say something short and sharp. Adrenaline pumped. He knew she was trying to chain the door against him. The metallic scrape of a key being inserted into the lock was preternaturally loud as she grabbed the chain again.

Before she could slot it into place the door swung open, pushing her back a half step. Normally, the half step back wouldn't have fazed her, but with the weird shakiness of the virus she was definitely not her normal, athletic self and had to clutch at the hall table to help with her balance. Something crashed to the floor; glass shattered. She registered that when she had grabbed at the table her shoulder must have brushed against a framed watercolor mounted on the wall.

Lucas frowned. "Don't move."

Ignoring him, she bent down and grasped the edge of the frame.

Lean fingers curled around her upper arms, hauling her upright. "Leave that. You'll cut yourself."

Too late. Curling her thumb in against her palm, she made a fist, hiding a tiny, stinging jab that as far as she was concerned was so small it didn't count as a cut. She blinked at the bright porch light. "I didn't give you permission to come in, and you don't have the right to give me orders."

"You *did* cut yourself." He muttered something in Medinian. She was pretty sure it was a curse word. "Give me the watercolor before you do any more damage."

Her grip on the watercolor firmed, even though his request made sense. If she got blood on the painting it would be ruined. "I don't need your help. Get your phone and go."

"You look terrible."

"Thanks!"

"You're as white as a sheet."

He released her so suddenly she swayed off balance. By the time she recovered he had laid claim to her sore thumb and was probing at the small cut. But she still had the painting. "Neat trick."

His gaze was oddly intent. "There doesn't seem to be any glass in it."

He wrapped a handkerchief around her thumb and closed her fingers around it to apply pressure. "How long have you been sick?"

Her jaw tightened. She was being childish, she knew, but she hated being sick. It literally brought out the worst in her. "I'm not sick. Like I said before, all I need is a good night's sleep, so if you don't mind—"

The brush of his fingers against her temple as he pushed hair away from her face distracted her.

"Does that hurt? Don't answer. I can see that it does."

He leaned close. Arrested by his nearness, she studied the taut line of his jaw, suddenly assaulted by a myriad of sensations—the heat from Lucas's body, the clean scent of his skin, the rasp of his indrawn breath. That was one of the weird things about the virus: it seemed to amplify everything, hearing, scent, emotions, as if protective layers had been peeled away, leaving her senses bare and open.

In a slick move, he took the watercolor while her attention was occupied by the intriguing shape of his cheekbones, which were meltdown material.

A small sound informed her that he had placed the painting on the hall table. Out of nowhere her stomach turned an uncomfortable somersault. "I think I'm going to be sick."

His hand closed around her upper arm, and the heat from his palm burned through the cotton sweatshirt. Then they were moving, glass crunching under the soles of her slippers as he guided her out of the entrance hall into the sitting room. Another turn and they were in the bathroom.

Long minutes later, she rinsed her mouth and washed her face. She had hoped that Lucas would have left, but he was leaning against the hallway wall looking patient and composed and drop-dead gorgeous. In contrast she felt bedraggled and washed-out and as limp as a noodle.

Disgust and a taut, burning humiliation filled her. It was a rerun of Thailand, everything she had never wanted to happen again.

He folded his arms across his chest. "I'm guessing this is a relapse of the virus."

Keeping one hand on the wall for steadiness, she made a beeline for her bedroom. "Apparently. This is the first recurrence I've had." Her head spun and for a split second she thought she might be sick again, although she was fairly certain there was nothing left in her stomach. Two more wavering steps then the blissful darkness of her bedroom enfolded her. "Don't turn on the light. And don't come in here. This is *my* room." And as such it was off-limits to men who didn't love her.

"You should have told me you were still ill."

Her temper flashed, but if it was measured on a color spectrum it would have been a washed-out pink, not the angry red it had been earlier in the evening. She didn't have the energy for anything more and she was fading fast. "I didn't *know* I was still ill."

"That's some temper you've got."

Her teeth would have gritted if she'd had the strength. "Inherited it from my mother." She dragged her coverlet back. "She'll be home soon." The thought filled her with extreme satisfaction. She hadn't been able to kick Lucas's butt out, but Margaret Ambrosi would. Especially if she found him in her little girl's room.

Gingerly she sat on the side of the bed. Now that the stomach issue was over her attention was back on her head, which was pounding. What she needed was another painkiller, because the last one had just been flushed.

Dimly, she registered that despite her express order, Lucas *was* in her room. "I told you not to be here."

He crouched down and eased her slippers off her feet. "Or what? You'll lose that famous temper?"

"That's right." A shiver went through her at the burning heat of his hands on her feet. The chill on her skin made her realize that the next stage of the virus was kicking in. Oh, goody, she thought wearily, Antarctic-cold shivers followed by sweats that rivaled burning desert sands. Exactly how she always wanted to spend a Saturday night.

"I'll take the risk. I survived Thailand, I can survive this."

He pulled her to her feet. Her nose bumped against his shoulder. Automatically, she clutched his lean waist and leaned into his comforting strength. She inhaled, breathing in his scent, and for a crazy moment all she wanted to do was rest there.

A split second later, the sheet peeled back, Lucas eased her into bed and pulled the sheets and coverlet over her.

With a sigh, she allowed her head to sink into the feather pillow. "All I need is another one of the painkillers on the bathroom vanity and some water and I'll be fine." It was surrender, she knew it, but she really did need the pill.

She registered his near silent footfalls as he walked to the bathroom, the hiss of water as he filled the glass, then he was back. His arm came around her shoulders as he propped her up so she could take the pill and drink the water. When she was finished he set the glass down on her bedside table.

She settled back on the pillows. "You know what? You're good at this."

"I had lots of practice in Thailand. Do you need anything else?" His voice was closer now, the timbre low and deliciously gruff.

It was the kind of velvety masculine rumble that, if they had been in bed together, would have invited a snuggling session. Then suddenly she remembered. Lucas was with Lilah now; he no longer wanted her. If he felt anything for her, it had to be pity. A weak, watered-down version of fury roared through her.

She peeled her lids open and peered at Lucas, ready to read him the riot act, then forgot what she was about to say because there was a strange, intent expression on his face. "Nothing. You can leave. Phone's on the coffee table. That was what you came for, wasn't it?"

He was so close she could feel the heat blasting off his body, see his gaze sliding over her features, cataloging her white face and messy hair. For shallow, utterly female reasons she wished that her face was glowing instead of chalky-white and that she had taken the time to brush her hair. Mercifully, the strong painkiller finally kicked in, taking the heat out of the ache in her head and dragging her down into sleep. "I don't want you here."

It was a lie. The virus had made her so weak that she was fast losing the strength to keep up the charade, even to herself.

"I'm staying until I know you'll be all right."

"I would like you to leave. Now." The crisp delivery she intended was spoiled by the fact that the words ran together in a drunken, blurred jumble.

She was certain the soft exhalation she heard had something to do with amusement, which made her even more furious. The mattress shifted as he planted a hand on either side of her head and leaned close. "What are you going to do if I don't? Make me leave?"

For a crazy moment she thought he was actually flirting with her, but that couldn't be. "Don't have to," she mumbled, settling the argument. Her eyelids slid closed. "You've already gone."

Silence settled around her, thick, heavy, as the sedative effect of the pills dragged her down.

"Do you want me back?"

The words jerked her awake, but they had been uttered so quietly she wasn't sure if she had imagined them or if Lucas had actually spoken.

She could see him standing in her bedroom doorway. Maybe she had been dreaming, or worse, hallucinating. "I took codeine, not truth serum."

"It was worth a try."

So he *had* asked the question.

She pushed up on one elbow. The suspicion that he was sneakily trying to interrogate her while she was drowsy from the pills solidified. Although she couldn't fathom why he would be interested in what she really thought and felt now. "I don't know why you're bothering. Thank you for helping me, but please leave now."

He shook his head. "You're…different tonight."

Different? She had been dumped. She had committed the cardinal sin of making love with her ex and could quite possibly be pregnant.

"Not different." Turning over, she punched the pillow and willed herself to go to sleep. "Real."

Six

Ten days later, Carla strolled into the Ambrosi building in Sydney.

When she reached her office, her assistant, Elise, a chirpy blonde with a marketing degree and a formidable memory for names and statistics, was in the process of hanging up the phone. "Lucas wants you in his office. *Now*."

A jolt of fiery irritation instantly evaporated the peace and calm of four days spent recuperating at her mother's house, the other five in the blissful solitude of the Blue Mountains at a friend's holiday home. "Did he say why?"

Elise looked dreamily reflective. "He's male, hot *and* single. Does it matter?"

Nerves taut, Carla continued on to her desk and deliberately took time out to examine the list of messages and calls Elise had compiled in her absence. Keeping her bag hooked over her shoulder, she checked her calendar and noted she had two meetings scheduled.

When she couldn't stall any longer, she strolled to Sienna's old office, frowning at the changes Atraeus money had already made to her family's faltering business. Worn blue carpet had been replaced with a sleek, dove-gray weave. Fresh paint and strategically placed art now graced walls that had once been decorated solely with monochrome prints of Ambrosi jewelry designs.

Feeling oddly out of place in what, from childhood, had been a cozily familiar setting, she greeted work colleagues.

Directing a brittle smile at Sienna's personal assistant, Nina—Lucas's PA now—she stepped into the elegant corner office.

Lucas, broad shouldered and sleekly powerful in a dark suit with a crisp white shirt and red tie, dominated a room that was still manifestly feminine as he stood at the windows, a phone held to one ear.

His gaze locked with hers, he terminated the call. "Close the door behind you and take a seat."

Suddenly glad she had made an extra effort with her appearance, she closed the door. The sharp little red suit, with its short skirt and fitted V-necked jacket, always made her feel attractive and energized. It probably wasn't the best idea for dealing with Lucas, but she hadn't worn it for him. She had a job interview at five with Alex Panopoulos, and she needed to look confident and professional. His upmarket Pan department stores were branching into jewelry manufacture and he had been chasing her all week to come in for an interview.

She hated the idea of leaving Ambrosi Pearls, but she had to be pragmatic about her position. When Constantine had offered the company back to Sienna on her wedding day they had held a family meeting. In essence, they had agreed to honour their debts, so the transfer of the company to The Atraeus Group had gone through as planned. With Sienna's marriage to Constantine binding both families together, combined with Constantine's assurance that he would keep the company intact, it had seemed the most sensible solution.

As a consequence, Carla now owned a block of voting shares. They would assure her of an income for the rest of her life, but they gave her no effective power. Her current personal contract as Ambrosi Pearls's public relations executive was up for renewal directly after Ambrosi's new product launch in a week's time. She didn't anticipate that Lucas would renew it. Her tenure as "The Face of Ambrosi" was just as shaky, but as she provided that service for free to help the company save money, it was no skin off her nose if Lucas no longer wanted her face on the posters.

Annoyance flickered in Lucas's gaze when she didn't immediately sit. He replaced the phone on its base. "I didn't expect you back in so soon."

She lifted a brow. "I felt okay, so there was no point in staying at home."

"I've been trying to reach you all week. Why didn't you return my calls?"

She shrugged. "I was staying with friends and didn't take my phone." She had left the phone at her apartment on purpose. The last thing she had needed was to have a desperately low moment and make the fatal mistake of trying to call or text Lucas.

There was a small charged silence. "How are you?"

"Fine. A couple of days in bed and the symptoms disappeared." She smiled brightly. "If that's all…"

"Not exactly." His gaze rested on her waist, where the jacket cinched in tight. "Are you pregnant?"

Despite her effort at control, heat flooded her cheeks. "I don't know yet. I have a test kit, but it's early to get an accurate reading."

"When will you know?"

She frowned, feeling distinctly uncomfortable with the subject and the way he was regarding her, as if she was a concubine who had somehow escaped the harem and he had ownership rights. "I should know in another couple of days. But whether I'm pregnant or not, it needn't concern you."

Actually, she could find out right that minute if she wanted. The test kit had said a result could be obtained in as early as seven days. She had studied the instructions then chucked the box in the back of one of her drawers. She still felt too raw and hurt to face using the kit and discovering that not only had she lost Lucas, her life was about to take a huge, unplanned turn. In a few days, when she felt ready, she would do the test.

Anger flickered in his gaze. "You would abort the child?"

"No." She felt shocked that he had even jumped to that conclusion. If there was a child, there was no way she would do anything other than keep the baby and smother it with love for the rest of its life. "What I meant is that *if* there is a child, I've decided that you don't have to worry, because you don't need to be involved, or even acknowledge—"

"Any child of mine would be acknowledged."

The whiplash flatness of his voice, as if she had scraped a raw nerve, was even more shocking. Carla sucked in a breath and forced herself to loosen off the soaring tension. She was clearly missing something here. "This is crazy. I don't know why we're discussing something that might never happen. Is that all you wanted to know?"

"No." He propped himself on the edge of the desk. "Have a seat. There's something else we need to discuss."

There were three comfortable client seats; she chose the one farthest away from Lucas. The second she lowered herself into the chair she regretted the decision. Even though he wasn't standing, Lucas still towered over her. "Let me guess—I'm fired in a week's time? I'm surprised it took you so long to get around to—"

"I'm not firing you."

Carla blinked. Constantine had fired Sienna almost immediately, although his reasons had been understandable. Continuing on as CEO of a company in Sydney while he was based in Medinos had not been viable.

His gaze flicked broodingly over the crisp little suit. "Do you always dress like that for work?"

His sudden change of tack threw her even more off balance. She realized that from his vantage point he could see more than the shadowy hint of cleavage that was normally visible in the vee of the jacket. She squashed the urge to drag the lapels together. "Yes. Is there a problem?"

He crossed his arms over his chest. "Nothing that an extra button or a blouse wouldn't fix."

She shot to her feet. "There is nothing wrong with what I'm wearing. Sienna was perfectly happy with my wardrobe."

He straightened, making her even more aware of his height, the breadth of his shoulders, the incomprehensible anger simmering behind midnight-dark eyes.

"Sienna was female."

"What has that got to do with anything?"

"From where I'm standing, quite a lot.

She didn't know what was bothering him. Maybe a major deal had fallen through, or even better, Lilah had dumped him. Whatever it was she would swear that he was behaving proprietorially, but that couldn't be. He had dumped her without ceremony; he had made it clear he didn't want her. To add insult to injury, the tabloids were having a field day reporting his relationship with Lilah.

His gaze dropped once again to the vee of her jacket. "Who are you meeting today?"

Temper soaring at the lightning perusal, the even more pointed innuendo, she reeled off two names.

"Both male," he said curtly.

"Chandler and Howarth are contemporaries of my father! And I resent the implication that I would resort to using sex to make sales for Ambrosi, but if you prefer I could turn up for work in beige. Or, since this conversation is taking a medieval turn, maybe you'd prefer sackcloth and ashes."

His mouth twitched at the corners and despite her spiraling anger she found herself briefly mesmerized by the sudden jolt of charm. Lucas was handsome when he was cool and ruthless, but when he smiled he was drop-dead gorgeous in a completely masculine way that made her go weak at the knees and melt.

"You don't own anything beige."

"How would you know?" she pointed out, glad to get her teeth into something that could generate some self-righteous anger.

She wasn't vengeful, nor did she have a desire to hurt Lucas. It was simply that she was black-and-white in her thinking. They were either together or they weren't, and she couldn't bear the underlying invitation in his eyes, his voice, to be friends now that he had decreed their relationship was over. "As I recall, you were more interested in taking my clothes off than noticing what I was wearing. You had no more interest in my wardrobe than you had in any other aspect of my life."

His brows jerked together. "That's not true. You were the one who decreed we had to live separate lives."

Her hands curled into fists. "Don't say it didn't suit you."

"It did, at the time."

"Ha!" But the moment of triumph was hollow. She just wished she had realized she wasn't built for such a shallow, restricted relationship.

Pointedly, she checked her wristwatch. "I have a meeting in ten minutes. If there's nothing else, I need to go. With the product launch in two days' time, there's a lot to do."

"That's what I wanted to talk to you about. We've made some changes to the arrangements for the launch party. Nina will be heading up the team running the promotion."

Not fired, Carla thought blankly. Sidelined.

She took a deep breath and let it out slowly, but when she spoke her voice was still unacceptably husky. "Some product launch without the most high-profile component, or have you forgotten that I'm 'The Face of Ambrosi'?"

Broodingly, Lucas surveyed Carla's perfect face, exquisite in every detail from exotic eyes to delicate cheekbones and enticing mouth. Add in the outrageously sexy tousle of dark hair trailing down her back and she was spectacularly irresistible.

Ambrosi had cut costs and cashed in on Carla's appeal, but he found himself grimly annoyed every time he noticed one of the posters. "It's hard to miss when your face is plastered all over the front of the building."

And in every one of the perfumed women's magazines he had been forced to flick through since he'd stepped into Sienna Ambrosi's front office.

Triumph glowed briefly in her gaze. "You can't sideline me. I have to be there." She began ticking off all the reasons he couldn't surgically remove her from the campaign.

His frustration levels increased exponentially with every valid reason, from interviews with women's magazines to a promotional stunt she had organized.

"I have to be there—it's a no-brainer. Besides, the costuming has all been completed to my measurements."

He cut her off in midstream. "No."

Carla's eyes narrowed. "Why not?"

Not a subject he was prepared to go live on, he thought, gaze fixed on the sleek fit of her red suit.

Every time he saw one of the posters, he had to fight the irrational urge to rip it down. The idea that Carla would do a promotional show in the transparent, pearl-encrusted creation he had viewed in front of an audience filled with voyeuristic men was the only no-brainer in the equation.

Over his dead body.

He felt as proprietary as he imagined a father would feel keeping his daughter from hormonal teenage boys. Not that his feelings were remotely fatherly. She could threaten and argue all day; it wasn't going to happen.

"You haven't been well, and you could be pregnant," he said flatly. "I'll do the interviews, and I've arranged for a model to take your place for the promotion. Nina is hosting the promotional show. Elise will take care of the styling."

Styling. He gripped the taut muscles at his nape. A week ago he didn't even know what that meant.

"I'm so well I'm jumping out of my skin. I'm here to work. The launch is *my* project."

"Not anymore."

Silence hung heavy in the air. Somewhere in the office a clock ticked; out on the street someone leaned on a car horn. Carla groped for the fire-engine-red bag that matched her suit.

Lucas's stomach clenched when he saw tears glittering on her lashes. Ah, damn... He resisted the sudden off-the-wall urge to coax her close and offer comfort. He had expected opposition—a fight—but he hadn't been prepared for this level of emotion. Somewhere in the raft of detail involved with taking over Ambrosi and figuring out how to handle Carla, he had forgotten how passionately intense and protective she was about her family and the business. Although how he could forget a detail that had seen *him* sidelined in Carla's life, he didn't know. "Carla—"

"Don't." She turned on her heel.

Jaw clenched against the need to comfort her and soothe away the hurt, he reached the door first. His hand landed on the cream-and–gilt-detailed panel of the door, preventing her from opening it. "Just one more thing. My mother and Zane fly in tomorrow. I've organized a press conference to promote The Atraeus Group's takeover of Ambrosi and the product launch, then a private lunch. As a family member and PR executive your presence is required at both."

She stared blankly ahead. "Will Lilah be there?"

"Yes."

Lucas had to restrain himself from going after Carla as she strode out of his office. His jaw tightened as he noted the outrageously sexy red heels and the enticing sway of her hips as she walked. The fact that he had lost his temper was disturbing, but ten days kicking his heels while she had disappeared off the radar had set him on edge. The second he had seen her in the red suit he had lost it. He had been certain she wasn't wearing anything but a bra under the tight little jacket, and he had been right.

Closing the door, he prowled back to the window and held aside the silky curtains that draped the window, feeling like a voyeur himself as he watched Carla stroll out onto the street and climb into the sports car that was waiting for her.

He had questioned her assistant extensively about her meetings, then, dissatisfied with her answers, had looked both Chandler and Howarth up on the internet.

Elise had been correct in her summation. Both men were old enough to be her father. Unfortunately, that didn't seem to cut any ice with him. They were men, period.

At a point in time when he should have been reinforcing

the end of their relationship by keeping his distance, he had never felt more possessive or jealous.

Instead of moving to Sydney, he should have stepped back and simply kept in touch with Carla. If she was pregnant, whether she told him or not, he would soon have known. Instead he had grabbed at the excuse to be close to her.

The fact that he had lost control to the extent that he had made love to Carla after they had broken up, *without protection,* still had the power to stun him.

Worse, he found the idea that they could have made a baby together unbearably sexy and appealing.

Maybe it was a kickback to his grief and loss over Sophie, but a part of him actually hoped Carla was pregnant.

He dropped the curtain as the taxi merged into traffic. Broodingly, he reflected that when it came to Carla Ambrosi, he found himself thinking in medieval absolutes.

For two years one absolute had dominated: regardless of how risky or illogical the liaison was, he had wanted Carla Ambrosi.

Despite breaking up and replacing her with a new girlfriend—a woman he had not been able to bring himself to either touch or kiss—nothing had changed.

Seven

Carla checked the time on the digital clock in her small sports car. She had ten minutes to reach Alex Panopoulos's office and rush hour was in full swing, the traffic already jammed.

On edge and impatient, Carla used every shortcut she knew, but even so she was running late when she reached the dim underground garage.

Late for an interview that was becoming increasingly important, she grabbed her handbag and portfolio and exited the car.

Her heels tapped on concrete as she strode to the elevator, just as a sleek dark car cruised into a nearby space. The tinted driver's side window was down, giving her a shadowy glimpse of the driver. The car reminded her of the vehicle Lucas's security detail used when he was in town.

Frowning, she stepped into the elevator and keyed in the PIN she had been given. She punched the floor number, then wished she hadn't as the doors slid shut, nixing her view of the driver before he could climb out of the car. Maybe she was paranoid, or simply too focused on Lucas, but for a split second she had entertained the crazy thought that the driver could be Lucas.

She kept an eye on the floor numbers as they lit up. She caught her reflection in the polished steel doors. The scene with Lucas accusing her of dressing to entice replayed in her mind.

Hurt spiraled through her that he clearly had such a bad opinion of her and was so keen to get rid of her that he had replaced her both personally and professionally. She wondered if he intended to escort Lilah to the event, then grimly decided that of course he would.

As a publicity stunt, the move couldn't be faulted. The media would love Lilah fronting for Ambrosi and the further evidence of her close relationship with Lucas. Ambrosi couldn't ask for a better launch gimmick…except maybe an engagement announcement at the launch party.

Her chest squeezed tight on a pang of misery. Suddenly, that didn't seem as ludicrous or far-fetched as it should, given that Lucas and Lilah had only been publicly dating for a couple of weeks. Lucas was legendary for his ruthless efficiency, his unequivocal decisions. If he had decided Lilah was the one, why wait?

The elevator doors opened onto a broad carpeted corridor. Discreetly suited executives, briefcases in hand, obviously leaving for the day, stepped into the elevator as she stepped out.

The receptionist showed her into Alex's office.

Twenty minutes later, the interview over, Carla stepped out of the lift and strode to her car. She had been offered the job of PR executive for Pan Jewelry, but she had turned it down. Five minutes into the interview she had realized that

Alex hadn't wanted her expertise; he had wanted to utilize her connection with the Atraeus family. Apparently, he could double his profit base in two years if they allowed Pan to trade in the luxury Atraeus Resorts.

She had been prepared to withstand his smooth charm, possibly even reject an attempt at seduction. She had done that before, on more than one occasion. Alex had made it clear he was prepared to deal generously with her in terms of position and salary, including a free apartment, if she came to him.

Stomach churning at the sexual strings that were clearly attached to his offer, and because she had missed lunch, Carla tossed her portfolio and purse on the backseat of her car. Flipping the glove box open, she found the box of cookies she kept there for just such an emergency. Part of the reason she had ended up with an ulcer was that she had a high-acid system. She had to be careful of what she ate, and of not eating at all. Stress coupled with an empty stomach was a definite no-no. Popping a chunk of the cookie in her mouth, she drove out of the parking garage.

The car she had thought could possibly belong to Lucas's security guy was no longer in its space, but, as she took the ramp up onto the sunlit street, the distinctive dark sedan nosed in behind her.

Spine tingling with a combination of renewed anger and the flighty, unreasoning panic of knowing someone was following her—no matter how benign the reason—she sped up. The car stayed with her, confirming in her mind that it *was* one of Lucas's men snooping on her.

Still fuming at his high-handed behavior, she pulled into her apartment building. When the sedan slid past the entrance and kept on going, she reversed out and made a beeline for Lucas's inner-city apartment.

Twenty minutes later, after running the gauntlet of a concierge and one of Lucas's security detail, she pressed the buzzer on Lucas's penthouse door.

It swung open almost immediately. Lucas was still dressed in the dark pants and white shirt he had worn to the office that morning, although minus the tie and with the shirt hanging open to reveal a mouthwatering slice of taut and tanned torso. He leaned one shoulder against the door-jamb, unsubtly blocking her from barging into his apartment.

"Tell me that wasn't you following me."

"It wasn't me following you. It was Tiberio."

"In that case, do you really want to have this discussion in the hallway, where anyone can overhear?"

Cool amusement tugged at his mouth. "I rent the entire floor. The other three apartments are all occupied by my people."

"Let me rephrase that, then. Do you really want to have this discussion where your employees can overhear what I'm about to say?"

His jaw tightened, but he stepped back, leaving her just enough room to march past him. She was in the hallway, strolling across rug-strewn wooden floors into an expansive, airy sitting room before she had time to consider the unsettling fact that Lucas might not be alone. With his shirt hanging open and his sleeves unbuttoned it was highly likely he had company.

Her stomach churned at the thought. She'd had plenty of time on the drive over to consider that Lilah could be here.

She breathed a sigh of relief when she registered that the sitting room, at least, was unoccupied, although that didn't rule out the bedrooms. Until that moment she hadn't known just how much she dreaded seeing Lilah in Lucas's home, occupying the position in his life that until a few days ago she had foolishly assumed was hers.

Fingers tightening on her purse, she surveyed the sitting room with its eclectic mix of artwork and sculpture. Some she knew well; at least two she had never seen. "Nice paintings."

But then that had been one of the things that had attracted her to Lucas. He wasn't stuffy with either his thinking or his enjoyment of art.

As her gaze was drawn from one new painting to the next, absorbing the nuances of line, form and color, her stomach tensed. "A new artist?"

"You know me." His gaze was faintly mocking as he walked through an open-plan dining area to a modern kitchen and opened the fridge. "I'm always on the lookout for new talent."

It occurred to her that the artist could be Lilah, who painted in her spare time, and jealousy gripped her. Before she could stop herself she had stepped closer to the nearest of the new paintings, so she could study the signature. S. H. Crew, not L. Cole.

Her knees felt a little shaky as she moved on to the next painting, also by S. H. Crew. For some odd reason, the thought that Lilah might appeal to Lucas on a creative, spiritual level was suddenly more sharply hurtful than her physical presence would have been.

Lucas loomed over her, the warm scent of his skin, the faint undernote of sandalwood, making her pulse race. "Is it safe to give you this?"

"Not really." Jaw clenching against an instant flashback of the scene on Medinos when she had dashed water over Lucas, and the lovemaking that had followed, she took the glass of ice water. She strolled the length of the sitting room and drifted into a broad hall that served as a gallery. She sipped water and pretended to be interested in the paintings that flowed along a curving cream wall that just happened to lead to the master bedroom. "So why did you have me followed?"

He strolled past her and stood, arms folded over his chest, blocking her view of his bedroom. "I wanted to see what you were up to. Tell me," he said grimly, "what did Panopoulos offer you?"

She blinked at the mention of Panopoulos's name, but it went in one ear and out the other. She was consumed with suspicion because Lucas clearly did not want her to see into his bedroom, and the notion that Lilah was there, maybe even in his bed, was suddenly overwhelming.

Setting the water down on a narrow hall table she marched past him. Lucas's hand curled around her arm as she stepped through the door, swinging her around to face him, but not before she had ascertained that his bedroom was empty. And something else that made her heart slam hard against the wall of her chest.

What he hadn't wanted her to see. A silk robe she had left at his apartment by mistake the last time she had been here almost three months ago, and which was exactly where she had left it, draped over the back of a chair. The aquamarine silk was wildly exotic, sexy and utterly feminine. No woman would have missed its presence or significance and allowed it to remain. The robe was absolute proof that Lilah had never been in Lucas's bedroom.

Her heart beat a queer, rapid tattoo in her chest. "You haven't slept with her yet."

Lucas let her go, his gaze glittering with displeasure. "Maybe I was in the process of getting rid of your things before I invited her over."

Anger flaring, she backed up a half step. The cool solidity of the door frame stopped her dead. "I'm here now, you can hand it to me personally."

"Is that a command, or are you going to ask me nicely?"

Wary of the banked heat in Lucas's gaze, which was clearly at odds with the coolness of his tone, she controlled her temper with difficulty. "I just did ask you nicely."

"I'm willing to bet you were nicer to Alex Panopoulos when you walked into his office in that suit. Did you finally agree to sleep with him?"

"*Sleep* with him?" The words came out as an incredulous yelp. She couldn't help it, she was so utterly distracted by the fact that Lucas thought she could be even remotely interested in Alex Panopoulos, a man she barely tolerated for the sake of business. "Well, I haven't jumped into his bed, yet. Does that make you feel better about me?"

Hot anger simmered through her, doubly compounded by the humiliating fact that Panopoulos *had* wanted to sleep with her.

With a suddenness that shocked her, Lucas leaned forward and kissed her. The sensual shock of the kiss, even though she had half expected it and had goaded him into it, sent a wave of heat through Carla. Until that moment, she hadn't understood how much she had wanted to provoke him, how angry she was at his defection. She was also hurt that he still didn't know who she was after more than two years, and evidently didn't have any interest in knowing, when she was deeply, painfully in love with him.

She blinked, dazed. At some point, she realized, probably that first time they had met, something had happened. After years of dating men and knowing they weren't right, she had taken one look at Lucas and chosen him.

That was why she had broken almost every personal rule she'd had and slept with Lucas in the first place, then continued with the relationship when she knew any association with him would hurt her family. If she had been sensible and controlled she would have stepped back and waited. After all, if a relationship had legs it should stand the test of a little time. But she hadn't been able to wait. She had wanted him, needed him, right then, the same way she needed him now.

Two years. She blinked at the immensity of her self-deception. She had buried the in-love thing behind the pretense that theirs was a modern relationship between two overcommitted people with the added burden of some crazy family pressures. Anything to bury the fact that the sporadic interludes with Lucas in no way satisfied her need to be loved.

Her arms closed convulsively around his neck. She shouldn't be kissing him now, not when she wanted so much more, but in that moment she ceased to care.

"What's wrong?" Lucas pulled back, his gaze suddenly heart-stoppingly soft. "Am I hurting you?"

"No." *Yes.* Her hands tangled in the thick black silk of his hair and dragged his mouth back to hers. "Just kiss me."

Long minutes later they made it to the bed. She dragged his shirt off his shoulders and tossed it aside. Her palms slid across his sleek, heavy shoulders and muscled chest. Giddy pleasure spun through her as he removed her clothing, piece by piece, and she, in turn, removed his.

Time seemed to slow, then stop as she fitted herself against him and clasped his head, pulling his mouth to hers, needing him closer, needing him with her. Late-afternoon sun slanted through the shutters, tiger striping his shoulders as his gaze linked with hers and she suddenly knew why making love with Lucas had always been so special, so important. For those few minutes when they were truly joined it was as if he unlocked a part of himself that normally she could never quite reach, and he was wholly hers. In those few moments she could believe that he did love her.

Cool air swirled around naked skin as he sheathed himself. Relief shivered through her as they flowed together. She was utterly absorbed by the feel of him inside her, his touch and taste, the slow, thorough way he made love to her, as if he knew her intimately, as if they did belong together.

Aside from those few minutes on Medinos it had been long months since they had last made love, and she had missed him, missed this. As crazy as it seemed, despite everything that had gone wrong, everything that was still wrong, this part was right.

His head dipped, she felt the softness of his lips against her neck. Her stomach clenched, the slowly building tension suddenly unbearable as she tightened around him. She felt his raw shudder. In that moment her own climax shimmered through her with an intense pleasure that made tears burn behind her lids, and the room spun away.

Long minutes later the buzzer at the front door jerked her out of the sleepy doze she had fallen into. With smooth, fluid movements, Lucas rolled out of bed, snagged his clothes off the floor and walked through to the adjoining bathroom. Seconds later, he reappeared, fastening dark trousers around narrow hips as he strolled to the door.

Carla didn't wait to see who it was. Snatching up her clothes, including her bra, which had ended up hooked over a bedside lamp, she hurried into the bathroom to freshen up and change. Her clothes were crumpled and her hair was a tumbled mass, but she couldn't worry about that. Her priority was to leave as quickly as possible.

Slipping into her shoes, she searched and found her bag on the floor just outside the bedroom door. She must have dropped it when Lucas had kissed her there. Her cheeks burned with embarrassment as she marched through the sitting room where Lucas was talking in low, rapid Medinian to two of his security personnel.

Lucas said her name. She ignored him and the curious looks of the men, in favor of sliding through the open door and making a dash for the elevator.

Relief eased some of her tension when she saw that the doors were open. Jogging inside, she jabbed the ground floor button as Lucas appeared in the corridor.

"Wait," he said curtly.

The doors closed an instant before he reached the elevator. Heart pounding, Carla examined her reflection in the mirrored rear wall and spent the few seconds repairing her smudged mascara. She winced at her swollen lips and the pink mark on her neck where Lucas's stubble must have grazed her. She looked as if she had just rolled out of bed.

The elevator stopped with a faint jolt. Shoving her mascara back in her bag, Carla strolled quickly through the foyer, ignoring the concierge, who stared at her with a fascinated expression.

She almost stopped dead when she saw Lilah sitting in a chair, flipping through a magazine, obviously waiting. Pretending she hadn't noticed her, Carla quickened her step. Now the two security staff talking with Lucas in hushed, rapid Medinian made sense. Lilah had wanted to go up to Lucas's apartment, but they had known Carla was there.

Mortified, she dimly registered Lilah's white face, the shock in her eyes, as she pushed the foyer doors wide. The sound of traffic hit her like a blow. The sun, now low on the horizon, shone directly in her eyes, dazzling her, a good excuse for the tears stinging her eyes. Her throat tightened as she started down the front steps.

As she stepped onto the sidewalk a hand curved around her arm, stopping her in her tracks.

Her heart did a queer leap in her chest as she spun. "Lucas."

Eight

Carla wrenched free. Lucas was still minus his shirt, his hair sexily tangled. If she looked rumpled, he definitely looked like he had just rolled out of the love nest. "How did you get down so fast?"

"There's a second, private lift."

Her fingers tightened on the strap of her bag. "More to the point, why did you bother?"

His gaze narrowed. "I won't glorify that with an answer. What did you think you were doing running out like that?"

Now that the initial shock of Lucas chasing after her was over, she was desperate to be gone. She needed to be alone so she could stamp out the crazy notion that kept sliding into her mind that there was still a chance for them. She had to get it through her skull that there was no hope. She was the one who got lost in useless emotion, while Lucas remained coolly elusive.

Her gaze flashed. "We were finished, weren't we?" *In*

more ways than one. "Or was there something else you wanted?"

Heat burned along his cheekbones. "You know I never viewed you that way."

"How, then?"

He said something low and taut in Medinian that she was pretty sure was a swear word or phrase of some kind. Not for the first time it occurred to her that for her own peace of mind she really should learn some of that language.

His palm curved around the base of her neck, his fingers tangling in her hair. A split second later his mouth closed over hers.

A series of flashes, the slick, motorized clicking of a high-speed camera jerked them apart. A reporter with an expensive-looking camera had just emerged from a parked car.

A shudder of horror swept Carla. When the press recognized her they would put one and one together and make seven. Before she arrived back at her apartment they would have her entangled in a second-time-around affair with Lucas. By morning they would have her cast off and pregnant or, more probably, since Lucas was involved with Lilah, caught up in some trashy love triangle.

Most of it, unfortunately, was embarrassingly true.

A strangled sound jerked her head around. Bare meters away, directly behind Lucas, Lilah was caught in an awkward freeze-frame.

Carla's stomach lurched as if she'd just stepped into a high-speed elevator on its way down. That was a definite "go" on the love triangle.

Lilah spun on her heel and walked quickly away.

With a final, manic series of clicks the reporter slid back into the car from which he had emerged. With a high-pitched whine reminiscent of a kitchen appliance the tiny hatchback sped away.

Lucas swore softly, this time in English, and released his grip on her nape. His gaze was weary. "Did you know he was out here?"

Her temper soared at what she could only view as an accusation. She gestured at her crumpled clothing and hair, the smeared makeup. "Do I look like I'm ready to be photographed by some sleazy tabloid reporter?"

Lucas's brows jerked together. "You did it once before."

A tide of heat swept her at his reference to her admittedly outrageous behavior in making their first breakup public and the resulting scandal that had followed. "You deserved that for the way you treated me."

"I apologized."

He had apologized. And she had forgiven him, then continued to sleep with him. There was a pattern there, somewhere.

His head jerked around as he spotted Lilah climbing into a small sedan. Slipping a cell phone out of his pants pocket, he punched in a number.

Carla blinked at his sudden change of focus. Feeling oddly deflated and emptied of emotion, she rummaged in her purse to find her car keys. "Before you ask the question, the reporter didn't follow me. Why would he? I'm not your girlfriend."

Lucas frowned and gave up on the call, which clearly wasn't being picked up.

He was no doubt calling Lilah, trying to soothe her hurt and explain away his mistake. Despite the fact that Carla knew she was the one in the wrong for sleeping with Lucas, she found she couldn't bear the thought of Lucas trivializing what they had just shared.

He had the nerve to try the phone number again.

A red mist swam before her eyes. Before she even registered what she was about to do, her hand shot out, closed around the phone and she flung it as hard as she could onto the road. It bounced and flew into several pieces. A split second later a truck ran over the main body of the phone, smashing it flat.

There was a moment of silence.

Lucas's expression was curiously devoid of emotion. "That was an expensive phone."

"So sue me, but I find it insulting and objectionable that the man I've just slept with should phone another woman in my presence. You could have at least waited until I had left."

His gaze narrowed. "My apologies for accusing you of calling the press in. I forgot about Lilah."

"Something you seem to be doing a lot lately. I don't know what you're doing out here with me when you should be concentrating on getting back with her."

A swirling breeze started up, making her feel chilled. She rubbed at the gooseflesh on her arms, suddenly in urgent need of a hot bath and an early night. Technically, she was still recovering from the viral relapse and under doctor's orders to take it easy, not that she would tell Lucas that. She was supposed to take an afternoon nap if she could fit it in. Ha!

She started toward her car. Lucas stepped in front of her, blocking her path.

She stared at his sleek, bare shoulders and muscled chest, the dark line of hair that arrowed down to the waistband of his pants. She was tired, and her body still ached and throbbed in places from what they had done in his penthouse apartment. What they had done was *wrong,* but that didn't stop the automatic hum of desire.

"I have no plans on 'getting back' with Lilah. Do you intend to sleep with Panopoulos?"

She went still inside at the first part of that sentence, although she felt no sense of surprise that Lucas was breaking up with Lilah. If he could gravitate back to her so easily then clearly there wasn't much holding them together. Then a second thunderbolt hit her.

Lucas was jealous.

Make that *very* jealous. She didn't know why she hadn't seen it before, but the knowledge demystified his overbearing reaction to her job interview with Alex Panopoulos. It also cast a new light on the dictatorial way he had decided that she would no longer be "The Face" or act in the promotional play she had planned to stage as part of Ambrosi's product launch. She had thought he was downgrading her both personally and professionally because he didn't want her, but the opposite was true.

A glow of purely feminine pleasure soothed over the hurt he had inflicted by demoting her. The launch was *her* baby. She had meticulously planned every detail, always shooting for perfection, and she needed to be there to make sure everything went smoothly. She still didn't like what he had done, but she understood his reasoning now and, because it involved his emotions for her, she would allow him to get away with being so high-handed.

Her chin came up at the question about Alex Panopoulos, although it no longer had any sting. "You're not my boyfriend," she said flatly. "You have no right to ask that question."

Maybe not. But that situation was about to change.

Lucas's jaw locked as he controlled the surge of cold fury at the thought of Carla and Panopoulos together. When he had asked her before she had said she hadn't slept with him, and he believed her, but he knew Alex Panopoulos. He was wealthy and spoiled and used to having what he wanted. If he wanted Carla, he wouldn't give up.

His hands curled into fists at the almost overwhelming urge to simply pick Carla up and carry her back up to his apartment and his bed. Instead, he forced himself to still-ness as Carla climbed behind the wheel of her sports car and shot away from the curb.

He was finished with caveman tactics. Finesse was now required.

He examined his options as he took the stairs into his apartment building and strode through the foyer. They were not black-and-white, exactly, but close.

He stepped into the elevator, which Tiberio was holding for him. It was a fact that ever since he had first seen Carla he hadn't been able to keep his hands off her. His attempt to create distance and sever their relationship had backfired. Instead of killing his desire, distance had only served to in-crease it to the point that the very thing he had been trying to avoid happened: he lost control.

He could deny the story the tabloids would print and which would no doubt hit the stands by morning, or he could allow the story to stand. If he took the second option, Car-la's name would be dragged through the mud. He would not allow that to happen.

Until that afternoon, he had been certain about the one thing he didn't want: a forced marriage to Carla Ambrosi.

But that had been before she had waved Alex Panopou-los in his face.

The elevator door slid open. Jaw tight, Lucas strode to his apartment and waited for Tiberio to swipe the key card.

He walked through to his bedroom, every muscle lock-ing tight as he studied the rumpled bed. He picked up the sexy, exotic silk wrap, his fingers closing on the silk. Her delicate feminine scent still clung to the silk, the same scent that currently permeated the very air of his room and would now be in his bed.

If she had wanted to force his hand, he reflected, she could have done it at the beginning, when the media had published the story about the first night they had spent together. Instead, she had walked away from him. He was the one who'd had to do the running.

He had gotten her back, but only after weeks of effort. His fingers tightened on the silk. It was an uncomfortable fact that he wanted Carla more now than he had in the beginning. With each encounter, instead of weakening, his need had intensified.

Now Panopoulos had entered the picture.

Alex was a clever man who had leveraged a modest fortune into an impressive retail empire. Lucas was aware that he wouldn't miss the opportunity to enhance his bid to place his stores in Atraeus resorts by marrying close to his family.

Lucas reached for his cell phone, and remembered that Carla had destroyed it. He shook his head at the irrational urge to grin. The destruction of personal property, especially his, shouldn't be viewed as sexy.

He found the landline then, irritated because his directory had been on his dead cell and he had to ring his PA on Medinos to find the unlisted number. Frustrating minutes later, he made the call. Panopoulos picked up almost immediately.

Lucas's message was succinct and direct.

If Panopoulos offered Carla any kind of position within his company, or laid so much as a finger on her, he would lose any chance at a business alliance with The Atraeus Group. Lucas would also see to it personally that a lucrative business deal Panopoulos was currently negotiating with a European firm The Atraeus Group had a stake in, deVries, would be withdrawn.

Panopoulos's voice was clipped. "Are you warning me off because Constantine is now married to Carla's sister?"

"No." Lucas made no effort to temper the cold flatness of his reply. "Because Carla Ambrosi is mine."

The instant he said the words satisfaction curled through him. Decision made.

Carla was his. Exclusively his.

He was over making excuses to be with her. He wanted her. And he would do what he had to to make sure that not Panopoulos or any other man went near her again.

Terminating the call, Lucas propped the phone back on its rest.

Panopoulos was smart; he would back off. Now all Lucas had to do was talk to Lilah, then deal with the press and Carla.

Carla wouldn't like his ultimatum, but she would accept it. The damage had been done in the instant the reporter had snapped them on the street.

The following morning, after a mostly sleepless night, Carla dressed for the scheduled press conference and luncheon with care. Bearing in mind the elegance of the restaurant Lucas had booked, she chose a pale blue dress that looked spectacular against her skin and hair. It was also subtly sexy in the way it skimmed her curves and revealed a hint of cleavage. High, strappy blue heels made her legs look great, and a classy little jacket in powder-blue finished off the outfit.

Normally she would dress in a more low-key way for a press conference, but any kind of meeting with Lucas today called for a special effort. The heels were a tad high, but that wasn't a problem; she had learned to balance on four-inch stilettos from an early age. She figured that by now that particular ability was imprinted in her DNA.

She decided to leave her hair loose, but took extra care with her makeup in an effort to hide the faint shadows under her eyes.

Minutes later, after sipping her way through a cup of coffee, she stepped out of her apartment. As she locked the door, she noticed a familiar sleek sedan parked across the entrance to her driveway, blocking her in. Her tiredness evaporated on a surge of displeasure.

As she marched toward the car she could make out the shadowy outline of a man behind darkly tinted windows. It would be one of Lucas's security team, probably the guy who had tailed her to her interview with Alex Panopoulos.

Temper escalating, she bent down and tapped on the passenger-side window. Tinted glass slid down with an expensive hum. Glittering dark eyes locked with hers and a short, sharp jab of adrenaline shot through her. Lucas.

Dressed in a gray suit with a metallic sheen and a black T-shirt, his hair still damp from his shower, Lucas looked broodingly attractive. His hair was rumpled as if he'd run his fingers through it. He looked edgy and irritable, the shadow on his jaw signaling that he hadn't had time to shave.

The irritating awareness that still dogged her despite her repeated efforts to reprogram her mind kicked in, making her belly clench and her jaw set even tighter. "What are you doing here?"

"Keeping the press off." Lucas jerked his head in the direction of a blue hatchback parked on the opposite side of the street.

With an unpleasant start, Carla recognized the reporter who had snapped them outside Lucas's apartment the previous evening. "He wouldn't be here if he wasn't following you."

"He arrived before I did."

Her stomach sank. That meant the press would be going

all out with whatever story they could leverage out of that kiss. "Even more reason for you not to be here."

He leaned over and opened the passenger door. "Get in."

Carla gauged the time it would take to dash to her small garage, open the door and back her convertible out. With the reporter just a few fast steps away it would be no contest.

The flash and whir of the camera sent a second shot of adrenaline zinging through her veins as she slid into the passenger seat and slammed the door. The thunk of the locks engaging coincided with the throaty roar of the engine as the vehicle shot away from the curb. Seconds later, they were on the motorway heading into town and forced to an agonizing crawl by rush-hour traffic.

Carla relaxed her death grip on her purse, strapped on her seat belt and checked the rearview mirror. Anything but acknowledge the fact that she was once more within touching distance of Lucas Atraeus.

And riding in his car.

Although this wasn't his personal car. His taste usually ran to something a little more muscular and a lot faster, like the Maserati, but the intimacy still set her on edge and recalled one too many memories she would rather forget.

The first time they had made love had been in a car.

Two years ago he had given her a lift home from a dinner at a restaurant, a family meet-and-greet following Constantine and Sienna's first engagement.

Accepting a lift with Lucas, when she had expected to be delivered home the same way she had arrived, via hired limousine service, had seemed safe despite his bad-boy reputation with the tabloids. Plus there was the fact that recently he had been photographed on two separate occasions, each time with a different gorgeous girl.

Despite telling herself that he was clearly not on the hunt, when she slid into his car, she had felt a deliciously edgy kind of thrill. Lucas was gorgeous in a dangerous, masculine way, so she was more than a little flattered to be singled out for his attention.

It had taken a good half hour to reach her apartment during which time Lucas had played cruising music and asked her about her family and whether or not she was dating.

When they'd reached her place it was pitch-dark. Instead of parking out on the street, Lucas had driven right up to her garage door and parked beneath the shelter of a large shade tree. An oak overhung the driveway and blocked the neighbor's view on one side. Her security lights had flicked on as Lucas turned off the engine, although they remained encapsulated in darkness since the garage blocked the light from reaching the car.

With the music gone, the silence took on a heavy intensity, and her stomach had tightened on a kick of nerves because she knew in that moment that despite her frantic reasoning to the contrary, he *did* want to kiss her. If Lucas was just dropping her home, he wouldn't have driven right into her driveway, and so far up it that the car was partially concealed.

He had barely touched her all night, although she had been aware that he had been watching her and, admittedly, she had played to her audience.

But all of the time she had flirted and played she had been on edge in a feminine way, her nerves tingling. She was used to being pursued, that went with the fashion industry and the PR job. But Lucas was in a whole different league and she hadn't made up her mind that she wanted him to catch her.

She had turned her head, bracing herself for the jolt of eye contact, and his mouth caught hers, his tongue siding right in. A burning shaft of heat shot straight to her loins and she went limp.

Long seconds later, he had released her mouth. She gulped in air and then his mouth closed on hers again and she was sinking, drowning. Her arms closed convulsively around his neck, her fingers tangling in his hair, which was thick and silky and just long enough to play with. Not a good idea, since playing with Lucas Atraeus was the dating equivalent of stroking a big hunting cat, but the second he had touched her, her normal rules had evaporated.

She'd felt the zipper of her silk sheath being eased down her spine, the hot shock of his fingers against the bare skin of her back.

He'd muttered something in Medinian, too thick and rapid for her to catch, and lifted his head, jaw taut. "Do you want this?"

She realized he was holding on to control by a thread. The realization of his vulnerability was subtly shocking.

From the first her connection with Lucas had been powerful. Cliché or not, she had literally glanced across the restaurant and been instantly riveted.

Head and shoulders above most of the occupants of the room, all three Atraeus brothers had been compelling, but it had been Lucas's faintly battered profile that had drawn her.

She had let out a shuddering breath, abruptly aware of what he was asking. Not just a kiss. Somehow they had already stepped way beyond a kiss.

He'd bent his head as if he couldn't bear not to touch her. His lips feathered her throat, sending hot rills of sensation chasing across her skin, and abruptly something slotted into place in her mind.

She had been twenty-four, and a virgin, not because she had been consciously celibate but for the simple reason that she had never met anyone with whom she wanted to be that intimate. No matter how much she liked a date, if they couldn't knock her sideways emotionally, she refused to allow anything more than a good-night kiss.

Making love with Lucas Atraeus hadn't made sense for

a whole list of logical reasons. She barely knew him, and so there was no way she could be in love, but instead of recoiling, she'd found herself irresistibly compelled to throw away her rule book. On an instinctive level, with every touch, every kiss, Lucas Atraeus felt utterly right. "Yes."

A car horn blasted, shattering the recall, jerking Carla's gaze back to the road.

"What's wrong?"

Lucas's deep, raspy voice sent a nervy shock wave through her. His gaze caught hers, dispatching another electrical jolt. "Nothing."

His phone vibrated. He answered the call, his voice low. A couple of times his gaze intercepted hers and that weird electrical hum of awareness zapped her again, so she switched back to watching the wing mirror. Once she thought she spotted the blue hatchback and she stiffened, but she couldn't be certain.

"He's not behind us. I've been checking."

Which raised a question. "You said he got to my place before you did, so how did you know he was there?"

Constantine inched forward in traffic, braked, then reached behind to the backseat and handed her a newspaper, which had been folded open.

The headline, Lightning Strikes Twice for Atraeus Hatchet Man, sent her into mild shock, although she had been expecting something like it.

They hadn't made the front page, but close. A color photo, which had been taken just as Lucas had kissed her, was slotted directly below the story title.

Her outrage built as she skimmed the piece. According to the reporter, the romantic fires had been reignited during a secret tryst while she'd been on Medinos. An "insider" had supplied the tidbit that the wedding had literally thrown them together and they were now a hot romantic item. Again.

Although the speculation that Lucas would pop the question was strictly lighthearted. According to the "source," if Carla Ambrosi hadn't had what it took to keep Atraeus interested the first time around, the "reheat" would be about as exciting as day-old pasta.

Carla dropped the newspaper as if it had scorched her fingers. The instant she had seen her name coupled with Lucas's she should have known better than to read on.

Two years ago when Lucas had finished with her after that one night, she had been angry enough to go to the press. They'd had a field day with speculation and innuendo. Her skin was a lot thicker now, but the careless digging into her personal life, and the outright lies, still stung.

Reheat.

Her jaw tightened. If she ever found out who the cowardly "insider" was, the next installment of that particular story could be printed in the crime pages.

Folding the newspaper, she tossed it on the backseat. "You should have called me. You didn't have to show up on my doorstep."

Making it look like there really was substance to the story.

"If I'd called, you would have hung up on me."

She couldn't argue with that, because it was absolutely true.

Lucas signaled and made a turn into the underground parking garage beneath the Ambrosi building.

Carla was halfway out of the car, dragging her bag, which had snagged on a tiny lever at the base of the seat, when movement jerked her head up. A man with a camera loomed out of the shadows, walking swiftly toward them. Not the guy in the blue hatchback, someone else. The pale gleam of a van with its garish news logo registered in the background.

Lucas, who had walked around to open her door, said

something curt beneath his breath as she yanked at the strap. The bag came free and she surged upright.

"Smile, Mr. Atraeus, Ms. Ambrosi. Gotcha!"

The camera flashed as she lurched into Lucas.

The touching was minimal—her shoulder bumped his, he reached out to steady her—but the damage was done. In addition to the kiss outside Lucas's apartment the tabloids now had photos of Lucas picking her up from her apartment then delivering her to work.

The day-old pasta had just gotten hotter.

Nine

When Carla stepped out of her office to attend the press conference later on that morning, one of Lucas's bodyguards, Tiberio, was waiting for her in the corridor.

Lucas wasn't in the office. He had left after dropping her off that morning, so there was no one to interpret. After a short, labored struggle with Tiberio's fractured English, Carla finally agreed that, yes, they would both follow Lucas's orders and Tiberio could drive her to the press conference and see her safely inside.

On the way down to the parking garage, she decided that she was secretly glad Lucas had delegated Tiberio to mind her. She had been dreading dealing with the paparazzi when she arrived at the five-star hotel where the press conference was being held.

To her surprise, Tiberio opened the door on a glossy black limousine, not the dark sedan Lucas's security usually drove. When she slid into the leather interior, she was startled to discover that Lucas was already ensconced there, a briefcase open on the floor, a sheaf of papers in his hand.

The door closed, sealing her in. Lucas said something rapid to Tiberio as he slid behind the wheel. There was a discreet thunk, followed by the low hum of the engine.

She depressed the door handle, when it wouldn't budge, her gaze clashed with Lucas's. "You locked it."

His expression was suspiciously bland. "Standard security precaution."

Daylight replaced the gloom of the parking garage as they glided up onto the street. Her uneasiness at finding Lucas in the car coalesced into suspicion; she was beginning to feel manipulated. "Tiberio said you had ordered him to mind me, that he was supposed to drop me at the press conference. He didn't say we would be traveling together."

Lucas, still dressed in the silver-gray suit and black T-shirt he had been wearing that morning, but now freshly shaved, retrieved a cell phone from his briefcase. "Is there a problem with going together?"

She frowned. "After what happened, wouldn't it be the smart thing to arrive separately?"

Lucas's attention was centered on what was, apparently, a swanky new phone. "No."

Her frustration spiked as he punched in a number and lifted the phone to his ear then subsided just as quickly as she listened to his deep voice, the liquid cadences of his rapid Medinian. Reluctantly fascinated, she hung on every word. He could be reciting a grocery list and she could still listen all day.

Minutes later, the limousine pulled into a space outside the hotel entrance. When she saw the media crush, she experienced a rare moment of panic. Publicity was her thing; she had a natural bent for it. But not today. "Isn't there a back entrance we can use?"

Lucas, seemingly unconcerned, snapped his phone closed and slipped it into his pocket.

She flashed him an irritated look. "The last thing we need right now is to be seen arriving together, looking like we *are* a couple."

"Don't worry, the media will be taken care of. It's all arranged."

Something about his manner brought her head up, sharpened all her senses. "What do you mean, 'arranged'? If the media doesn't see me for a few days, the story will die a death."

"No, it won't," Lucas said flatly. "Not this time."

The door to the limousine popped open. Lucas exited first. Reluctantly Carla followed, stepping into the dusty, steamy heat of midtown Sydney.

The media surged forward. To Carla's relief they were instantly held at bay by a wall of burly men in dark suits.

Lucas's hand landed in the small of her back, the heat of his palm burning through her dress, then they were moving. Carla kept her spine stiff, informing Lucas that she wasn't happy with either the situation or his touch, which seemed entirely too intimate.

The glass doors of the hotel threw a reflection back at her. Lucas stood tall and muscled by her side, his gaze with that grim, icy quality that always sent shivers down her spine. With the other men flanking them in a protective curve, she couldn't help thinking they looked like a trailer for a gangster flick.

The doors slid open, and the air-conditioned coolness of the hotel foyer flowed around her as they walked briskly to a bank of elevators. A security guard was holding an empty elevator car. Relief eased some of her tension as they stepped inside.

Before the doors could slide closed a well-dressed female reporter, microphone in hand, cameraman in tow, side-stepped security and grabbed the door, preventing it from closing.

"Mr. Atraeus, Ms. Ambrosi, can you confirm the rumor that Sienna Atraeus is pregnant?"

There was a moment of confusion as security reacted, forcing the woman and her cameraman to step back.

Lucas issued a sharp order. The doors snapped closed and she found herself alone with Lucas as the elevator lurched into motion.

Carla's stomach clenched at the sudden acceleration.

Sienna pregnant.

"Constantine phoned me earlier to let me know that Sienna was pregnant and that it was possible the story had been leaked."

A hurt she had stubbornly avoided dealing with hit her like a kick in the chest.

She didn't begrudge Sienna one moment of her happiness, but it was a fact that she possessed all the things that Carla realized *she* wanted. Not necessarily right now, but sometime in the future, in their natural order, and with Lucas.

But Lucas was showing no real signs of commitment.

Blankly, she watched floor numbers flash by. If she were pregnant she had to assume there would be no marriage, no happy ending, no husband to love and cherish her and the child.

She became aware the elevator had stopped. She sucked in a deep breath, but the oxygen didn't seem to be getting through. Her head felt heavy and pressurized, her knees wobbly. Not illness, just good old-fashioned panic.

Lucas took her arm, holding her steady. The top of her head bumped his chin, the scrape of his stubbled jaw on the sensitive skin of her forehead sending a reflexive shiver through her. She inhaled, gasping air like a swimmer surfacing, and his warm male scent, laced with the subtle edge of cologne, filled her nostrils.

Lucas said something curt in Medinian. "Damn, you *are* pregnant."

A split second later the elevator doors slid open.

Fingers automatically tightening around the strap of her handbag, which was in danger of sliding off her shoulder, she stepped out into a broad, carpeted corridor. Lucas's security, who must have taken another elevator, were waiting.

Lucas's hand closed around her arm. "Slow down. I've got you."

"That's part of the problem."

"Then deal with it. I'm not going away."

She shot him an icy glare. "I thought leaving was the whole point?"

He traded a cool glance but didn't reply because they had reached the designated suite. A murmur rippled through the room as they were recognized, but this time, courtesy of the heavy presence of security, there was no undisciplined rush.

Tomas, Constantine's PA, and Lucas's mother, Maria Therese, were already seated. Carla took a seat next to Lucas. Seconds later, Zane escorted Lilah into the room.

Her stomach contracted as the questions began. The presence of a mediator limited the topics to the Atraeus takeover of Ambrosi, Ambrosi's new collection and the re-creation of the historic Ambrosi pearl facility on the Medinian island of Ambrus. However, when Lucas rose to his feet, indicating that the press conference was over, a barrage of personal questions ensued.

Lucas's fingers laced with hers, the contact intimate and unsettling as he pulled her to her feet. When she discreetly tried to pull free, wary of creating even more unpleasant speculation, he sent her a warning glance, his hold firming.

As they stepped off the podium the media, no longer quietly seated, swirled around them. The clear, husky voice of a well-known television reporter cut through the shouted questions. A microphone was thrust at Lucas's face.

The reporter flashed him a cool smile. "Can you confirm or deny the reports that you've resumed your affair with Carla?"

Lucas pulled her in close against his side as they continued to move at a steady pace. His gaze intersected with hers, filled with cool warning. "No official statement has been issued yet, however I can confirm that Carla Ambrosi and I have been secretly engaged for the past two years."

The room erupted. Lucas bit out a grim order. The security team, already working to push the press back, closed in, forcing a bubble of privacy and shoving Carla up hard against Lucas. His arm tightened and she found herself lifted off her feet as he literally propelled her from the room.

Shock and a wave of edgy heat zapped through her as she clung to his narrow waist and scrambled to keep her balance. Seconds later they were sealed into the claustrophobic confines of what looked like a service elevator, still surrounded by burly security.

Carla twisted, trying to peel loose from his hold. Lucas easily resisted the attempt, tightening his arms around her. In the process she ended up plastered against his chest. The top button of her dress came unfastened and his hand, which was spread across her rib cage, shifted up so that his thumb and index finger sank into the swell of one breast.

As if a switch had been thrown, she was swamped by memories, some hot and sensuous enough that her breasts tightened and her belly contracted, some hurtful enough that her temper roared to life.

Lucas's gaze burned over the lush display of cleavage where the bodice of her dress gaped. "Keep still," he growled.

But she noticed he didn't move his hand.

She was *not* enjoying it. After the humiliation of the previous evening the last thing she needed was to be clamped against all that hot, hard muscle, making her feel small and wimpy and tragically easy. Unfortunately, her body wasn't in sync with her mind. She couldn't control the heat flushing her skin or the automatic tightening of her nipples, and Lucas knew it.

The doors slid open. Before she could protest, they were moving again, this time through the lower bowels of the hotel. A door off a loading bay was shoved wide and they spilled out onto a walled parking area where several vehicles, including a limousine, were parked.

Her fury increased. Here was the back entrance she had needed an hour ago.

Hot, clammy air flowed around her as she clambered into the limousine, clutching her purse. Lucas slid in beside her, his muscled thigh brushing hers. She flinched as if scalded and scooted over another few inches.

His gaze flashed to hers as they accelerated away from the curb. "All right?"

His calm control pushed her over the edge. She reached for her seat belt and jammed the fastenings together. "Secretly *engaged?*"

A week ago an engagement was what she had longed for, what she would have *loved*. "Correct me if I'm wrong, maybe I blacked out at some stage, but I don't ever remember a proposal of marriage."

She caught Tiberio's surprised glance in the rearview mirror.

Lucas's expression was grim. A faint hum filled the air as a privacy screen slid smoothly into place, locking them into a bubble of silence.

She stared at Lucas, incensed. Thanks to the mad dash

through the hotel, her hair had unwound and was now cascading untidily down her back, and she was perspiring. In contrast, Lucas looked cool and completely in control, his suit *GQ* perfect. "An engagement is the logical solution."

"It's damage control, and it's completely unnecessary." She remembered her gaping bodice and hurriedly refastened the button. "I may not be pregnant."

Her voice sounded husky and tight, even to herself, and she wondered, a little wildly, if he could tell how much she suddenly wanted to be pregnant.

"Whether you're pregnant or not is a consideration, but it isn't an issue, yet."

Something seized in her chest, her heart. For a crazy moment she considered that he was about to admit that he was in love with her, that he didn't care if she was pregnant or not, he couldn't live without her. Then reality dissolved that fantasy. "But what the newspapers are printing is. Do you know how humiliating it is to be offered a forced marriage?"

Irritation tinged with outrage registered in his expression. "No one's *forcing* you to do anything. Marriage as an option can't be such a shock. Not after what happened on Medinos. And last night."

"Well, I guess that puts things in perspective. It's a *practical* option."

Her mood was definitely spiraling down. Practicality spelled death for all romance. Cancel the white wedding with champagne and rose petals. Bring on the registry office and matching gray suits.

"I wouldn't propose marriage if I didn't *want* to marry you."

Her gaze narrowed. "Is that the proposal?"

His expression was back to remote. "It isn't what I had planned, but, yes."

"Uh-huh." She drew a deep breath and counted to ten.

"The biggest mistake I made was in agreeing to sleep with you."

Suddenly he was close, one arm draped behind her, his warm male scent laced with the enticing cologne stopping the breath in her throat. "On which occasion?"

She stared rigidly ahead, trying to ignore the heated gleam in his eyes, the subtle cajoling that shouldn't succeed in getting her on side, but which was slowly undermining her will to resist.

That was the other thing about Lucas, besides the power and influence he wielded in the business world. When he wanted he could be stunningly seducingly attentive. But this time she refused to be swayed by his killer charm. "All of them."

He wound a strand of her hair around one finger and lightly tugged. She felt his breath fanning her nape. "That's a lot of mistakes."

And she had enjoyed every one of them.

She resisted the urge to turn her head, putting her mouth bare inches from his and letting the conversation take them to the destination he was so blatantly angling for—a bone-melting kiss. "I should never have slept with you, period."

He dropped the strand of hair and sat back, slightly, signaling that he had changed tack. "Meaning that if you had played your cards right," he said softly, "you could have had marriage in the beginning?"

Ten

Like quicksilver the irresistible pull of attraction was gone, replaced by wrenching hurt. "Just because I didn't talk about marriage, that didn't mean I thought it would never be on the agenda for us. And what is so wrong with that?"

Silence vibrated through the limousine. She saw Tiberio glance nervously in the rearview mirror. She turned her head to watch city traffic zip by and registered that her stomach felt distinctly hollow.

Glancing at her watch, she noted the time. She'd only had coffee for breakfast and it was after one. She would be eating lunch soon, which would fix the acid in her stomach, but she couldn't wait that long. Fumbling in her purse, she took out the small plastic bag that contained a few antacid tablets and a couple of individually packaged biscuits. After unwrapping a slightly battered biscuit, she took a bite.

"Marriage is on the agenda now," Lucas reminded her. "I need an answer."

She hastily finished the biscuit and stuffed the plastic bag back in her purse.

Lucas watched her movements with an annoyed fascination. "Do you usually eat when marriage is being proposed?"

"I was hungry. I needed to eat."

"I'll have to remember that should I ever have occasion to propose again."

She closed the flap on her purse. Maybe it was childish not to tell him that she had ended up with an ulcer, but it was no big deal and she was still hurt that he hadn't ever bothered to check up on her after he had deposited her on the plane home from Thailand. The memory of his treatment of her, which had been uncharacteristically callous, stiffened her spine. "I don't know why you want marriage now when clearly you broke up with me because you didn't view me as 'wife' material."

His gaze was unwavering, making her feel suddenly uncomfortable about giving him such a hard time.

"As it happens, you've always fulfilled the most important requirement."

She was suddenly, intensely conscious of the warmth of his arm behind her. "Which is?"

Her breath seized in her throat as Lucas cupped her chin with his free hand. She had a split second to either pull back or turn her head so his mouth would miss hers. Instead, hope turned crazy cartwheels in her stomach, and she allowed the kiss.

Long, breathless minutes later he lifted his head. "You wanted to know why marriage is acceptable to me. This is why."

His thumb traced the line of her cheekbone, sending tingling heat shivering across the delicate skin and igniting a familiar, heated tension. His mouth brushed hers again, the kiss lingering. The stirring tension wound tighter. Reflexively, she leaned closer, angling her jaw to deepen the kiss. Her hand slid around to grip his nape and pull him closer still.

When he finally lifted his head, his gaze was bleak. "Two months without you was two months too long. What happened on Medinos and in my apartment is a case in point. I want you back."

Carla released her hold on his nape and drew back. Her mouth, her whole body, was tingling.

It wasn't what she wanted to hear, but the hope fizzing inside refused to die a complete death.

Lucas had tried to end their relationship; it hadn't happened. She hadn't chased him. If he had truly wanted an end, she was in no doubt that he would have icily and clinically cut her out of his life.

He hadn't been able to because he couldn't resist her.

He might label what held them together as sex; she preferred to call it chemistry. There was a reason they were attracted to each other that went way beyond the physical into the area of personality and emotional needs. Despite their difficulties and clashes, at a deep, bedrock level she knew they were perfect for each other.

That they had continued their relationship for two years was further proof that whatever he either claimed or denied, for Lucas she was different in some way. She knew, because she had made it her business to check. Lucas was only ever recorded by the tabloids as having one serious relationship before her, a model called Sophie, and that had been something like five years ago. The fact that he wanted the marriage now, when a pregnancy was by no means certain, underlined just how powerfully he did want her.

It wasn't love, but everything in her shouted that it had to be possible for the potent chemistry that had bound Lucas to her for the past two years to turn to love.

She was clutching at straws. Her heart was pounding and her stomach kept lurching. There was a possibility that Lucas might never truly love her, never fully commit himself to the relationship. There was a chance she was making the biggest mistake of her life.

But, risky or not, if she was honest, her mind had been made up the second she'd heard his announcement to the press.

She loved Lucas.

If there was a chance that he could love her, then she was taking it.

Lucas activated the privacy screen. When it opened, he leaned forward and spoke in rapid Medinian to Tiberio. He caught the skeptical flash of his chief bodyguard's gaze in the rearview mirror as he confirmed that they would be making the scheduled stop at the jewelers.

However, the wry amusement that would normally have kicked up the corners of his mouth in answer to Tiberio's pessimism was absent. When it came to Carla, he was beginning to share Tiberio's doubts. She hadn't said yes, and he was by no means certain that she would.

Carla, who was once again rummaging in her handbag, stiffened as the limousine pulled into the cramped loading bay of a downtown building. "This isn't the restaurant."

Lucas climbed out as Tiberio opened the door then leaned in and took Carla's hand. "We have one stop to make before lunch."

As Carla climbed out he noted the moment she spotted the elegant sign that indicated this was the rear entrance to the premises of Moore's, a famous jeweler. A business that just happened to be owned by The Atraeus Group.

Her expression was accusing. "You had this all planned."

"Last night you knew as well as I that the story would go to press."

Her light blue gaze flashed. Before she could formulate an argument and decide to answer his proposal with a no, Lucas propelled her toward the back entrance.

Frustration welled that he hadn't been able to extract an answer from her *and* that he couldn't gauge her mood, but he kept a firm clamp on his temper. An edgy, hair-trigger temper that, until these past two weeks, he hadn't known existed.

He offered her his arm and forced himself to patience when she didn't immediately take it.

Clear, glacial-blue eyes clashed with his. "What makes you think I'm actually going to go through with this?"

Lucas noted that she stopped short of using the word *charade.* "I apologize for trying to bulldoze you," he said grimly. "I realize I've mishandled the situation."

He had used business tactics to try to maneuver Carla into an engagement. He had assumed that when he proposed marriage she would be, if not ecstatic, then, at least, happy.

Instead, she was decidedly *unhappy,* and now he was being left to sweat.

He acknowledged that he deserved it. If patience was now required to achieve a result, then he would be patient. "The ring is important. I need you to come inside and choose one."

"I suppose we need one because we've been *secretly engaged* for two years, so of course you would have loved me enough to buy a ring."

Ignoring Tiberio's scandalized expression, he unclenched his jaw. *"Esattamente,"* he muttered, momentarily forgetting his English. "If you don't have a ring, questions will be asked."

"So the ring is a prop, a detail that adds credence to the story."

The door popped open. A dapper gray-haired man, elegant in a dark suit and striped tie, appeared along with a security guard. "Mr. Atraeus," he murmured. "Ms. Ambrosi. My name is Carstairs, the store manager. Would you like to come this way?"

Keeping his temper firmly in check, Lucas concentrated on Carla. If she refused the ring, he would arrange for a selection to be sent to his apartment and she could choose one there. What was important was that she accept his proposal, and that hadn't happened yet. "Are you ready?"

Her eyes clashed with his again, but she took his arm.

Jaw clenched, Lucas controlled his emotions with a forcible effort. Fleetingly, he registered Tiberio's relief, an exaggerated expression of his own, as he walked up the steps and allowed Carla to precede him into the building.

She would say yes. She had to.

The turnaround was huge, but now that he had made the decision that he wanted her in his life permanently, he felt oddly settled.

Like it or not he was involved, his feelings raw, possessive. Sexually, he had lost control with Carla from the beginning, something that had never come close to happening with any other woman.

It was also a blunt fact that the thought of Carla with Panopoulos, or any man, was unacceptable. When he had walked into that particular wall, his reaction had cleared his mind. Despite everything that could go wrong with this relationship, Carla was his.

If he had to be patient and wait for her, then he would be patient.

Carla stepped into the room Carstairs indicated, glad for a respite from the odd intensity of Lucas's gaze and her own inner turmoil. For a fractured moment, she had been an inch away from giving up on the need to pressure some kind of admission out of Lucas and blurting out "yes." She would marry him, she would do whatever he wanted, if only he would keep on looking at her that way. But then the emotional shutters she had never been able to fathom had come crashing down and they had ended up stalemated again.

The room was an elegant private sitting room with sleek leather couches offset by an antique sideboard and coffee tables. Classical music played softly. The largest coffee table held a selection of rings nestled in black velvet trays.

Carstairs, who seemed to be staring at her oddly, indicated that she take a seat and view the rings, then asked if she would like coffee or champagne. Refusing either drink with a tight smile, she sat and tried to concentrate on the rings. Lucas, who had also refused a drink, paced the small room like an overlarge caged panther, then came to stand over her, distracting her further.

His breath stirred her hair as he leaned forward for a closer look. Utterly distracted by his closeness, she stared blindly at the rings, dazzled by the glitter but unable to concentrate, which was criminal because she loved pretty jewelry. "I didn't think you were interested in jewelry."

"I'm interested in you," he said flatly. "This one."

He picked out a pale blue pear-shaped stone, which she had noticed but bypassed because it occupied a tray that contained a very small number of exquisite rings, all with astronomical price tags.

He handed it to her then conferred briefly with Carstairs. "It's a blue diamond, from Brazil. Very rare, and the same color as your eyes. Do you like it?"

She studied the soft, mesmerizing glow of the diamond, but was more interested in the fact that he had picked the ring because it matched her eyes. She slipped the ring on her finger. Wouldn't you know, it was a perfect fit and it looked even better on. "I love it."

His gaze caught hers, held it, and for a moment she felt absurdly giddy.

"Then we'll take it." He passed Carstairs his credit card.

Yanking the ring off, she replaced it on its plush velvet tray and pushed to her feet, panic gripping her. "I haven't said yes yet."

Lucas said something in rapid Medinian to Carstairs. With a curt bow, the store manager, who could evidently speak the language, left the room, still with Lucas's card, which meant Lucas was buying the ring, regardless. Simultaneously, an elegant older woman in a simple black dress collected the remaining trays and made a swift exit along with Tiberio, leaving them alone. The blue ring, she noticed, was left on the coffee table.

In the background the classical music ended. Suddenly the silence was thick enough to cut.

Carla shoved to her feet and walked to the large bay window. She stared out into the tiny yard presently dominated by the limousine, and the issue she'd been desperate to ignore, which had hurt more than anything because it had cut into the most tender part of her, surfaced. As hard as she had tried for two years to be everything Lucas could want or need, it hadn't been enough. When the pressure had come on to commit, he hadn't wanted *her*. He had wanted Lilah, who in many ways was her complete opposite: calm, controlled and content to keep a low profile.

In retrospect, maybe she had tried too hard and he hadn't ever really seen her, just the glossy, upbeat side that was always "on." The one time he had truly seen her had been in Thailand. She had been too sick to try to be anything but herself, and he had run a mile. "What about Lilah?"

"I spoke to Lilah last night. Zane is taking care of her."

She met his gaze in the window. "I thought you were in love with her."

He came to stand behind her. "She was my date at the wedding, that was all. And, no, we didn't sleep together. We didn't kiss. I didn't so much as hold her hand."

Relief made Carla's legs feel as limp as noodles. He pulled her back against him in a loose hold, as the palm of one hand slid around to cup her abdomen.

"Marriage wasn't on my agenda, with anyone, but the situation has…changed. Don't forget it's entirely possible you're pregnant."

Lucas's hold tightened, making her intensely aware of his hard, muscled body so close behind her. Their reflection bounced back at her, Lucas large and powerfully male, herself paler and decidedly feminine. "I can't marry solely for a baby that might not exist! There has to be something more. Sienna is married to a man she loves. A man who loved her enough that he kidnapped her—"

"Are you saying you want to be *kidnapped?*"

She stared at the dark, irritable glitter of Lucas's eyes, the tough line of his jaw. Her own jaw set. "All I'm saying is that Constantine loves Sienna. It matters."

There was an arresting look in his eyes. "You love me."

Eleven

Carla inhaled sharply at the certainty in Lucas's voice, feeling absurdly vulnerable that, after two years of careful camouflage, she was so transparent now. She was also hurt by his matter-of-fact tone, as if her emotional attachment was simply a convenience that smoothed his path now. "What did you expect, that I was empty-headed enough that I was just having sex with you?"

"Meaning that was how I was with you?" His grip on her arms gentled. "Calm down. I didn't know until that moment. I'm…pleased."

"Because it makes things easier?"

"We're getting married," he said flatly. "This is not some business deal."

He didn't make the mistake of trying to kiss her. Instead he released her, walked over to the coffee table and picked the ring up.

The diamond shimmered in the light, impossibly beautiful, but it was the determined set to Lucas's jaw, the rock-solid patience in his gaze, that riveted her. "What if I'm not pregnant?"

"We'll deal with that possibility when we get to it."

Her jaw tightened. She didn't want to create difficulties, but neither could she let him put that ring on her finger without saying everything that needed to be said. "I'm not sure I want marriage under these conditions."

"That's your choice," he said flatly, his patience finally slipping. "But don't hold out for Alex Panopoulos to intervene. As of yesterday he has reviewed his options."

The sudden mention of Panopoulos was faintly shocking. "You warned him off."

"That's right." Lucas's voice was even, but his expression spoke volumes, coolly set with a primitive gleam in his eyes that sent a faint quiver zapping down her spine.

Just when she thought Lucas was cold and detached he proved her wrong by turning distinctly male and predatory.

It wasn't much, it wasn't enough, but it told her what she needed to know: Lucas was jealous. Given his cool, measured approach to every other aspect of his life, if he was jealous then he had to feel something powerful, something special, for her.

It was a leap in the dark. Marriage would be an incredible risk, but the past two years had been all about risk and she had already lost her heart. It came down to a simple choice. She could either walk away and hope to fall out of love with Lucas or she could stay and hold out for his love.

Her chin came up. When it came down to it she wasn't a coward. She would rather try and fail than not try at all.

"Okay," she said huskily, and extended her hand so he could slide the ring on her finger.

The fit was perfect. She stared at the fiery blue stone, her chest suddenly tight.

Lucas lifted her fingers to his lips. "It looks good."

The rough note in his voice, the unexpected caress, sent a shimmering wave of emotion through her. "It's beautiful."

He bent his head. Before she could react, he kissed her on the mouth. "I have good taste."

Despite her effort to stay calm and composed and not let Lucas see how much this meant to her, a wave of heat suffused her cheeks. "In rings or wives?"

He grinned quick and hard and dropped another quick kiss on her mouth. "Both."

Lucas shepherded Carla into the backseat of the limousine, satisfaction filling him at the sight of the ring glowing on her finger.

She loved him.

He had suspected it, but he hadn't known for sure until she had said the words. Her emotional involvement was an element he hadn't factored in when he had decided on marriage. He had simply formulated a strategy and kept to it until she had capitulated.

Now that he knew she loved him and had agreed to marry him, there would be no reason to delay moving her in with him. No reason to delay the wedding.

Marriage.

Since Sophie's death, marriage had not been an option, because he had never gotten past the fact that he still felt responsible for the accident.

It had taken a good year for the flashbacks of the accident to fade from his mind, another six months before he could sleep without waking up and reliving that night.

Sometimes, even now, he still woke up at night, reliving their last argument and trying to reinvent the past. He had avoided commitment for the simple reason that he knew his own nature: once he did commit he did so one hundred per-

cent and he was fiercely protective. The night Sophie had
died, he had been blindsided by the fact that she had aborted
his child. He'd allowed her to throw her tantrum and leave.
Maybe he was overcompensating now, but he would never
allow himself, or any woman he was with, to be put in that
situation again.

Until Carla, he had avoided becoming deeply involved
with anyone. The week in Thailand had been a tipping point.
Caring for Carla in that intimate situation had pushed him
over an invisible boundary he had carefully skirted for five
years. He hadn't liked the intense flood of emotion, or the
implications for the future. He knew the way he was hard-
wired. For as long as he could remember he had been the
same: when it came to emotion it was all or nothing.

Now that Carla had agreed to marry him and it was possible that he would be a father, if not in the near future, then
sometime over the next few years, he was faced with a double
responsibility. He could feel the possessiveness, the desire
to cushion and protect already settling in.

With Sophie he hadn't had time to absorb the impact of
her pregnancy because it had been over before he had known
about it. She hadn't given him a chance. With Carla the situation was entirely different. He knew that she would never
abort their child. She would extend the same fiercely protective, single-minded love she gave her family to their baby.

Any child Carla had would be loved and pampered. Unlike Sophie, she would embrace the responsibility, the chills
and the spills.

It was an odd moment to realize that one of the reasons
he wanted to marry Carla was that he trusted her.

During the drive to the restaurant Lucas had booked,
Carla wavered between staring with stunned amazement at

the engagement ring and frantically wondering what Lucas's mother was going to think.

Like every other member of the Atraeus family, Maria Therese would know that Carla and Lucas had more than a hint of scandal in their past. Plus, the first and only time they had met, Lucas had been dating Lilah.

Lucas, who had been preoccupied with phone calls for the duration of the short trip to the restaurant, took her arm as she exited the limousine. "Now that we're engaged, there is one rule you will follow—don't talk to the press unless you've cleared it with me."

Carla stiffened. "PR is my job. I think I can handle the press."

Lucas nodded at Tomas, who was evidently waiting for them at the portico of the restaurant. "PR for Ambrosi is one thing. For the Atraeus family the situation is entirely different."

"I think I can be trusted."

His glance was impatient. "I know you can handle publicity. It's the security aspect that worries me. Every member of my family has to take care, and situations with the press provide prime opportunities for security breaches. If you're going to be talking to the press, a security detail needs to be organized. And by the way, I've booked you into the hotel for the launch party. We leave first thing in the morning."

Carla stopped dead in her tracks, a small fuzzy glow of happiness expanding in her chest. Lucas had obviously taken care of that detail before he had asked her to marry him, righting a wrong that had badly needed fixing. She knew she wouldn't be in charge of running the show, but that was a mere detail. She would still be able to make sure everything came off perfectly and that was what mattered. She was finally starting to believe that this marriage could work. "My contract as Ambrosi's public relations executive is up for renewal next week."

"It's as good as signed."

"That was almost too easy."

His arm slid around her waist, pulling her in against his side as they walked into the restaurant. "I was going to renew it anyway. You're damn good at the job, and besides, I want you to be happy."

Her happiness expanded another notch. It wasn't perfection yet—she still had to deal with that emotional distance thing that Lucas constantly pulled—but it was inching closer.

Maria Therese, Zane and Lilah were already seated at the table. Carla's stomach plunged as Lucas's mother gave her a measuring glance. With her smooth, ageless face and impeccable fashion sense, the matriarch of the Atraeus family had a reputation for being calm and composed under pressure. And with her late husband's affairs, there had been constant media pressure. "Does your mother know how long we've been involved?"

"You're an Ambrosi and my future wife. She'll be more than happy to accept you into the family."

Carla's stomach plunged. "Oh, good. She knows."

The resort chosen for the product launch was Balinese in style. Situated in its own private bay with heavy tropical gardens, it was also stunningly beautiful.

The hotel foyer was just as Carla remembered it when she had originally investigated the resort for the launch party. Constructed with all the grandeur of a movie set, it was both exotic and restful with a soaring atrium and tinkling fountains.

When Carla checked in at the front desk, however, she found that the guest room that had originally been booked for her had been canceled and there were no vacancies. Every room had been booked for the launch.

Lucas, casual in light-colored pants and a loose gauzy white shirt that accentuated his olive skin and made his shoulders look even broader, slipped his platinum card across the counter. "You're sharing with me. The suite's in my name."

So nice to be told. Even though she understood that Lucas was behaving this way because he was still unsure of her and he wanted to keep her close, there was no ignoring that it was controlling behavior. Pointedly ignoring the interruption, she addressed the receptionist. "Are you sure there are no rooms left? How about the room that was originally booked for Lilah Cole?"

Lilah had originally been slated to attend the launch. As the head designer she had a right to be there, but she had pulled out at the last minute.

The receptionist dragged her dazzled gaze off Lucas. "I'm sorry, ma'am, there was a waiting list. The room has already been allocated."

Carla waited until they were in the elevator. The feel-good mood of the two-hour drive from Sydney in Lucas's Ferrari was rapidly dissolving. Maybe it was a small point since they were engaged, but she would like to have been asked before Lucas decided she would be sharing his room. Lucas's controlling streak seemed to be growing by leaps and bounds and she was at a loss to understand why. She had agreed to marry him; life should be smoothing out, but it wasn't. Lucas was oddly silent, tense and brooding. Something was wrong and she couldn't figure out what it was.

Lucas leaned against the wall, arms folded over his chest, his gaze wary. "It's just a hotel room. I assumed you would want to share."

"I do."

Lucas frowned. The relaxed cast to his face, courtesy of an admittedly sublime night spent together in his bed, gone. "Then what's wrong? You already know that Lilah and I were not involved."

"It's not Lilah—"

The doors slid open. A young couple with three young children were waiting for the elevator.

Lucas propelled her out into the corridor. "We'll continue this discussion in our room."

Their luggage had already been delivered and was stacked to one side, but Carla barely registered that detail. The large airy room with its dark polished floors, teak furniture and soaring ceilings was filled with lush bouquets of roses in a range of hues from soft pinks to rich reds. Long stemmed and glorious, they overflowed dozens of vases, their scent filling the suite.

Dazed, she walked through to the bedroom, which was also smothered with flowers. An ice bucket of champagne and a basket crammed with fresh fruit and exquisitely presented chocolates resided on a small coffee table positioned between two chairs.

Lucas carried their bags into the bedroom. The second he set them down she flung her arms around him. "I'm sorry. You organized all this—it's beautiful, gorgeous—and all I could do was complain."

His arms closed around her, tucking her in snugly against him. The comfort of his muscled body against hers, the enticement of his clean scent, increased her dizzy pleasure.

The second she had seen what Lucas had done, how focused he was on pleasing her, the notion that there was something wrong had evaporated. Now she felt embarrassed and contrite for giving him such a hard time.

Carla spent a happy hour rearranging the flowers and unpacking. By the time she had finished laying out her dress for the evening function, Lucas had showered, changed into a suit and disappeared, called away to do a series of interviews.

A knock on the door made her frown. When she opened it a young woman in a hotel uniform was standing outside with a hotel porter. After a brief conversation she discovered that Lucas had arranged for the items to be delivered for her perusal. Anything she didn't want would be returned to the stores.

Feeling a bit like Alice falling down the rabbit hole, Carla opened the door wider so the porter could wheel in a clotheshorse that was hung with a number of plastic-shrouded gowns. At the base of the clotheshorse were boxes of shoes from the prominent design stores downstairs. She signed a docket and closed the door behind the hotel employees.

A quick survey of the gowns revealed that while they were all her size and by highly desirable designers, they were definitely not her style. Two had significantly high necklines, one a soft pink, the other an oyster lace. Both were elegant and gorgeously detailed, but neither conformed to her taste. The pink was too ruffled, like a flapper dress from the 1920s, and the oyster lace was stiffly formal and too much like a wedding gown.

The other boxes contained matching shoes and wraps and matching sets of silk underwear. She couldn't help noticing that none of the shoes had heels higher than two inches.

As dazzled as she was by the lavish gifts, nothing about any of them fitted her personality or style. Each item was decidedly conventional and, for want of a better word, boring, like something her mother would have worn.

Her pleasure in unwrapping the beautiful things was dissolving by the second. Aside from the underwear, which was sexy and beautiful, it was clear that Lucas had had one thought in mind when he had had the things sent up: he was trying to tone her down. That brought them back to the original problem. Despite the engagement, Lucas still didn't accept her for who she was. If he couldn't accept her, she didn't see how he could ever love her.

She found her phone and jabbed in the number of Lucas's new phone. He picked up on the second ring, his voice impatient.

She cut him off. "I'm not wearing any of these dresses you've just had sent up."

"Can we discuss this later?" The register of his voice was low, his tone guarded, indicating that he wasn't alone.

Carla was beyond caring. "I'm discussing it now. I resent the implication that I dress immodest—"

"When did I say—"

"I'm female and, newsflash, I have a *figure*. I do not buy clothes to emphasise sex appeal—"

"Wait there. I'm coming up."

A click sounded in her ear. Heart pounding, she snapped her phone closed, slipped it back in her bag and surveyed the expensive pile of items. Hurt squeezed her chest tight.

She had repacked the shoes and started on the underwear when the door opened.

Lucas snapped the door closed behind him and jerked at his tie. "What's the problem?"

Carla glanced away from the heated irritation in his gaze, his ruffled hair as if he'd dragged his fingers through it, and the sexy dishevelment of the loose tie.

She picked up the pink ruffled number. "This, for starters."

He frowned. "What's wrong with it?"

She draped the gown against her body. "Crimes against humanity. The fashion police will have me in cuffs before I get out of the elevator."

He pinched the bridge of his nose as if he was under intense pressure. "Do you realize that on Medinos, as your future husband I have the right to dictate what you wear?"

For a moment she thought he was joking. "That's *medieval*—"

"Maybe I'm a medieval kind of guy."

She blinked. She had been wanting to breach his inner barriers, but now she was no longer sure she was going to like what she'd find. The old Lucas had been a pussycat compared to what she was now uncovering. "I buy clothes because they make me look and feel good, not to showcase my breasts or any other part of my anatomy. If that means I occasionally flash a bit of cleavage, then you, and the rest of Medinos, are just going to have to adjust."

She snatched up the pink silk underwear, which in stark contrast to the dress was so skimpy it wouldn't keep a grasshopper warm. "Are these regulation?"

He hooked the delicate thong over one long brown finger. "Absolutely."

Carla snatched the thong back and tossed the pink underwear back in its box. Retrieving the list of items she had signed for, she did what she had been longing to do—ripped it into shreds and tossed the pieces at Lucas. The issue of clothing, as superficial as it seemed, ignited the deep hurt that Lucas still viewed her as his sexy, private mistress and not his future wife. "You can have your master plan back."

Lucas ignored the fluttering pieces of paper. "What master plan?"

"The one where you turn me into some kind of perfect stuffed mannequin and put me in a room on Medinos with one of those wooden embroidery frames in my hand."

Lucas rubbed the side of his jaw, his gaze back to wary. "Okay, I am now officially lost."

"I resent being treated as if I'm too dumb to know how I

should dress. This is not digging gold out of rocks or sweaty men building a hotel, this is a *fashion* industry event."

His jaw took on an inflexible look she was beginning to recognize. "We're engaged. Damned if I'm going to let other men ogle you."

She threw up her hands. "You're laying down the law, but you don't even know what I plan to wear tonight."

Marching to the bed, she held up a hanger that held a sleek gold sheath with a softly draped boat-shaped neckline. "It's simple, elegant, shows no cleavage—and, more to the point, I like it."

"In that case, I apologize."

Feeling oddly deflated, she replaced the dress on the bed. When she turned, Lucas pulled her into his arms.

Her palms automatically spread on his chest. She could feel the steady pound of his heart beneath the snowy linen of his shirt, the taut, sculpted muscle beneath. Her heart rate, already fast, sped up, but he didn't try to pull her closer or kiss her.

"It wasn't my intention to upset you, but there is one thing about me that you're going to have to understand—I don't share. When it comes down to it, I don't care what you wear. I just don't want other men thinking you're available. And from now on the press will watch you like a hawk."

"I'm not irresponsible, or a tease." She released herself from his hold. The problem was that she had never understood Lucas's mood swings; she didn't understand him. One minute he was with her, the next he was cut off and distant and she needed to know why, because that distance frightened her. Ultimately it meant it was entirely possible that one day he could close himself off completely and leave her.

She began carefully rehanging the dresses, needing something to do. "Why did you never want any kind of long-term relationship with me? You planned to finish with me all along."

He gripped his nape. "We met and went to bed on the same night. At that point marriage was not on my mind."

"And after Thailand it definitely wasn't."

"I compressed my schedule to be with you in Thailand. Taking further time off wasn't possible."

"What if I'd been *really* ill?"

His gaze flashed with impatience. "If you had been ill, you would have contacted me, but you didn't."

"No."

"Are you telling me you *were* ill and didn't contact me?" he asked quietly.

"Even if I was," she said, folding the oyster silk lingerie into the cloud of tissue paper that filled the box, "you didn't want to know because looking after me in Thailand was just a little too much reality for you, wasn't it?"

"Tell me more about how I was thinking," he muttered. "I'm interested to know just how callous you think I am."

Frustration pulling at her, she jammed the lid on the box. Lucas had cleverly turned the tables on her, but she refused to let up. It suddenly occurred to her that Lucas's behavior was reminiscent of her father's. Roberto Ambrosi had hated discussing personal issues. Every time anyone had probed him about anything remotely personal he had turned grouchy and changed the subject. Attack was generally seen as the most effective form of defense.

She realized now that every time she got close to what was bothering Lucas, he reacted like a bear with a sore head. If he was snapping now, she had to be close. "If I wasn't what you wanted before," she said steadily, "how can I be that person now?"

There was a small, vibrating silence. "Because I realized you weren't Sophie."

Carla froze. "Sophie Warrington?"

"That's right. We lived together for almost a year. She died in a car accident."

Carla blinked. She remembered the story. Sophie Warrington had been gorgeous and successful. She had also had a reputation for being incredibly spoiled and high maintenance. She had lost a couple of big contracts with cosmetic companies because she had thrown tantrums. She had also been famous for her affairs.

Suddenly, Carla's lack of control in the relationship made sense. She was dealing with a ghost—a gorgeous, irresponsible ghost who had messed Lucas around to the point that he had trouble trusting any woman.

Let alone one who not only looked like Sophie but who was caught up in the same glitzy world.

Twelve

Half an hour later, after taking her medication with a big glass of water, she nibbled on a small snack then decided to go for a walk along the beach and maybe have a swim before she changed for the evening function. It wouldn't exorcise the ghost of Sophie Warrington or her fear that Lucas might never trust enough to fall in love with her, but at least it would fill in time.

Winding her hair into a loose topknot, she changed into an electric blue bikini and knotted a turquoise sarong just above her breasts. After transferring her wallet to a matching turquoise beach bag, she slipped dark glasses on the bridge of her nose and she was good to go.

Half an hour later, she stopped at a small beach café, ordered a cool drink and glimpsed Tiberio loitering behind some palms. She had since found out that Tiberio wasn't just a bodyguard, he was Lucas's head of security. That being the case, the only logical reason for him to be here was that Lucas had sent him to keep an eye on her.

Annoyed that her few minutes of privacy had been invaded by security that Lucas hadn't had the courtesy to advise her about, she finished the drink and started back to the resort.

The quickest way was along the long, curving ocean beach, which was dotted with groups of bathers lying beneath bright beach umbrellas. As she walked, she stopped, ostensibly to pick up a shell, and glanced behind. Tiberio was a short distance back, making no attempt to conceal himself, a cell phone held to his ear.

No doubt he was talking to Lucas, reporting on her activities. Annoyed, she quickened her pace. She reached the resort gardens in record time but the fast walk in the humidity of late afternoon had made her uncomfortably hot and sticky. She strode past the cool temptation of a large gleaming pool. Making an abrupt turn off the wide path, she strode along a narrow winding bush walk with the intention of losing herself amongst the shady plantings.

Beneath the shadowy overhanging plants, paradoxically it was even hotter. Slowing down, she unwound her sarong and tied it around her waist for coolness and propped her dark glasses on top of her head.

Footsteps sounded behind her, coming fast. Annoyed, she spun, and came face-to-face with Alex Panopoulos.

Dressed in a pristine business suit, complete with briefcase, his smooth features were flushed and shiny with perspiration.

She frowned, perversely wondering what had happened to Tiberio, and suddenly uncomfortably aware of the brevity of her bikini top. "What are you doing here?"

Alex set his briefcase down and jerked at his edgily patterned tie. "I just arrived and was walking to my chalet when I saw you."

She frowned, disconcerted by the intensity of his expression and the fact that he had clearly run after her. "There was no need. I'll see you tonight at the presentation."

"No you won't. My invitation was rescinded."

"Lucas—"

"Yes," he muttered curtly, "which is why I wanted to talk with you privately."

His gaze drifted to her chest, making her fingers itch with the need to yank the sarong back up. "If it's about the job—"

"Not the job." He stepped forward with surprising speed and gripped her bare arms. This close the sharp scent of fresh sweat and cologne hit her full force.

His gaze centered on her mouth. "You must know how I feel about you."

"Uh, not really. Let me go." She tried to pull free. "I'm engaged to Lucas."

"Engagements can be ended."

A creepy sense of alarm feathered her spine. He wasn't letting go. She jerked back more strongly, but his grip tightened, drawing her closer.

The thought that he might try to kiss her made her stomach flip queasily. Alex had frequently made it clear that he was attracted to her, but she had dismissed his come-ons, aware that he also regularly targeted other women, including her sister, Sienna.

Deciding on strong action, she planted her palms on his chest but, before she could shove, Panopoulos flew backward, seemingly of his own accord. A split second later Lucas was towering over her like an avenging angel.

Alex straightened, his hands curling into fists.

Lucas said something low and flat in Medinian.

Alex flinched and staggered back another step, although Lucas hadn't either stepped toward him or touched him.

Flushing a deep red, Panopoulos lunged for his briefcase and stumbled back the way he'd come.

With fingers that shook slightly with reaction, Carla untied the sarong, dragged it back over her breasts and knotted it. "What did you say to him?"

Lucas's gaze glittered over her, coming to rest on the newly tied knot. "Nothing too complicated. He won't be bothering you again."

"Thank you. I was beginning to think he wasn't going to let go." Automatically, she rubbed at the red marks on her arms where Panopoulos had gripped her just a little too hard.

With gentle movements, Lucas pushed her hands aside so he could examine the marks. They probably wouldn't turn into bruises, but that didn't change the cold remoteness of his expression.

"Did he hurt you?"

"No." From the flat look in his dark eyes, the grim set to his jaw, Carla gained the distinct impression that if Panopoulos had stepped any further over the line than he had, Lucas wouldn't have been so lenient. A small tingling shiver rippled the length of her spine as she realized that Lucas was fiercely protective of her.

It was primitive, but she couldn't help the warm glow that formed because the man she had chosen as her mate was prepared to fight for her. In an odd way, Lucas springing to her defense balanced out the hurt of discovering how affected he'd been by Sophie Warrington. To the extent that his issues with her had permeated every aspect of his relationship with Carla.

His hand landed in the small of her back, the touch blatantly dominant and possessive, but she didn't protest. She was too busy wallowing in the happy knowledge that Lucas hadn't left it to Tiberio to save her. Instead, he had interrupted what she knew was a tight schedule of interviews and come after her himself. Despite the unpleasant shock of the encounter, she was suddenly glad that it had happened.

When they reached the room, Lucas kicked the door shut and leaned back against the gleaming mahogany and drew her close.

Carla, still on edge after the encounter, went gladly. Coiling her arms around his neck, she fitted her body against the familiar planes and angles of his, soaking in the calm reassurance of his no-holds-barred protection.

Tangling the fingers of one hand in her hair, Lucas tilted her head back and kissed her until she was breathless.

When he lifted his head, his expression was grim. "If you hadn't tried to get away from Tiberio, Panopoulos wouldn't have had the opportunity to corner you."

She felt her cheeks grow hot. "I needed some time alone."

"From now on, while we're at the hotel you either have security accompany you, or I do, and that's nonnegotiable."

"Yes."

He cupped her face, his expression bemused. "That was too easy. Why aren't you arguing?"

She smiled. "Because I'm happy."

A faint flush rimmed his taut cheekbones and suddenly she felt as giddy as a teenager.

"Damn, I wish I didn't have interviews." His mouth captured hers again.

She rose up into the kiss, angling her jaw to deepen it. This time the sensuality was blast-furnace hot, but she didn't mind. For the first time in over two years Lucas's kiss, his touch, felt absolutely and completely right.

He wanted her, but not just because he desired her. He wanted her because he *cared*.

* * *

Carla showered and dressed for the launch party. Lucas walked into the suite just as she was putting the finishing touches to her makeup.

"You're late." Pleasurable anticipation spiraled through her as he appeared behind her in the mirror, leaned down and kissed the side of her neck.

His gaze connected with hers in the mirror. "I had an urgent business matter to attend to."

And she had thrown his busy schedule off even further because he'd had to interrupt his meetings to rescue her.

The happy glow that had infused her when he'd read Panopoulos the riot act reignited, along with the aching knowledge that she loved him. It was on the tip of her tongue to tell him just how much when he turned and walked into the bathroom. Instead she called out, "I'll see you downstairs."

Minutes later, with Tiberio in conspicuous attendance, she strolled into the ballroom, which was already filled with elegantly gowned and suited clients, the party well under way.

She threaded her way through the crowd, accepting congratulations and fielding curious looks. When she walked backstage to check on the arrangements for the promotional show, Nina's expression was taut.

She threw Carla a harassed look. "A minor glitch. The model we hired is down with a virus, so the agency did the best they could at short notice and sent along a new girl." She jerked her head in the direction of the curtained-off area that was being used as dressing rooms.

Dragging the curtain back far enough so she could walk through, Carla stared in disbelief at the ultrathin model. She was the right height for the dress, but that was all. Obviously groomed for the runway, she was so thin that the gown, which had originally been custom-made for Carla, hung off her shoulders and sagged around her chest and hips.

Carla's assistant, Elise, was working frantically with pins. The only problem was, the dress—an aquamarine creation studded with hundreds of pearls in a swirling pattern that was supposed to represent the sea—could only be taken in at certain points.

To add insult to injury, the model was a redhead and nothing about the promotion was red. Everything was done in Ambrosi's signature aquamarine and pearl hues. The color mix was subtle, clean and classy, reflecting Ambrosi's focus on the luxury market.

"No," Carla said, snapping instantly into work mode, irritated by the imperfections of the model and the utter destruction of the promotion that had taken her long hours of painstaking time to formulate. "Take the pins out of the dress."

She smiled with professional warmth at the model and instructed her to change, informing her that she would be paid for the job and was welcome to stay the weekend at Ambrosi's expense, but that she wouldn't be part of the promotion that evening.

Clearly unhappy, the model shimmied out of the gown on the spot and walked, half-naked and stiff backed, into a changing cubicle. At that point, another curtain was swished wide, revealing the gaggle of young ballet girls, who were also part of the promotion, in various states of undress.

Tiberio made a strangled sound. Clearly unhappy that he had intruded into a woman's domain, he indicated he would wait in the ballroom.

Elise carefully shook out the gown, examined it for signs of damage and began pulling out the pins she'd inserted. "Now what?" She indicated her well-rounded figure. "If you think I'm getting into that dress, forget it."

"Not you. Me."

Nina looked horrified. "I thought the whole point of this was that you weren't to take part."

Carla picked up the elegant mask that went with the outfit and pressed it against her face. The mask left only her mouth and chin visible.

Her stomach tightened at the risk she was taking. "He won't know."

Thirteen

Carla stepped into the gown and eased the zipper up, with difficulty. The dress felt a little smaller and tighter than it had, because it had been taken in to fit the model who was off sick.

She fastened the exquisite trailing pearl choker, which, thankfully, filled most of her décolletage and dangled a single pearl drop in the swell of her cleavage.

Cleavage that seemed much more abundant now that the dress had been tightened.

She surveyed her appearance in the mirror, dismayed and a little embarrassed by the sensual effect of the too-tight dress.

Careful not to breathe too deeply and rip a seam, she fastened the webbed bracelet that matched the choker and put sexy dangling earrings in her lobes. She fitted the pearl-studded mask and surveyed the result in the mirror.

With any luck she would get through this without being

recognized. A few minutes on stage then she would make her exit and quickly change back into her gold dress and circulate.

Elise swished the curtain aside. "It's time to go. You're on."

Lucas checked his watch as he strolled through the ballroom, his gaze moving restlessly from face to face.

Tiberio had informed him that Carla was assisting the girls backstage with the small production they had planned. He had expected no less. When it came to detail, Carla was a stickler, but now he was starting to get worried. She should have been back in the ballroom, with him, by now.

He checked his watch again. At least Panopoulos was out of the picture. He had made certain of that.

Every muscle in his body locked tight as he remembered the frightened look on Carla's face as she'd tried to shove free of him. When he'd seen the marks on Carla's arms, he had regretted not hitting Panopoulos.

Instead, he had satisfied his need to drive home his message by personally delivering the older man to the airport and escorting him onto a privately chartered flight out.

Panopoulos had threatened court action. Lucas had invited him to try.

Frowning, he checked the room again. He thought he had seen Carla circulating when he had first entered the room, but the gold dress and dark hair had belonged to a young French woman. He was beginning to think that something else had gone wrong since the heart-stopping passion of those moments in their room and she had found something else to fret about.

The radiant glow on her face when he'd left her had hit him like a kick in the chest, transfixing him. He could remember her looking that way when they had first met, but gradually, over time, the glow had gone. He decided it was a grim testament to how badly he had mismanaged their relationship that Carla had ceased to be happy. From now on he was determined to do whatever it took to keep that glow in her eyes.

A waiter offered him a flute of champagne. He refused. At that moment there was a stir at one end of the room as Nina, who was the hostess for the evening, came out onto the small stage.

Lucas leaned against the bar and continued to survey the room as music swelled and the promotional show began. The room fell silent as the model, who was far more mouth-wateringly sexy than he remembered, moved with smooth grace across the stage. *Floor show* wasn't the correct terminology for the presentation but he was inescapably driven to relabel the event.

Every man in the room was mesmerized, as the masked model, playing an ancient Medinian high priestess, moved through the simple routine, paying homage to God with the produce of the sea, a basket of Ambrosi pearls. With her long, elegant legs and tempting cleavage, she reminded him more of a Vegas dancer than any depiction of a Medinian priestess he had ever seen.

His loins warmed and his jaw tightened at his uncharacteristic loss of control. He had seen that dress on the model who was supposed to be doing the presentation. At that point the gown, which was largely transparent and designed so that pearl-encrusted waves concealed strategic parts and little else, had looked narrow and ascetically beautiful rather than sexy. He hadn't been even remotely turned-on.

The model turned, her hips swaying with a sudden sinuous familiarity as she walked, surrounded by a gaggle of young ballet dancers, all carrying baskets overflowing with free samples of Ambrosi products to distribute to clients.

Suspicion coalesced into certainty as his gaze dropped to the third finger of her left hand.

He swallowed a mouthful of champagne and calmly set the flute down. The mystery of his future wife's whereabouts had just been solved.

He had thought she was safely attired in the gold gown, minus any cleavage. Instead she had gone against his instructions and was busy putting on an X-rated display for an audience that contained at least seventy men.

Keeping a tight rein on his temper, he strode through the spellbound crowd and up onto the stage. Carla's startled gaze clashed with his. Avoiding a line of flimsy white pillars that were in danger of toppling, he took the basket of pearls she held, handed them to one of the young girls and swung her into his arms.

She clutched at his shoulders. "What do you think you're doing?"

Grimly, Lucas ignored the clapping and cheering as he strode off the stage and cut through the crowd to the nearest exit. "Removing you before you're recognized. Don't worry," he said grimly, "they'll think it's part of the floor show. The Atraeus Group's conquering CEO carrying off the glittering prize of Ambrosi Pearls."

"I can't believe you're romanticizing a business takeover, and it is *not* a floor show!"

He reached the elevator and hit the call button with his elbow, his gaze skimmed the enticing display of cleavage. "What happened to the model I employed?"

"She came down with a virus. The replacement they sent didn't fit the dress. If I hadn't stepped in, the only option would have been to cancel the promotion."

A virus. That word was beginning to haunt him. "And canceling would have been such a bad idea?"

"Our events drive a lot of sales. Besides, I'm wearing a mask. No one knew."

"*I* knew."

She ripped off the mask, her blue gaze shooting fire. "I don't see how."

He took in the sultry display of honey-tanned skin. Cancel the Vegas dancer. She looked like an extremely expensive courtesan, festooned with pearls. *His* courtesan.

It didn't seem to matter what she wore, he reflected. The clothing could look like a sack on any other woman, but on Carla it became enticingly, distractingly sexy. "Next time remember to take off the engagement ring."

The elevator doors opened. Seconds later they had reached their floor. Less than a minute later Lucas kicked the door to their suite closed.

"You realize I need to go back to the party."

He set her down. "Just not in that dress."

"Not a problem, it's not my color." Carla tugged at the snug fit of the dress. Fake pearls pinged on the floor. A seam had given way while Lucas was carrying her, but on the positive side, at least she could breathe now. She eyed Lucas warily. "What do you think you're doing?"

He had draped his suit jacket over the back of a couch, loosened his tie and strolled over to the small business desk in the corner of the sitting room. She watched as he flipped his laptop open. "Checking email."

The abrupt switch from scorching possessiveness to cool neutrality made her go still inside. She had seen him do this often. In the past, usually, just before he would leave her apartment he would begin immersing himself in work—phone calls, emails, reading documents. She guessed that on some level she had recognized the process for what it was; she just hadn't ever bothered to label it. Work was his cop-

ing mechanism, an instant emotional off button. She should
know. She had used it herself often enough.

She watched as he scrolled through an email, annoyed at
the way he had switched from blazing hot to icy cool. Lucas
had removed her from the launch party with all the finesse
of a caveman dragging his prize back to the fire. He had
gotten his way; now he was ignoring her.

The sensible option would be to get out of the goddess
outfit, put on another dress and go downstairs and circulate
before finding her gold dress and handbag, which she had
left backstage. But that was before her good old type A personality decided to make a late comeback.

Ever since she had been five years old on her first day at
school and her teacher, Mrs. Hislop, had put daddy's little
girl in the back row of the classroom, she had understood one
defining fact about herself: she did not like being ignored.

Walking to the kitchenette, she opened cupboards until
she found a bowl. She needed to eat. Cereal wasn't her snack
of choice this late, but it was here, and the whole point was
that she stayed in the suite with Lucas until he realized that
she was not prepared to be ignored.

She found a minipacket of cereal, emptied it into the bowl
then tossed the packaging into the trash can, which was
tucked into a little alcove under the bench.

Lucas sent her a frowning glance, as if she was messing
with his concentration. "I thought you were going to change
and get back to the party."

She opened the fridge and extracted a carton of milk.
"Why?"

"The room is full of press and clients."

She gave him a faintly bewildered look, as if she didn't
understand what he was talking about, but inwardly she was
taking notes. He clearly thought she was a second Sophie, a

party girl who loved to be the center of attention. "Nina and Elise are taking care of business. I don't need to be there."

"It didn't look that way ten minutes ago."

She shrugged. "That was an emergency."

Aware that she now had Lucas's attention, she opened the carton with painstaking precision and poured milk over the cereal. Grabbing a spoon, she strolled out into the lounge, sat on the sofa and turned the TV on. She flicked through the channels till she found a talk show she usually enjoyed.

Lucas took the remote and turned the TV off. "What are you up to?"

Carla munched on a spoonful of cereal and stared at the now blank screen. Before the party she had found reasons to adore Lucas's dictatorial behavior. Now she was back to loathing it, but she refused to allow her annoyance to show. She had wanted Lucas's attention and now she had gotten it. "Considering my future employment. I'm not good with overbearing men."

"You are not going to work for Panopoulos."

She ate another mouthful of cereal. He was jealous; she was getting somewhere. "I guess not, since I have an iron-clad contract I signed only yesterday."

Lucas tossed the remote down on the couch and dispensed with his tie. "Damn. You must be sleeping with the boss."

"Plus, I have shares."

"It's not a pleasing feminine trait to parade your victories." He took the cereal bowl from her and set it down on the coffee table. Threading her fingers with his, he pulled her to her feet.

More pearls pinged off the dress as she straightened. A tiny tearing sound signaled that another seam had given. "You shouldn't take food from a woman who could be pregnant."

His gaze was arrested. "Do you think you are?"

"I don't know yet." She had left the test kit behind. With everything that had happened, taking time out to read the instructions and do the test hadn't been a priority.

"I could get used to the idea." Cupping her face, he dipped his head and touched his mouth to hers.

The soft, seducing intimacy of the kiss made Carla forget the next move in her strategy. Before she could edit her response, her arms coiled around his neck. He made a low sound of satisfaction, then deepened the kiss.

Hands loosely cupping her hips, he walked her backward, kiss by drugging kiss, until they reached the bedroom. She felt a tug as the zipper on the dress peeled down, then a loosening at the bodice. More pearls scattered as he pulled the dress up and over her head and tossed it on the floor.

"The dress is ruined." Not that she really cared. It had only been a prop and it had served its purpose, in more ways than one.

"Good. That means you can't wear it again."

Stepping out of her heels, she climbed into bed and pulled the silk coverlet over her as she watched him undress. With his jet-black hair and broad, tanned shoulders he looked sleek and muscular.

The bed depressed as he came back down beside her. The clean scent of his skin made her stomach clench.

He surveyed the silk coverlet with dissatisfaction. "This needs to go." He dragged it aside as he came down on the bed. One long finger stroked over the pearl choker at her throat down to the single dangling pearl nestled in the shadowy hollow between her breasts. "But you can keep this on."

She had forgotten about the jewelry. Annoyed by the suggestion, which seemed more suited to a mistress than a future wife, she scooted over on the bed, wrapping the coverlet around her as she went. "You just destroyed an expensive gown. If you think I'm going to let you make love to me while I'm wearing an Ambrosi designer orig—"

His arm curled around her waist, easily anchoring her to the bed. "I'll approve the write-off for it."

Despite her reservations, unwilling excitement quivered through her as he loomed over her, but he made no effort to do anything more than keep her loosely caged beneath him.

"Whether we make love or not," he said quietly, "is your decision, but before you storm off, you need to know that I've organized a special license on Medinos. We're going to be married before the week is out."

"You might need my permission for that."

Something flared in his gaze and she realized she had pushed him a little too hard. "Not on Medinos."

"As I recall from Sienna's wedding, I still have to say yes."

Frustration flickered in his gaze and then she finally got him. For two years she had been focused on organizing their time together, taking care of every detail so that everything was as perfect as she could make it, given their imperfect circumstances. Lucas had fallen in with her plans, but she had overlooked a glaring, basic fact. Lucas was male; he needed to be in control. He now wanted her to follow the plan he had formulated, and she was frustrating him.

He cupped her face. "I have the special license. I don't care where we get married, just as long as it happens. Damned if I want Panopoulos, or any man, thinking you're available."

Unwilling delight filtered through the outrage that had driven her ever since she had realized that Lucas had developed a coping mechanism for shutting her out. The incident with Alex seemed a lifetime away, but it had only been hours.

She understood that in Lucas's mind he had rescued her for a second time that day, this time from a room full of men. As domineering and abrasive as his behavior was, in an odd way, it was the assurance she so badly needed that he cared. After watching him detach and walk away from her for more than two years, she wasn't going to freeze him out just when she finally had proof that he was falling for her.

"Yes."

His gaze reflected the same startled bemusement she had glimpsed that afternoon. "That's settled, then."

Warmth flared to life inside her. The happy glow expanded when he touched his lips to hers, the soft kiss soothing away the stress of dealing with Lucas's dictatorial manner. Sliding her fingers into the black silk of his hair, she pulled him back for a second kiss, then a third, breathing in his heat and scent. The kiss deepened, lingered. The silk coverlet slid away and she went into his arms gladly.

Sometime later, she woke when Lucas left the bed and walked to the bathroom, blinking at the golden glow that still flooded the room from the bedside lamp. Chilled without his body heat, she curled on her side and dragged the coverlet up high around her chin.

The bed depressed as Lucas rejoined her. One arm curled around her hips, he pulled her back snug against him. His palm cupped her abdomen, as if he was unconsciously cradling their baby.

Wistfully, her hand slipped over his, her fingers intertwining as she relaxed back into the blissful heat of his body. She took a moment to fantasize about the possibility that right at that very moment there could be an embryo growing inside her, that in a few months they would no longer be a couple, they would be a family. "Do you think we'll make good parents?"

"We've got every chance."

She twisted around in his grip, curious about the bitter note in his voice. "What's wrong?"

He propped himself on one elbow. "I had a girlfriend who was pregnant once. She had an abortion."

"Sophie Warrington?"

"That's right."

"You told me about her. She died in a car accident."

There was silence for a long, drawn-out moment. "Sophie had an abortion the day before she died. When she finally got around to telling me that she'd aborted our child before even telling me she was pregnant, we had a blazing argument. We broke up and she drove away in her sports car. An hour later she was dead."

Carla blinked. She hadn't realized that Lucas had split with Sophie before she had died. She smoothed her palm over his chest. "I'm sorry. You must have loved her."

"It was an addiction more than love."

Something clicked into place in her mind. Lucas had once used that term with regard to her. She hadn't liked it at the time, because it implied an unwilling attraction. "You don't see me as another Sophie?"

His hand trapped hers, holding it pressed against his chest so she could feel the steady thud of his heart. "You are similar in some ways, but maybe that's how the basic chemistry works. Both you and Sophie are my type."

Her stomach plunged a little. There it was again, the unwilling element to the attraction.

She knew he hadn't considered her marriageable in the beginning, because in his mind marriage hadn't fitted with the addictive sexual passion she had inspired in him. Admittedly, she hadn't helped matters. She had been busy trying to de-stress in line with her doctor's orders and keep their relationship casual but organized until the problems between both families had been rectified. In the process she had given him a false impression of her values. He had gotten to know who she really was a little better in the past few days, but that was cold comfort when she needed him to love her.

Fear spiked though her at the niggling thought that, if he

categorized her as being like Sophie, it was entirely possible that he wouldn't fall in love with her, that he would always see her as a fatal attraction and not his ideal marriage partner.

If she carried that thought through to its logical conclusion, it was highly likely that once the desire faded, he would fall for the kind of woman that in his heart he really wanted. "What happens when I get old, or put on weight, or…get sick?"

Physical attraction would fade fast and then where would they be?

She cupped his jaw. "I think I need to know *why* you can't resist me, because if what you feel is only based on physical attraction, it won't last."

He stoked a finger down the delicate line of her throat to her collarbone. "It's chemistry. A mixture of personality and the physical."

She frowned, her dissatisfaction increasing. "If you feel this way about me then how could you have been attracted to Lilah?"

As soon as she said Lilah's name, she wished she hadn't. Despite having Lucas's ring on her finger, she couldn't forget the weeks of stress when Lucas had avoided her then the sudden, hurtful way he had replaced her with Lilah.

"If you're jealous of Lilah, you don't need to be."

"Why?" But the question was suddenly unnecessary, because the final piece of the puzzle had just dropped into place. Lucas hadn't wanted Lilah for the simple reason that he had barely had time to get to know her. She had been part of a coldly logical strategy. An instant girlfriend selected for the purpose of spelling out in no uncertain terms that his relationship with Carla was over.

Fourteen

Carla stiffened. All the comments he'd made about her not needing to worry about Lilah and the quick way he had ended his relationship with her suddenly made perfect sense. "I have no reason to be jealous of Lilah, because you were never attracted to her."

His abrupt stillness and his lack of protest were damning.

"You manufactured a girlfriend." Her throat was tight, her voice husky. "You picked out someone safe to take to the wedding to make it easy to break up with me. You knew that if I thought you had fallen for another woman I would keep my distance and not make a fuss."

He loomed over her, his shoulders blocking out the dim glow from the lamp. "Carla—"

"No." Pushing free of his arms, she stumbled out of bed and struggled into her robe.

She yanked the sash tight as another thought occurred, giving her fresh insight into just how ruthless and serpentine

Lucas had been. "And you didn't pick just anyone to play your girlfriend. You were clever enough to select someone from Ambrosi Pearls, so the relationship covered all bases and would be in my face at work. That made it doubly clear to me that you were off-limits. It also made it look like you wanted her close, that you couldn't bear to have her out of your sight."

The complete opposite of his treatment of her.

Through the course of their relationship she had been separated and isolated from almost every aspect of his personal and business life.

Suddenly the room, with its romantic flowers, her clothes and jewelry draped over furniture and on the floor, emphasized how stupid she had been. Lucas's silence wasn't making her feel any better. "You probably even wanted to push me into leaving Ambrosi, which would get me completely out of your hair."

He shoved off the bed, found his pants and pulled them on. "I had no intention of depriving you of your job."

She stared at him bleakly, uncaring about that minor detail, when his major sin had been his complete and utter disregard for her feelings and her love. "What incentive did you offer Lilah to pose as your girlfriend?"

"I didn't pay Lilah. She knew nothing about this beyond the fact that I asked her to be my date at Constantine's wedding. That was our first, and last, date."

He caught her around the waist and pulled her close. "Do you believe me?"

She blinked. "Do you love me?"

There was the briefest of hesitations. "You know I do."

She searched his expression. It was a definite breakthrough, but it wasn't what she needed, not after the stinging hurt of finding out that he had used Lilah to facilitate getting rid of her.

His gaze seared into hers. "I'm sorry."

He bent and kissed her and the plunging disappointment receded a little. He was sorry and he very definitely wanted her. Maybe he even did love her. It wasn't the fairy tale she had dreamed about, but it was a start.

A few days ago she had been desperate for just this kind of chance with Lucas. Now too she was possibly pregnant. She owed it to herself and to Lucas to give him one more chance.

After an early breakfast, Carla strolled into the conference room Ambrosi had booked for its sales display. Lucas had phone calls to make in their suite, then meetings with buyers. Carla had decided to make herself useful and help Elise put together the jewelry display and set out the sales materials and press kits.

The fact that, if Lilah had been here, setting up the jewelry would have been her job was a reminder she didn't need, but she had to be pragmatic. Lilah was likely to be a part of the landscape for the foreseeable future, and she probably wasn't any happier about the situation than Carla. They would both have to adjust.

Security was already in place and lavish floral displays filled the room with the rich scent of roses. Elise had arranged for Ambrosi's special display cases to be positioned around the room. All that remained was for the jewelry, which was stored in locked cases, to be set out and labeled.

Elise, already looking nervous and ruffled, handed her a clipboard. "Just to make things more complicated, last night Lilah won a prestigious design award in Milan for some Ambrosi pieces. The buzz is *huge*." She snapped a rubber band off a large laminated poster. "Lucas had this expressed from the office late last night." She unrolled the poster, which was a blown-up publicity shot of Lilah, looking ultrasleek and gorgeous in a slim-fitting white suit, Ambrosi pearls at her lobes and her throat. With the pose she had struck and her calm gaze square on to the camera, Carla couldn't help thinking she looked eerily like the Atraeus bride in the portrait both she and Zane had studied at the prewedding dinner.

Elise glanced around the room. "I think I'll put it there, so people will see it as soon as they walk into the room. What do you think?"

Carla stared at the background of the poster. If she wasn't mistaken Lilah's image was superimposed over a scenic shot of Medinos—probably taken from one of the balconies of the *castello*. It was a small point, but it mattered. "Lucas ordered that to be done *late* last night?"

If that was the case, the only window of time he'd had was the few minutes after he had abducted her from the party when he had suddenly lost all interest in her because he had been so absorbed with what he was doing online.

Ordering a poster of the gorgeous, perfect Lilah.

Elise suddenly looked uncertain. "Uh, I think so. That's what he said."

Carla smiled and held out her hand. "Cool. Give the poster to me."

Elise went a little pale, but she handed the poster over.

Carla studied the larger-than-life photo. Her first impulse was to fling it into the ocean so she didn't have to deal with all that perfection. With her luck, the tide would keep tossing the poster back.

"I need scissors."

Elise found a pair and handed them over. Carla spent a happy few minutes systematically reducing the poster to an untidy pile of very small pieces.

Elise's eyes tracked the movement as Carla set the scissors down. She cleared her throat. "Do you want to sort through the jewelry, or would you prefer I did that?"

"I'm here to help. I'll do it."

"Great! I'll do the press kits." She dug in her briefcase. "Here's the plan for the display items. With all of the other publicity about, uh, Lilah, our sales have gone through the roof. We've already received orders from some of the attending clients so some of that jewelry is for clients and not for display. With any luck, they've kept the orders separate."

Carla slowly relaxed, determinedly thinking positive thoughts as she checked off the orders against the packing slip and set those packages to one side. Her mood improved by the second as she began putting the display together, anchoring the gorgeous, intricate pieces securely on black velvet beds then locking the glass cases. Lilah may have designed most of the jewelry, but they were Ambrosi pieces and she was proud of them. She refused to allow any unhappiness she felt about Lilah affect her pride in the family business.

A courier arrived with a package. Elise signed for it, shrugging. "This is weird. All the rest was delivered yesterday."

Carla took the package and frowned. The same courier firm had delivered it, but this one wasn't from the Ambrosi warehouse in Sydney. The package had been sent by another jeweler, the same Atraeus-owned company from which Lucas had purchased her engagement ring. That meant that whatever the package contained it couldn't be either an order for a customer or jewels for the launch.

Anticipation and a glow of happy warmth spread through her as she studied the package. She had her ring, which meant Lucas must have bought her something else, possibly a matching pendant or bracelet.

Her heart beat a little faster. Perhaps even matching wedding rings.

The temptation to open the package was almost overwhelming, but she managed to control herself. Lucas had bought her a gift, his first real gift of love, without pressure or prompting. She wasn't about to spoil his moment when he gave her the special piece he had selected.

She studied the ring on her finger, unable to contain her pleasure. She didn't care about the size of the diamond or the cost. What mattered was that Lucas had chosen it because it matched her eyes. Every time she looked at the ring she remembered that tiny, very personal, very important detail. It was a sign that he was one step closer to truly loving and appreciating her. After what had happened last night, how close they had come to splitting up again, she treasured every little thing that would help keep them together.

Elise finished shoving boxes and Bubble Wrap in the bin liner the hotel had provided. She waggled her brows at the package. "Not part of the display, huh? Looks interesting. Want me to take it to Lucas? I'm supposed to take the Japanese client he's meeting with to the airport in about ten minutes."

"Hands off." Carla's fingers tightened on the package. Despite knowing that Elise was teasing her, she felt ridiculously possessive of whatever Lucas had bought for her.

A split second later, Lucas strolled into the conference room. Immediately behind him, hotel attendants were setting up for morning tea, draping the long tables in white tablecloths and setting out pastries and finger food. Outside, in the lobby, she could hear the growing chatter. Any minute now, buyers and clients would start pouring into the conference room and there would be no privacy. The impulse to thrust the package at Lucas and get him to open it then and there died a death.

Lucas's gaze locked with hers then dropped to the glossy cut-up pieces of poster still strewn across the table. He lifted a brow. "What's that?"

"Your poster of Lilah."

There was a moment of assessing silence.

Lucas was oddly watchful, recognizing and logging the changes in her. As if he was finally getting that she was a whole lot more than the amenable, compartmentalized lover he had spent the past two years holding at a distance.

In that moment Carla knew Lilah had to go completely, no matter how crucial she was to Ambrosi Pearls. If she and Lucas were to have a chance at a successful marriage, they couldn't afford a third person in the equation.

Lucas lifted a brow. "What's in the package?"

"Nothing that won't keep." She pushed the package out of sight in her handbag then briskly swept all the poster fragments into the trash.

Whatever Lucas had bought her, she couldn't enjoy receiving it right at that minute, not with the larger-than-life specter of Lilah still hanging over them.

The weekend finished with a dinner cruise, by the end of which Lucas was fed up with designer anything. Give him steel girders and mining machinery any day. Anything but the shallow, too bright social whirl that was part and parcel of the world of luxury retailing.

He kept his arm around Carla's waist as they stood on the quay, bidding farewell to the final guests.

Carla was exhausted—he could feel it in the way she leaned into him—and her paleness worried him. The last thing she needed was another viral relapse.

He had insisted she fit in a nap after lunch. It had been a struggle to make her let go of the organizational reins, but in the end he had simply picked her up and carried her to their room. He had discovered that there was something about the masculine, take-charge act of picking Carla up that seemed to reach her in a way that words couldn't.

She had been oddly quiet all day, but he had expected that. He had made a mistake with the poster. The second he had walked into the conference room that morning and seen the look on Carla's face he had realized just how badly he had messed up. He had grimly resolved to take more care in future.

Her quietness had carried over into the evening. He had debated having her stay in their suite and rest, but in the end he had allowed her to come on the cruise for one simple reason. If he left her behind, she might not be there when he returned.

Lucas recognized Alan Harrison, a London buyer and the last straggling guest.

He paused to shake Lucas's hand. "Lilah Cole, the name on everyone's lips. You might have trouble holding on to her now, Atraeus. I know Catalano jewelry in Milan is impressed with her work. Wouldn't be surprised if they try and spirit her away from you."

Lucas clenched his jaw as Carla stiffened beside him. "That won't happen for at least two years. Lilah just signed a contract to take on the Medinos retail outlet as well as head up the design team."

"Medinos, huh? Smart move. Pretty girl, and focused. Got her in the nick of time. Another few days and you would have lost her."

Carla waited until Harrison had gone then gently detached herself from his hold. "You didn't tell me you had renewed Lilah's contract."

There was no accusation in her voice, just an empty neutrality, but Lucas had finally learned to read between the lines. When Carla went blank that was when she was feeling the most, and when *he* was being weighed in the balance.

Two years, and he hadn't understood that one crucially important fact. "I offered her the Medinos job a couple of days ago. If I'd realized how much it would hurt you I would have let her go. At the time removing her to Medinos for two years seemed workable, since I'll be running the Sydney office for the foreseeable future and we'll be based here."

"You did that for me." There was a small, vibrating silence and he was finally rewarded with a brilliant smile. "Thank you."

"You're welcome." Grinning, he pulled her into his arms.

Carla slipped out of her heels as she walked into their suite. Her feet were aching but she was so happy she hardly noticed the discomfort.

Lucas had finally crossed the invisible line she had needed him to cross; he had committed himself to her, and the blood was literally fizzing through her veins.

Maybe she should have felt this way when they had gotten engaged, but the reality was that all he'd had to do was say words and buy a ring. As badly as she had wanted to, she hadn't felt secure. Now, for the first time in over two years, she finally did.

The fact that he had arranged for Lilah to work in Medinos because they would be based in Sydney for two years had been the tipping point.

He had made an arrangement to ensure their happiness. He had used the word *they*. It was a little word, but it shouted commitment and togetherness.

Two years in Sydney. Together.

Taking Lucas by the hand, she pulled him into the bedroom, determinedly keeping her gaze away from the bedside bureau where she had concealed the package that had arrived that morning. "Sit down." She patted the bed. "I'll get the champagne."

He shrugged out of his jacket and tossed it over a chair before jerking at his tie. "Maybe you shouldn't drink champagne."

"Sparkling water for me, champagne for you."

"What are we celebrating, exactly?"

"You'll see in a minute."

He paused in the act of unbuttoning his shirt. "You're pregnant."

The hope in Lucas's voice sent a further shiver of excitement through her. Not only did he want her enough that he had bought her a wonderful surprise gift, he really did want their baby. Suddenly, after weeks, years, of uncertainty everything was taking on the happy-ever-after fairy tale sparkle she had always secretly wanted.

Humming to herself, she walked into the kitchen and opened a chilled bottle of vintage French champagne. The label was one of the best. The cost would be astronomical, but this was a special moment. She wanted every detail to be perfect. She put the champagne and two flutes on a tray and added a bottle of sparkling water for herself. On the way to the bedroom, she added a gorgeous pink tea rose from one of the displays.

She set the tray down on the bedside table as Lucas padded barefoot out of the bathroom. In the dim lamp-lit room with his torso bare, his dark dress trousers clinging low on narrow hips, his bronzed, muscular beauty struck her anew and she was suddenly overwhelmed by emotion and a little tearful.

Lucas cupped her shoulders and drew her close. "What's wrong?"

She snuggled against him, burying her face in the deliciously warm, comforting curve of his shoulder. "Nothing, except that I love you."

There was a brief hesitation, then he drew her close. "And I love you."

Carla stiffened at the neutral tone of his voice then made an effort to dismiss the twinge of disappointment that, even now, with this new intimacy between them, Lucas still couldn't relax into loving her.

She pushed away slightly, enough that she could see his face and read his expression, but she was too late to catch whatever truth had been in his eyes when he had said those three little words.

Forcing a bright smile, she released herself from Lucas's light hold, determined to recapture the soft, fuzzy fairy-tale glow. "Time for the champagne."

Lucas took the bottle from her and set it back down on the tray.

He reeled her in close. "I don't need a drink."

His head dipped, his lips brushed hers. She wound her arms around his neck, surrendering to the kiss as he pulled her onto the bed. Long seconds later he propped his head on one elbow and wound a finger in a coiling strand of her hair. "What's wrong? You're like a cat on hot bricks."

Rolling over, Carla opened the bureau drawer and took out the courier package. "This came today."

The heavy plastic rustled as she handed it to Lucas. Instead of the teasing grin she had expected, Lucas's gaze rested on the courier package and he went curiously still.

A sudden suspicion gripped her.

Clambering off the bed she took the package and ripped at the heavy plastic.

"Carla—"

"No. Don't talk." Tension banded her chest as she walked out to the kitchen, found a steak knife in the drawer and slit the plastic open. A heavy, midnight-blue box, tied with a black silk bow, the jeweler's signature packaging, tumbled out of layers of Bubble Wrap onto the kitchen counter.

Not an oblong case that might hold a necklace, or a bracelet. A ring box.

Lucas loomed over her as she tore the bow off. Maybe

it was a set of wedding rings. Lucas wanted an early wedding. It made sense to order the rings from the same place they had bought her engagement ring.

"Carla—"

She already knew. Not wedding rings. She flipped the jewelry case open.

A diamond solitaire glittered with a soft, pure fire against midnight-blue velvet.

Fingers shaking, she slid the ring onto the third finger of her right hand. It was a couple of sizes too small and failed to clear her knuckle. The bright, illusory world she had been living in dissolved.

The ring had never been meant for her. The elegant, classic engagement ring had been selected and sized with someone else in mind.

Lilah.

Fifteen

Carla replaced the ring in its box and met Lucas's somber gaze head-on. "You weren't just dating Lilah to facilitate making a clean break with me, were you? You intended to marry her."

Lucas's expression was calmly, coolly neutral. "I had planned to propose marriage, but that was before—"

"Why would you want to marry Lilah when you still wanted me?" She couldn't say *love,* because she now doubted that love had ever factored in. Lucas had wanted her, period. He had felt desire, passion: lust.

"It was a practical decision."

"Because otherwise you were worried that when Constantine and Sienna tied the knot you might be pressured into marrying me."

Impatience flashed in his gaze. "No one could pressure me into marriage. I wanted you. I would have married you in a New York second."

Realization dawned. "Then lived to regret it."

"I didn't think what we had would last."

"So you tied yourself into an arrangement with Lilah so you couldn't be tempted into making a bad decision."

His brows jerked together. "There was no 'arrangement.' All Lilah knew was that I wanted to date her."

"With a view to marriage."

"Yes."

Because she wouldn't have gone out with him otherwise. Certainly not halfway across the world to a very public family wedding.

Hurt spiraled through her that Lucas hadn't bothered to refute her statement that marrying her would have been a bad decision. And that he had so quickly offered Lilah what she had longed for and needed from him.

Throat tight, eyes stinging, Carla snapped the ring box closed and jammed it back into the courier bag. She suddenly remembered the odd behavior of the manager of Moore's. It hadn't been because their engagement was so sudden, or because of the scandal in the morning paper. The odd atmosphere had been because Lucas had bought *two* engagement rings in the same week for two separate women.

Blindly, she shoved the courier bag at Lucas. "You were going to propose to her *here,* at this product launch." Why else would he have requested the ring be couriered to the hotel?

Carla remembered the flashes of sympathy in Lilah's gaze on Medinos, her bone-white face outside of Lucas's apartment when the reporter had snapped Carla and Lucas kissing. Lilah had expected more than just a series of dates. She wouldn't have been with Lucas otherwise.

"You were never even remotely in love with Lilah."

"No."

Her head jerked up. "Then, why consider marriage?"

His expression was taut. "The absence of emotion worked for me. I wasn't after the highs and lows. I wanted the opposite."

"Because of Sophie Warrington."

"That's right," he said flatly. "Sophie liked bright lights, publicity. She loved notoriety. We clashed constantly. The night of the crash we argued and she stormed out. That was the last time I saw her alive. I shouldn't have let her go, should have stopped her—"

"If she wasn't your kind of girl, why were you with her?"

"Good question," he said grimly. "Because I was stupid enough to fall for her. We were a mismatch. We should never have been together in the first place."

Carla's jaw tightened. "You do still think I'm like her," she said quietly. "Another Sophie."

His expression was closed. "I…did."

The hesitation was the final nail in the proverbial coffin. Her stomach plummeted. "You still do."

"I've made mistakes, but I know what I want," Lucas said roughly.

"Me, or the baby I might possibly be having?" Because if Lucas still didn't know who she was as a person, the baby seemed the strongest reason for marriage. And she couldn't marry someone who saw his attraction to her as a weakness, a character flaw. She stared blankly around the flower-festooned room. "If you don't mind, I'd like to get some sleep."

Stepping past Lucas, she walked into the bedroom and grabbed a spare pillow and blanket from the closet.

"Where are you going?"

"To sleep on the couch."

"That's not necessary. I'll take the couch."

She flinched at the sheer masculine beauty of his broad shoulders and muscled chest. She had fallen in love with a mirage, she thought bleakly, a beautiful man who was prepared to care for her but who, ultimately, had never truly wanted to be in love with her. "No. Right now I really would prefer the couch."

His fingers curled around her upper arms. "We can work this through. I can explain—"

She went rigid in his grip. The pillow and blanket formed a buffer between them that right now she desperately needed because, despite everything, she was still vulnerable. "Let me go," she said quietly. "It's late. We both need sleep."

His dark gaze bored into hers, level and calm. "Come back to bed. We can talk this through."

She fought the familiar magnetic pull, the desire to drop the pillow and blanket and step back into his arms. "No. We can talk in the morning."

A familiar cramping pain low in her stomach pulled Carla out of sleep. A quick trip to the bathroom verified that she had her period and that she was absolutely, positively not pregnant.

Numbly, she walked back to the couch but didn't bother trying to sleep. Until that moment she hadn't realized how much she had desperately needed to be pregnant. If there was a child then there had been the possibility that she could have stayed with Lucas. Now there wasn't one and she had to face reality.

Lucas had broken up with Sophie when she had aborted his child. He had also proposed marriage when he had thought she could be pregnant. For a man who had gone to considerable lengths to cut her out of his life, that was a huge turnaround. She could try fooling herself that it was because he loved her, even if he didn't quite know it, but she couldn't allow herself to think that way. She deserved better.

Now she knew for sure she wasn't pregnant. There were no more excuses.

Her decision made, she opted not to shower, because that would wake Lucas. Instead, she found her gym bag, which was sitting by the kitchen counter and which contained fresh underwear, sweatpants, a tank and a light cotton hoodie. She quickly dressed and laced on sneakers. Her handbag with all her medications was in the bedroom. She couldn't risk getting that, but she had a cash card and some cash tucked in her gym bag. That would give her enough money and the ID she needed to book a flight back to Sydney. She had plenty of medication at home, so leaving the MediPACKs in her purse wasn't a problem. She would collect her hand-bag along with the rest of her luggage from Lucas when he got back to Sydney.

Working quickly, she jammed toiletries into the sports bag. She paused to listen, but there was no sound or move-ment from the bedroom. She wrote a brief note on hotel paper, explaining that she was not pregnant and was there-fore ending their engagement. She anchored the note to the kitchen counter with the engagement ring.

Picking up the sports bag and hooking her handbag over her shoulder, she quietly let herself out of the room.

Within a disorientingly short period of time the elevator shot her down to the lobby. The speed with which she had walked away from what had been the most important adult relationship of her life made her stomach lurch sickly, but she couldn't go back.

She couldn't afford to commit one more minute to a man who had put more creative effort into cutting her out of his life than he ever had to including her.

A small sound pulled Lucas out of a fitful sleep.

Kicking free of the tangled sheet, he pushed to his feet and pulled on the pair of pants he'd left tossed over the arm of a chair.

Moonlight slanted through shuttered windows as he walked swiftly through the suite. His suspicion that the sound that had woken him had been the closing of the front door turned to certainty when he found a note and Carla's engagement ring on the kitchen counter.

The note was brief. Carla wasn't pregnant. Rather than both of them being pushed into a marriage that clearly had no chance of working, she had decided to give him his out.

She had left him.

Lucas's hand closed on the note, crumpling it. His heart was pounding as if he'd run a race and his chest felt tight. Taking a deep breath, he controlled the burst of raw panic.

He would get her back. He had to.

She loved him, of that fact he was certain. All it would take was the right approach.

He had messed up one too many times. With the double emotional hit of discovering that he had intended to propose to Lilah then the shock of discovering that she wasn't pregnant, he guessed he shouldn't be surprised that she had reacted by running.

Like Sophie.

His stomach clenched at the thought that Carla could have an accident. Then logic reasserted itself. That wouldn't happen. Carla was so *not* like Sophie he didn't know how he could have imagined she was in the first place.

But this time he would not compound his mistake by failing to act. He would make sure that Carla was safe. He would not fail her again.

He loved her.

His stomach clenched as he examined that reality. He couldn't change the past; all he could do was try to change the future.

Sliding the note into his pocket along with the ring, he strode back to his room to finish dressing. He pulled on shoes and found his wallet and watch. The possibility that he could lose Carla struck him anew and for a split second he was almost paralyzed with fear. Until that moment he hadn't understood how necessary Carla was to him.

For more than two years she had occupied his thoughts and haunted his nights. He had thought the affair would run its course; instead his desire had strengthened. In order to control what he had deemed an obsession, he had minimized contact and compartmentalized the affair.

The strategy hadn't worked. The more restrictive he had become in spending time with Carla, the more uncontrollable his desire had become.

She wasn't pregnant.

Until that moment he hadn't known how much he had wanted Carla to be pregnant. Since the out-of-control lovemaking on Medinos, the possibility of a pregnancy had initiated a number of responses from him. The most powerful had been the cast-iron excuse it had provided him to bring her back into his life. But as the days had passed, the thought of Carla losing her taut hourglass shape and growing soft and round with his child had become increasingly appealing. Along with the need to keep Carla tied close, he had wanted to be a father.

Pocketing his keys, he strode out of the suite. Frustration gripped him when he jabbed the elevator call button then had to wait. His gaze locked on the glowing arrow above the doors, and he scraped at his jaw, which harbored a five-o'clock shadow.

Dragging rough fingers through his rumpled hair, he began to pace.

He couldn't lose her.

Whatever it took, he would do it. He would get her back.

He recalled the expression on Carla's face when she had found the engagement ring he had ordered for Lilah,

her stricken comment that Constantine had wanted Sienna
enough that he had kidnapped her.

Raw emotion gripped him.

Almost the exact opposite of his behaviour.

Carla walked quickly through the lobby, which was empty
except for a handful of guests checking out. She had wasted
frantic minutes checking the backstage area. It had been
empty of possessions, which meant either Elise or Nina had
her things.

Too fragile to bear the stirring of interest she would cause
by waiting inside, she avoided the concierge desk and made
a beeline for the taxi stand.

Not having her medication wasn't ideal. She hadn't taken
any last night, and now she would go most of the day without them. Antacids would have to do. She could wait out the
short flight to Sydney and the taxi ride home, where there
was a supply of pills in her bathroom cupboard.

A pale-faced group of guests, obviously catching an early
flight out, were climbing into the only taxi waiting near the
hotel entrance. Settling her gym bag down on the dusty pave-
ment, she settled herself to wait for the next taxi to turn into
the hotel pickup area.

Long seconds ticked by. She glanced in at the empty reception area, her tension growing, not because she was desperate to escape, she finally admitted to herself, but because
a weak part of her still wanted Lucas to stride out and stop
her from going.

Not that Lucas was likely to chase her.

Shivering in the faint chill of the air, she stared at the
bleak morning sky now graying in the east as a cab finally
braked to a halt beside her.

She slipped into the rear seat with her bag, requested
the cab driver take her to the airport and gave the hotel en-

trance one last look before she stared resolutely at the road unfolding ahead.

Why would Lucas come after her, when she was giving him the thing he had always valued most in their relationship, his freedom?

Lucas caught the flash of the taxi's taillights as it turned out of the resort driveway and the panic that had gripped him while he'd endured the slow elevator ride turned to cold fear.

Sliding his phone out of his pocket, he made a series of calls then strode back into the hotel and took the elevator to the rooftop.

Seconds later, Tiberio phoned back. He had obtained Carla's destination from the taxi company. She was headed for Brisbane Airport. He had checked with the flight desk and she had already booked her flight out to Sydney.

The quiet, efficient way Carla had left him hit Lucas forcibly. No threats or manipulation, no smashed crockery or showy exit in a sports car, just a calm, orderly exit with her flight already arranged.

He felt like kicking himself that it had taken him this long to truly see who she was, and to understand why she was so irresistible to him. He hadn't fallen into lust with a second Sophie. He had fallen in love for the first time—with a woman who was smart and fascinating and perfect for him.

Then he had spent the past two years trying to crush what he felt for her.

Issuing a further set of instructions, Lucas settled down to wait.

Carla frowned as the taxi took the wrong exit and turned into a sleepy residential street opposite a sports field. "This isn't the way to the airport."

The driver gave her an odd look in the rearview mirror

and hooked his radio, which he'd been muttering into for the past few minutes, back on its rest. "I have to wait for someone."

Carla started to argue, then the rhythmic chop of rotor blades slicing the air caught her attention. A sleek black helicopter set down on the sports field. A tall, dark-haired man climbed out, ducking his head as he walked beneath the rotor blades.

Her heart slammed in her chest. She had wanted Lucas to come after her. Contrarily, now that he was here, all she wanted to do was run.

Depressing the door handle, she pushed the door wide and groped for the cash in the side pocket of her gym bag. She shoved some money at the driver, more than enough to cover his meter, and dragged the sports bag off the backseat. A split second later the world flipped sideways and she found herself cradled in Lucas's arms.

Her heart pounded a crazy tattoo. The strap of the sports bag slipped from her fingers as she grabbed at his shoulders. "What do you think you're doing?"

His gaze, masked by dark glasses, seared over her face. "Kidnapping you. That's the benchmark, isn't it?"

Her mouth went dry at his reference to the conversation they'd had when she had listed the things Constantine had done that proved his love for Sienna. Her pulse rate ratcheted up another notch.

She stared into the remote blankness of the dark glasses, suddenly terribly afraid to read too much into his words. "If you're afraid I'm going to do something silly or have an accident, I'm not. I'm just giving you the out you want."

"I know. I read the note." He placed her in the seat directly behind the pilot. "And by the way, here it is."

He took out a piece of the hotel notepaper, tore it into

pieces and tossed it into the downdraft of the blades. The scraps of paper whirled away.

"What are you doing now?" she asked as he started to walk away from the chopper.

The noise muffled his reply. "Getting your shoes and makeup and whatever else it is that makes you happy."

Seconds later, he tossed her sports bag on the floor at her feet and belted himself in beside her.

"Where are we going?" She had to yell now above the noise from the chopper.

Lucas fitted a set of earphones over her head then donned a set himself. "A cabin. In the mountains."

A short flight later the helicopter landed in a clearing. Within minutes the pilot had lifted off, leaving them with a box stamped with the resort's logo on the side. Lucas picked it up. She guessed it was food.

Carla stared at the rugged surrounding range of the Lamingtons, the towering gum trees and silvery gleam of a creek threading through the valley below. "I can't believe you kidnapped me."

"It worked for Constantine."

Her heart pounded at his answer. It wasn't quite a declaration of love, but it was close.

She followed Lucas into the cabin, which was huge. With its architectural angles, sterile planes of glass and comfortable leather couches it was more like an upscale executive palace than her idea of a rustic holiday cottage.

He placed the box on a kitchen counter then began unloading what looked like a picnic lunch. A kidnapping, Atraeus-style, with all the luxury trappings.

Frustrated by his odd mood and the dark glasses, she walked outside, grabbed her sports bag and brought it into the house. She could feel herself floundering, unable to ask the questions that mattered in case the hope that had flared to life when he had bodily picked her up and deposited her in the helicopter was extinguished. "It's not as if this is a real kidnapping."

He stopped, his face curiously still. "How 'real' did you want it to be?"

Sixteen

"We're alone. We're together." Lucas reached for calm when all he really wanted was to pull her close and kiss her.

But that approach hadn't worked so far. Carla had actually tried to run from him, which had altered his game plan somewhat. Plan B was open-ended, meaning he no longer knew what he was doing except that he wasn't going to blow this now by resorting to sex. "We can do what we should have done last night and talk this out. Have you eaten?"

"No." She stared absently at the rich, spicy foods and freshly squeezed juice he had set out then began rummaging through her gym bag just in case there was a stray pack of antacids in one of the pockets.

Lucas, intensely aware of every nuance of expression on Carla's face, tensed when she picked up the phone on the counter. "What's wrong? Who are you calling?"

She frowned when the call wasn't picked up. "Elise. She can get me some medication I need."

"What medication?" But suddenly he knew. The small bag of snacks she carried, her preoccupation with what she was eating and the weight loss. "You're either diabetic or you've got an ulcer."

"The second one."

He could feel his temper soaring. "Why didn't you tell me?"

"You weren't exactly over the moon when I got ill in Thailand."

"You had a virus in Thailand."

"And the viral bacteria just happened to attack an area of my stomach that was still healing from an ulcer I had two years ago. Although I didn't find that out until the ulcer perforated and I got to hospital."

He felt himself go ice-cold inside. "You had a perforated ulcer?" For a split second he thought he must have misheard. "You could have died. Why didn't you tell me?"

Her gaze was cool. "After what happened in Thailand I didn't want you to know I was sick again." She shrugged. "Mom and Sienna didn't know about you, so it was hardly likely they would call you. Why would they? You had no visible role in my life."

That was all going to change, he thought grimly. From now on he was going to be distinctly, in-your-face visible.

He felt like kicking himself. In Thailand he had distanced himself from Carla when she was sick because the enforced intimacy of looking after her had made him want a lot more than the clandestine meetings they'd had through the year. Pale and ill, sweating and shivering, Carla hadn't been either glamorous or sexually desirable. She had simply been *his*.

He had wanted to continue caring for her, wanted to keep her close. But the long hours he had spent sitting beside her bed, waiting for her fever to break, had catapulted him back to his time with Sophie.

He had not wanted her to be that important to him. He hadn't wanted to make himself vulnerable to the kind of guilt and betrayal his relationship with Sophie had resulted in. He could admit that now.

"When was the last time you had your medication?"

She punched in another number. "Lunch, yesterday. That's why I'm calling the resort. Either Nina or Elise can go to the suite and find my handbag, which is where I keep my Medi-PACKs. I'm hoping Tiberio or one of your other bodyguards could drive up with it."

"If you think I'm taking two hours to get you the medication you need, think again." Lucas's cell was already in his hand. He speed dialed and bit out commands in rapid Medinian, hung up and slipped the phone back in his pocket. "Our ride will be here in fifteen minutes."

She slipped her phone back in her handbag. "I could have waited. It's not that bad. I just have to manage my stomach for a few weeks."

"You might be able to wait, but *I* can't. What do you think it did to me to hear that you almost died in hospital?"

"I didn't *almost* die." She grimaced. "Although it wasn't pleasant, that's for sure. It wasn't as if I wasn't used to dealing with the ulcer. It just got out of hand."

He went still inside. "How long did you say you had the ulcer?"

"Two years or so."

Around the time they had met. His jaw tightened at this further evidence of how blind he had been with Carla. He knew ulcers could be caused by a number of factors, but number one was stress. In retrospect, the first time they had made love and he had found out she was a virgin he should have taken a mental step back and reappraised. He hadn't done it. He hadn't wanted to know what might hurt or upset

Carla, or literally eat away at her, because he had been so busy protecting himself.

"News flash," she said with an attempted grin. "I'm a worrier. Can't seem to ditch the habit."

He reached her in two steps and hauled her close. "The woman I love collapses because she has a perforated ulcer," he muttered, "and all you can say is that it *wasn't pleasant?*"

Carla froze in Lucas's arms and, like a switch flicking, she swung from depression and despair to deliriously happy. She stared, riveted by his fierce gaze, and decided she didn't need to pinch herself. "You really do love me?" He had said the words last night but they had felt neutral, empty.

"I love you. Why do you think I couldn't resist you?"

"But it did take you two years to figure that out."

"Don't remind me. Tell me how you ended up with the ulcer."

"Okay, here it goes, but now you might fall out of love with me. I'm a psycho-control-freak-perfectionist. I worked myself into the ground trying to lift Ambrosi's profile and micromanage all of our advertising layouts and pamphlets. When I started color coordinating the computer mouses and mouse pads, Sienna sent me to the family doctor. Jennifer gave me Losec and told me to stop taking everything so seriously, to lighten up and change my life. A week later, I met you."

"And turned my life upside down."

"I wish, but it didn't seem that way." She snuggled in close, unable to stop grinning, loving the way he was staring at her so fiercely. "All I knew was that I was running the relationship in the exact opposite way I wanted, supposedly to avoid stress. If you'd arrived in my life a couple of weeks early, you would have met a different woman."

"I fell in love with you. Instantly."

She closed her eyes and basked for just a few seconds. "Tell me again."

"I love you," he said calmly and, finally, he kissed her.

During the short helicopter ride, Lucas insisted on being given a crash course on her condition. When they reached the doctor's office, which was in a nearby town, Carla took Losec and an antibiotic under the eagle eye of both the doctor and Lucas.

At Lucas's insistence, the doctor also gave her a thorough checkup. Twenty minutes later she was given a clean bill of health.

They exited the office and strolled around to the parking lot to wait for the rental vehicle that Tiberio, apparently, had arranged to have delivered.

Lucas had kept his arm around her waist, keeping her close. "How are you feeling?"

"Fine." She leaned on him slightly. Not that she needed the support, but she loved the way he was treating her, as if she was a piece of precious, delicate porcelain. She could get used to it.

Lucas cupped her face, his fingers tangling in her hair. "I need to explain. To apologize."

Carla listened while Lucas explained about how her illness in Thailand had forced him to confront the guilt and betrayal of the past and had pushed him into a decision to break off with her.

His expression was remote. "But as you know, I couldn't break it off completely. When Constantine told me he was marrying Sienna, I knew I had to act once and for all."

"So you asked Lilah to accompany you to the wedding."

"She was surprised. Before that we had only ever spoken on a business level."

"But she guessed what was going on the night before the wedding."

"Only because she saw us together." He pulled her close, burying his face in her hair. "I'm not proud of what I did but I was desperate. I didn't realize I was in love with you until I read the note you left in the hotel room and discovered that you had left me. It was almost too late."

He hugged her close for long minutes, as if he truly did not want to let her go. "I've wasted a lot of time. Two years."

"There were good reasons we couldn't be together in the beginning. Some of those reasons were mine."

He frowned. "Reasons that suited me."

Gripping her hands gently in his, he went down on one knee. "Carla Ambrosi, will you marry me and be the love of my life for the rest of my life?"

He reached into his pocket and produced the sky-blue diamond ring, which he must have been carrying with him all along, and gently slipped it on the third finger of her left hand.

Tears blurred Carla's eyes at the soft gleam in Lucas's gaze, the intensity of purpose that informed her that if she said no he would keep on asking until she was his.

Emotion shimmered through her, settled in her heart, because she *had* been his all along.

"Yes," she said, the answer as simple as the kiss that followed, the long minutes spent holding each other and the promise of a lifetime together.

* * * * *

LET'S TALK
Romance

For exclusive extracts, competitions
and special offers, find us online:

f facebook.com/millsandboon

◉ @millsandboonuk

🐦 @millsandboon

Or get in touch on 0844 844 1351*

For all the latest titles coming soon, visit
millsandboon.co.uk/nextmonth